CW01262405

THE LAST DOORBELL

WILLIAM PARKER

Deixis Press

Copyright © William Parker 2024
All rights reserved.

The right of William Parker to be identified as the author of this work has been asserted by him in accordance with the Copyright, Designs and Patents Act 1988.

This book is a work of fiction. Names, characters, businesses, and incidents either are products of the author's imagination or are used in a fictitious manner. Any resemblance to actual persons, living or dead, events, or locales is entirely coincidental.

First published in 2024 by Deixis Press
www.deixis.press

ISBN 978-1-917090-00-1 (HB)
ISBN 978-1-917090-01-8 (PB)

Typeset using Monticello Pro by
Palimpsest Book Production Ltd, Falkirk, Stirlingshire

Cover design by Deividas Jablonskis

THE LAST DOORBELL

WILLIAM PARKER

In memory of Geoffrey Peck, inspirational teacher.
1929 – 2023

PART 1

CHAPTER 1

September 1995

The wind arrived during the night. It came whistling down from the North Sea, buffeting the Isle of Thanet before descending upon the red-tiled roofs of Sandwich. We were old acquaintances by then, so I knew its presence warned of the imminent arrival of autumn and dark evenings; it demanded that we prepare for orange flames in the grate, for singing central heating pipes, damp leaves underfoot, caps and scarves, coats with collars turned up and hands thrust deep into pockets. As it bullied its way into Bridget's high-walled garden for a second long day, it rocked the marble urns on their plinths and stripped the geraniums of their last blooms, swirling them into a miniature tornado before relaxing its grip and depositing the crimson confetti by the French doors of the drawing room.

'Right on time,' I said to myself. It was the end of September and the geraniums had to be helped to hibernate into the greenhouse.

It would be for the last time. Alexander, in his small,

sparsely furnished bedroom at the top of the stairs, was dying, and so this would be the last September in the big house in Fisher Street for all of us. I'd been pretending to myself that it couldn't be true but in my heart of hearts I knew it was. I'd had ample time to prepare; I'd known the old man for sixteen years and not a month had passed since the day we met when he hadn't told me that 'it's only a matter of time now, dear boy – a few months at the most'. He was ninety-two and had lived on for ten months since the death of Bridget, his wife. She had died the previous November in the nursing home down in the bay. Theresa, our housekeeper, and Alexander had sent her there for just a few days to give everyone a rest from the dementia that had been relentlessly stealing her from us over the past few years.

It hadn't been my decision to move her. I didn't want it. I'd raced along the M2 from London when Theresa phoned to tell me she'd suffered a heart attack trying to get back onto the bed from which she'd fallen. By the time I reached her, she was tossing about on a high single bed in a room overlooking the winter-grey sea beyond a desolate garden where white plastic chairs were stacked on a desert of weather-blackened decking. She was kicking the sheets from her body to expose her bare legs and a diaper while talking schoolgirl French in a loud outraged voice, desperate to make herself understood, demanding to be returned to her mother and father and a home she'd left seventy years before. She'd calmed down as I sat by her bed holding her hand, and having been assured that she was comfortable and quite stable, I'd kissed her cheek and promised to be back in the morning. But she had died alone in the middle of the night while I lay awake just a mile or two away, wondering whether I should be with her. It wouldn't be the same for Alexander. I swore to myself I'd be with him when he died.

Theresa was away on holiday. I wish I'd asked her not to go – she answered to me and not to Alexander; it had been a long time since he had been able, or indeed wanted, to make any decisions. 'You'll have to ask our young friend,' he would say to anyone with a demand. 'He's in charge here, thank God!' Since she'd left the week before, it had occurred to me that Theresa knew he was dying and had lost her nerve. She'd nursed Bridget and perhaps couldn't muster the strength for this final struggle that would also find her out of a job. I'd employed people to help me while she was away, a rota of three local women who had been assuring me for quite some time that it 'can't be long before the end'. Death's midwives, they were, and I needed them. They had all witnessed this same scene many times before, and they went about their duties with an efficiency and serenity that comforted me, reminding me that what was happening was inevitable, and for them not much more than a matter of routine. For poor Alexander, it would be a release.

In those last lonely weeks, I started drifting into the kitchen for their company during the long evenings after Alexander had settled into his bed. Yvonne would sit straight-backed at the kitchen table all night long, a tabloid crossword in front of her as she knitted a pullover for her baby grandson. She'd tell me of her new lover and the serial infidelities of her husband that had eventually driven her away from the marital home. Rita talked of her adopted son, his addiction to heroin, and of the bungalow on the cliffs at Kingsdown, lost when her ex-husband went bankrupt. And Anne, big-bosomed with pearly-white teeth in an open smile, talked of her struggle to afford the upkeep of her beloved horse. Until the very last few days, she took to bringing homemade soup that, propped up by pillows, Alexander had been able to sip from a mug held in two unsteady hands.

As we had always done, I dressed for dinner that last night, although I was alone. I bathed as usual, donned the suit that Alexander had had made for me in Savile Row and came down to sit in the drawing room to drink the first of my several gin and tonics. As my Marks and Spencer's chicken Kiev warmed in the oven, Alexander and Bridget's aristocratic ancestors eyed me from their rococo frames on the walls and the first fire of autumn flickered in the grate. The curtains, made from the chintz that Bridget had brought back from a trip to India thirty-five years before, were drawn against the dark, the sudden cold and the howling wind. I laid out the dishes on the hotplate, served myself using the crested silver cutlery and ate half-heartedly, a large white napkin draped across my knees. A bottle of Alexander's favourite wine – a Tavel rosé supplied by his wine merchants in Bristol – comforted me through the lonely meal. Upstairs, the old man was falling into a deeper state of unconsciousness with every passing hour. Much later, I took a bottle of port from the cellar and went up to sit at the end of his bed. In the early hours, while the wind keened loudly in the chimney, I watched his chest rise and fall, ready at any moment for the movement to stop.

∼

'Monsieur?' asked a waiter in an immaculate white shirt and black waistcoat. The young man's A-level French immediately deserted him. He looked up with sad, fearful eyes.

'Could I have an omelette please, with French fries and a glass of white wine and some sparkling water? Thank you. Er – merci.'

Nervous and ill at ease, he'd been forced by hunger and a sudden rainstorm to enter the restaurant and had sat himself down at an anonymous table tucked into a corner by the window.

It was his very first visit to Paris. It had seemed to him such a seductive idea – to throw his customary caution to the wind and embark on the journey alone. Paris was a childhood dream; he'd promised himself the glories of the Louvre and the Orangerie, he'd visit Versailles, sit in pavement cafés, and watch elegant Parisians go about their business while he quaffed a 'demi-carafe'. He'd wear a big scarf, smoke untipped cigarettes and ostentatiously read Camus and Sartre. He was quite sure that he'd be taken for a student at the Sorbonne.

But as he looked at the white tablecloth, the stiff, folded napkin and the two wine glasses competing for his attention, the dream, already terminally ill, finally succumbed to reality. He felt his head begin to sink towards the table, and to his intense dismay he realised that he was wishing that he'd not come to Paris at all.

'You're English,' said a mellifluous, patrician voice from the adjoining table. 'Is it your first visit?'

'Yes – yes, it is.'

'How wonderful! It'll be one of the best experiences of your life. Most beautiful city in all the world.' The elderly gentleman relaxed back into his seat, observing the stranger over the detritus of his lunch with quizzical, kindly eyes. As his hands played nonchalantly with a creased napkin, a large gold signet ring bearing a coronet caught the dazzle from the sunlight reflecting off the rain-soaked pavement outside. 'A toast to your visit,' he said as he raised a glass of port way above his head, paused for a second, and transferred it to his lips. His eyes twinkled and the aquiline face broke into a friendly, reassuring smile.

'My name's Bellaghy. Alexander Bellaghy. Spelt with a GH. Pronounced as though it's a little sigh of contentment...'

~

I drank the whole bottle of port and then fell into a drunken slumber in the wicker chair at the end of Alexander's bed and only woke as I began an involuntary slide towards the floor. The old man's talking clock with the Japanese accent told me it was four in the morning. I'd stayed up for him. If he'd gone during the night, I could tell myself that he'd not died alone. The following morning, I had a sick headache that not even a walk along the river in the driving wind was able to budge.

Late morning found me dozing on Alexander's highbacked chair in the drawing room. Outside, the wind was subsiding. I'd fallen into a state of lethargy induced by my hangover, but I was also procrastinating, conscious that the moving of the geraniums would probably signal the beginning of the dismantling of this grand old house – the beginning of the scattering of the contents so conscientiously collected and loved by Bridget and Alexander over the years.

Beside the chair, there was an eighteenth-century wine cooler, acting as a side table. Deep cigarette burns and water stains from a whisky glass marked the surface that an eyeglass, huge ashtray and the light from a lamp had been unable to protect. Round the feet of the chair, the green carpet had been subjected to years of punishment – spills, mostly of port and tea, unseen by failing eyes. The fruitless endeavours of housekeepers and cleaners to scrub away the damage had left the carpet faded and threadbare. Until a few short weeks before, Alexander had now and again made his own way down the stairs from his bedroom – a slow, measured descent, his impending arrival announced by the changing tones of the tapping of his walking stick against first, the skirting board, then the drawing-room door and finally the legs of his chair.

∼

The young man found himself adopted for that first visit to Paris. At the same time as being a little discomfited by the realisation that he was so recognisably English, he was almost pathetically grateful to have his cherished dreams of a long weekend immersed in Parisian culture restored. He quickly discovered in Alexander the ideal companion, one more than willing to humour his rambling dissertations on the causes of the French Revolution and to empathise with his passion for eighteenth-century France. Paris was Alexander's great love too.

'I had business interests in the city,' Alexander said as that first meeting, accompanied by glasses of port and cups of coffee that were never allowed to run dry, stretched late into the afternoon. 'I spent so much time here that I decided to buy myself a little pied-à-terre. You'll see it – five floors up in a small street in Montparnasse. The studio right next door to me was used by Modigliani in the twenties.' Alexander paused to enjoy the delighted reaction, lit another cigarette and, attracting the waiter's attention, ordered yet more port. 'Leave the bottle on the table, dear chap – it'll save me waving my arms around. Anyway, when I retired, I found myself quite unable to part with the little place. I feel free in a way I don't in London. I suppose I rather indulge myself here – in the pleasures of the spirit and the emotions.'

Later, when the young man came to know him better, he was to discover that his new friend's rather odd little turn of phrase should also have included the pleasures of the flesh. Tucked away in the depths of his pocket address book, Alexander kept the telephone number of one or two establishments close to the Bois de Boulogne where a gentleman might spend a pleasurable hour or two after a good dinner. Bridget, it seemed, preferred to turn a blind eye to certain things that she regarded as unimportant, and to devote herself to the glories of her pretty garden in Sandwich.

'I'll show you some of the things I know will interest you. You're here for such a short time and we can't do it all, but trust me. The Eiffel Tower and the Folies Bergère will just have to wait!'

In awed silence they looked down at Napoleon's tomb, took in the glories of the stained-glass windows of the Sainte-Chapelle hidden in the depths of the Palais de Justice, giggled at the number of times the otherwise unintelligible guide in the Conciergerie mumbled *'condamné a mort'* and, standing together in a dark courtyard with a miserly little fountain, wondered at the awful cruelty of Marie Antoinette's last journey to the scaffold in the Place de La Concorde. They went to Versailles and for years after, Alexander quoted the stunned, monosyllabic reaction to the Hall of Mirrors – 'Wow!' Alexander, once he'd become aware of his companion's love for French painting of the eighteenth century, was able – as a true connoisseur himself – to lead him straight to the galleries in the Louvre where they found the painters they'd talked of the evening before – Fragonard, Hubert, Chardin, Élisabeth Vigée Le Brun.

They sat outside Les Deux Magots and watched fire-eaters and flamenco dancers on the wide pavements; they walked through the Jardin du Luxembourg and disagreed loudly about where the new government of Margaret Thatcher might lead, and on the last night of the young tourist's visit, they dined at La Coupole where they overstayed their welcome, ignoring the pleas of the waiter to free the table as he gesticulated at the long, patient Friday night queue at the entrance.

'Do you think we ought to order a second bottle of rosé?' Alexander had said, leaning conspiratorially towards his young companion.

'I think it's probably for the best.'

And it was soon after the bottle arrived that Alexander knocked over a glass for the second time in two days. He cuffed it with the sleeve of his jacket as he reached for his packet of cigarettes, and in his desperation to retrieve the glass as it rolled towards the edge of the table, his hand gave it a mighty flick. It spun off at great speed into space before landing with an ear-piercing smash on the tiled floor below, momentarily silencing the cavernous room.

The next morning, before embarking on his journey home, the young man called at Alexander's apartment for breakfast and to say his goodbyes and thank yous. He tried to avoid the disapproving glances of the concierge sitting in her dark little room full of plastic flowers by the main door. Very late the previous night, she had witnessed the tipsy 'milord anglais' being escorted back to his quarters by the verbose young Englishman who, quite the worse for wear himself, had been unable to find the light switch in the pitch black on his way out, and had been forced to call out for assistance.

Alexander, dressed in a Prince of Wales check suit with a floppy polka-dot handkerchief in the breast pocket, opened the door to his apartment and waved him into the sitting room with a theatrical flourish. The young man settled himself into a blue damask-covered chair pulled up to a circular mahogany table and attacked a croissant still warm from the boulangerie in the street below. As he sipped coffee enthusiastically from a white bone-china cup, his hand strayed carelessly to a large magnifying glass in the centre of the table. He picked it up, casually turning it round as huge letters from the newspaper beneath it filled the round frame and then receded as he put it down.

'I see very badly,' Alexander said abruptly. 'Glaucoma. I've left it too late. My fault really – no patience with doctors. Saw every eye specialist in Harley Street and ignored them all. Silly fool! Nothing to be done about it now, I'm afraid.'

The floor-to-ceiling windows in Alexander's small, book-lined sitting room high above the roofs of Montparnasse had been flung wide open. Bright sunshine cascaded into the room and the chill wind of an early October morning caught the yellow curtains, sending them billowing like the sails of an ocean-going yacht. A smell of freshly ground coffee and eau-de-Cologne retreated under the onslaught of the chilly air. Yesterday's *Daily Telegraph*, anchored against the breeze by the magnifying glass, flapped against the table.

'Listen, you're not too busy at the moment – struggling young actor and all that. No doubt you could do with a little bit of cash, so why not come over once a week to the house in Eaton Square and help me with my bits and pieces? Spot of letter writing, read some stuff to me, go over my list of stocks and shares. Come and be my eyes, so to speak.'

∼

I was fighting against sleep in the depths of Alexander's huge chair. It smelled of him. An almost imperceptible trace of cigarettes, eau-de-Cologne, shoe polish, starched collars and whisky, combining to make something that was indefinably Alexander. It put me in mind of Paris. I needed to savour it, store it away so that it was always with me, a memory more evocative and precious than a photograph.

Looking out into Bridget's garden, it occurred to me that she would be pleased that I'd not abandoned it to grow wild. The lawn had recently been mowed and met the flowerbeds in a straight, trimmed line. Alyssum and a late flourish of blue campanula were still growing showily between the York stones, terracotta pots brimmed with white busy Lizzies, and purple petunias, only a little past their best, vied for attention with the yellowing hosta and a large fuchsia bush that had fastidiously held its own against the elements unleashed on it earlier. The wind, so punishing just an hour or two before, had quite suddenly died to nothing. The rhododendron was stilled, and the old magnolia tree seemed to be catching its breath, perhaps readying itself for a second harrying.

The doorbell rang. I raised myself from the chair and my half-sleep. A pale, sickly-looking youth with dark, unwashed hair stood on the pavement when I opened the door.

'Is my mum here?' Feral, intelligent eyes, peering over my shoulder, darted about, absorbing the contents of the hall behind me.

'Your mum?'

'Rita... She's got some money for me. Said she'd leave it with you.'

'No, no. She's not due in till later. I'll say you called and–'

'She said for you to give me the money,' he interrupted, eyes locked firmly onto my face.

'I really can't help you at the moment. Come back later and Rita will sort it out.' I closed the door firmly before he could reply, unnerved by the hunger and controlled desperation that hung about the youth. I returned to the chair, eased off my shoes and drew my knees up to rest under my chin.

I was conscious that I was struggling to do the right thing by Alexander. I wanted to be with him when he went, but I'd no idea when that moment might be. After all the years together, I felt it was one of my last duties to him – the very last being to fulfil the promise of a funeral service devoid of any religious symbolism. 'It's a job for the dustbin men,' he used to say to me. 'If it were allowed, I'd have my remains put into a black bag and left in the alleyway at the back with the rest of the garbage!'

Anne, seated in the kitchen, was reading the paper when I entered, one hand resting on her cheek while the fingers of the other played with her long dark curls. 'Can't I make you a little something to eat for lunch? It's going to be a long day, you know,' she said with a sympathetic smile.

'I'm really not hungry, thanks, Anne, but there is something you could do for me – could you help move the geraniums into the greenhouse?' I asked her, 'a sort of last favour in memory of Her Ladyship? There's nothing for us to do upstairs.'

There was a collection of pots by the greenhouse door. 'Some of these have been blown to hell and back again, Anne. Wish I'd got myself together to move them before the storm.' I reached for the greenhouse door and realised I'd left the key inside the house. As I walked across the lawn, the sun came out and immediately banished the premonition of autumn with its warmth.

It was as I opened the door from the garden into the hallway that I heard the noise. Tapping, drumming, knocking, pummelling. I thought I could hear infant feet scurrying to and fro, restless, near to panic, looking to escape. Surely, that's what I was hearing – the sound of tiny shoes on floorboards? But no, it was much more than that, something building towards a crisis – windows shook in their frames, hinges sung discordantly, shutters banged against glass panes and then threw themselves back to knock and thud against masonry. It was as though some malignant force was attempting to rip the house from its ancient foundations. I couldn't make sense of the kaleidoscope of sounds that assaulted my ears and looked through the garden door towards the sky, seeking confirmation of the return of the storm. But all was still, becalmed, at rest after the torture of the night before. With a dread realisation, I suddenly knew that the sound was coming from Alexander's room above my head.

'It's Rita's son – that strange, wild boy,' I told myself. 'He's in Alexander's room!' Outrage and fear drove me in just a few bounds up the flight of stairs and onto the landing outside the room. A window afforded me a look down into the garden, and I saw Anne's questioning face gazing up towards me. The door to the bedroom was slightly ajar. The noise stopped. All was still again. I stood in a white-hot silence looking at the brass doorknob, wondering what chaos I might find beyond.

And then, with an overpowering certainty, I knew that Alexander was alone, and I knew why I was there. 'I will take a step towards the door, I will push it, it will swing open, and as my eyes come to rest on his face, the life will drain from him, and I will have been granted my wish – I will have been with him when he died.' I took the step and placed a flat, shaking palm against the door. I pushed it. It swung open. As my eyes came to rest upon the figure on the bed, the head, already deep within the pillows, moved almost imperceptibly sideways and downwards at the same time as a last, weary but accepting sigh escaped the parted lips.

Then I heard my voice calling to Anne, who was already beside me.

'Bless him,' she said as she squeezed my hand. 'He's gone. He's gone…'

∼

It really did happen like that – someone, something granted me my wish to be with my dear old friend Alexander for his last moments.

I've had the odd mystic experience in the past – I was quite led astray by a long-lasting experiment with an Ouija board in my teens, and at about the same time, I remember the extraordinarily real presence of my mother talking sense to me in a dream some little while after her death. 'It's time to get over your grief now – time to move on,' she'd said to me in a kind but forthright little speech as she sat on a park bench holding both my hands between hers.

But now, looking back at both the Ouija business and the dream I had of my sweet mama, I'm more than willing to put it all down to adolescent angst rather than anything else. I really don't have time for the so-called paranormal – as soon as someone starts off on a ghostly yarn in a reverential voice, I'm likely to have to stifle a yawn in the same way that I do if I'm presented with a conspiracy theory about JFK's assassination, Diana's death in that underpass in Paris, or YouTube evidence of absolutely not a single plane being flown into the Twin Towers (the CIA blew them both up). If I were to find myself reading the two or three pages I've just presented to you, I'd be likely to snap the book shut with a groan. It's just not my thing. But I crave your indulgence. The truth is, I'm not embellishing anything that happened on that last day of my old friend's life; that's how it was, plain and simple. Make of it what you will.

Having said that, it is important to me that I fess up and tell you that although the deathbed scene is quite how I remember it, I'm being less than forthright with one or two other little paragraphs in my opening. The very beginning of my little Parisian essay begs your indulgence and asks that it be allowed to sit on the page uncorrected for a brief moment – but I make you a firm promise. I'll return to it later, and I will be telling you the truth.

CHAPTER 2

November 1978

'You should be an 'ore, Benjamin. You will make munai. Lots of munai.'

It's just over three months since the above declaration was aimed at me, and right now, as I stand on the pavement that runs past a splendid, double-fronted Georgian house in Hampstead, I'm having difficulty believing that I've had the guts to act upon it and got myself together to be here.

I don't *have* to do this, of course. I can turn my back and walk away from this green door that stands below a warm light shining from a large delicate spider's web of a fanlight – and no harm done. I can change my mind any time I like. But, once I press that brass doorbell, it's done. Then I guess I'm in. No going back.

Holy fuck, am I really going to follow this through? Now I've located the door and confirmed that the address scribbled on my piece of paper really exists, I'm going to walk across to the churchyard on the other side of the road, see if I can't find a quiet place to sit in the dark, and have another think about this for half an hour or so. A last chance to change my mind. A very last chance. Shit – I've been doing this delaying thing from the moment I closed the door behind me at home three quarters of an hour ago.

I'll just lock my door, even though I might not actually be going anywhere.

I'm on the Tube to Hampstead, though I don't have to get out there – might go on to Golders Green.

Here I am at Hampstead, very early, so I think I'll walk up the six hundred steps to ground level to give me more time to think things through, and besides, it's jolly good exercise. Time for a cup of coffee, and you know something? I'm committed to nothing at all yet. Absolutely nothing.

But I'm here now, outside the house. Early, early, early. I just needed to make sure of my bearings. I'm ready to come back a little later. Nearly half an hour still before I'm due. Oh Christ, I'm not sure I can do this. Give me the peace of a bench in the dark damp graveyard to gather my wits and my courage...

∼

Edouard's outrageous suggestion had come out of the blue, apropos of nothing at all. A non sequitur. He was spotting me in the gym, a veritable Greek god standing above the bench on which I was stretched out while I stared up his shorts and grew slightly distracted – and a mite embarrassed, to be honest – at the memory of some of the things he'd introduced me to during the previous evening. He was encouraging me to handle a weight a great deal heavier than my puny frame could handle, and as his words sank in, my first confident push upwards slowly ground to a halt as the bar developed a nasty little wobble and started an agonisingly slow descent towards my chest. I heard myself utter a wheezy 'Heeeeelp!' as Edouard grabbed the bar, expertly and swiftly directing it back onto the stand, thereby narrowly averting an embarrassing scene that would undoubtedly have thrilled the less sympathetic members of the YMCA.

'You talking to me?' I said, sitting up to check he wasn't making a flirty aside to someone close by.

'Yes, Benjamin – to you.'

'Oh, I don't think so, Edouard – not really my sort of thing.' A short silence followed, accompanied by a lopsided grin on the handsome face below the tight golden curls. 'You're joking, aren't you? I'm hardly gigolo material, and I don't really think I have the right sort of personality – and aren't I a bit old?' I said, rubbing my biceps whilst glancing around, relieved that no one seemed to have witnessed my fall from grace.

'What are you talking about? Too old? Don't be reediculous! You are twenty-one – twenty-two? I am twenty-five and going very strong with it. Zere ees plenty of interest still. And besides, you know how it ees – different people like different things. *Chacun à son gout,* as we say in France.' *No accounting for taste*, I quickly decided was the correct translation as the little ghost of a compliment disappeared into the ether.

Well, I thought he was talking bollocks, of course, sending me up, or at the very least showing off, which is rather his thing – Edouard, the wickedly handsome French aristo (or so he says) with no discernible means of support, pumping up his chest while his battered

1950's white Rolls Royce collects a ticket on a double yellow line in Bedford Square.

So, by the time I left the gym later that afternoon and sulkily sat myself down on the Tube, I had decided that our bit of banter had been a barely disguised put-down, delivered because the handsome bugger obviously felt I needed to be put in my place. Perhaps he thought I was daring to entertain a little dewdrop of a dream about my being a Hephaistíon to his Alexander. I truly wasn't. The whole thing was far too new and exotic for me to be going off on one, since it was all built on the shallowest of foundations. In fact, there were no foundations at all – I was just hopelessly grateful for the attention of the newcomer in the gym that everyone was talking about. I suppose it was great for my ego – though I do absolutely know I'm not at all in the same league as him on the looks front. It's not that I'm incapable of turning a head, but I don't think I'm in the A-team like he is.

The truth is, a few months on, my little dalliance with Edouard really hadn't turned out to be very much more than a one- or two-night stand. That was okay; right from the beginning I knew I could be dropped at a moment's notice and that his little dig was probably the beginning of the end, a little preparation for the inevitable rejection. So off I went in a huff, with what had started as a near-compliment a full raging insult by the time I climbed the stairs to my bedsit. I opened the door and flung myself into the saggy old armchair lodged between the window and my two gas rings. No more Edouard, even if he was gagging for it, I told myself – though he quite obviously wasn't.

But funnily enough, it wasn't quite the end of my

French marquis. Looking out of the window a few evenings later, what do I spot? Nothing other than the white Rolls Royce – far below, on the other side of Kennington Park Road, parked at a jaunty angle, with its wheels taking up a selfishly large and surely illegal amount of the pavement. Its driver was leaning nonchalantly against the bonnet, a tight white tee-shirt showing off his assets. He was looking up towards me, legs crossed, and hands folded across his impressive pecs. No call to the communal phone in the hallway beforehand, no ring on the doorbell. Just standing there taking the unlikely chance that I'd glance out and notice him. Which I did. Arrogant French tart. But fun to see him again, I guess – and there *was* the slightest quickening of the pulse, to be honest. Anyway, I went down to let him in but, without any explanation, found myself being whisked away from my little attic – perfectly suitable in itself for a tryst – to an anonymous, dark cul-de-sac in Streatham, for God's sake, where my education continued with some complicated manoeuvres involving the reclining passenger seat, an open window and an instruction to be aware of the gear stick.

'You should become an 'ore, Benjamin,' he said again during the mopping-up operation, 'there will be munai for you in eet…'

What is the bugger going on about? I thought to myself without bothering to answer back.

Later, as his vast – and really rather ridiculous – car glided to a halt outside my bedsit, Edouard had fumbled about the dashboard, found a pen and a scrap of paper before jotting down a number from memory. 'This ees the number of Alan who ees the owner of the massage agency that I am working for. Think about what I have been saying. Call him sometime.'

∼

I caught up with him again the other day in the King's Road. He was driving an old Mini – in even worse shape than the white Rolls-Royce – with a punishingly loud exhaust. No idea what's happened there. First time I've seen him for a month or two; he's changed gyms already, no doubt seeking pastures new – though I've bumped into him at the Gay Saturday at the Markham Arms once or twice, and we always have a bit of a chat. Nice while it lasted, no hard feelings, and certainly not even the slightest twinge of an aching heart on my behalf, though an invitation back to the cul-de-sac in Streatham might still be acceptable. For old time's sake. And because he's very, very accomplished at all those gymnastic goings-on. I'm rather grateful, too; I like the fact that he's helped to dispel the ice-maiden, Mother Teresa persona that I seem to have been quite unfairly labelled with at the gym before his arrival. Some of the guys are definitely looking at me with fresh, might I say envious, eyes. A little something of the now absent Edouard's charisma has rubbed off on me, I think.

But the extraordinary thing is that a week or two after he'd scribbled down that number in the car, I found that Edouard's suggestion from the weights room was still with me, bouncing around in my head. The fantasy first entertained me and then morphed into becoming the compliment that it was perhaps meant to be all along, and I got into the habit of happily dusting it down and buffing it up every now and again, generally feeling rather pleased about the whole thing every time I recalled the heavy accent. *You should be an 'ore, Benjamin.* I began to think that in some way it reflected rather well on me.

And so I started playing with the idea, wondering what it might be like, what it would entail; whether it really might be possible to endure the wandering, lustful hands of complete strangers, allowing contact without desire. A quite reasonable occurrence if you're pissed, of course. Who the hell hasn't woken up of a Sunday morning, stretched a lazy arm out across the bed only to encounter a great lump of an appallingly unattractive stranger that you don't remotely recall from the night before? But to do it sober? Everything all planned out and agreed upon, a business arrangement?

Actually, I'd better come clean at this point and declare that I have, just once or twice, flirted in a very ineffectual sort of way with a bit of what I imagined was whoring. Twice, I think, unless there's the odd occurrence that I'm not remembering. Both times after making a little bit too free with a beverage or two – so perhaps that might indicate that I always have been, in fact, just a little bit taken by the idea of the oldest profession, even before Edouard came along. If I'm being honest, I do recall a memory from quite some time ago. A bald portly gentleman with a handlebar moustache, wearing a yachting club blazer sidled up to me on the pavement opposite Centre Point as everyone was spilling out of Bang and asked me whether I might go back to his hotel with him. 'Cost you a fiver,' I heard myself reply without a pause, aiming high right from the start. Don't quite remember how that evening panned out exactly, seeing as I was much the worse for wear – a harbinger of things to come – but there's a vague memory of a dimly lit hotel room drowning in soft furnishings at the Marble Arch end of Oxford Street, room service with a waiter wearing a disapproving, knowing look, a switch from my usual lager to a smooth red wine, followed by some rather cursory goings-on.

Then there's a much sharper recollection of a bouncing cheque a week later. Yes, a cheque. What sort of tart accepts cheques for £5, for Christ's sake? There's quite a lot I'm probably going to have to learn if I'm entering the business of pressing odd doorbells of an evening, that's for sure.

Another evening, deciding not to wait for the night bus, I jumped, quite pissed again, into one of the unlicensed cabs touting for business outside Heaven, and halfway to Kennington, announced to the Asian driver that I didn't have a penny to my name and a blow job would be my preferred method of payment. He was very angry and seemed quite disturbed by the whole thing.

'Not possible! Not possible!' he shouted when we got there, pulling angrily at the handbrake and frenetically winding down the window. 'You pay the fare *and* you give blow job!'

'Oh, go on then…'

～

It's the utter lack of money that I can't stand anymore. That's the real reason I'm probably about to stand with my finger over a doorbell in Hampstead. The relentless poverty with no end in sight. I'm just no longer sure how excited I can pretend to be about packing my things into the beaten-up old leather suitcase I've inherited from

Pa, handing the keys to my room over to a stranger who's answered an ad I've pinned up at The Dance Centre, and setting off for somewhere in the north for two or three months in the middle of winter. God knows, I've not been at it for very long, but it's getting me down already. Every bloody job pays the Equity minimum and I spend the whole time wondering what on earth I'm going to do when the run ends and I'm heading home with not a measly penny saved. I'll admit something now – quite out of the blue, a month or two back, the whole thing started to feel a bit foolish. I guess my commitment to my 'art' has begun to look a bit shaky. Or else I'm growing up.

Anyway, the whole poverty thing has been building for a while now. It came to a head at the end of August when I was sunbathing in the park with Charlie Sanderson and found myself rather vehemently voicing my growing disillusionment. 'My dear chap – the stage is one's *raison d'être* – one must be prepared to sacrifice one's all for it,' he said after I'd finished a ten-minute moan. Well, I bloody well lost it. I shouldn't have, of course, but he's so fucking pompous – one day last winter I bumped into him on the Tube, wearing his ludicrous blue cape, pen in hand, head town. 'Good morning,' I said. 'Can't talk,' he boomed à la Tyrone Guthrie, showing me a flat palm as though he was stopping traffic. 'I'm just completing a crucial scene…' Silly old fart. Four years out of drama school and only the one job so far. Acting ASM at The Queen's in Hornchurch. Still going on about understudying Philip Madoc playing Othello and scrubbing the black off his back in the shower after the end of the show. That was nothing more than the duties of an ASM, but he made it sound as though they were preparing to run off into the sunset together once the final curtain came down. Philip this, Philip that and Philip almost certainly unable to recall his name just a few weeks after the end of the run.

Anyway, back to the park, and out of the window went my usual Little Miss Nice. 'Oh, for fuck's sake,' I hollered louder than I intended, 'could you possibly keep your old clichés to yourself just this once?' I was trying to inject a vaguely jokey feel into it, but it came out all raw and wrong and nasty – which is a description of me at that very moment, I suppose. I couldn't help myself. But Jesus Christ, as he sat there, stretching out into one of his yoga positions, pontificating away, it had just occurred to me that the cost of another cup of tea in one of the stained old mugs from the park caff was too much of an extravagance. Quite unsurprisingly, Charlie decided to take umbrage at my general tone, shook his big tartan rug out, packed it into his purple crochet bag – all the while employing a deathly silence – and then flip, flap, flopped away across the lawn with half a white bum cheek hanging out of his far too brief, far too tight white shorts. I'll have to apologise, of course. He meant no harm, but sometimes he just gets on my tits – but much more importantly, it was the moment that revealed to me that I'm really struggling. I've thought it over countless times since.

It's not just about the money. I guess that's what I'd like to believe is the problem. The fact is, it doesn't suit me. It doesn't suit who I am – not really. Probably never has. I'm too much of a scaredy cat. Too much of a cowardy custard. I mean, come on, let's face it – here we have a person with a long history of being frightened as fuck of everything – panic attacks, dry mouth, sweaty palms and gurgling stomach, and he sets himself up with a life to be conducted in front of an audience. How fucking mad is that? How on earth did I think that was going to work out? That is *not* cutting one's coat according to one's cloth, or whatever it is they say. That's what has been catching up with me for a while. But the problem is – who am I going to be if I don't want all that anymore? What will I do instead? I'm no good at anything else. The real truth is this, though – I may have won the cup for best actor of my year at drama school, but just because I might be good at it doesn't mean it works for me, does it? It doesn't mean I have to do it.

∼

I'm going to admit something now that I haven't really given much thought to since it happened, but in this new mood, and seeing how things are turning out, it's time to air this thing out loud – well, 'on paper' out loud. When I got home from the run of *Rock Nativity* in Exeter last Christmas, I remember climbing the stairs up to the bedsit and being absolutely thrilled to see, on the threadbare carpet outside my door, an envelope which I knew contained the keys to the room and some rent money. But it also held a scrawled note from Krista, my temporary lodger and companion in class at The Dance Centre, thanking me for the use of the room over Christmas – with a PS saying '*Agent phoned as I was leaving. Contact ASAP. Audition for Pitlochry tomorrow morning. One Shakespeare piece and a modern American.*'

My heart sank so low and with such force I'm surprised

it didn't crash through the floorboards and land up in Nurse Sue's flat in the basement. Truly. Warning sign, perhaps, that things weren't as they should be for an ambitious young actor? And it wasn't the first time that had happened – it was just the worst and the most recent, and it sort of stopped me in my tracks. Well, it is ghastly, of course, turning up to some hired church hall to do a turn to a desk behind which there are three or four people counting the minutes away till they can get their hands around a nice glass of something in the pub next door. Oh God. Trying to raise one's voice against a tinny piano in a room with the acoustics of a World War Two hangar and battling to pick up a few dance steps with legs that quite suddenly are refusing every command one makes of them – two left feet, when only yesterday one was a veritable Gene Kelly during Arlene's class at The Dance Centre in Floral Street. But the awful thing was that it wasn't just the idea of the audition itself – it was the whole idea of setting off again...

Oh shit – I'm just feeling a bit jaded at the moment, that's all. And if that encourages me to ring the bell in front of me, perhaps it's all for the good.

When I left drama school nearly three years ago, I just thought that life was going to be so exciting, surrounded by wonderful opportunities and big, showbiz characters. I thought I'd be drawn in and become part of it all. The whole thing would be an upward trajectory. Assistant stage manager in Farnborough, the odd commercial which would keep things economically afloat, then small telly bits and pieces before the film roles started to arrive.

Dream on. Now the whole thing seems rather naff. It's such an egocentric world. Sounds like a generalisation,

I know, but it's true – whether you belong to the world of the musical tour or the more highbrow three-weekly rep set. The first lot spend their working lives in digs inevitably called something like 'The Ivor Novello Guest House', run by camp old ex-dancer couples desperate to share their fading memories with their guests over a cooked breakfast. *'Harry Secombe sat in that chair, you know. Yes, the very chair you're sat in now...'* There are little marble fountains and gnomes sitting on white gravel in the front garden and signed, sepia-coloured photos of sultry, long forgotten leading ladies and panto dames covering every inch of the staircase wall leading up to the bedrooms where an alarming shot of static is delivered to the clientele every night as they slip between the nylon sheets; there's endless gossip about developing affairs that might be over by the time the show reaches the Wolverhampton Grand, and forthright political views are aired, lifted straight from the pages of the *Daily Mail* about how Margaret Thatcher would change everything in the country for the better if only people were sensible enough to give her a chance.

I've always known about the naffness, of course, but learned to laugh it off while making a decision to be amused by the fact that I felt not quite a part of that world, not joining in with the boys and girls from the chorus talking about the upcoming production of *Snow White on Ice* in Blackpool and the possibility of lots of extra work at Pinewood and the BBC TV Centre before the start of the summer season.

Putting my general fearfulness and snobbish contempt to one side, though, there's going to be a big fat problem if the Conservatives win the next election. I was so sure

Labour was safe last year, but this Winter of Discontent has nibbled away at their support. Tory austerity will eventually mean the end of those jolly queues at the labour exchange in Strutton Ground, that's for sure. If she gets in, there might well be an end in sight to sitting around over endless cups of coffee comparing notes about being 'pencilled in' for a Coke commercial, about provisional Equity cards, the Redgraves and their Workers Revolutionary Party, dance classes with Arlene and Matt in Covent Garden, auditions for weekly rep in Scarborough, a radically alternative Shakespeare at the Citizens in Glasgow set in the Maasai Mara or a new musical in town based on *Tom Brown's School Days* and so on and on and on. No more hanging out with glamorous actresses with fiery hair, blood-red lips and chihuahuas in handbags and their 'Shweetie-pie! Lovely-to-shee-you's'. Just recently it seems those funny 's' sounds have become quite obligatory for any aspiring actress. Typical conversation on the stairs leading up to an audition room – 'Who'sh the director?'

'Shtuart Beshton.'

'Really? Heavensh! I don't know why he'sh ashked to shee me for thish role. He knowsh my work – sheen me on shtage sheveral timesh.'

Fuck. Maggie will put an end to all that silliness if she gets in. Well, she might not be able to get rid of it completely, but she sure as hell won't be subsidising it!

∼

Stopped on a double yellow line in the King's Road, Edouard was looking gloriously tanned in the battered Mini that seemed to have replaced the Rolls Royce. He'd just come back from a two-week holiday in the Canaries.

'So what sort of money do you earn then, Edouard, when you do your bits and pieces?'

'Alan's agency ees charging the client £100 and you 'ave to give him £10 for each of the bookings. Then the rest is for you…' he said, sweeping his hand through his blond curls while looking at himself admiringly in the cracked wing mirror.

'£90. You make £90 every time you're sent to someone?'

'That's right.'

'Holy shit.'

CHAPTER 3

So I rang it. It was one of those doorbells that needs a lot of pressure from a determined thumb rather than a finger, before a half-hearted electric current engages with some far away basement bell. Eventually, there was a reluctant staccato rasp in the distance. I remember it well. But momentous as it was for me and my future, I'm going to have to admit that the nitty-gritty of what happened that first evening is a good deal hazier than it could be. Well, it's a hell of a time ago now, but it's extraordinary that the lead-up – the journey to Hampstead, the churchyard, the drawn-out coffee beforehand is still absolutely, indelibly printed in my memory. I *am* going to put something down for you here, but I can't promise strict accuracy when it comes to the details. It's just too long ago, and too many similar memories from those few months have been collected and messily filed away. That's not to say that many of the characters I met in the next few months aren't as clear as day, including this first gentleman. What I'm trying to tell you here is that most of those evenings proceeded in the same sort of way, and I promise you that it always turned out to be the most uninteresting part of what I have to relate.

A shadow bounced about the skylight above me on the other side of the door. There was the sound of a patient, steady unlocking, and a chain being freed before being let fall along the inside frame. The early middle-aged face that then appeared bore an open, relaxed smile. This, perhaps, was a routine weekly occurrence here of no import, my arrival no more unusual than that of a chiropractor or podiatrist. A glass hung lackadaisically from his fingers; he wore monogrammed maroon slippers, and his blue shirt had damp patches at the front after what had perhaps been a hasty shower; the buttons strained a little against a girth beginning to spread, there were gold cuff-links at his wrists and a stiff collar liberated from a tie.

'Tony.' He dropped the keys into his pocket and stretched out his hand. I was on the point of correcting him, telling him my name, when he said, 'And you are?'

'Oh – Ben. I'm Ben. How are you?'

'I'm well, jolly well. Yes, absolutely. Give me your coat, Ben.'

I slipped off my jacket, tangling the straps of my small canvas bag in the arms as I did so. 'Whoops-a-daisy,' I said as I struggled to separate them before handing him the jacket. He deposited it onto a hook in the darkness to the side of the door.

'Do come on up and let's get you an oversized gin and tonic – will that do the trick do you think?' He'd already made it over to the bottom of a grand flight of stairs. 'You come far, old chap?' There was a clink from the ice in his glass and a pause in his journey as his hand met the banister. He turned, his eyes swiftly spanning me from top to bottom, asking themselves if I'll do. He started his ascent. I was scurrying behind, keeping up, the eager beginner wanting to please.

'Oh, that would be lovely. Er, yes, Kennington, actually. Not too far really. Straight up on the Northern Line. Didn't need to change at Camden, which was just great...' I was already talking too much, trying to delay some moment that was bound to catch up with me in the very near future.

We were climbing a dark mahogany staircase, panelling stretching out above us, with eighteenth and nineteenth century portraits so close to each other they were practically touching, a jigsaw puzzle of ancestors.

'Gosh. Lovely pictures! Are they family?' Silence. *Shit. Shut up. None of my business. Christ, I've a lot to learn. Nerves getting the better of me.* We reached a great room then, oozing culture and comfort, on the first floor. It ran the whole length and width of the house, with two deep, long, low sofas laden with cushions at either side of a flaming fire.

I seated myself, straight-backed, on the very edge of the sofa he waved me towards, depositing my scruffy little bag carefully at my feet, which bizarrely made me think of the Queen about to grant her weekly audience to the Prime Minister. My host went straight across to a table groaning under the weight of dozens of enticingly shaped bottles. There was a meticulously tidy row of cut-crystal tumblers which reflected the soft light from the lamps dotted about the room; lemon wedges decorated a saucer, and a silver pot brimmed with ice, a pair of tongs by the side. He'd been preparing for me, so I was no chiropractor, no podiatrist after all. My drink was already being poured. 'Back in a jiffy. Just checking all's okay upstairs,' he said, placing a glass in my hand before swiftly exiting. He left me to gawp at my surroundings and to wonder whether Alan from the agency was being phoned to be informed that the young man who had just arrived *'really doesn't pass muster, old chap. Not my sort at all...'* Perhaps it was going to be all right, though – a generous drink had, after all, been delivered into my hands, and I'd made it up the first flight of stairs.

A pair of tall Regency mirrors dominated the two mantelpieces in the room; there were low-hanging chandeliers and leather-bound volumes in wall-to-ceiling bookcases. Ranged on the coffee table in front of me was a great tome called *The Vatican* with Michelangelo's *Pietà* dominating the frontispiece; next to it was another called *The Paintings of Delacroix* with bare-breasted Liberty holding her flag over the barricades of revolutionary Paris. They sat between neatly arranged copies of *Country Life*, *House and Home* and *Vogue*. A large tapestry – a representation of *Diana the Huntress discovered by Actaeon*, after Titian – covers an entire wall. One of my favourite paintings – it was in the National Gallery of Scotland, and I was patting myself on the back for recognising it. But I'd have to keep it to myself – a show-off question that was designed to reveal my knowledge might have made me feel good about myself but would probably be well out of order. Old money here – a man who'd inherited rather than bought his furniture, I reckoned. A banker? Barrister? Someone in the arts – the curator of a museum, a gallery owner, or perhaps an aristo in his London house? I liked all that; it appealed to my snobby side.

A marble-topped table behind the sofa that faced me had layers of photos in silver frames; one was of my host, bordering on cuteness – younger, less fleshy with darker and slightly more hair – top hat held out, ever so slightly campily – to the side as his other arm encircled his bride possessively and pulled her towards him; they were descending a sweeping flight of steps under a portico that led up to the great doors of some grand church in the City. Pride of place, in the middle of the table, was taken by a close-up of a pretty, flaxen-haired teenager who looked away from the camera as her fingers played with a string of pearls at her neck. Next to her, in a slightly less ornate frame, there was a boy in a canoe, arms holding a paddle aloft, unaware of the camera as he battled with a swift-flowing current. He had golden locks above chiselled features that hinted at a public-school confidence and sense of entitlement. I was in the home of a family man, then, who allowed himself to play freely now that the kids had flown, and the wife was away.

When Tony returned, there was no attempt to join me on the sofa, for which I was grateful. He sat opposite me and we embarked on a conversation – he asked straight questions that just for a while hinted at a real interest in the young man on his sofa, questions about school, university – 'Oh, drama school! Interesting, interesting. Theatre's one of my passions...' There was a lot of slow noddings of the head – 'Gosh, gosh, interesting life you're leading, Ben' – but the chat surely was no more than good manners, just a way of getting us from A to B. My large, and very generous gin was hitting the spot. Enough time elapsed for me to relax into the cushions behind me; I stretched out my legs and crossed them underneath the coffee table. I was beginning to feel at home, becoming loquacious about singing lessons and voice teachers. Then he interrupted me.

'How about that little massage, then?'

I think you'll be gathering here that I'm a bit of an open book. There's no made-up moniker, no effort at anonymity, at covering up where I've come from and what I'm doing – even while I'm thinking that if Tony really is this pleasantly behaved man's name, he's an idiot to let on. I, on the other hand, am pretending nothing, hiding less. I bet Edouard invents a new persona for every customer, fantasy and lies taking flight night after night. But even if I was to decide to try and hide myself, I don't think I would succeed. I don't know why. Frightened of eventually being caught out or looking ridiculous, failing to play the game correctly? Or some honest, forthright part of my character that refuses to vanish? A peculiar thing that, when guile, dishonesty and make-believe are the essential ingredients of the oldest profession.

The bedroom was another flight of stairs further up. As he ushered me into the room, I see that it's not just the lemon wedges downstairs that have been prepared – the chintz curtains have been drawn against the dark outside, the tall lamps on either side of the bed have been turned on and dimmed and a large crisp white bath-towel has been spread across one half of the bed. A blue dressing gown had been draped across the wide stool at the foot of the bed and the smell of soap and eau-de-Cologne that hung in the air told of the fading damp warmth of the recently vacated shower in the en suite. The meticulous preparation made me even more nervous; I was an amateur out of my depth and once again, I was whispering to myself, promising that I really didn't have to do this. The door to the room was ajar, the great flight of stairs awaited me, the chain on the front door hung loose and I'm sure it was not relocked after I entered. I could still run from here any time I liked.

Tony was taking his clothes off. Cuff-links were removed and placed with a clink in a little lacquer box on a chest of drawers – I caught myself silently asking why he had bothered to put them on again after his shower. Braces were slipped from shoulders, trousers unbuttoned and let fall to the floor. He stepped free, picked them up, shook them till they found their crease; then they were folded in half and anchored with his chin while he stretched out to the back of a chair for the hanger that already held the jacket. A tall wardrobe with delicate floral carvings à la Grinling Gibbons was opened, and the reunited suit was gently guided into it. Then he was leaning over the bed, smoothing the towel with both hands, now wearing nothing but a voluminous pair of striped red-and-blue boxer shorts – the sort you might purchase from one of those old establishments in Jermyn Street perhaps at the same time as placing an order for your tailored shirts.

He turned to look at me as he climbed onto the bed, a note of puzzlement crossing his features when he realised that I had not shed any of my own clothes. I paused, took a silent breath and found myself stripping off. Quickly, I was standing there in nothing but the white gym shorts that I'd been wearing under my jeans, clutching the canvas bag (a roll of kitchen towel and massage oil within) to my naked chest as though it might help to hide my vulnerability. I prized it away and tentatively placed it on the edge of the bed. Then I found myself taking a leaf out of his book by picking up and folding my clothes before placing them on top of his dressing gown on the stool. I thought better of it when I noted with alarm the grubby denim jeans and the once white tee-shirt turned grey by a hundred mixed-colour washes clashing with the pristine blue silk. I scooped them up and let them drop to the floor before moving across to the side of the bed.

I survived it – more than survived it. Slightly over an hour after I'd rung that dainty doorbell, I was back on the Northern Line, the empty train careering south as it rattled out a song of congratulations. The wallet in my back pocket contained more notes than it had ever done before. *Easy-peasy, that was, you clever young man!* I told myself as I peered into its leathery depths to check, once again, that there really was one hundred pounds in crisp new notes snuggled up together where just a while ago there had been nothing.

∼

And so it began. Two or three times a week, in the early evening, I would steel myself to descend the stairs from my room in the attic to the communal phone on the landing in the middle of the house, press a coin into the box and ring Alan to inform him that I was 'available'. I'd creep back up the stairs and leave my door ajar so I could hear the phone ring when he called me back, crossing my fingers and praying hard that the other occupants of the house wouldn't be hogging the line with long-distance calls. Earlier that summer, Yong, the medical student who lived in a tiny room on the landing below me, had discovered that a glitch in the system, encouraged by a piece of deftly manipulated wire, meant he was able to phone his parents and friends in Singapore without having to fill the box with coins. Hours of his sing-song voice drifting up the stairs throughout the night had sent me nearly crazy, until I'd gently knocked on his door one Saturday morning to tell him, eyes wide with innocent alarm, that 'A man from British Telecom came round this morning to inform us that it has been discovered that our phone is being abused, apparently. They're in the process of working out who might be owing what – and they're saying that by far the major part of what's owed has been spent on international calls! Isn't that the strangest thing? What do you think has been going on?' He was much less on the phone after that – essential now that I was working from home and quite reliant on it.

∼

And the business? The ins and outs of what I got up to? The routine I was to get used to over the next few weeks and months? All quite straightforward, really, uncomplicated and not at all memorable. At least for those first few sessions, there would have been the application of a little oil, followed by a loitering start on the shoulders before a stealthy descent to the middle of the back. Then the legs – a little time spent on feet and calves before the suggestion of the removal of boxer shorts followed by a straightforward pummelling of the buttocks for a minute or two and a request to the client to turn onto his back. A lot of circular rubbing of stomach and kneading of thighs would follow, the hand steadily rising along the inner leg to the point where the intrepid tip of a finger might dare to probe the side of a bollock. Testing the waters, as it were. If that all went to plan, after not more than ten to fifteen minutes the proceedings might very well be brought to an end with a politely outstretched hand, an averted eye, and a firm, no-nonsense grip. A few weeks on, perhaps a little more complicated than that, with the elastic of my own shorts receiving the odd twang from a wandering hand before I might consent to their removal, usually after the client's suggestion of an ever so slightly enhanced fee.

∼

I'm being modest with my words here and sparing detail, but what I'm trying to say is that we're not really referring to much more than a bit of slap and tickle. What took place that first evening in Hampstead and most of the following evenings over those few short months certainly wouldn't suffice in the present day. A perfunctory act, with no comparison to what might happen now with practiced young Brazilians with oversized egos, great pride in their gym-acquired assets and no inkling of shame, with cocky northerners being summoned by mobiles and ex-marines with a no-nonsense, businesslike attitude; apps with photos and maps, and coded phrases that hint at requirements and desires that I'm too old to have ever known the meaning of – a world away from the fumblings of the gauche young amateur of all those years ago.

You have to understand that it was indeed a more innocent age in many ways. My few weeks of compulsory training at Alan's hands – no employment offered without the paper certificate that boasted a pass – had given me the rudimentary skills of the masseur, and a training in what to say if I was ever to feel that things were getting out of control. *'Excuse me, sir, but I'm asking you to understand that I'm only here to give you a massage...'* I'm not quite sure how that would have gone down had I been faced with a large, powerfully built and determined gentleman who was unwilling to take no for an answer, but luckily, I was never faced with that situation. Very lucky, really, since I was a rather fey young man whose time in the gym hadn't had that much effect on my slight frame. But the words I'd been told to say if I ever felt I was in trouble seemed to give me enough confidence to convince myself that I was well armed against any unpleasantness.

Of all the various gents that I bumped into in those months, there was not one that lit any type of fire in my loins, apart perhaps from a near-silent, very young German aristo at the Ritz squeezing in a little erotic pleasure while his mother took off for a stroll along Old Bond Street – 'You heff to be ze queeeckest before she is coming beck to zer room...' That did quite appeal, I suppose – something about the general panic around the need to be done and dusted within a quarter of an hour or so and the naughtiness of a teenager doing things on the bed his mother (a countess, no less) would be sleeping in later that night. 'A queeecky.' But truthfully, of all the others, I don't remember the details

– unless they were particularly gory – because they were of no interest to me.

~

'Bad, bad idea. It will ruin you, Ben – it will ruin your life.'

That was Aurelio's opinion, delivered in the lilting Gibraltarian accent that had so endeared me to him from the moment we first met. We were sitting at the pine table in his kitchen in the large mansion flat in Bloomsbury that he shared with five other students. It was one or two days after my visit to Hampstead and I was busy turning the incident into an amusing anecdote, boasting about what had happened and not yet quite facing up to the fact that there were to be other assignations. That's a bit like comparing notes straight after the first night of an under-rehearsed, badly written production that should never have seen the light of day. In the middle of celebrating, the realisation dawns that you may have got away with the opening night, but you've now got to perform the same wretched piece the next evening, and the evening after that, and the one after that. A lingering look of anxiety came across my face; Aurelio's half-hearted laugh had disappeared as his large grey eyes darkened.

'You have no idea what you are getting into – you're too delicate a sort of person to be able to handle it. At the very least, you'll get used to the money and not know when to stop and become thoroughly jaded by the whole thing – I promise this will be a disaster. I really don't understand how you think you can do such a thing. And I also don't quite know why you've left it till now to tell me about it, either. How long was this bloody massage course you did?'

'Oh, not that long. A few weeks. I didn't think to tell you – it's not really that important.'

'Not important? You've been training to become a fucking rent boy and not telling me about it? Jesus, I really–'

'Rent boy? Come on, Lelo – it's hardly as though I'm hanging around the railings at Piccadilly Circus winking at men in grey macs! And I can't believe that *you* are preaching to me about morals. You're the one who took me to my first sauna, remember – and it was you who showed me how to navigate my way round Hampstead Heath in the middle of the night. Now, for some reason, you think you've got the right to start moralising about–'

'It's not about morals, Ben, it really isn't. It's just that you're such an innocent. Unworldly. And I don't want you to get hurt, that's all.'

'Fucking hell, I'm twenty-two, not a sixteen-year-old virgin!'

'Okay, okay – things may have changed a bit, but can I just remind you of what you were like barely a year or two ago? Remember our first night? I finally manage to pick you up at Bang after chasing you up and down every fucking floor of the building for the whole goddam evening. I bring you home and sit here at this table with you till the sun comes up, trying to work out how the hell I'm going to get you from kitchen to bedroom. Jesus – I must have had the patience of a saint! Finally, we climb into bed and ten minutes later you're still clutching the waistband of your underpants as though they were a chastity belt and requesting that the light be turned out "at least for a bit". God, those startled eyes shining through the gloom. And then the hesitant, fearful voice, "Aurelio, I think I ought to tell you – I haven't really done much of this sort of thing before…" No shit, Sherlock…'

CHAPTER 4

I was a thoroughly inefficient tart. Talentless. Hopeless at the arts of seduction and totally immune to any pleasure from the physical goings-on that I allowed myself to be subjected to. I truthfully don't know how I got away with it, and indeed, I'm not sure that I would have if I'd tried to carry on for more than three or four months.

I wasn't like any of the other lads I came across who were also working for Alan's agency. They were all seriously on the make but also seemed to manage to get a modicum of enjoyment from what they were doing. I remember once turning up at one of the Park Lane hotels to find that three of us had been summoned to a vast and gaudy suite to entertain an extraordinarily obese member of one of the royal families of the Middle East and being taken aback by what seemed like the genuine enthusiasm displayed by my colleagues. They were scampering about naked, laughing, poking fun at the vast blob of a prince who didn't seem to take any offence as he lay stretched out on a bed the size of Saudi Arabia, wearing a pair of massive Y-fronts and a vest the width of a schooner's mainsail. His desires seemed to be satisfied quite innocently by having strawberries from a silver bowl popped into his mouth while his hand floated just above his private parts without ever quite coming into contact with them. 'Plop!' the boys were shouting with each little delivery. I couldn't give myself to the moment in quite the same way and found myself rather self-consciously placing the fruit firmly and deliberately onto the extended tongue before wiping my fingers politely on a napkin, like a particularly diligent waiter serving afternoon tea at Fortnum and Mason's. At the end of the evening, an aide presented all three of us with a tight wad of notes each. My companions spent a few minutes expertly flicking through their bundles, a pleased, deserving look lighting up their faces. They had obviously visited before, and knew they were onto a winner. I accepted with delight that this was a cash reward way beyond what had been agreed, folded the notes up tight and pushed them into the top pocket of my denim jacket. No vulgar counting out of money for me. But the greatest difference between me and my companions was that while they hailed taxis to take them off to spend their ill-gotten gains in the fleshpots of Soho, I was walking down to Trafalgar Square to catch the night bus home. A soon as I got in, my notes, counted at least three times to convince myself I really was in receipt of £800, were placed in a tin money box, ready for a transfer to the bank at the earliest opportunity the next morning.

∼

Aurelio was wrong. My short winter and spring of whoring was the cleverest thing I ever did, and not just for the reasons that I will soon be revealing to you. Of course, there were a few downs as well as ups, but surely, that was to be expected. Sensitised, traumatised, foully cut open by the experience, I was not. That's not to say that I wasn't touched by my friend's concern. It wasn't the most likely thing for a perpetually frightened, law-abiding young man with little experience in the ways of the world to find himself doing. I guess it could easily have been a disaster.

A talentless tart I may have been, but my saving grace was my ability to talk. It may well have started off as an attempt to delay what inevitably was to follow once I arrived at a client's premises, but almost anywhere I landed up, the conversation flowed. It wasn't long before I was recognised for being the sort of company that might amuse a companionless man over dinner in a hotel, very often the various 'goings-on' of the first one or two meetings being put to one side in the pursuit of intellectual rather than physical companionship. Quite soon, Alan took to phoning me if he ever felt that some old pussycat of a punter was more lonely than he was horny, and that I might be the perfect choice to go along to soothe a soul rather than a body. Tart with a heart of gold, and all that.

It's a long time ago, but I still think fondly of Roddy Halliday – which might well have been his real name – and the conversation that bounced about the walls of the dining room at the Grosvenor Hotel, close to his flat in Belgravia, where we began to dine regularly. I'd meet him there, usually taking a place at a table for two in the corner a little while before his arrival. I never quite found out exactly what he did, but I do remember him being taken aback by the fact that I knew so much about the Middle East. Wonderful conversations I had with him – about Constantinople, the Sykes-Picot Agreement, the Hashemites, the Ba'athists in Iraq and Syria and Israel's occupation of the West Bank. Me showing off about one of the things that I'm most interested in, and him more than allowing me my passion. The lack of a wife would have got in the way of a career in the Foreign Office in those days, so my assessment that he may have been a diplomat was, in hindsight, unlikely to be right, and I somehow knew that questions about his exact employment were not to be asked. I loved him thinking I was rather knowledgeable, humouring my excitement while he enjoyed my wide-eyed wonder at something he also knew so much about. 'How do you know this stuff, Ben? How *on earth* do you know this stuff?' he'd often say to me, shaking his head with a puzzled smile.

Our initial meetings at his place, with the unmemorable fumblings that had obviously been so unimportant, were quite quickly put behind us and never mentioned again once we began to meet away from his flat. It may have become a different type of assignation, but at the end of each evening, he never failed to slip an envelope into the pocket of my jacket as we rose from the table.

One night, after he'd found my pocket as usual, I removed the envelope from my jacket and pressed it back into his hand. 'Perhaps, just this once, we won't bother with that?'

'Oh – n-not short of readies tonight, then, Ben?' he said, thrusting the envelope back into his pocket, blushing and flustered and obviously embarrassed by any conversation about a financial transaction.

'Correct. Not short of readies tonight…'

After a time, as he began to feel less pressure to keep

me amused – don't ask me why, he was paying for my companionship, after all – his eyes would sometimes well up over the dessert wine when he allowed himself to reminisce about Nick, the great love of his life. They'd been on a driving holiday together in Italy when Nick had swerved to avoid a head-on collision with a teenager showing off his recently acquired driving skills to his girlfriend; they'd left the road and hit a tree. Roddy had emerged without a scratch, but Nick had been killed instantly. I got the impression that somehow, he couldn't stop blaming himself, guilty to find himself the one to be spared. He was a warm, generous-hearted man who really should have found another partner but, ten years on, lived resolutely alone in his well-ordered flat, high above Buckingham Palace Road.

That was a rather different experience, but with the other more conventional arrangements, I have to say that I was quite incapable of understanding what pleasure anyone might take in the visit of a young man who was unlikely to be enjoying what he was being paid for – the uninterested body, putting up with the invited, but unwanted attention. I've never craved that for myself; couldn't see the point. I think I probably looked down on these perfectly nice people, thinking of them as being of a certain age and past their best – strange to think that most of them would have been a lot younger than I am now. When I think back to it, I'm more than aware that there was often an unkindness in my attitude; perhaps it was something I used to keep me on top of the situation. It became a regular trick of mine, as I stood over some old gentleman – stretched out on his front with eyes closed, gently moaning with pleasure – to amuse myself with my reflection in a nearby mirror by crossing my eyes and sticking out my tongue. Not very nice of me.

It wasn't all plain sailing, of course. You can't do what I was doing without coming up against the odd surprise. People's peccadillos don't shock me in the least any longer, but back then, the whole thing was a fairly steep learning curve.

Quite early on in those few months, I rang the bell of a house in a street off Clapham Common and almost immediately, as though he had been waiting for my arrival with his hand on the latch, the door was opened by a rather harassed-looking gentleman dabbing at beads of sweat on his forehead with a large white handkerchief. He looked from side to side, up and down the street before ushering me in under his arm, as though I were a member of the Resistance meeting a contact on a perilous mission somewhere in occupied France.

'You're a schoolteacher,' he said breathlessly, before I was able to do my usual over-hearty introduction.

'No, no, I'm not actually. I'm an unemployed actor, resting, as they say–'

'No, you're not. You're a schoolteacher.'

'No, truthfully, I'm not. You must be thinking of someone else–'

'I've been a very, very naughty boy, sir, and I wouldn't be at all surprised if you were to have to give me the slipper on my bare backside…'

'Oh…'

Just a few minutes later, I was upstairs in the marital bedroom, half-heartedly swinging a slipper against a large purple bottom while wondering what on earth the world was coming to. At least the man had had the decency, before my arrival, to lay the inevitable family photos face down on his wife's dressing table.

Plumbers and accountants, MPs and judges, policemen and social workers. Some were quite open about who they were, others less so, but with a nose like mine, it didn't take much more than a glance around a room to figure out a thing or two. A well-known TV chat-show host made no attempt to hide his identity – 'Lovely, lovely, lovely!' he'd shout at the critical moment, before putting on a dressing gown, pouring me a drink and settling down to find out as much about me as possible – I found myself being questioned in as much detail as a celebrity in front of the cameras on his wildly popular show. Sweet man. Made me feel important. A lion tamer from Tbilisi (not quite sure if I went along with this) wearing black leggings; an oleaginous jeweller late at night in Hatton Garden who delivered a horribly wet, unwelcome kiss to my mouth as soon as I stepped inside his premises; a diplomat from behind the Iron Curtain who summoned me to a hotel and never took his fear-filled eyes off the door to the room for the short time I was there, and a rotund celebrity cook with the eyes of a sad teddy bear who patted the space on the bed next to him and told me he 'really just wanted a bit of a chat...'

∽

'His name is Mr Herschmann. Spelt H-E-R-S-C-H-M-A-N-N. Okay? 34. Horsfield. Crescent. West. Hampstead. Tube. Seven. Thirty. This. Evening.' Alan was using his dictating voice, nearly every word a sentence. It brought out the residue of a South African accent in a way that didn't happen in ordinary conversation. 'Side door.' The voice returned to its usual, undoubtedly fake, plummy accent. 'Knock hard. Quite deaf. One of our regulars. First name's Herman. Second name Herschmann.' The light bulb above the phone had pinged off as I'd reached for the receiver, so I'd found myself writing in the semi-darkness, hoping the biro was recording enough info onto my notepad to get me to my destination. 'Yes, I know – Herman Herschmann,' said Alan. 'Sort of rhymes with itself. Sounds like a monster character from a fairy tale. Funny the names that parents decide to burden their kids with, but there you go. You got all that then, Ben?'

'Yep – yep. Got it all.' I was a bit frightened of Alan. Had been right from the start. I guess it was because I knew he had the ability to grant or take away at a moment's notice. He could be moody, too, and a bit capricious in his treatment of us – I was aware that he'd recently taken against a lad who was no longer earning any pennies as a result. Alan hadn't been honest with him by telling him to clear off, so Jo had sat at home by the phone night after night until he realised that he was being punished, that no punters were being put his way. Apparently, he'd been called into the office some while before and Alan had backed him into a corner, asking him if he 'could give him a helping hand with this,' as he pointed down to an unpleasant-looking bulge in his trousers. The lad hadn't wanted to do it, which might seem a bit odd given the general nature of our employment, but there you go, he just wasn't willing to provide a free quickie, I suppose. I wouldn't have wanted to either, which is why the story had put me on edge with my dealings with Alan.

'Want to repeat it, then?'

'Yeah, sure. Herman Herschmann. 34, Horsfield Crescent. West Hampstead Tube. 7.30 this evening. Door to the side of the house. Knock hard.'

'Good. All set, then. Oh – one last thing, though. The fee's double for our Herman. £200.'

'Oh, okay. Why's that then, Alan?'

'Because he's the ugliest old fucker you'll ever come across in your life.'

∽

Well, old Hermie rather took to me. I've no idea why. Probably something to do with the gift of the gab thing. Perhaps I'm doing myself down a little here because I suppose I was quite cute in a way that I wouldn't have been at all aware of at the time. My idea of cute would have been just about any of the other lads who belonged to Alan's stable of young men – pretty, streetwise urchins from the East End with flat stomachs and bright, darting eyes looking for any opportunity for financial enhancement; squaddies from the Brigade of Guards accepting cash to help bury the truth of their shameful desires from themselves; already well-paid cabin crew needing more to sustain their hedonistic lifestyles and foreign, exotic guys like my old friend Edouard, and Zvonimir, who'd wanted out of Yugoslavia and told an unlikely tale of political asylum granted after an eight-hour swim after throwing himself overboard from a warship in the Adriatic. To me, the middle-class goody-goody-two-shoes boy from the Home Counties, my companions in crime possessed an extraordinary daredevil glamour that I wanted to be part of, at least for a while. But for all of us, it must have felt like just a passing moment, a journey towards an unknown destination, but with many of them not able to get off the ride once it had picked up speed. God knows where they all are now. There must be lots of survivors, but so many of those lads will have been totally fucked up, first by smashed childhoods – handed over to the care system by parents beyond coping – and then by drink and drugs, following their mums and dads into abusive relationships while the relentless passing of looks and health and finally, hope, took their toll.

I wasn't one of them. I don't think I was, anyway. But fuck knows – perhaps I've not got that quite right. Stockbroker belt Surrey adolescence it might have been for me, but Mum was a drinker all right, and Pa tried to rise above it and pretend it wasn't happening. Still does, really – it's not up for discussion, even now, all these years after she died. Sometimes, when I visit him, I feel as though we're two characters in a Pinter play – speaking words that sound like one thing while meaning something quite different.

'The wallflowers are looking particularly good this year, Pa,' I said to him last week.

'Yes, aren't they just – got them from a new nursery this time. I like the mixed variety better…' Mum, in the little gaps in her drinking, loved the garden, and it dawned on me as I drove away from Pa that my comment was a clumsy subconscious attempt at remembrance, a hint that we might someday be allowed to talk about her. It would have passed Pa by, of course, sat in his chair after our lunch, his hand impatiently spread across the *Daily Telegraph* on his knee as he waited for me to announce my usual 'Best be off'. Pa has a look in his eyes that tells me he's a thousand miles away, but he's not, of course – he sits, to this day, in the same house we moved into when we first came home from the Middle East nearly twenty years ago. He seems to be in a perpetual state of dry-eyed mourning for a lost life, every passing year rendering him less capable of moving on. No, it wasn't ideal, my childhood, but somehow, I look at the chaos of those young guys' lives and never felt that there was a comparison to be made. I've always told myself that I was just an observer for a little while. And I definitely knew when to move on.

But back to Herman. *He's not* that *hideous*, I told myself as I followed him into what was quite obviously a consulting room in the basement of a large house in West Hampstead. Below his crusty bald pate, the old man, slightly unsteady on his feet perhaps after getting up too quickly from an early evening nap, had a long, languorous face, like that of a retired bloodhound, not exactly unpleasant or unkind, but with a look around the jowly mouth that suggested disapproval, and that a telling off for a quite minor misdemeanour wasn't far off. Herman had vast ears which seemed quite a pointless waste, since every sentence I ever uttered to him had to be loudly and slowly repeated – he would inevitably berate me, using a tone both impatient and disappointed, for my 'veeery pawr deection'. Perhaps the ears had been forced to grow larger over the decades in the hope of catching at least a little of what was being said to him. They were great flowery protuberances made up of a multitude of folds and creases; they gave him the appearance of having been the victim of some failed artistic experiment by an ambitious exponent of origami.

The room he 'practised' in, although in the basement of the house, was large and airy. There was a chaise-longue pushed up against the mantelpiece with a tartan rug thrown over it, and at the top end, where a head might repose during a consultation, was a large, rather battered leather winged armchair where no doubt Herman sat taking note of what might come tumbling from a patient's subconscious. Behind his chair was a standard lamp covered by a silk shawl that had been thrown haphazardly over the top of the shade, scorch marks showing where the bulb had burned into it; above the mantlepiece hung a good painting – a bright-eyed man looking out of the canvas with a face held slightly to one side, holding a pipe near to his mouth, as though he had just taken it out to comment on something.

'That's a beautiful picture, Hermie,' I said to him, a few weeks after we'd first become acquainted.

'Vhat?'

'A beautiful picture – that,' I said, stabbing a finger aggressively towards it while wondering at the same time what had happened to me since I was somehow beginning to ape Hermie's mannerisms.

'My fazzer. Dead at Auschwitz.'

'Oh my God! I'm so sorry.'

'Sorry? Sorry for vhat? Zis is your fault?'

Below the picture, on the mantelpiece, a bronze bust of what I took to be the same man propped up a row of books and files so disorganised that they threatened to fall to the floor at any moment. At the far end of the room, the French windows opened onto an unkempt-looking garden; it was a constant worry to me that since there were no curtains, Frau Herschmann (if she existed) might at any time descend into the garden from the rooms above. I had a frightful image of her cupping her hands against her forehead and peering into the room during one of my 'consultations' with her husband, only to find herself in receipt of a very severe shock from which she might never recover. I spent most of my few visits (for there was to be more than one) to old Hermie rehearsing in my mind a plunge onto the threadbare Persian carpet followed by a roll under the chaise-longue should an elderly lady wielding a pair of secateurs come into view.

I saw Hermie Herschmann several times before deciding to call it a day. Each time I went, I allowed myself to row back a little from my first opinion that he really was not *that* bad and slowly began to understand that the doubling of the fee in Hermie's case might be justified.

'Zer door is open! It is open! You heff to push it haaard!' he called in annoyance on what turned out to be my last visit. I'd knocked a couple of times, as usual, before getting a response. He was on the far side of the room once I'd managed to push open the rather stiff door, wearing a pair of very baggy and none too clean underpants and a string vest so low-slung that his nipples could be seen amongst the long white hairs that started at his Adam's apple and petered out somewhere just north of his knees. By this time in our relationship, three or four visits in, Hermie had decided that he had a great passion for me. Hence the state of undress on my arrival. 'You heff zer body of a sportsman,' he'd inform me in a cross voice, somehow making an intended compliment sound like a criticism. I didn't have the body, but we'll let that pass.

He embarked upon a slow journey towards me, a slightly sideways stagger, one shoulder leading the way, from a corner of the room towards the opposite one. As he approached me, he began to moan appreciatively. A long string of drool made its way out of the corner of his mouth and stretched its way towards the carpet. Trembling hands reached out even though I was still quite a few feet away and a small, but clearly audible fart escaped him, no doubt due to the general atmosphere of heightened excitement that my presence had encouraged.

No – I'm not sure that I can do this again, I told myself as he closed in on me and I found myself taking backward steps towards the wall behind. I felt my dick declare a state of emergency and start to shrink into my abdomen out of harm's way. A hand reached out and a puzzled then disappointed look came over Hermie's face as his fingers delved about, searching in vain for signs of a reciprocal fervour.

'I am just vondering,' he said, scratching his cheek, 'vezzer it might be you don't realise zat perhaps you are not so attracted to me as you seenk you are. Is zis possible?'

'Golly, Hermie. That's a really interesting idea. It hadn't occurred to me, that, but I wonder if there might be something in it...'

Holy fuck. Mr Herman Herschmann was at the very top of his profession, according to Alan. An expert in the toings and froings of the troubled mind, and yet unable to master the most basic elements of self-awareness. I don't know. Perhaps an inability to put your ego to one side and see through to the truth of yourself doesn't necessarily cancel you out as a therapist. But when, years later, it eventually came time for me to lie along a chaise-longue, I couldn't help but check for signs of an untrustworthy sense of self in the person sat in the chair opposite.

CHAPTER 5

It was going swimmingly, my new career. At the small branch of Barclays close to my bedsit on Kennington Park Road, the middle-aged lady behind the counter – all lacy blouses, tight auburn curls and pencilled-in eyebrows, more like an old-fashioned chemist's assistant than a cashier – dropped her surly attitude and started to view me with fresh eyes.

Long ago, she'd decided to adopt a look of deep disapproval whenever I appeared, her lips growing thin and the corners of her mouth turning down – as though she felt I was in need of a shower. Latterly, quite unable to keep her feelings to herself about the long-term unemployed, she'd taken to allowing herself a sad, disappointed sigh while stamping my giro. This might well be followed by another, slightly longer and angrier, as she counted out my money. With an impatient, dismissive push of her hand, the measly few notes and coins would be shunted through the grille, creating an unfriendly clatter that confirmed the feeling that I was being reprimanded for my indolence. But in the space of just a week or two, she'd gone from making sure never to catch my eye, to a nodding of the head in recognition of my presence and then, in early January, we'd ended up with something approaching a 'teeth and tits' showbiz smile of approval as soon as I was spotted coming through the door. Quite right too, with the vast amounts I was squirreling away.

I began to indulge in a little retail therapy, deciding that two pairs of Levi's 501 jeans would be permitted to be in my possession at the same time (that didn't pass Aurelio by, who didn't comment but whose eyebrows involuntarily lifted at the sight of the stiff, unfaded denim beneath a new plaid shirt). The days of waiting at the laundrette in my underpants for my only pair to dry were over; I upgraded myself to a service wash instead of having to sit growing dizzy for an hour or two as I watched my clothes tumbling round and round in a silver drum. I'd hand in my large blue canvas bag and return much later to collect a bundle of nicely folded, warm, dry clothes from the mop-wielding, monosyllabic Edna, or the efficient and seemingly rather prim proprietor, Mrs Scott – though the first time I'd entrusted my Y-fronts, jeans and vests to her, I'd gone into the unusually empty premises, gingerly calling out her name before pushing the door at the back. It had slowly swung open, hinges squealing, to reveal her on her knees administering an enthusiastic blow job to a tall gentleman in a grey suit; he was steadying himself against the onslaught, arms outstretched against the drying machines that whirled and whined approvingly behind his back, his face wearing an ecstatic expression not unlike that of Saint Sebastian during his martyrdom. They were far too busy to be aware of having been caught *in flagrante*; I leapt back through the door, too shocked to think of closing it, and dashed outside still gripping my canvas bag as though it were a lifebelt.

I walked once round the block before going back in, having decided that Mrs Scott's dedication to the matter in hand would be bringing an end to the proceedings quite quickly and indeed, by the time I returned, the gentleman was readjusting his tie, and she was patting her perfect hair back into submission. As I handed over my smalls, an animated discussion had taken off between the two about the benefits to the business of the deal he'd obviously just closed for a new set of tumble dryers. I suspect Mrs Scott's bobbing head in the back room was part of an attempt to secure a discount. Naughty old thing – but hey, it's certainly not for me to accuse her of behaving like a floozy. Let him who is without sin cast the first stone and all that.

It's difficult to describe the joy of suddenly, after years of having to be so careful, of being able to treat oneself. I bought myself a black leather waistcoat from an emporium in Kensington High Street, together with several shirts and a light-brown pair of boots with heels. The shoes turned out to be a fashion faux pas on account of my inexperience; they were abandoned forever after their first outing when I heard a disparaging aside from some fashion queen to his companion as they leant up against the bar of The Salisbury in St Martin's Lane. I played with the idea of returning them but couldn't quite convince myself that I was never going to wear them; they took to moving house whenever I did, never being taken out of the box they'd originally come in, which was consigned to the bottom of various wardrobes around South London. There they remained for over two decades, a pair of Sleeping Beauties in perfect condition but for a sad layer of dust over the box, until I presented them to a charity shop just a few years ago. There were other extravagances – I started to have my hair cut at Smile in Knightsbridge, but took fright when on my third visit Michel, with the cupid lips, tiny waist and wildly bouffant hair, asked me if I'd 'enjoyed my last creation?'.

I resisted an urge to tell him to pull himself together and decided to revert to Abdul and his no-nonsense barber's next to the library at Kennington Cross.

It lasted just for a flash, the urge to spend money and impress; I indulged a fleeting image of myself parading around in fancy designer clothes from Selfridges with a Rolex flashing at my wrist. I thought a car might be necessary, though I didn't then drive, and I allowed myself to imagine I might be the mystery man about town with the odd photographer snapping me for the Tatler society pages with some celeb (who, for fuck's sake?) on my arm as we stepped from a limo together. But it wasn't to be, because the fantasy couldn't take hold, especially when I got round to thinking about the inevitable press speculation about the mysterious young man's background. Holy shit – imagine the whole caboodle eventually coming to light in the *News of the World*? *'Supermodel taken for a ride by an underworld rent boy.'* Anyway, I couldn't get my head round the person in a white suit that I conjured up in the first-class lounge at Heathrow, propping up the bar with champagne and oysters embedded in ice spread out in front of him. I never really wanted to eat out in fancy restaurants – still don't. I like good, ordinary grub like shepherd's pie with beans and chips and plenty of it – not colourful bits and pieces of nothing, daintily arranged left of centre on a too-large plate. Not only could I not imagine sunning myself beside the helipad on some yacht anchored off Capri, but I also wasn't attracted to who that person might be. What on earth was I doing entertaining those sorts of fantasies? Christ, I'd been a student revolutionary just a tiny while ago!

I guess that even with the odd flight of fancy, I've always been anchored in some sort of reality. In the end, by far the most successful purchase of those months was a little black-and-white telly that I bought for the bedsit. That also took to following me round South London, but it was greatly loved and appreciated for all the years I owned it. Quite recently, for old times' sake, I turned on my old friend in the spare room and the screen flickered for a moment before it went blank, save for a tiny dot of light that hung on for a second or two as it finally gave up the ghost.

Wait, though. I'm going on as though there were stuffed envelopes every day making their way across the counter, thousands of readies accruing in the account, with the bank manager desperate to invite me into the side room at the branch to offer me coffee (brought in by Miss Lacy Blouse who'd leave the tray on the table and take backward steps out of the room) and to persuade me to take out an investment portfolio under his auspices. But of course, I wasn't really after any of that – the whole adventure had come about because I was fed up with being dirt poor, remember. I had no money. It pissed me off and I took measures to adjust the situation. That's all, really.

So, came the moment when a nice healthy surplus had been saved and I was able to slack off. By early April, less time was being spent turning down the volume on my new telly to enable me to hear the phone in the hall, and I was beginning to contemplate what might follow the end of this little period in my life.

It didn't take much to get me to start neglecting the phone. Aurelio may not have been entirely right about the effect my little money-making scheme would have on my psyche, but somewhere in the back of my mind, I was never quite able to dismiss the look of worry that I'd seen on his face the day I'd told him of my plans, even though the new pair of denims gracing my thighs may have had him daring to reappraise the situation. More important than that, the idea that I fancied I was doing something exciting and daring had begun to pall.

There was a choice to be made. Either I stuck to my initial bargain with myself and put an end to my money-making spree, having devoted myself to it for a sensible amount of time, or I carried on. And what would that mean?

In the end, certain things helped push me firmly towards a decision.

∼

The billiard cue was pointed in my direction, singling me out at the bar. 'What the fuck are you lookin' at, mate?' An ominous silence hung in the smoke, broken eventually by a slow nod. 'You don't belong here, you fuckin' poof – you're just poncing about playing at this, ain't ya?' The boy launched the cue into the air; it made a half circle and the thin end landed in his hands as it came down. It was raised to the side of his head like a baseball bat ready to take the impact of a ball. Now it was a weapon and he was edging towards me. 'You've no fuckin' idea, have you? No fuckin idea...'

I'd clocked the tall, dark-blond squaddie type in the grey tracksuit pants as soon I'd arrived an hour before. Deep-blue eyes, hard as steel. He was wearing a tee-shirt exposing biceps and tattoos; a pint glass was gripped firmly in one hand with an elbow out to the side with a cigarette pinched between thumb and index finger in the other as he waited for his turn at the table. I'd been amusing myself with the fantasy that, beneath the bravado, he was a little boy lost and I might be the one to help soften and soothe him. Diamond Lil's got his eye on him too – he's at his usual space atop a stool at the bar, like a vulture weighing down the branch of a tree, waiting to spread his wings and glide down towards his prey.

Just before my squaddie had turned on me, he'd started a rowdy game of pool with one of the other regulars, ignoring the thirsty look of the two or three elderly potential punters ranged along the bar. They were trying to ingratiate themselves by laughing too loud at the players' lewd comments and calling out their names when a ball was pocketed. 'Yes! Good fuckin' shot, Mickey – fuckin' nice one!' Posh man, dumbing down for the evening, not for the first time. I employed the same sort of tricks in these lads' company in an attempt to pretend to myself that I was part of their world. Up to this point, I was being ignored, looked through as though I didn't exist. Neither potential punter, lover nor mate. Mickey was right, of course. I was just an ex-public schoolboy playing a game.

'Cut it out, Mickey. Back off.' Leon's voice at the

reception desk boomed above the Bay City Rollers track playing to the tiny, permanently redundant dance floor. He'd interrupted the shuffling of a pack of cards and his finger was jabbing at Mickey, mirroring the billiard cue. 'Any fuckin trouble, an' you're outta here. Leave the kid alone.'

'I'm jokin', Leon,' said Mickey using an exaggerated, exasperated tone. He twirled the cue round in his hands and then let it slip slowly through his fingers till the end hit the floor. He leaned on it, chin resting on the chalked end. 'Just 'avin' a little laugh an' a joke, ain't I? Jesus fuckin' Christ, Leon. A joke, a fuckin' joke. Takin' the piss, like...'

'Well, it don't fuckin' well sound like it to me. Remember – I know you, Mickey, I know you. Just bear it in mind, mate – one fuckin' call to the ol' bill and you're back in the slammer where you belong – so watch it. Fuckin' cunt.'

'Fer fuck's sake, Leon–'

'Shut it. Fucking shut it.'

I was at the Up and Down club on the edge of Soho, a scruffy dive in Little Newport Street reached through a nondescript door, the buzzer with exposed wires hanging off the door-frame. It was one of the late-night clubs where some of the lads congregated between, or instead of bothering to find, tricks. It was also a place where an intrepid punter might try his luck. A steep ascent of a narrow staircase delivered you to Leon on reception where his vast frame was draped across a stool in front of a desk. A fag dangled from a mouth of gold and brown teeth and a voluminous stomach, barely contained within a nastily stained tee-shirt, hung heavily over the top of his trousers. Plastered flat onto the top of his head, fooling no one, was a toupée, as compromised as the threadbare carpet on the stairs that led up to him. The long dark greasy strands clashed with what was left of his white hair where they met at the bulbous neck. He was a mess, but today he was my hero. I think he had a soft spot for me – the very same thing that had inflamed Mickey was probably what Leon liked about me. I was sticking by Leon for protection for a while, lest the danger hadn't quite receded, but I was determined not to look in the least disturbed by what had just happened at the billiard table, and I really didn't want to be seen slipping away, tail between my legs. I placed a faux-friendly hand on Leon's shoulder as I bent over the desk, pretending to take an interest in his game of patience while eyeing the flight of stairs as though it were a bobsleigh run. It was there to whizz me away from danger when I judged that enough time had gone by to allow a nonchalant yawn, a bored look at my watch and a speedy exit.

∼

Twenty minutes later, I was huddled under the shelter of the bus stop at the top of Whitehall, my hands pressed into my armpits and the collar of my damp denim jacket turned up in a futile quest to keep out the unexpectedly cold wind of an early April night. Sharp drizzle-laden gusts were pestering my feet while I concentrated my gaze at the bottom of Nelson's Column, waiting for the welcome sight of the N87 to come into view.

I gratefully jumped into the warmth when the bus arrived and made my way upstairs to the seat at the front.

I was alone but for a comatose punk couple taking up the whole row of the rear seats, both clutching empty wine bottles and leaning against each other with their heads rolled back, yellow and purple mohican spikes stabbing the window behind. Their mouths were wide open, and they were so helplessly unconscious that if the bus were to plunge off Westminster Bridge into the night-black waters of the river it probably wouldn't be enough to bring them round. With the sleeve of my jacket, I wiped from the window enough of the condensation to give me a glimpse of the bus's progress, and settled back, knees lodged against the windscreen ledge as I embarked on a post-mortem of the evening's events at The Up and Down. I was glad to be away and I knew that Mickey at the pool table was right. I didn't belong. I was playing a game. I was just a silly posh poof from Surrey out of my depth and desperate to belong to a group of lads I had nothing in common with. I was an outsider – like Diamond Lil – and I didn't want to land up where he was.

I was not at all like him really, but the thing we had in common was that we were acting a part. Sure, he'd been at it for very much longer than I had – doing tricks forever, of course, but also playing at belonging, convincing himself he was one of the gang. He was not, and the life he'd led had left him jaded and cruel, with a clever tongue that spared no one. A sharp, unkind wit wouldn't spare him his comeuppance forever, though. The lads laughed at him behind his back, and sometimes to his face, but he could look after himself in a verbal catfight, give as good as he got, and up to now he'd been able to command some sort of respect. He was a loudmouth – he hadn't bothered to learn my name, because I was of no interest to him, but he needed an audience tonight, and just before the pool table incident, I was being subjected to an onslaught from his usual position at the bar. He was perched on a high stool, wine glass in hand, legs crossed once over his thighs and again round his calves, the fumes from the menthol cigarette poised between long fingernails at war with those of the roll-ups of his co-workers.

'Fuck that old bastard!'

He was showing off about last night, needing to inform anyone who was prepared to listen that he was still in the running, capable of turning a trick. 'The stuff he wanted from me – I ended up asking for double! Dirty old sod – but he's so fucking hung up on me he'll just about pay anything I ask. I reckon that was half his weekly wages he put into my hands last night. Nasty old perv. Fuck, I hate the cunt. Who the fuck does he think he is, dribbling and pawing at me?'

In between punters Diamond Lil flirted with the boys, sometimes striking lucky if one of them was in need of shelter or too drunk to make it home. But the odds were against him because he was in his late thirties, he was stuck and beginning to look ridiculous and the punters were few and far between; he'd been hanging around Soho long enough to have lost contact with anything to do with his previous existence. In my mind's eye, I saw a camp skinny lad from Huddersfield arriving in London twenty years ago, nervously clutching a small suitcase neatly packed by his mother, to take up a position as trainee porter in one of the better London hotels. He's the pride and joy of his parents, mouthing off to anyone who'll listen about their son's escape from the blighted northern town that they've hardly ever left. He has wonky teeth, a stud in his ear and a shock of blond highlights among a rigid hair-sprayed fringe concealing a forehead illuminated by acne. Actually, he'd been around too long for me to have that image anywhere near right – I wondered what a delicate-looking seventeen-year-old, fresh off the train from the north, looked like in the late fifties? Anyway, now he was an aging rent boy and the sheen of youth had worn off. The look was all wrong; the highlights had been toned down, but he sported a ridiculous bob, had recently added a diamond stud to his nose to go with the one in his ear, and he wore gawdy rings on his fingers and a chunky gold chain round his neck, spanking-clean white trainers together with an immaculately laundered grey tracksuit that he no doubt hoped looked like Mickey's but that sure didn't work in the same way. He was a figure of fun, and he didn't know it because he was too bound up fooling himself. The old man he was deriding was his only customer and his only means of support.

∼

I was on the point of being lulled to sleep by the warmth and the motion of the bus when I was suddenly being pushed over towards the empty seat beside me as a body was inserted into the space I was forced from.

'Fucking freezing out there! Jesus. You got a fag, mate?' It was Mickey, breathing beer and fag fumes over me, and so close his lips were practically touching my ear. I was gripped by fear, stiffening and readying myself for violence.

'Er – no. I don't smoke actually...' Damn the nice boy

from Surrey who just couldn't help revealing himself. Silence for a while then, with a leg forcefully and pointedly pressed up against mine.

'Where you off to then?' he said eventually, suddenly placing his hand on my thigh and squeezing it to the point of pain.

'Er – Kennington, actually. I live in Kennington.'

'Oh yeah? Where's that? You all by yourself there?'

A wink, then. I couldn't believe it. He must have left the club just after me and followed me onto the bus. He'd been hiding downstairs, waiting to make a move on me. And I thought he didn't like me. Wow, this was crazy.

'Hey – you got a fag?' He was up and heading to the back of the bus towards the sleeping couple.

'You got a fag?' he shouted again, taking the young man by the shoulders and shaking him until his elaborately constructed mohican wobbled from side to side and threatened to collapse. A pair of eyes briefly opened and struggled to focus. 'Na. No fags.' They closed again, Mickey let go of the shoulders and the head slumped, returning to its position against the back window.

'Fuckin' 'ell! What are they on? Could use some of that for myself. Look at the fuckin' state of them! Jesus Christ!' he said loping back down the bus and throwing himself back onto the seat beside me. Another hard squeeze to my thigh, which might have been a deliberate cruelty rather than a suggestion of passion. I couldn't suppress a sharp intake of breath, but Mickey ignored it.

'Am I staying with you tonight, then?'

'Yes, if you want...' My mouth dried as the words came from me. There was not yet much desire in this decision, just uncharacteristic daredevilry. But whose eyes might I widen with this tale in a few days' time? Who would I be if I had this wild boy in my bed, if he got to really want me, dropped the bravado, stared into my eyes and swapped the profanities for honeyed words? I was off on the excitement of it, picturing myself at the Up and Down at all hours, Mickey's constant companion as I watched him playing pool with his mates, perhaps taking up the game myself as I played the part of a gangster's moll. A part of his life. Cherished. Unquestioningly accepted by all.

∼

Just a little later, in the early hours, a knife had materialised as if from nowhere. It was at my throat as I was pushed, naked, up against the wardrobe in my room.

'I haven't got any money here, Mickey, honestly. I don't keep–'

'Fuck off, mate, fuck off. Don't give me that. Where's the money? Tell me or you're gonna get cut.'

It was all going to be all right, too, just a little while before. He'd softened as we'd left the bus, as though the macho image was an act that could be left on the seat to travel on through South London now that there was no one there to see and judge him. When I closed the door of my room and locked it against the outside, he'd put his arms round me and kissed my neck; the lad that had threatened me just a few hours before had been banished.

'God wasn't making little green apples the day he made you,' he'd whispered. Not an expression that I'd ever heard before or quite understood, but I took it as an endearment.

Just before daybreak, with the birds starting their dawn chorus, I'd woken to a space beside me growing cold and the sound of a drawer being opened on the other side of the room. Sitting up and adjusting my eyes to the semi-dark, I was able to make out the shape of a rounded back; a naked figure on its knees, head buried in the chest of drawers, arms out to the sides as his hands rummaged their way through my clothes. Was he sleep-walking, looking for a tee-shirt to stave off the cold of my unheated room? Or had he fallen over, struggling to find his way to the bathroom on the landing below? Perhaps he'd woken with a need to quench his thirst after the excitement of the early hours? I said nothing, lay back and closed my eyes wondering what to do, struggling against a moment of doubt that surely could soon be explained away. I made up my mind to pretend sleep, wait for him to return to the bed and throw his arms around me again. But the sound grew sharper, busier, then more desperate as another drawer was opened and impatient, determined hands pushed things from side to side and knocked against the back panel of the drawer. Something was thrown halfway across the room then, and I heard a whispered, frantic 'Fuck!'

I pushed myself up onto my elbows, no longer able to keep up the pretence of sleep. 'Mickey? You okay?'

And then I'm being pulled, naked, from the bed; powerful arms with pinching fingers hold my own behind my back. The light is switched on, and I see again the mean face that I saw at the pool table in the 'Up and Down.'

'You've had your fun and now you've gotta pay, you

fucking, toffee-nosed poof. Just give me the money and I'll fuck off out of here and leave you alone, okay? Got it?' A measured tone, spelling out the demand – polite compared to what was to come during the next half hour or so, or however long the bloody thing went on for. Then the pleading, the trying to convince him that there was only the money in my wallet that he'd found and already emptied. It was now lying, splayed open on the floor in the middle of the room, like the forlorn carcass of some small bird stripped of its feathers. Over and over again I was telling him I was a person who didn't keep cash in the room and please, please to just go now and I won't mention any of this to anyone, not ever, but perhaps, if he was just to come back a bit later, after the bank had opened, I could maybe get more money, and I promise to give it to him when he knocks on the door, I really would, but go now, please, and leave me alone? And then there's the knife, suddenly produced from his bomber jacket, and it's up against my throat, nicking the edge of my chin, and I'm looking at my ridiculous skinny nakedness in the long mirror and despising myself and this sullied, silly room, and I'm more frightened than I have ever been in my life.

And a long, long time later, after he's grabbed my hair and used it to bury my face in the mattress and ram it against the wall, he sits astride my chest, and he pinches my nose hard and shoves a hanky that came out of my drawer into my mouth while I struggle to breathe. Then, at last his face changes again as greed and desperation subside and pure anger arrives, and I know he realises that there is no money. He loses patience and wants to punish, and he slaps my face with his palm and then with the back of his hand, to and fro, to and fro until my face is numb and my bleeding nose wets my chin and cheeks. I'm thinking of the couple downstairs who have just moved in, imagining if they are pulling their blankets up round their necks, looking up at the ceiling and pretending not to hear but then whispering to each other, wondering whether to call the police, and I'm half hoping they've noticed nothing because if I ever come out of this room, I won't be able to bear the shame and the questions that will be asked and then have to be answered with a truthfulness which will drag this time of horror into a living reality forever.

But now, quite suddenly, he gets off me, reaching for his pants, his track suit bottoms; he's wrestling his arms into his tee-shirt, dragging it down over his abs, then pulling on his trainers without loosening the knots, stamping them impatiently against the floor until they succumb to his feet, and all the time he's swearing that I'm as good as dead for what I've done to him, what I've cheated him of.

'You owe me one, you fucking poof; you fucking owe me, cunt, shit-arsed fairy bastard...'

I unlock the door and walk down the stairs with his stuttering breath on my neck and the knife prodding at my back, and it must be that there are ears pressed up against doors as I go by on my way to let him out, and I find myself whistling tunelessly under my breath, trying to convince myself and my neighbours that nothing untoward is taking place. When I open the front door, I stand politely to one side to let him out as though I'm an Edwardian bell boy operating a lift, and the cold air of the morning shocks me when it hits my damp, bloodied face. He walks down the short path to the pavement and when he reaches the road, he looks to left and right and breaks into a run without ever looking back at me.

CHAPTER 6

'Ben – have you any idea what time it is?' Aurelio's mellow tones have been replaced with something a little harsher.

'It's morning, I think.'

'That's right.' A pause followed by the faintest sound coming down the line of a mattress spring complaining while a bedside clock is being checked. 'Four-thirty in the frigging morning.'

'Oh. Is it? Is it really?'

Another shorter pause and an intake of breath. The dawning at the other end of the line that something is amiss.

'Ben – are you okay?' I'm not able to answer, but there's immediate comfort in the familiarity of my friend's voice, even though he might be angry. 'Ben? For fuck's sake answer me. Ben? Are you still there?'

'Yes. I'm here.'

'What the fuck's up? Are you alright for Christ's sake? What's happened?'

'Yea, yea – I'm fine actually, Lelo. I just wanted to have a bit of a chat, really. That's all. Just a chat…'

∼

At no time during the next day, or come to think of it, any time after, did my sweet friend Aurelio even hint at a '*told you so*'. Not that I remember very clearly anything that might have been said during the passing of those first hours after the 'incident' – as we later learned to call it.

I'd crept back up the stairs once Mickey had gone, holding a cupped hand under my chin to catch the shaming stream of blood from my nose and forehead that wouldn't be stopped, while praying fiercely that no one would crack their doors open on any of the three landings. I didn't want anyone to be witness to my humiliation and fear. The key in my door turned with a reassuring clunk when I locked it, but even then, I had to try the handle to make sure no one, friend or foe, could come in. I sat down in the old armchair and began to pull absentmindedly but determinedly at the innards already escaping from an open wound in the arm – as though it had become necessary for me to add to the chaos that my visitor had left behind. I don't know how long I sat there, but I know I was waiting for a new day, praying for the clarity that the dawn might bring. I needed it to help dismiss what had taken place. Daylight would normalise things, distance me from what had happened.

Later, having sat for an acre of time staring at the tangled bedclothes under the harsh light of the single bulb which now hung free of its broken shade, I eventually allowed my eye to wander and settle on a solitary ten-pence coin, lying like a reprimand on the carpet next to my empty wallet. '*Okay. Enough of sitting here doing nothing*', it seemed to be saying. I picked it up, unlocked the door very slowly and precisely, as though I was defusing a Second World War bomb and tiptoed out of the room into the cold gloom of the hallway to make my way down to the phone. I didn't want the noise of the coin clattering into the box, didn't want to be seen or spoken to, didn't want to be asked if I was all right and most of all, I didn't want my faltering voice to be heard being directed into the receiver.

When Aurelio arrived not very long after, the knock at the front door sounded as though it was apologising for the disturbance, two short shudders reverberating around the house hoping to alert only me, the waiting presence at the top.

I'd said nothing to the figure at the door. I didn't want him to see me, pressing a hanky to my nose with one hand as the fingers of the other started to busy themselves with freeing hair and eyebrows of the congealed blood from the gash on my forehead. I took a few steps back and then vaulted up the stairs two by two in the dark with Aurelio trying to keep up with me while asking questions in a rasping whisper.

'What the fuck–' Aurelio's eyes widened as he walked from the dark hallway into the battlefield of a room now lit by the first tentative rays of the morning sun. As I closed the door, his eyes turned from the bloodied, crumpled sheets on my bed and came to rest on my face.

'Jesus, Ben. Holy fuck! Oh my God, Ben!'

Then he put his arms round me. 'You poor, poor thing,' he said as I started to cry.

∼

Aurelio had quickly taken control of the situation, sitting me in the armchair before dabbing and wiping my face with a dampened tea-cloth while wearing a serious, but somehow comforting look on his face that put me in mind of Miss Carson, the matron at prep school.

'You going to tell me what's happened here, Ben?'

'In a minute, just a minute, not straight away. Just let me catch my breath...'

'Okay. Are we going to call the police? I think that–'

'No! Please, not that. I just couldn't bear it, I really couldn't–'

'Calm down, calm down. Okay, no police for the moment.'

He'd packed my laundry bag with clothes picked from the debris of my upside-down room and whisked me away in his old Renault 4, even though I thought I'd put my foot down firmly, once the tears had stopped, about being quite all right and wanting to stay put.

∼

It took me a few days to get back to Kennington. I quickly got used to Aurelio's cosseting at Gordon Mansions and didn't want to let it go too soon. I was seduced by the Mediterranean attention to all things dietary ('You've had a shock. You've got to eat to grow your strength back.'). There were comforting soups, a slowly braised beef casserole, morning porridge and toast and endless cups of coffee, croissants and pastries which flowed onto the long pine table in the kitchen. 'Jesus, Lelo – where did you learn to cook like this?' I'd asked him halfway through the week whilst spooning into my mouth a large portion of a particularly good moussaka.

'I didn't learn. It's just within me, that's all. Sort of culinary common sense...'

After the weekend, when I found myself alone in the flat, two or three calls a day would come in from my host between lectures, firstly to check on my progress, and then to give detailed instructions about warming things up after their removal from the fridge. On his return every evening there would be a meticulous attention to detail while cleaning and redressing my wounds, followed by an affectionate but careful ruffling of the hair on the undamaged side of my head.

Busbee, Aurelio's much-loved companion, resolutely refused to accept that I wasn't much of a cat lover and insisted on making a home on my lap. I quickly took to the companionship of the old lady with the loud purr and allowed myself to be treated as a daybed. While Aurelio was out at college, I spent long hours in his room, watching TV and sitting in a chair at the window observing the activity in the street below while taking some sort of pleasure in not being a part of what was going on. Within a few days, I'd become quite acclimatised to life in the big flat with its five student inhabitants – the bustle of the early evenings in the kitchen with Aurelio stirring something tasty on the hob while his flatmates also came in to prepare their suppers, chatting round the table before making their way back to their rooms with steam rising from plates of pasta on trays. Later, Aurelio and I would spend the evening sprawled in front of the telly on the huge cushions that drowned his mattress on the low bed before climbing under the duvet together, where a loving, but platonic, arm would be draped along my back for the duration of the night.

After a thorough appraisal the day after my arrival, a definite decision was taken to do fuck all about what had happened. No sitting in police stations waiting to be interviewed, no visiting and questioning of anyone at the Up and Down, no hunting down of erstwhile colleagues in other dubious dives to ask if they'd seen the bruiser who'd done me over. *'Let sleeping dogs lie'* seemed to be the general advice of all and sundry. The attention and understanding of the lads in the flat helped put it to bed for me. Notes were compared. Owen, though large and impregnable-looking, had been thoroughly beaten up just last summer on the seafront in Llandudno by three boys from the local rugby club after he'd said a drunken 'Hi handsome!' to one of them; Jeff had recently been relieved of his wallet while his pants rested round his ankles for just a little too long on Hampstead Heath, Frank had endured years of teasing about his aversion to any type of rough and tumble in the playground at his school in Newcastle, and David had needed six stitches to the back of his head having been pushed off a bar-stool in Hartlepool last Christmas by a very pretty miner who'd accused him of looking at him for a little too long. So, once it had been discussed over rather too many beers on my first evening, what more was to be said about the incident? I'd been 'queer-bashed'. That's all. Robbed as well actually, but it happens in a life. I got it into perspective. I didn't know how it could come about, but even the idea that a six-foot-something psycho might take to banging on my door and demanding money sometime in the future didn't seem to faze me too badly, card-carrying coward though I undoubtedly am.

'It's not that I've learned some sort of lesson, Lelo. Not really.' I was in the hall, taking my leave of Gordon Mansions. My laundry bag was full of clothes fresh out of the flat's communal washing machine with Tupperware containers of Bolognese sauce and chili con carne balanced among a collection of nicely packaged fruit from Marks and Spencer's. Aurelio had done both a shop and a cook to make sure I was not going to go hungry on the assumption, which I thought I'd go along with, that once I was on my own, I'd be quite incapable of looking after myself. 'It's just that I don't think I need to know anything more about that life,' I said as I put my arms around him at the door.

'What life?'

'You know – the whole rent boy thing. There's a few quid in the bank now and there wouldn't be if I'd not done what I did.' No accusation had come from Aurelio, but perhaps I felt I had to justify myself and my choices. 'It's been "informative" shall we say? Some bubble's popped now, though, and that's okay. Time to move on.'

I didn't know quite what I'd be facing on my return to the bedsit, though Aurelio had told me he'd 'popped over' between lectures one day during my week away, so I suspected that the worst would have been dealt with. I'd opened the door with my heart racing, but I needn't have feared. Typical of him that the room was not only spotless, but quite a bit cleaner than it had ever been. He'd obviously visited more than once, because my bed-linen, miraculously free of bloodstains, was back on the bed – he'd sneaked all the stuff back to Gordon Mansions without my knowledge and put them in the washing machine. The sheet and blankets at the top corner of the bed had been invitingly turned back, and the pillows and cushions arranged at a jaunty, welcoming angle with two towels neatly folded and placed at the bottom of the now barely recognisable (turned from miserable grey to a healthy salmon pink) continental quilt that I'd inherited with the room. A brand-new lightshade hung proudly from the ceiling in the centre of the room, and on the table under the window, next to my little telly – an unlikely survivor of the onslaught – a chipped vase that had been collecting cobwebs under the sink had been given a new lease of life; it had been washed and filled with yellow tulips just on the point of breaking into full bloom. There was the smell of polish, and of lavender coming from a saucer of pot-pourri on the little bedside table, of newly vacuumed carpet and freshly laundered bedclothes. The poster of my bête noire, the Chilean dictator Augusto Pinochet and his fascist cohorts, with its angry words of defiance – *'el pueblo unido jamás sera vencido'* – had disappeared. It had been a feature of my life ever since Salvador Allende had been overthrown in 1973.

At some point during the encounter with Mickey, I remember stretching out my hand, grasping at the wall as I was being swung round and round. Then the sound of ripping paper. Now, in its place, Blu-Tacked to the wall, was a vast print of *The Lady of Shalott* by Waterhouse. I don't quite know why Aurelio chose it for my room, a picture of a lady with flaming auburn hair adrift in a boat on a lake, looking with trepidation somewhere beyond the crucifix and flickering candles at the prow. Perhaps it reminded him of my state of mind after the 'incident'. It wouldn't have occurred to me to have her take the place of the cruel military goons with their lantern-jaws and dark sunglasses, but I loved her presence immediately – this damsel who now so dominated my room that she had turned it into a sober, softer space, distanced from the events of a few days ago.

~

I wanted to put off what I knew I had to do. It would have been so easy to procrastinate – to have a cup of coffee, sit in the armchair (duct tape now covering the split in the arm) and marvel at the changes that Aurelio had made to my little room. But as soon as I'd taken my clothes from the laundry basket and added them to what Aurelio had made sure were neatly folded piles in the chest of drawers, I forced myself from the room and went down to make the phone call I'd been planning for most of the previous week.

'I think you're making a mistake, Benjamin, I really do. I think you'll regret it.' There was a hint of annoyance in Alan's voice. 'You've been making bloody good money, you know. Why give it all up now?'

'Just time to move on really, Alan, but I'm ever so grateful you gave me the opportunity–'

'Yes, well a bit of a waste of our time and money, actually, when we've paid for your massage course. Wasn't free, you know. You do know that, don't you? You're not going to be earning the sort of money you have been with us, that's for sure. I doubt you're going to find things particularly easy out in the real world. Actors like you are two a penny...'

~

'How do you feel about the pink satin shorts and the Rollerblades?'

It was early evening and I was in the very grand

basement of a building at the top of Old Bond Street. I'd come down through the semi-dark to a small, brightly lit office next to the kitchens, past long bars framed in chrome and banked with glinting bottles and polished glasses, smoky mirrored walls and crimson-carpeted stairways. I'd passed a vast dance floor overlooked by balconies, silent and empty as yet, but with the lights around the edge already flashing in expectation of the punters who would be be queuing along the street outside in a few hours' time, with fingers crossed that they would be picked to enter the most exciting venue in London. They'd be the chosen few, joining the too rich or too famous to have to wait in line. In the early evening, this cavernous, silent space seemed to be holding its breath, preparing itself for what the midnight hours might bring – the promise of intrigue, glamour and sexual opportunity. The Embassy Club. I was at the nerve centre of this operation, being interviewed for a job as a waiter by the manager, David Yardley, who was lounging deep in a chair that was tilted back on two legs. His fingers were laced behind his head and his long, be-denimed legs were crossed and hoisted up onto the desk in front of him. He was giving me the compliment of his full attention, ignoring the phone that was ringing off the hook and the continual interruptions of a purring fax.

'Oh! Sort of fine about them, really,' I said brightly. 'The pink satin shorts are definitely not a problem, but I've really not that much experience with Rollerblades, if I'm being honest. I'm a quickish learner, though. Are they an absolute requirement of the job?' I was already catastrophising about an involuntary plunge down the flight of stairs I'd just come down, drinks taking leave of my tray to float momentarily above me, followed by another gash to my forehead that would make my recent misfortunes at Mickey's hands seem no more serious than a trimming of my toenails. And all observed by the most fashionable crowd in London.

'Let's see how you go,' David said to me as my very short interview ended with what seemed to be success. 'Wednesday and Sunday evenings are your nights off and we'll start you on the dance-floor balcony without the Rollers...'

So that was that. A new job, and quite a change too. £10.00 a night plus tips rather than the hundreds I'd grown used to over the last few months – and starting the very next day when I was rather hoping for just a breather to savour the victory. A proper job. The first one I'd had – save for treading the boards – since gagging on the whale meat I had to chop up in Anne Miller's pet shop back home in Surrey while I was a drama student.

Anyway, I found my feet quite quickly – aided by the fact they were in white trainers rather than Rollerblades. I sailed away into this new world without much difficulty, save for a hiccough on my very first evening when I approached a customer and asked him if I could get him a drink. He looked quite delighted, patted my bottom while beaming me a smile, and replied that a Harvey Wallbanger would be just the thing. 'That will be one hundred and thirty-seven pounds and fifty-four pence please, sir,' I said to him as I handed it over. (That's not the right figure, of course, but it may as well have been since the amount was preposterously enormous.)

'What?'

'One hundred and thirty-seven pounds and fifty-four

pence please, sir,' I repeated, my voice beginning to trail off. And then I'm thinking I've asked this geezer if he wants a drink and he's got quite the wrong end of the stick. 'A drink for you, sir?' delivered in a no-nonsense tone, with raised eyebrows and without a smile is the correct approach. But 'Would you like a drink?' said with a shy girly smile while curling a lock of your hair round a finger is open to misinterpretation. First-night nerves.

'Shit! I thought you were offering to buy me a drink! I thought my luck was in!'

'I'm so sorry, sir. I think there's been a bit of a misunderstanding – I'm a member of staff here...' As if it wasn't blindingly obvious! Jesus – what the hell did the twat think I was doing, silver tray in hand and standing there naked save for a few inches of satin shorts stretched across my arse?

∼

The satin shorts didn't last. Within a few days I'd graduated to wearing black trousers and serving in the restaurant, where it was felt my social skills might be better used. My waitering skills, however, were severely lacking and there was a lot to be learnt. But I was thoroughly indulged by the manager, Nadia, a petite American with a voluptuously rounded figure and luscious curly black hair that framed a beautiful face with ruby lips and skin like a nineteenth century porcelain doll, and who, with the patience of a saint, took me under her wing and became a lifelong friend. Nadia was my kind of girl. She'd run away from an America being traumatised by the Vietnam war, a veteran of campus demonstrations and sit-ins, burning draft cards and rubber bullets – and hence a troubled relationship with the authorities. She'd fetched up in a more benign Europe and made it her home, marrying and divorcing a bent cop who turned out to be gay (not by any means her last husband – she was prone to making bad mistakes in her choice of partners) in order to keep the immigration toughs at bay, before helping to run an alternative independent cinema, a bookshop and a host of other things and then finally landing up as the hat-check girl at the Embassy. That meant for a while she had the power of life and death; smile at Nadia and you might get inside.

But David Yardley knew a good thing when he saw it and she was soon making her way up the hierarchy. By the time I bumped into her she was in charge of the restaurant, the hub of the club, a most valued employee, even though she had a tendency to ask me now and again to hold the fort, guard the till and its takings while she went off, often accompanied by some gobsmackingly famous rock star, to 'powder her nose' in the little office behind the kitchen.

They were great days. I stayed on and off for a year, getting a little more efficient at my job and being entrusted with the till when Nadia had better things to do. I flirted with the celebs who'd make their way down to the restaurant where Nadia seemed to be a confidante of most of them. It was an occupation a great deal more glamorous than the one I'd just left – though the crash in wages took a little getting used to, of course. The place was staffed by 'aspiring' young actors with buff bodies (not sure if I was one of those. Perhaps my promotion to black pants was actually a demotion). There was a lot of general naughtiness of the druggy and sexy kind, nearly all of which passed me by, meaning I missed quite a lot of the fun. I'd been a tart for only a short while and my general innocence seemed to be still very much intact, for some inexplicable reason.

'Why don't you and I have a lovely session in the broom cupboard,' a particularly cute young waiter, the wayward son of a diplomat, said to me sometime near the beginning of my employment. 'That would be so nice, but I don't think it's going to be possible. We're very busy this evening – Elton's in the restaurant at the moment, and I really need to be on the ball.'

'Just a quickie. Go on.'

'No – I don't think that's a very good idea.' To just about anyone else, it certainly would have been the most splendid idea, but there we go. Stupid, really. I regretted it later, especially since I had a feeling that Elton would have understood a gap between the main course and dessert if things had been properly explained to him.

The whole drugs thing totally passed me by. I was completely unaware of what the shuffling to and fro between bar and loos, the snifflings and dusting down of noses, the heightened sense of bonhomie of the people returning to the restaurant after a break between courses with a suddenly acquired translucent quality of the skin on a cheek meant. One of the co-owners of the club had taken a shine to the 'new boy in the restaurant' and persuaded me to go home with him at the end of an evening. I sat around drinking champagne on a huge sofa somewhere off Kensington Church Street trying to get an avalanche of powder to go up my nose which quite failed to make the slightest difference to my frame of mind. I left in the early hours, perhaps unaware that I was less tired and much chattier than I usually was at five in the morning, leaving behind a disconsolate gentleman who must have assumed that the evening would be all his once he'd got me steering a rolled up twenty-pound note towards a thin white line on a glass coffee table. Wasn't my thing, I guess.

∼

But I've digressed.

Just two or three days into my new job, I was woken mid-morning, after just a few hours' sleep (the club closes at 3am) by frantic yelling from the landing. It was Yong, who was holding the phone out towards me as though clutching the head of a snake that was trying to bite him. That was his general demeanour for many months before enough time had elapsed for him to realise that there was to be no astronomical phone bill to be divided between the residents of 89, Kennington Park Road. Come to think about it, it's rather extraordinary that he picked up the phone in the first place. More extraordinary still is that I didn't ignore his shouts and found myself throwing back my bedclothes in a panic (*Who the fuck's dead in a car crash now and what am I expected to do about it?*) and pulling on my jeans. It was my middle of the night, so I was falling out of my room heavy-limbed with sleep, doing up buttons while stumbling down the stairs to take the call – this, even though I'd decided quite firmly on a post-whoring independence and a liberation from the shackles imposed by the payphone on the landing. I think I was caught off guard. Wanted the bloody shouting to stop above all else. Infernal racket.

'Ben – I'm going to ask you the greatest favour.' It was

Alan, and the reasons why I wouldn't be able to grant a 'greatest' favour were immediately flooding my brain.

'I don't think I can, actually, Alan. I've got to be–'

'Just this once, mate. There's no one else around who can do this for us and he's one of our best punters and actually a real sweetheart. I think you'll like him and–'

'But I'm working, Alan. I've got a job that starts at 7.30 every evening so it's just out of the question.' As I said it, I realised that it was Wednesday and my first night off. But I was still not going to do it. That all belonged to a past life.

'Couldn't you take the night off?' Wanker.

'Not really, no. Don't think I can.'

'Please? You've no idea how big a favour it'd be...'

∽

So bugger me if eventually I didn't find myself saying 'yes', for God's sake. I don't know why. Against everything I'd decided. What a pussycat of a pushover person I was. I don't know – perhaps I did think I owed the fucker a favour. Perhaps I just wanted silence, to get off the phone and to cancel later. Perhaps I thought of the niceness of an extra few pounds for one little last time. But anyway, for whatever reason, the definite 'no' morphed into a 'yes'.

I'm conscious that there are a few doorbells in my story, perhaps a few too many, so I'll try to keep them to a minimum from now on. But this last doorbell that I've reluctantly been persuaded to ring is of supreme importance. This doorbell changes my life.

PART 2

CHAPTER 7

May 1979

It's not the first time that Alexander has found himself waiting for the doorbell to be rung by a young man that he has never met before, and he's having to admit to himself that in the last year or two, it seems to have become more of a habit than he'd ever intended. It's far from sliding out of control, but it's certainly on a different level to what it has ever been in the past. But why the hell not? Surely an old chap is entitled to a little bit of fun now and again, and where's the bloody harm in it all? Still, when tonight's adventure is over, he's minded to cut it back to once or twice a month rather than the weekly occurrence it's threatening to become. Is it really alright that these little interludes have become such a highlight? Has he fallen into a bit of a mundane routine?

He had promised himself, after all, that when he properly retired, resigning from the board of Thoroughcoat Property Investments and winding down his other business commitments eight years ago, there would be more foreign travel; both he and Bridget would get about more, go to places they'd never been before. He'd hung on at the company for much longer than he should have, but it had rather become his life, and he wasn't at all sure how things would shape up once he'd given up the chairmanship.

Now, it's all much of a muchness – even the foreign trips don't really vary. Well, not at all in the last few years, if the truth be told. He has kept the little apartment close to the Jardin de Luxembourg in Paris, and visits often for the joy of the city and a small business interest he maintains there, but apart from that, they still often find themselves at the Villa de France in Tangier at the end of May, where they're able to observe the unchanging staff growing old along with the faithful clientele. Alexander and Bridget are quite used to the scenes that greet them on their arrival – the ululating chambermaids who spill down the stairs as their taxi comes to a halt, pushing their way past the porters and doormen in their blue-and-white-striped djellabas to embrace them like long-lost family members, the fond kiss to both cheeks delivered to them by Djemal at reception and Ahmed's welcome to the dining room on every first evening of their stay – the deep bow from the waist to Alexander, with palm momentarily flattened on his heart, followed by the gentlest raising of Bridget's hand to his lips as if he were administering the kiss of life to an exhausted sparrow. Year in, year out, the comfort of the expected.

But not this year, thinks Alexander. Why not Reid's in Madeira? Just for a change. Or further south in Morocco – La Mamounia in Marrakesh would be nice, but it's already a little late in the season. Too hot for Bridget, now. They could stay further afield than

Marrakesh, though – that cool, wonderful place high up in the Ourica Valley with its magical views, the ice-cold swimming pool used by no one, and the chef's famous omelettes. No chance there for the sort of little favours that might accompany room service, of course. They can be quite bewitching, those peasant Berber boys, but certainly less willing to '*have a go*' than their suburban counterparts. But that's not a make-or-break thing. He can go without for a week or two.

Their lives now, in old age, follow an orderly, predictable rhythm, that's for sure, and hence the rumblings of his discomfort. Times are split between Sandwich and Belgravia; Bridget motors them up to Eaton Square on Sunday afternoon after they've taken tea at 4 – although recently she's sometimes been managing to persuade Alexander to delay their departure till Monday morning. He'd initially complained and resisted but has now partly come round to her way of thinking, since it does mean that he's been able to extend his time on the course at Royal St George's, and now and again even pick up another game at Prince's next door. He's proud of his handicap, but not at all sure how much longer he is going to be able to continue, with his eyesight going downhill as rapidly as it is. Same goes for the horse. The combined age of man and beast is not that far off one hundred. He's seventy-seven, and Flight is eighteen. Is he really going to replace his dear old friend when the time comes? And is he up to it – indeed, he might well have to be replaced first!

Would it be possible for him to settle himself into a new seat, learn to compromise all over again with a younger, perhaps less reliable horse? They've been a good team for the last ten years, but circumstances are threatening that now. While following the hunt at a leisurely pace last March (more out for the ride these days, rather than the chase itself), he'd quite failed to catch sight of a low-hanging bow while concentrating on a hedge approaching fast that had to be jumped. The branch had beaten him about the head like an East End thug and unseated him, leaving his tall frame stretched out on a grassy knoll some distance behind the other riders. Pride basically intact due to the lack of witnesses; mount and horseman relatively unscathed, luckily. This time. Bloody eyes.

Bridget falls into a near silence these days once the car nears Eaton Square. She itches for the garden in Sandwich, even during the winter when she's quite unable to stop herself pottering in the greenhouse, inspecting the geraniums and then foraging about in the borders, cutting things back even when Midge, the garden help, advises her to leave well alone till the spring. Summer provides her with a blessedly full programme of garden works and being wrenched from her beloved patch beyond the French windows of the sitting room becomes more and more difficult. She's long fallen out of love with London and can't see the point of the weekly visit. Hence the delay till Monday, and her departure, just the right side of the rush hour, back to the country as soon as tea has been taken on Wednesday afternoon. Alexander follows on the next morning by train. And hence the time for a little dalliance after dinner.

Maria has cleared the dinner things away together with the little folding mahogany table that she lays beneath the bookcase at seven o'clock every evening now that they no longer bother with the dining room. She's said her goodnights and departed, the front door gently clicking closed behind her. Alexander has settled himself with an air of excited anticipation deep into the cushions of the sofa with the remains of the bottle of Tavel rosé that he always swears is going to see him through two evenings and never does. Well, he's leaving in the morning, and is he really going to leave a perfectly good wine to compromise itself in the Frigidaire?

He draws back his cuff, squints deeply at the watch on his wrist and makes a guess at the time, then takes a long draft from the wine glass that he picks up from the side table. He finds his other hand patting the space beside him, a subconscious rehearsal for the moment, if all goes to plan, when the youth on the sofa opposite might accept the summons to join him by his side. His fingers caress the half-full glass that is now anchored between his knees, gently tracing the outline of the large 'B', surmounted by a coronet, engraved on its side. 'Silly old Pa!' the old man says out loud, remembering his father's vainglorious excitement at the push upstairs from Commons to Lords that Churchill had used to get rid of a host of old MPs in the hope of winning the election after the war. Didn't work, of course, because he'd been trounced by Attlee, but old Sir Willy Lowther had loved all the trappings of his new status. The boy from Northern Ireland made good. For his title, he'd taken the name of the village where the family had settled with a grant of land during the time of Cromwell and added that of his old constituency. William, 1st Baron Bellaghy of Holland Park no less! The new peer – encouraged by his second wife, thrilled to find herself promoted from the wife of a knight to a peeress of the realm – had rushed off to various establishments in Mayfair to arrange a swift delivery of stationery, silver cutlery, glasses and plates, towels and sheets, suitcases and crimson velvet slippers, the whole lot embossed and engraved with 'B's topped by a baron's coronet.

There's time before the young man is due. Time enough for a quick think about the speech that he's preparing for the wedding anniversary celebration next week. He'll make people laugh. That is what's required, and indeed, it's the only part of the whole proceedings he's looking forward to. A good speech. Time to shine. Something for people to laugh at, unlike the efficient, staid soliloquies about property development he finds himself delivering on a regular basis to the Upper House.

A party to celebrate a golden wedding anniversary had seemed a marvellous idea in January, absolutely splendid, and Bridget had been thrilled too; she had become positively girly for three or four days after he'd first made the suggestion and had remained committed to the idea for much longer than he had. But that was January, and now it feels like the most dreadful idea. Talk about cold feet. There's no way out, of course – they've got to do the bloody thing now. Oh God – hordes of people from the past all turning up at the front door expecting to be wined and dined. And the expense of the damned thing! Positively crippling, especially when you've belatedly decided you don't want it in the first place. There had even been a brief discussion in the car on Monday about cancelling the whole thing. 'We really can't, darl, not now. And you'll love it when all the old crocks show up. I know you...' he'd said to the anxious face beside him as she'd lost herself and shot across a red light on the Camberwell Road after he'd mentioned the monstrous marquee. It's to be erected on Monday next week, downstairs, beyond the dining-room doors that open onto the lawn.

∼

The hullabaloo around the party has made Alexander more aware of a change that he's noticed in his wife recently. The rather straightforward, no-nonsense, almost masculine approach to life that Bridget has always shown is changing. There's an anxiety that has crept up on her recently that has been entirely lacking throughout their married life; now he is having to accommodate endless questions about how many caterers can fit into what's not much more than a galley kitchen, about wines, napkins, gaps between courses, the supplying of cutlery and most important of all, who's to sit where. 'What about the placements? Are we sort of going to be ranking people – cards at every place setting, do you think?'

'Oh, darl, come on – we're not the Sun King holding court at Versailles, for heaven's sake! Yes, we'll place people, but we'll put them next to chums, of course.' Enough to drive an old gent quite doolally tap, this endless worrying.

'Sorry. Didn't mean to snap.' A noisy silence. Alexander can practically hear the whirring of his wife's unquiet brain before the inevitable resumption of uneasy questions.

'Do we give them a drink as they step outside into the marquee? Or should it be at the front door so they can mingle there and take their time coming down, do you think, Alecky? And will there be someone to collect the coats and things?'

'Darl, please,' he says, quite unsuccessfully trying to eliminate the sound of irritation in his voice. 'Do stop going on about it. There's to be staff to take charge of all that sort of thing. And none of it is at all important anyway.'

'All three Guinnesses are coming, aren't they? Oh dear...'

'Yes, but we'll spread them out, so no one has to endure them undiluted.' *God, what a nightmare*, thought Alexander to himself as a vision of Bridget's Irish cousins presented itself to him. Six marriages between them, and all clinging with a relentless snobbery to the titles bestowed on them by their long divorced first husbands. The marchioness now married to a committed fraudster, the countess to a bigamist and the viscountess to a jazz trumpeter as black as the night from New Orleans. All four surviving husbands, past and present, devoted to collecting as large a slice as possible of the Guinness millions that the very silly girls had inherited from their papa. Plenty to go around though, even once the present partners move on from the ancient trio.

'And we can't have that dreadful old tart Margaret of Argyll on the same table as Frances Rutland, Alecky. They've not spoken since the scandal.'

'Darl – leave it to me, will you? Margaret of Argyll certainly hasn't been invited – Ian Argyll's coming and as you well know, she's absolutely persona non grata with all the Campbells, especially the ex-stepson. Bit rich after they used all her father's inheritance to rebuild Inveraray after the fire, but there we are. Anyway, we hardly know the old girl.' Alexander calls to mind an evening party some years ago given by an Aitken in Smith Street where he'd had to rescue a terminally bored-looking Harold Macmillan from Duchess Margaret's embrace. She was sucking up to him like mad, hands patting and tapping at his shoulders and thighs, desperate for his attention. The poor old girl was not quite wise enough to realise that the attention she craved was never to be on offer.

She had found it quite impossible to shake off the notoriety that had followed her for the last fifteen years, ever since 'the photograph' had done the rounds. In it, she was seen to be on her knees, naked but for a string of pearls, fellating a gentleman whose head disappeared off the top of the picture. Was this cabinet member Duncan Sandys, a member of the Royal Family, Douglas Fairbanks Jnr? For quite a few months, there was an unquenchable blaze of suggestions going round in polite, but outraged society, as to whom the startlingly well-endowed gentleman might be. A divorce from the duke was quick to follow, the scandal then opened up to public scrutiny by the discussion in the court of the fabled photo and the judge's comments about the duchess's 'disgusting sexual activities'.

'Most unedifying,' Bridget had declared, lowering *The Telegraph* to the table in front of her and then pushing it disdainfully to one side during a breakfast at the height of the scandal. 'Sheila Holland says it all went wrong after Margaret banged her head very hard on a low door at Belvoir Castle. Turned her into an absolute nympho, apparently. Can't get enough of it now. On the other hand, Clara Newton, who's known her for centuries, says she was always up for a go. Guardsmen, high court judges, ticket collectors, fly fishermen from the castle river, the king of the Belgians, anyone at all...'

Perhaps someone had thought it might be amusing to pair up the old premier and the infamous duchess. It hadn't worked. 'She don't tell no jokes! None at all!' the incredulous old man had said as Alexander steered him towards a sofa peopled by a younger, much more entertaining crowd. He'd looked over later to see a fresh-faced, newly elected Margaret Thatcher sat at Harold's feet, legs curled up beneath her, an elbow resting on the sofa as she looked up adoringly at the old man who was holding forth, back in his métier.

'We'll have to think of a way of withdrawing her invitation, Alecky...'

'Darl – how many times do I have to tell you? She's not bloody coming, for fuck's sake!'

'Okay, dear. But there's no need to raise your voice...'

∼

Alexander is now beginning to come to terms with what is really bothering him about their party next week – all his old friends who won't be there. There's a wind about, these days, sharpening with every month that goes by, sweeping so many of his chums off their feet and carrying them away. All so bloody arbitrary. Every chair within the marquee will be filled, of course, but he'll cast his eye around and be taken aback by the memory of everyone who should be present and is not. And won't it be the saddest thing to address his witty speech to only half a room, a room full of survivors? God, the people who have gone! Wonderful Debbo Devonshire will be here, representing Mitfords past and present, but how he misses dear Nancy – one of the greatest of losses. He remembers his last visit to her house in Versailles after she'd given up on her treatment in London. He'd sat in the garden with his old friend, now so frail that it had been a struggle for her to step out into the sunlight of an early summer's day.

'Why the unmown lawn, Nancy?' He was looking out at what the passionate gardener now allowed to grow wild.

'I like it that way,' she'd said, firmly. 'Just to let it be, to let it do its own thing, to return to nature.' There had been a silence then, cups of English tea balanced on laps as the two old friends surveyed the garden together, both aware that this would be their last meeting.

'Did you know that the Japanese have no word for wilderness?' she said after a long pause. 'After their defeat in the war, it was found that wherever they'd been, they left these perfect little gardens, shrines to orderliness. Bizarre, really – the barbarity and the delicacy all mixed up. Right now, I want the wilderness. I like the poppies growing through the waving grass. If I were strong enough to stand in the middle of it all under a parasol, I'd imagine myself transported into one of Monet's paintings of meadows.' She'd stretched her hand out then, and placed it on his, resting on the arm of the canvas chair; an overtly affectionate gesture not quite in keeping with the Nancy he'd known for so long. Another long pause, as he allowed her hand to grow heavy on his. 'It's an extraordinary adventure, Alex, this business of dying. If only it came without the fucking pain…'

∼

Who else should be here but will be missing? Desmond Carmichael from the office in Waterloo Place, with his wicked sense of humour and a twinkle in the eye. Gone many years now. How Alexander had loved his company. A string of stories to make his colleagues laugh, but the best being his description, related to hysterical colleagues straight after the event, of the retrieval of a pen dropped on the boardroom floor during an important meeting with the newly rich Saudis; the view from underneath the heavy mahogany table of the impossibly prim Miss Elstromme's long legs crossed high above her thighs, her knickerless fanny giving him what looked like a wry, lopsided grin. His imitation of the sight, his mouth twisted to the side with eyebrows raised, never failed to amuse, however many times it was repeated in the happy hours spent at the bar of the Three Crowns in Babmaes Street after work.

A long list, with too many memories of fallen friends to dwell on now, apart from the most painful. Brilliant young Robert Greville, a great passion of Alexander's that he'd eventually had to accept was unrequited but that he had been able to steer towards a richly rewarding platonic, playful friendship. Just last summer, the young Oxford don had set out with two others in a small rowing boat from the beach at Ramsgate on a blissfully calm July day, never to return. He remembers the anguish of relatives and friends and the three days of waiting before the discovery of the lonely bodies washed up, miles apart, on the beach in Sandwich Bay.

Dearest Rachel and the memories of the illicit times they'd spent together still so fresh. Those endless afternoons and evenings here in Eaton Square once Bridget had returned to Sandwich. How they used to laugh over the continual thwarting of their plans when passion had overtaken them after a few drinks. How many times had they arranged a trip to The Royal Academy, a dinner at the Garrick, race meetings at Ascot or a visit to the latest 'five star' show in town, only to find their best intentions put to one side? A pre-event drink would almost always end up with them making their way towards the small room with the single bed that Alexander had inhabited since he and Bridget had admitted to each other, many years ago, that they were more comfortable not sharing a bed. How they giggled at the passion of two people in their seventies behaving like teenagers! And then the phone call from Edward Tollemy to tell him that he'd woken to find his wife dead beside him. There had followed a conversation between two heartbroken old men, openly sharing a grief with absolutely no need to acknowledge what had never been discussed.

Charlie Hinton will be missing too. Okay, he's not dead, but still a dreadful loss. He's recently fled the country for Cape Town without explanation. Some trouble with boys, Alex had heard, some of them really just a little too young. Silly bugger. Bloody hell – everyone's gone AWOL these days. How very hard it's becoming to keep the sadness at bay.

And Owen will not be here, of course. There will be no Owen. 'I have no son, now,' Alexander says to himself out loud. 'I truly have no son.'

'Oh, for fuck's sake, what's with this pointless

reminiscing?' he mutters, breaking the maudlin grip of his reverie. He takes a deep breath, sighs, and empties his glass before reaching for his notepad and pen on the coffee table in front of him. He begins to scribble down what has already formed in his head.

I would just like to say a most sincere and humble 'thank you' to all of our dear remaining friends who find themselves here, in Eaton Square, on a summer's evening instead of what they would really like to be doing at the start of their weekends. (Pause for laughter here.) You've got yourselves up in your smartest kit and been forced to raid the safe for the last of the family heirlooms; you've summoned your taxis and made your phone calls to housekeepers and given them the evening off, you've notified various young relatives that you are delayed in London overnight but will still be expecting them for a late lunch tomorrow. You then explain to them that the stay in town is unavoidable because you are seeing dear, though now rather befuddled old friends (take this out if Bridget doesn't like) from way back who are celebrating some anniversary or other, and it's proven quite impossible to get out of a commitment that seemed like quite a good idea when the invite arrived some months ago...

Alexander is relieved to find that he's beginning to enjoy himself, warming to the task, and wondering whether his little speech of welcome, and the joy he's going to take in its formation, might be enough to banish the melancholia that he had allowed to encroach on his evening.

There's a sharp, impatient rat-a-tat-tat from the doorbell in the hall.

'Good gracious,' he says out loud, springing youthfully

to his feet, before having to extend an arm to the back of the sofa to steady himself as the effect of the recently finished bottle of Tavel threatens to topple him. 'I'd quite forgotten about the young man who's coming…'

CHAPTER 8

Jesus – another doorbell! And I swore that I was through with all this. It's only a week or two since my last punter, but I feel so far away from the whole thing. I've moved on. I'm a waiter in a nightclub, I've got my first audition for months on Friday, and I'm feeling good about the future. What the hell has persuaded me to be standing here under a porch in Belgravia at the beginning of a thunderstorm? I think I must be still frightened of Alan, so I'm doing his bidding. Yes, that makes sense – I've been bullied into this. That's what's happened. But how can that really be? He has no power over me anymore, none whatsoever. I guess he's one of those people who casts a shadow and– *Oh stop going on. You're here, and it's for the last time. So ring the bloody doorbell.*

'Hello there, I'm Peter!'

And I'm Rupert Bear, but never mind, I think to myself while telling the elderly gentleman in front of me my real name. 'Ben. I'm Ben. How do you do?' He takes a step back from the open door and thrusts out his hand which I take and find myself vigorously shaking. He looks nice enough actually. Tall and upright in a dark green smoking jacket, with a kindly, slightly mischievous face with twinkly eyes, so that's okay. I think I probably won't be here all that long anyway – I can get this sorted quite quickly.

'Golly, it's blowing up a storm out there,' I find myself saying, slipping comfortably into my old ways.

'Well, come on in and I'll pour you a glass of wine. Actually rather cold for this time of the year, don't you think?'

'Yes indeed. Extraordinary the tricks the weather can play, isn't it?'

As I slip out of my damp jacket, I'm able to observe just how far I've come in a few months. I'm not nervous, only a bit disappointed that I've allowed myself to be here in the first place and just a little bored at the prospect of what's ahead; I'm suddenly aware I've developed an attitude that I don't approve of – a growing feeling of disdain that I've been successfully keeping at bay for some time. Perhaps it's the very thing that Aurelio was trying to warn me of a few months ago – the development of a certain contempt for anyone who opens the door to a stranger, anyone entertaining a fantasy about who I might be and whether I really want to be here. A little callous has been forming on my soul; I'm becoming cynical. I wonder if I'm still capable of returning an envelope of cash, like I did to Roddy Halliday just a few months ago? I know my way around these situations far too well now, and I'm pleased to be on the point of leaving it all behind. These days, I even know to take off my jacket and fling it towards a coat-stand by the door without being asked, and I'm much quicker to settle deep into a sofa while basking in a glow which might be the beginnings of a feeling of superiority. *I'm young, I'm cute and you're paying.*

I follow my host along a hallway where vast mezzotints are hung so close to each other they're practically touching, and enter a large drawing room. I've come full circle; the room puts me in mind of my very first client in Hampstead.

'I'm going to open an excellent bottle of Tavel that I have in the kitchen. I had a little with my dinner, so why don't we continue with another bottle? Are you partial to the grape?' I've no idea what a bottle of Tavel is and the question is a rhetorical one apparently, since the gentleman exits without waiting for an answer.

I sit back and look around me. How many times have I done this – an appraisal of my surroundings while my host goes out to seek something to encourage the evening towards conviviality? I'm in a comfortable room; self-assured, elegant, grand, and slightly more than well lived in. The mezzotint theme is carried on from the hallway with two rows of framed prints banked up on either side of a French commode on which sits an exquisite terracotta bust of an eighteenth-century lady. She has curls falling about her neck and great swirls with bows rising above her head à la Marie Antoinette – I reckon it might well be a copy of the famous representation of the queen by Boizot. The two large sofas have deep indentations at the fireside end, hinting at years of relaxed lounging; the cushions are flattened with age and use, and the once crisp colours of the flowers, picked out in needlepoint, have faded into an autumnal mellowness. The drawn silk curtains, a deep crimson, are faded and just beginning to fray at the edges where the sun has touched them, and the long footstool in front of me – needlepoint again – that nearly stretches the length of the two sofas is spotted with ink-stains and has an assortment of books, papers and notepads on it; there's a tumbler on its side spilling pencils and biros, elastic bands and a pair of nail scissors. A battered Roberts radio whispers *sotto voce* to nobody and next to it are several pamphlets entitled *House of Lords Weekly Hansard*. Beside them is a pile of *Financial Times* and *Daily Telegraphs*; they're neatly folded and alternating pink and white, weighed down by a large eyeglass that catches and throws the light back at a chandelier in the middle of the room.

Nosey, aren't I, taking all this in as soon as I can, making my judgements and working things out. But doesn't everyone? Yes and no, I suppose. The difference between me and my erstwhile colleagues at the Up and Down is, to be frank, my slightly obsessive interest in people and where they all come from. A sort of snobby thing that doesn't reflect on me all that well, perhaps. I certainly don't belong to the world that this gentleman who says his name is Peter comes from, but in some strange way I think I know about it. What I'm saying is I have enough knowledge to be able to put together a picture more skilfully than a lot of people. I'm a washout on the sexual front with these old chaps, no doubt, but boy, can I hold my own in a conversation.

I *am* nosey. Nosey about everything. Not just about what's going on in *Coronation Street* and about who might be having sex with anyone, anywhere in the world (always totally fascinating) – I'm as interested in all that as the next man. But for some reason, it's imperative for me to also be up to date with just about everything else there is to know, like the overthrow of Pol Pot in Cambodia and the flight of the Shah from Iran. I need to read endless opinions about the impact Thatcher's new government might have on the country, about the plight of the very few Jews left in Iraq, and why after the division of the subcontinent, India manages to maintain a democracy and Pakistan doesn't. I need to know why certain colours in Inigo Jones' portraits are fading and sometimes radically changing and those in Zoffany's aren't. You know why? Well, I might as well tell you since I've brought it up – old Inigo loved experimenting with new, unknown pigments to mix his oils, but two hundred years later, it's caught him out and now his ghost employs a myriad of people in conservation who are trying to recreate the original hues.

I'm a bit of an oddball, that's for sure. I can spend endless hours in Kennington library amusing myself by working out how many times the children of the former king of Greece are descended from Queen Victoria (three times). Who the fuck needs to know that? Yesterday, I suddenly felt the urge to find something out about horses – to know who first climbed onto the creature's unwilling back. How long ago? And where did this happen? Central Asia, it turns out, about 3,500 years ago! It's the strangest thing, this need for knowledge, some of it quite pointless, because I'm not the slightest bit clever; I steer away from any questionnaire in a paper that wants to test my IQ. I'm quite sure it would be well below average, and a confirmation of the fact would upset me.

~

What happened later? After Peter had come back into the room with the open bottle and we'd had a glass or two? It's no good me going into detail about something I really don't remember – I'd be making it up and I'm not going to do that. Funny, this, isn't it? Is my amnesia about reluctance, or was everything so straightforward, so routine and unimportant that I couldn't be bothered to store the memory? But if I could remember, I would be reticent about sharing the experience, let's be honest. I don't want to write about it, and I don't really know why. Perhaps it feels like a disloyalty now. To both of us. Peter and myself. But I will try and sketch it out knowing that we're not going for any accuracy whatsoever here – just a little notepad impression of what this and a few other similar times might have been like.

∼

I'm relieved when, after not very long, we re-emerge from the bleak little back bedroom with the tiny window, furnished by not much more than a chest of drawers, a rather utilitarian wardrobe at odds with just about everything else, a narrow single bed that reminded me of the sort you might find in a prep-school dorm and a side table and lamp. Like I've said before, an elderly gentleman would never be my choice for a bit of rough and tumble, and now that I'm putting it all to one side, I'm able to come clean to myself and admit that I find it unpleasant. I've approached this and all the other times as though I'm running into the sea in Pembrokeshire on a perishingly cold April day ('I *can* do this! I'm holding my breath, but I can, I can, I can!') as I once did to show off to Pa, coming out congratulating myself, and at the same time making up my mind that it's never happening again.

In the room I vaguely remember there was not any charade about a massage, just a suffocating blackness once the side lamp went out, and then the clumsy and sharp bony elbows, knees and hips of a not very competent old performer getting in the way, and the pretence on my part of a mild, professional disinterest, then the turning away of a face to avoid a kiss, stolen glances at the luminous numbers on my watch-face to figure out how much longer this might have to be endured, and the galloping realisation that the thin veneer of guile and bravado that had seen me through the last three months was peeling away – the dawning of a conviction that this was to be the last time and that I was done, free of this and it could not, would not happen again.

I'm leaving then – I've taken the rolled-up banknotes from the old man's hand, thrust them into my back pocket and am speeding towards the front door with my arm stretching out to hook my jacket off the coat-stand. 'I love your prints! Wonderfully Napoleonic!' Just a passing comment on my way out, but Peter, following on behind me and doing up his cuff-links, stops and runs his hand through his hair. He folds his arms as he leans against the opposite wall to stare up at his collection, arranged in two rows, one on top of the other.

'Yes, they really are rather grand, aren't they?' he says slowly and emphatically, nodding his head, as though he's seeing them for the first time. 'And well done you on your dating – in fact, it's a gathering of the victors of Waterloo, plus George III, George IV and sundry horses. Most of the paintings they're copied from are in the Waterloo Chamber at Windsor Castle...'

Half an hour later, I'm still propping myself up in the

hallway casting my eyes up towards the prints while my host gives me a lecture on the development of printing techniques in the eighteenth century. By the time he's got around to explaining the difference between a print with explanatory scripts at the bottom (the painter, the printmaker and the noble subject with a dedication and date) and those with nothing at all, I'm totally on board and am in no hurry to leave. He's retrieved the eyeglass from the footstool in the drawing room, and I find myself clutching it while, under his direction, I take a detailed, close-up look.

'So – the prints with no script are called "before letters" and are actually more greatly prized since they are fresh off what were the newly engraved copper plates. Virginally pure, you might say, though it has to be said that the market is changing a bit now since the American collectors have started wading in. They, of course, like all the information at the bottom, which they think gives them more caché. The prints that are inscribed are referred to as "after letters" and... I say, old chap, why not slip your jacket back off and come and finish off that nice bottle of Tavel? Must be at least a glass each left...'

~

I'd have been mightily surprised to have been informed at the beginning of the evening that it wouldn't be me but my new acquaintance that would be calling time on my visit, but that's how it turned out. Late into the night, my host pleaded old age and the necessity to retire to his bed because he had to catch a train in the morning. By then, I wasn't in the slightest hurry to get away, especially after the decision had been taken that yet another bottle of that delicious Tavel (which I quickly learned is a wonderfully crisp, dark rosé) had become an absolute necessity, since there seemed to be so many things that needed to be discussed. I remember this part of the evening much more clearly than the time spent in the cramped little room – like a junior crew member's cabin on a yacht – where we'd started out. There was a heated debate, and general disagreement, about the brand-new Thatcher government; a coming together of minds about the ridiculousness of a belief in a merciful God and what it might be about the northern European temperament that had given rise to Protestantism. We talked of the Russian Revolution, and he listened intently to my opinion that while the Austro-Hungarian, French, British and Ottoman Empires had all collapsed or been wound down, the Tsarist Empire continued to thrive to this day, albeit under different management. I was in full flight, in my element, when he brought the evening to a close.

'Why not come back next week?' he asked me as he insisted on handing over yet another note – an over-generous contribution towards a taxi.

'Yes, okay, but–'

'Give me your phone number. No need to go through that rascal Alan, don't you think?'

∽

That was the beginning of it all. The beginning of the next sixteen years of my life. How bizarre that I didn't know it at the time, but how could I have done? I would have stared a little harder, and with a little more interest at 'Peter' when he first opened the door, I guess. I remember Mama telling me when I was quite small about the first time she saw my father. He'd walked into the office of the man she was secretary to in Baghdad and she'd glanced up, smiling politely at the figure whose blond hair was being ruffled by the breeze from the overhead fan. She'd indicated, with a polite smile and a flourish of her hand, a rattan chair for him to sit on. 'Do take a seat, Mr Teasdale. Mr Symonds-Jones will be with you in just a minute or two.' Then she'd lowered her eyes back to the typewriter. 'I would have taken a much better look, had I known how he was to figure in my life!' she used to say to me with a nostalgic smile.

I probably wasn't expecting a call back, and I don't remember waiting for it. The audition on the following Friday was for a rep season at the Theatre Royal in York and my agent was on the phone within a few hours informing me that I'd been offered a ten-week contract. Typical. No job ever materialised when you really needed it, but with the pressure off, finances settled, along it came. It was as though desperation in the audition room was a turn-off, like the smell of a blocked drain, while complacency smelled of roses. Anyway, what with juggling the excitement of the offer with the need to make sure that the Embassy Club would be willing to take me back on my return in October, another visit to the nice old gent in Eaton Square was not foremost in my mind.

When the call did come through, it took me by surprise and there was that momentary feeling of going back months and years, to a past time when I'd been held to ransom by the phone. 'I say, old chap, does no one answer the telephone in South London these days?' said the patrician voice with a slightly put-out tone.

'I beg your pardon – who is this, please?'

'It's Peter here. We met last week. Bonded over Russia and Waterloo. Just wondering if you might like to pay me another visit? I think you said you were relatively free most Wednesday evenings. Short notice now, I know, but it's not for the want of trying...'

Well, why not? I realised that there would probably be the unpleasant fumblings in the bedroom again, but I could man up for that and get it dealt with quite quickly. I know I said I never would again, but what the hell, the old gent had been such good company. At least I knew roughly what I was in for, and I wouldn't have to deal with Alan. There'd be the nice wine and all that great conversation to go with it. Money would be a definite bonus, too. Useful for the move to York – it would mean less digging too deep into the savings I'd accrued over the last few months. Strict bottom lines about no more whoring, therefore, quite swiftly put to one side.

I think we must have carried on where we left off the week before. Yes, there was certainly the vague unpleasantness of the trip to the back bedroom again, but before and especially after, there was a lot more wine, with me taking up what turned out in later years to be my usual position on the sofa opposite Peter. Alexander. (I'll come back to that. Eventually.) Shoes removed, cushions pummelled into position behind my back and legs hoisted up and crossed underneath me. Right from the start of that second meeting, I was in charge of the bottle (and remained so for the next decade and a half). For the first of many, many times I was directed towards the Frigidaire and was already at work on the corkscrew as I walked back into the room to deliver the chilled contents to the waiting glasses. Indeed, it wasn't long before I was the one who'd regularly be phoning Averys of Bristol to put in our monthly order. ('Ah! Mr Teasdale, how are you? And His Lordship? You're phoning just at the right time – we've just received a consignment of that port His Lordship's so fond of.')

∼

'It's not actually Marie Antoinette or by Boizot, no, but it's a jolly good guess of yours.' My third or fourth Wednesday evening visit, and we were standing, glass in hand, admiring the terracotta bust on the commode. Things had moved on apace, and I'd already graduated to being invited to dinner. Maria, who had a room in the basement flat next door and 'did' for the Bellaghys on a part-time basis when they were in town, was laying the table and gliding in and out of the room with lowered eyes, as though she was apologising for her very existence.

'Not quite sure if the experts would ever use the phrase "school of" or "circle of" about sculpture as they do with painting,' said Alexander, face tilted to one side, 'but it's certainly eighteenth-century French. You are an extraordinary young man. How the heck do you know who Boizot is?'

'Well, I love the era and pride myself on knowing these things – there's nothing I like better than checking out Christie's and Sotheby's before a big sale. I've learned so much by doing that. Unemployed actor with nothing better to do, so I think I've just imbibed an awful lot of knowledge by hanging around and asking loads of questions of all the posh people who work there. Boizot was just an inspired guess, really, and–'

'Yes, but very close, and quite wonderful that you know that stuff.' The old man gently placed his glass next to the bust of the young lady we were admiring, put his hands in his pocket and stared at me. 'What a strange young man you are. I'm really very pleased to have made your acquaintance, you know.'

∼

'I never took a single doctor's advice, silly bugger that I am. Up and down Harley Street for months on end trying to find someone who'd say what I wanted to hear. Took not a blind bit of notice – if you'll excuse the pun – and that's really not the best way to deal with glaucoma. Now I'm bloody well stuck with it. Left eye is almost completely shut down, and the right not much better.'

Our final dinner before I left for York, and it was now that Alexander, flicking his napkin at a non-existent fly, had sent his glass careering from the table to smash against the skirting board. Maria dashed into the room from her bolt-hole in the kitchen and cleared the smashed glass from the carpet. She brought another one to the table, which she half filled, her left arm placed neatly behind her back as she did so, like a dutiful sommelier in a top London hotel.

'Another one bites the dust, my dear girl. I'm so sorry,' Peter said wearily to Maria, as she caught my eye and smiled indulgently, knowing that the look was just between the two of us.

'Not to worry, my Lord, it is just a glass. Just a glass.'

'We'll have to buy some more, Maria, the rate I'm going through them.' Alexander took a large quaff, drowning his battered pride, and then used both hands to lower the glass to secure its position on the table. 'Best not to get anything expensive. A waste of time and money.' Maria left the room, practically walking backwards.

'Sorry about that, dear boy. Extraordinary the noise a breaking glass makes, isn't it?'

Just for a while, there was the tinkling of cutlery against crockery mercifully filling the unaccustomed silence. I refilled each glass carefully and modestly, more conscious now of the likelihood of spillages, while trying to decide whether I should comment or not. It was Alexander who broke the silence. With a world-weary sigh, he launched into the explanation of his condition and his attempts to find help – the string of meetings in Harley Street, followed by the trips to New York, Basel, a faith healer in Rio and then the small fortune spent on homeopathic remedies that made no difference. 'Nothing to be done,' he said as he finished. 'Just got to make the best of it, that's all. Nice to have your sympathetic ear though, Ben. You're a great comfort, you really are.'

～

I knew about the title by then, of course, so the 'my Lord' uttered by Maria didn't have me sliding off the seat in surprise. You can't be me and not have succumbed to curiosity, and less than an hour's research in the library had revealed all I needed to know. I'd found a battered copy of *Dod's Parliamentary Companion* and scanned the pages till I'd come across the right address in Eaton Square. '*Alexander Owen Lowther, Second Baron Bellaghy of Holland Park, created 1945. Educated at Winchester and Magdalene College, Oxford. Irish Guards. Ass Sec, War Cabinet (Mil) 1942 – 1945. US Legion of Merit. Succeeded his father 1952. Heir, his son, Owen, born 1936.*' There was a Lady Bellaghy mentioned too, a daughter of a 6th baronet, though I'd not seen much evidence of her. I guessed that the door next to Alexander's bedroom probably opened into a much more substantial room than the one he slept in.

At first, I didn't know whether the silence after the smashed glass was down to Alexander's embarrassment about his eyes or due to the fact that the noble handle to his name had unwittingly been revealed by Maria; anyway, I made a good pretence that this had passed me by. I'd already clocked the failing sight sometime before, though hadn't realised that it was quite so bad; I'd worked that out on the night I was leaving after our first meeting and he'd stared up at the prints in the hall. He must have been seeing very little, but was determined at that point that I was not to know. Pride, really, that's all. Much later in our friendship, I was to embark on a pointless struggle to try to get him to use a white stick when he went off alone for his daily constitutional along the Butts in Sandwich. Spectacular waste of time. I remember him once informing me over pre-dinner drinks in Sandwich that sometime the following week he was tempted to 'get the old Mini out of the garage and motor over to Woodnesborough to ride Flight for an hour or two'.

'You're thinking of *driving*?' I said, raising my eyebrows.

'Yes, I think so – mid-afternoon when it's not too busy.'

'Let me know when that might be happening, Alexander. It might be a day I plan not to be in Sandwich...' Typical of my old friend that he thought my remark so funny that he giggled to himself throughout dinner. He was extraordinarily stoical about the situation, really. There was a lot more sight in those early days of our friendship; what little was left was to disappear almost totally over the next few years.

Anyway, at the end of the evening, Alexander and I said our farewells (a handshake that turned into a hug and a tousling of the hair) and on a windy Sunday afternoon a day or two later I caught the train to York, probably thinking that my life must now be taking a radically different turn. I left my little room in Kennington with the usual trepidation and was not at all reassured, on reaching my digs in the suburbs of York, by the sight of my landlady. I knocked on the door sometime after 10 at night, fresh from the train with a suitcase by my side, and waited for what seemed like ten minutes before, through the frosted glass, I was able to make out the shape of a figure on the landing which swayed from side to side, then backwards and forwards before plunging head-first down the stairs. There was a pause while she was momentarily out of view, crumpled up round the doormat, before she got to her feet and let me in without saying a word.

She then sat heavily on a large pot containing a palm tree (the fronds splayed and slowly browning during the rest of my two months stay) from where she pointed at the ceiling above the hall, which I assumed was the direction in which I would find my lodgings. All was very much in order once I opened the door to the room, however, with the curtains drawn, the bedside lamp already turned on in welcome, and a fluffy white towel and flannel draped across a chair in the corner. There were profuse apologies in the morning, and an explanation of a birthday party with friends around the corner that had gotten a little out of hand. We became firm friends, and indeed, resolute drinking companions for the duration of my stay.

There had been somewhat of a renaissance in my feelings towards my chosen profession by the time I settled into rehearsals and grateful though I was for the change in my financial circumstances, I was very much putting the past few months behind me. It turned out to be a wonderful (though wet) summer in York, with me playing one of the mechanicals in a spirited rendition of *A Midsummer Night's Dream* followed by *The Boyfriend*, a rather camp production that saw the male members of the chorus scampering around in one-piece bathing suits throwing large beach-balls at each other.

∼

The letter from 'Peter' was waiting for me when I got back from York at the end of September. I remember unlocking the door and casting my eye around the room, thrilled and taken aback to find it had been left spotless, with a neat little pile of mail on the armchair the first thing to catch my eye. I'd handed the keys over before leaving in July to a sweet girl with freckles on a pretty face under blonde hair in pigtails who'd seen my ad for a ten-week let on the board in The Dance Centre. On the Sunday I was leaving, she'd arrived late, just at the point when I was beginning to fret about missing my train if I didn't leave *now*, right this very minute – fingers uncontrollably drumming against the suitcase I was sitting on while I waited for her just inside the front door. She was in tears, explaining to me that she'd decided to take time away from her boyfriend over the summer, and wanted her own space and time 'to re-evaluate her relationship'. She hadn't told me that when I'd decided, over the phone, to let her have the room, and I didn't want to hear it. I left with great trepidation, short of time, frazzled and unsympathetic, imagining a lovesick girl not able to look after herself, let alone my room, and as I hauled myself down to the Northern Line with my luggage getting more burdensome by the minute, I was already catastrophising about coming back to find Aurelio's work undone, and my precious four walls in a slightly worse state than they had been on the night of Mickey's criminal rampage.

Dried rose petals fell out of a folded page when I opened the purple envelope.

I haven't really spent much time here because I got back with Joel almost straight away. But the rent is paid and I'm really grateful your comfy room was available for me. Love and kisses, Becca xxx. P.S. I'm going into Jesus Christ Superstar at the Palace!! New cast!! Best thing ever!

'Peter's' short letter, bearing the seal of the House of Lords on the envelope, was under her note.

Can't remember when you are back, but I'm patiently waiting! Give me a call when you can. Come and have dinner. I have a proposition to put to you. Peter.

CHAPTER 9

'No strings,' Alexander had said as I came back into the sitting room brandishing another bottle on the evening of our reunion. He'd put the proposition of a trip to Paris to me as soon as Maria had said her goodnights and left for the evening. 'There's a nice little hotel called the Liberia on the opposite side of the street to my apartment in the rue de la Grande-Chaumière. I'll book you in there if you like; a little rough and ready, but warm and comfortable. Do come – it'll be such fun for an old man to show someone like you around. How about it? Go away and give it some thought.'

'I don't think that will be necessary, actually. I'd love to come,' I said, successfully covering my slight feelings of trepidation with a huge smile and the speed of my reply.

'Wonderful news! I have to be there for a business meeting on the Tuesday morning, so why don't you arrive mid-afternoon? And actually, there's a little more to my proposition, but it can wait till our first dinner in Paris.'

∼

So listen – my opening chapter, the story about a nervous, lonely young guy meeting a charming old aristo over dinner in Paris is really not so very far from the truth. It's just that I wasn't entirely alone right at the beginning of my trip, okay? The meeting in the restaurant is the story I tell those who might be just a little shocked at the truth. There's a little mishmash of truth and fantasy, but that's really the extent of my dishonesty, and I've cleared it all up with just a line or two. Therefore, once again, I pray your indulgence for something that surely isn't much more than a white lie. And don't bother asking why I felt the necessity of an untruth, since I'm not quite sure of the answer.

There was no little shadow cast by Alexander's letter to me on my return home from York, no wondering whether it might be the right or wrong thing to contact him, no feeling that things would be going backwards if I did. I also knew it was not a carelessness on his behalf that had him writing on House of Lords notepaper – it was an obvious hint I was meant to pick up on after Maria's slip, an act of forthright honesty and, of course, a risk. Our first meetings were in circumstances that would be highly compromising for him if it became general knowledge, after all, and he'd quite rightly not been forthcoming to me about his real name. But, of course, we'd made a real connection, and had met again seven or eight times before I left for York. Let's not pretend here – I could quite obviously see the advantages to me and I'm not so stupid as to have not realised that he might be a little smitten, so the whole thing could go wherever I wanted it to. Having said that, he'd certainly not lost his head, or his judgement. That was not

Alexander's way – he must have thought things through and decided to come clean with me.

∼

Just a day or two after the proposal had been put to me, I was on the train to Paris. A dream come true. No more shame about being in my mid-twenties and never having visited the City of Light!

I'd spent the previous few days packing a little holdall, putting things in and then taking them out again. Don't ask me how many times I checked my passport, my francs, the return tickets from Victoria to Dover, the plastic wallet containing the tickets for the hovercraft from Dover to Boulogne, and then the separate little folder for the tickets to the Gare du Nord in Paris. Alexander had told me very firmly (an index finger pointing skywards, as was his habit when making an important point) that I must remember to 'composter' the French train ticket. That meant having to find a machine on the platform at Boulogne that punches a little hole in it to enable me to embark. So important this, that it seemed I might well have risked life imprisonment in France if I got it wrong.

Oh, Jesus, the pain of travelling. Why am I so bad at it? What do I really think is going to happen if it goes wrong? If I miss a train or a flight, all that happens is I return home and have a different type of holiday, that's all. No one dies. Imagine the time I'd have wasted worrying if I'd had three weeks' warning instead of just a few days! I'd not been abroad since a trip to Crete some years ago; on that occasion, I thought I'd securely packed a rucksack, but it had somehow undone itself in transit and I was forced to run in circles around the baggage retrieval hall at Heraklion Airport gathering sundry bits and pieces coming up from the depths all jumbled up in everyone else's baggage – toothpaste and toothbrush separated by ten yards, a book about Trotsky appearing a minute later swiftly followed by a packet of anti-diarrhoea pills, some ointment in case of a herpes attack, two flowered shirts and even a pair of colourful underpants with an imprint of a banana and two plums on the front (fashionable at the time, would you believe) all looking rather surprised to find themselves travelling unaccompanied along the carousel. I've had a thing about packing ever since.

Perhaps my travel phobia is just a form of overwhelming excitement? God – the decisions to be made for this trip of just a few days. Was I to take my silly little skimpy vests? No – I decided that it was quite unlikely that I'd be hanging out at some gay nightclub. I really wouldn't know where to start with all that, though Aurelio was very keen to get me to experience the most infamous sauna in Europe situated 'somewhere near the Opera House, if my memory serves me well'. Should I take a nicely ironed shirt? Trainers and a pair of good shoes? What exactly to wear out to dinner with a peer of the realm? Ought I to buy a jacket for the trip? A pullover or two? Is Paris cold at the end of September, or surprisingly sultry? Might I find myself bathing my feet in the Seine, like something out of a Seurat painting, or lounging on the grass in the Jardin du Luxembourg, a figure from Manet's *Déjeuner sur l'herbe*? What books were to be packed in case I should find myself with time to kill alone, watching the world go by between a chapter or two of *Madame Bovary* from some pavement bistro on the Rive Gauche? I was initially worried about the sleeping arrangements, and so it was an immediate relief when Alexander had asked whether I'd like him to book me the hotel room. At the same time, I wasn't at all sure what was going to be expected of me.

The hovercraft crossing to Boulogne was quite different to what I was expecting. The announcements at the terminal and later by the cabin staff kept referring to our 'flight', which I suppose it was, as we were going to be floating on a cushion of air a few feet above the water for twenty-odd miles. The sea was so rough that there was a question mark about whether we would be able to leave at all, with me panicking about Alexander being put out and having to endure an endless wait at the Gare du Nord. But the weather calmed enough to allow us to board, and I was mightily relieved to find the first minute or two of the 'flight' quite extraordinarily smooth.

All hell broke loose, however, as soon as we left the safety of the harbour wall at Dover. Instead of rolling from side to side as happens on a ship, the motion was much more like being thrown upward into the air without warning, 'hovering' in a state of limbo for a while and then returning to earth with a bang and a wallop against a sea so hard and unforgiving it might as well be made of concrete. Of course, to my utter dismay, about halfway through the journey I found myself having to fix my eye onto the wall above the seat in front, at an advertisement of a man in a beret smoking a cigarette with the Eiffel Tower in the background. It became very hard work trying to prevent myself from emptying the contents of my stomach into the paper bag provided in the pocket in front of me. But the coastline of France eventually appeared outside the foam-splattered window, and I realised I was going to be able to leave my seat without making a fool of myself. Jesus. The traveller from hell, that's me. Days to pack a small holdall, unable to eat anything before embarking due to a general feeling of panic, and highly likely to be sick on the way. Hopeless.

The Paris-bound train was a different matter; so vast that it glided seamlessly out of the station in Boulogne, almost insinuating itself into movement, the actual moment of departure as silent and smooth as a boat on the calmest of lakes.

It grew gloriously dark as the train slid under the vast canopy above the Gare du Nord – just like the moment, full of promise, in the theatre when the lights dim before the curtain goes up. An impatient bustle of a queue for the door had formed quite a few minutes before our arrival, and once the train stopped, I found my excitement getting the better of me. The temptation to use elbows and a sharp corner of my holdall against the elderly couple in front of me who were blocking everyone's exit was almost overwhelming. They had their heads bowed over pointing fingers as they consulted a map of Paris, standing right in the middle of the aisle until a furious call of 'Madame, Monsieur!' from an exasperated businessman behind me finally broke the log-jam. Silly old farts.

The familiar figure beyond the far distant ticket barrier was leaning with both hands on a stick (not white, but of a sturdy walking variety), placed squarely between his feet; he was wearing a linen suit of the lightest blue – made in Hong Kong, he told me later, during the course of one afternoon on a business trip a few years before – with a large red hanky cascading from the top pocket of the jacket. I was still far away when the stick was raised into the air in greeting, and I upped my speed to reach him more quickly, happy and relieved to see a familiar face in a foreign city.

'Hello there, Peter,' I said, stretching out my hand. It was ignored; instead, he took both my shoulders firmly between his hands and a kiss was delivered to both cheeks. 'French custom,' he explained. 'Best you get used to it! How are you, dear boy? Wonderful that you're here!' My hair was ruffled then, which was fast becoming the usual way of greeting me.

The taxi that took us away from the station at speed rattled over the Paris cobblestones, the resulting tremor mirroring my own excitement. It flew past buildings I'd known all my life from photos, books and films, while Alexander gave directions to the driver in what appeared to be perfect French but without so much as a hint of an attempt at an accent. Just for a minute, I thought he might be taking the piss, but our driver was certainly not taking offence. Quite used to English milords, I suppose. 'I'm asking this nice chap to take us round the houses – the scenic route. Give you a chance to see a bit of the city.' The light was changing every few minutes, clouds and rain showers being overtaken by bright sunshine. Down the Rue de Rivoli we went, past the golden statue of Jeanne d'Arc on her horse, into the Place de La Concorde with its obelisk and fountains and a view up the Rue Royale to La Madeleine. We shot over the river on the Pont de la Concorde towards the Assemblée nationale then sped along the river for a while before turning right to dive into narrow streets where the buildings leaned towards each other as they stretched upwards toward the sky. Well-dressed couples, squeezed onto the narrowest of pavements, stared into the windows of shops containing the poshest of bric-a-brac, modern art, prints and framed cartoons, ancient books and eighteenth-century pieces of furniture polished to within an inch of their lives and so well restored that they might have been manufactured in the last day or so.

Alexander was looking at me with a smile on his face, a hand resting paternally on my knee while he basked in my excitement. 'You could see me!' I said. 'You waved to me as I came towards you along the platform–'

'It's the funniest thing, Ben, but yes, I really could. Just your outline, a shadow of something I completely recognised, something essentially you. It's probably because you're just so important.'

'Merci pour votre gentillesse, monsieur,' Alexander added as he fished around in his jacket pocket to locate the note that he had sorted out in advance – just one of the little tricks to help him hide the disability that I was quickly getting used to. The taxi had stopped before the large green door of an early nineteenth-century building in a narrow street of small restaurants and bookshops in Montparnasse. He punched a number onto a keypad to the side of the door which swung open. 'Bonjour, Madame Forestier,' he called to an enormous, cross-looking old lady I glimpsed through the window of a small dark room decked out in plastic flowers at the bottom of the stairs. My first Paris concierge. 'Five storeys up and no lift!' Alexander announced as he darted off ahead of me, three stairs at a time up the circular stairwell, pulling on the banister to haul himself up and holding his stick horizontally in his free hand. On the last level before we reached his apartment, a young man in uniform with a square, sunburned neck and military crew cut was knocking on a door, a bunch of carnations in a hand hidden behind his back, like a clichéd scene from a movie. A while later, walking along the Boulevard du Montparnasse looking for a taxi to take us to dinner, I was to see him again, leaning over a pavement table outside a brasserie to kiss the pretty young girl who'd emerged from the door to put her arms around him as we passed.

∼

'This, you'll find, is an excellent alternative to our old friend Monsieur Tavel.' Alexander was expectantly holding the glass into which I was pouring a dark-pink wine. 'It's a Béarn – from the slopes of the Pyrenees. I drink it all year round – in fact, whenever I dine here. Ignore anyone who says you should only drink rosé in the summer months. Piffle! Well, you know that already, of course. I adore this one, and so will you – you can practically taste the mountain air!' We were settled into a cosy niche in the Taverne Basque in the Rue du Cherche-Midi. My appetite had returned now that I sensed that all was going to be well with my visit. I'd unpacked my little suitcase in a room of the hotel opposite Alexander's front door and had even managed a snooze and a shower before once again passing the strict-looking Madame Forestier in her lair as I made my way up to a large pre-dinner gin and tonic waiting for me in the apartment. The meal, in a cosy, leather-upholstered booth of the Taverne Basque, was hearty and filling – a thick ham soup with cheese and bread, apparently called a garbure, then a no-nonsense, but delicious leg of lamb followed by an apple and prune tart.

Coffee was followed by Alexander's decision to call upon the services of another bottle and I sensed – not correctly, as it turned out – that this was the moment that he was to put to me the second part of his proposition. When it came to it, however, he seemed to be hesitating, not quite sure of himself; something that I'd not yet seen in this most straightforward of men. Then came an admission rather than the second part of the proposition.

'So, listen – I need to tell you something, Ben, before we go any further with our friendship.' There was a pause then, followed by a little clearing of the throat as his fingers started a delaying tactic with the base of the glass of wine, the contents tipping dangerously from side to side as Alexander seemed to look through and beyond the glass. 'When my father died,' he eventually said, having taken a large preparatory breath, 'I inherited a title from him. I don't for a minute suppose I have to explain to someone like you the ins and outs of the hereditary peerage, but it means that, as a peer, I'm able to attend the House of Lords, and some people address me as *my Lord*. It's of no importance, really, and my title's scarcely five minutes old, so we're not talking very grand and ancient here. Not really very relevant these days either, but it comes in useful now and again for jumping queues and reserving a table in fancy restaurants.'

There was another pause in which I attempted to arrange my face into one where new information appeared to be sinking in, followed by an expression both surprised and composed, as if the knowledge was interesting, not of great importance and quite unexpected. Quite a faceful. 'And I'd ask for your understanding for something else, and that is that I've not been able, for obvious reasons, to tell you my real name, which is Alexander. Not Peter. Alexander.'

'Well, yes, of course. I would have thought it very foolish if you'd used your real name when we first met–'

'Yes, and I'm telling you this now because I suspect you're going to be around for some time and also because, most importantly, I trust you implicitly. So that's that. Pour us another glass of that delicious wine would you, dear boy...'

By the time we left the Taverne Basque just before midnight, after the sole remaining waiter had pointedly wiped the table down for the third time and then positioned himself in by the door with one hand on his hip and the other throwing a bunch of keys into the air, we were both leaning on each other quite heavily and doing our best to wave down a string of taxis that refused to stop. A quite pointless debate about who was holding who upright ensued.

'I think we need to stand up by ourselves, Alexander, separately. It might be that the taxis are all whizzing by because we don't look like a very attractive proposition.'

'Good thinking, old chap. Good thinking...'

'*Nous vous nous pouvez déposer au coin*,' said Alexander as we approached the corner of the rue de la Grande-Chaumière in a taxi that had eventually dared to pick us up.

'What the hell does that mean?' I slurred.

'Oh shit – bit of a mouthful. Want him to drop us off

at the corner. I'll try it again. Slower, perhaps. *Pouvez-vous nous déposer au coin?* Yes, that's better. Sounds as though it's making more sense.'

∽

'I've a little more business to attend to today, and it's your last day so I'm going to leave you to your own devices,' Alexander announced over coffee and the croissants that I'd arrived with from the boulangerie next to the hotel.

'Business? I thought you had retired!'

'Oh, it's just a bit of fun really, something to keep me occupied in my dotage. I've a little interest in an Italian restaurant here – you'll see it later. We'll go there for dinner tonight.'

'What fun! You're part owner of a restaurant in Paris? Can't wait to see it, Alexander. And while we're talking business, what was the proposition you were going to put to me? I think you've been putting it off–'

'Not at all – but it can wait till breakfast tomorrow, before you leave to get the train back home. And why not try that sauna this evening, after our dinner? You'll be able to regale me with saucy stories for the next few weeks.'

∽

And so I found myself alone for a whole day in the greatest of European cities, but with the comfort of knowing that if I felt overwhelmed, I was free to go back to my hotel room or use the keys to Alexander's apartment that I'd tucked away in my pocket; I could scuttle back there at any time, like a rabbit taking refuge in his burrow.

It was a heavenly morning; I walked across the Jardin du Luxembourg under the eye of the medieval queens of France whose statues looked down towards the centre of the gardens. I sat down to sun myself in the unexpected warmth, smiling at small boys in corduroy pants and oversized caps, their mothers calling out 'Attention!' as they raced against model boats that were catching the wind in their sails and skimming across the surface to the far side of the pond in front of the Palais.

I ate a lunch in the autumn sunshine in the Place des Vosges in the heart of the Marais – steak frites ordered in a pre-rehearsed little snippet of French, in an accent I knew to be much better than Alexander's – before walking round the Île Saint-Louis and then going back to the Louvre for my second visit. I'd made my mind up beforehand that there was too much of Paris that I needed to see and so I wouldn't be staying for more than an hour, wouldn't be hunting out new treats, but reminding myself of just a few random things I'd seen and loved two days before with Alexander. Back to see a series of Fragonard paintings – of farm animals, tumbling clouds, a hay-wain, a gnarled old man and a waterfall in the Tivoli Gardens – sweetly lyrical pictures hinting at the dawn of Impressionism; my old friend Boizot's opulent bust of Marie Antoinette in the flesh, as it were, with her Habsburg chin and look of haughty disdain, and Perronneau's portrait of Madame de Sourquainville – her warmth and wit flowing out of the canvas to greet the viewer. And then an unexpected gallery devoted to eighteenth- and nineteenth-century British painters; Constable and Gainsborough, Lawrence, Raeburn and Turner, the room quiet, confident and understated after the dashingly effervescent qualities of the artists' European contemporaries.

～

'Ben – this is my old friend Enzo.' Alexander was already seated at a table on the pavement outside the Italian restaurant on the Quai des Orfèvres. I was just a little late, heady both from my day alone and also from a nap that had suddenly become a necessity after a day of exploring Paris on foot. The demi-carafe of white wine consumed at lunch, which then needed to be chased down by a glass of port, may also have played a part. Late afternoon, I'd found a stone bench on the banks of the Seine, warmed by the sun and so inviting that I wasn't able to pass by without prostrating myself along its length for a tiny moment. I woke up quite some time later with the sun going down and the surprisingly chilly onset of evening making its way into my bones. A brisk walk across the Île de la Cité had brought me back to life, and by the time I found Il Delfino just off the Pont Neuf, I was in celebratory mood, delighted that I'd not only done so much with my time, but also quietly pleased that I seemed to have mastered the art of finding my way around so easily, hopping on and off the metro once or twice as though I was a native of the city, the nervous tourist banished.

Enzo was in his early thirties, a tall and extremely handsome Sicilian with dark olive skin, piercing blue eyes and cheekbones high enough to dive off. He shook my hand and sat me at the small table opposite Alexander, his flat stomach against my back as he guided my chair into position. There was a theatrical flourish as he flicked open a white napkin that landed on my knee.

'Monsieur has ordered a bottle of wine already – it is good for you, the Pinot Grigio, or you prefer something else?'

'Oh – that's fine, thank you, Enzo. Looks like Alexander and I have identical tastes; I'll share the bottle with him, as usual.' I noticed that the pleasant smile on his lips didn't quite reach his eyes when he talked to me. During the course of our dinner he, the patron, hovered around our table more often than the waiter who'd taken our order, pouring wine and sparkling water, attending to our every need with an affectionate hand often coming to rest on Alexander's shoulder. They talked animatedly to each other, Alexander as usual making no compromises to sound French, and Enzo employing an accent so heavy that it might well be Italian he was speaking. I was unable to keep up with either of them; it was as though they were communicating in a private code that had been perfected over many years. Enzo met Alexander's gaze with an easy familiarity but seemed to be avoiding mine when I attempted to join the conversation.

'He's a dear friend,' whispered Alexander as Enzo broke away to take an order at an adjoining table whose occupants looked too important to leave to a young waiter who was in the first week of his professional life. 'His manner's a little too obsequious at the moment, though. Henriette – his wife – and I have mentioned it to him, but it's not quite sunk in yet. He needs to lighten up a bit. The restaurant's only been open a month or two so it's all very new to him – he's still finding his feet.' Later, as we left, I thanked him for looking after us so diligently. He took my proffered hand in his, but wasn't able to allow our eyes to meet, as though he was unsure quite how to relate to me. Alexander, just before stepping off the pavement into the taxi I'd hailed for him, ruffled his hair and Enzo, obviously used to the gesture, then glided his slender fingers through his long, curly black locks.

∼

It took me a little while to locate the Opera Euro sauna in a side street just off the Boulevard des Italiens. It was late when I got there; I didn't leave the restaurant after dinner with Alexander until a little after 10 and I'd asked the taxi driver to drop me at the front of the Opera house, too shy to mouth the name of the street nearby that I was actually heading for – La rue Louis-le-Grand – in case he worked out what I was really up to. As if he cared, for fuck's sake.

Once I'd found the unobtrusive doorway to the premises hidden away in the narrow street and handed over my money at reception, I immediately felt out of my depth with instructions about lockers and keys, a complementary soft drink to be exchanged for my entrance receipt, the swapping of wet towels for dry during the course of my visit and finally, complicated directions to the changing areas. Was the bruiser behind the desk speaking French? Perhaps he had the Paris equivalent of a thick East End accent? All quite impenetrable. Having finally located the long row of lockers in a changing area down two flights of dimly lit stairs, I had to ask a tired but contented-looking punter on his way out about how to use the key. I nodded appreciatively at the answer that I didn't understand, and returned to the reception area, having eventually worked out that I was meant to have picked up a token to operate the lock at the same time as my key. Finally, having succeeded in ramming my things into an impossibly small locker, I embarked on a struggle with a towel so tiny that it was difficult to secure it round my waist and so found myself getting into a state about the threat to my modesty in what I soon discovered to be the most immodest of places.

I had heard about continental goings-on, of course – how very much more relaxed things were in most parts of Europe compared to London – but still, the place was a revelation to any Brit who had ever experienced the constant policing by the staff of a sauna in London. 'Are you enjoying yourselves?' This overheard in a sauna in Endell Street in the West End just a few days before my Paris visit, addressed to a couple of young chaps by a strict Chinese orderly in a rather medical-looking white coat. He had his arms folded high across his chest, fingers tapping a bicep. A schoolmarm expression of disapproval had slowly taken over his face as he leant against the wall at the entrance to the shower where the guilty duo were entertaining each other with an abandon simply not permitted in the United Kingdom of Great Britain and Northern Ireland.

No rulings in this vast underground sauna about what might or might not be permissible, apparently. Jesus. Naked men everywhere, wandering endlessly in circles, along a myriad of dark passages, peering into cubicle after cubicle while assessing the goods inside. Stretched out on the narrow mattresses on the floor, the occupants were brazenly showing off their wares; moans and groans of pleasure emanated from those cubicles whose doors had been firmly closed, a casual towel flung over the top to inform the outside word that the occupants were busy.

The place contained two huge steam rooms and three saunas, and a large swimming pool surrounded by fabulously naff, neo-Romanesque mannequins of youths carrying amphoras on their shoulders releasing a stream of water back into the pool. The naked bottoms of much of the clientele were perched on precariously high stools all around the poolside bar where plastic vines bearing plastic grapes climbed plastic Doric columns.

I'd half expected to be alone in the place seeing that it was late on a Thursday evening, and surely Parisians have to go to bed for work in the morning like everyone else? I thought that the atmosphere at the tail-end of the evening might enable a shy young man to observe the goings-on while adopting an ice maiden persona, rising above the rough and tumble as though he might be Jane Goodall taking notes on the sexual behaviour of chimps. Well, I was trying to fool myself that my visit was to enable me to report back to Alexander, after all. A fact-finding visit. However, having sat demurely in the steam room with my knees anchored together for quite some time, I decided that a generalised peep around the premises was to be permitted, if only for the purpose of relating more accurately the events over breakfast.

I loosened up after a while in the steam room, though. Heaven's above, I thought, who was ever to know if I were to get up to a tiny little bit of mischief with one or two of those ever so nicely put together young men? Can't a boy have a little bit of fun when he's three-hundred-odd miles away from home? Who the hell's going to know anything about it? Good Lord, that exotic, erotic place. Not conducive to propriety. I'm not going to tell you exactly what I may have been up to at the moment that a curious, excited face came out of the mist to inspect the tangle of limbs on the slab of hot marble in the steam room, but it really was the most terrible shock when the features began to morph through the steam into something more familiar until, at a distance of about a foot, I realised I was being confronted by my housemate Yong (he of the long-distance telephone calls to Singapore) peering at me with a lecherous expression turning quickly to one of absolute horror. Neither of us *quite* far enough away from home, apparently.

~

'A "stipend", I think they call it.' Alexander was draining the last of his coffee from the large white bone-china cup he was caressing in both hands. He was in celebratory mode this morning, sitting opposite me at the table, the sunshine streaming in through the window of the apartment that he, aided by Enzo, had put together so lovingly; he was quite obviously pleased at my excitement and immediate acceptance of his idea of my becoming a helping hand with his 'bits and pieces'. I would be free to carry on working at the Embassy Club for now and could break off temporarily from our arrangement from time to time if a theatre job materialised. 'We'll be able to pick up the pieces any time you return from a job, don't you think? Besides, if you're working in London, it won't interfere very much. A second string to your bow and all that.' A flexible arrangement, in other words, all for the price of £70 a week for a job that would take up very little of my time – enough, with other little bits and pieces, to keep the wolf from my door. A brilliant gift of an idea, even if I'd already sensed that it might be in the offing.

'So, you come to me in Eaton Square every Wednesday morning, and be my eyes, so to speak. Help me with my list of stocks and shares, write out a few cheques, watch me sign them in the right place, tidy my desk up and read *The Telegraph* to me. Nothing onerous at all, but it has to be done, and if we're honest, I'm beginning to fall behind a little with things. Bloody eyes. Then, come back for dinner later on that same evening, enjoy a convivial bottle or two with me, and then Thursday morning, come back, flag down a taxi and see me onto the train at Charing Cross. How does that all sound?'

'Eminently doable. Wonderful arrangement! We'll firm it all up next week when we're back in London?'

'We will, dear boy–'

'Jesus – I'm going to have to go, or I'll miss my train.' I leant across the table and planted a kiss on both Alexander's cheeks. 'Thank you so, so much for making these few days so special. I adore Paris, and it's you that I'll always think of in the future as the person who introduced me to the city.'

'Well, you'll be coming with me in future, I think, practically whenever I do, so this morning's an adieu to the city rather than a goodbye.'

'Alexander – there is just one more thing before I go.' I was bending to grasp hold of the handle of my little case as I opened my mouth but realised that what I had to say couldn't be reasonably delivered as an aside from a standing position immediately before my exit, so I placed the case back down by my side with a thump and slid uneasily back into the seat I'd just left.

'What is it, old chap?'

'Well, the thing is this–' A long pause. Suddenly

tongue-tied. A look of the slightest confusion on Alexander's face.

'Come on – spit it out!' he said, looking puzzled and perhaps just a little concerned. 'What's up?'

'Well, it's really just that I think that with our new arrangements, the other stuff – the 'gymnastics', as it were, would probably have to stop and–'

'Gymnastics?'

'You know – the, er, the bedroom stuff. The thing is, it's not really my cup of tea and, er, it's probably not okay anymore for me to pretend that it is...' A look of surprise took over Alexander's face, but I was carrying on regardless. 'So – that might mean you want to change your mind about the whole thing? The stipend? I really would understand if that's the way it is. If, you know, it's really important to you to include that stuff with the list of stocks and shares and the tidying of the desk and the other things that I can be helpful with – the taxi to Charing Cross and all that? To tell you the truth, I'm sort of unsure that I would be able to manage the, er, sex thing from now on. Especially if I'm going to be around for ages, and we're going to become real mates...'

CHAPTER 10

'Bit of a cheek, really.' Alexander was muttering under his breath as the door closed on his young visitor rather more firmly than he'd intended. He paused, ear cocked, still holding the door-handle while he listened to the retreating echo of Ben's footsteps hurrying down the stairs. He couldn't quite make up his mind whether the boy might be running away out of sheer embarrassment and relief at what he'd just had the courage to say, or if he really was in danger of missing his train. Perhaps both.

Instead of making his way across the hall and into the sitting room to take refuge in his usual morning dose of the BBC (we might be in France, but Radio 4, the *Daily Telegraph* and coffee at the right strength and temperature are as essential as they are at home), he found himself standing in the kitchenette, hands buried deep in his pockets. Eventually he came to, and successfully located and reopened a jar before tipping some coffee beans into his palm and placing them in the grinder. The machine growled angrily in his hands; Alexander felt the same way. He was a man of habit, and he couldn't remember the last time he'd indulged himself with more than one cup of coffee at breakfast, but what had just happened with Ben had thrown him off balance – what on earth was it about the young man's departure that had so rattled him?

'Where's Enzo put the bloody filters, for God's sake? Oh, damn it, I had them last, of course I did. Fucking eyes! Ah, here they are…' Something slipped between his fingers. 'Oh – Jesus Christ!' He was making an infernal mess; a large portion of the ground coffee beans missed the filter, subjecting the tiled floor and his brogues to a dark-brown dusting. More intemperate growling would be needed from the grinder; Enzo or Rania would just have to clear up later.

He was put out, bemused, felt somewhat foolish. But there was something else, too. What was it, this heaviness in his chest? It was a feeling of loss, he decided, that then swelled into one of loneliness and regret; he was suddenly concerned that twenty minutes ago he'd reacted in a way that meant he might not see again the young man who'd just left. But wait – there had been no cross words, no sudden derailing of plans for the coming week, nothing had been broken that couldn't be fixed. For heaven's sake, it was hardly as though he'd lost his temper – something he was ashamed to admit that he was quite famous for. That had not happened; in fact, he was fairly certain he'd said nothing much more than 'You'd best be off, old chap – you're cutting it rather fine'. Not true, that – Ben was the nervous type who'd never be cutting anything fine. Alexander had been flustered, though, that was for sure. A little lost for words.

'Well bugger me! Isn't this *rejection*?' And when was the last time he'd experienced that? 'Silly old fool!' he called out to the room before laughing out loud, bemusement turning to something approaching amusement now that he was regaining his equilibrium, sat back at the table with the hot coffee doing its job. His ability to talk honestly to himself had always stood him in good stead and would do so again right now. 'At least the boy's got the courage to say what he wants – I put a proposition to him, and he's making his own terms!' He was relieved now that he'd had the sense to book Ben into L'Hotel Liberia, and that there could be no feeling that the boy had been taken advantage of. He was uncertain about how it had not happened, but indeed nothing of a sexual nature had taken place while he was here, and that granted Alexander a little solace. His pride had taken a battering but was basically still intact, though only really by accident – he'd never much liked sharing a bed the whole night long with anyone, even early in his marriage, which is why Ben was not staying in the apartment; he was the sort of man who was used to indulging himself in a nice little bit of sport of an evening before (and sometimes after) a good supper and rather a lot of wine, and then liked to be in possession of a whole bed alone, which afforded him the opportunity of reminiscing about the adventures that had just taken place while splayed out like a starfish, hands and feet luxuriating in the four far corners of the bed.

Now that Ben had left, however, he was coming to realise that the thing that was so captivating about the boy went far beyond his physical charms, sweet though they were; it had been marvellous fun showing him around and watching his enjoyment of just about *everything* – Alexander prided himself on knowing his history, but this young man, who had never been to Paris in his life, seemed to know as much about the city as he did, and somehow, in the midst of the boy's excitement, the sex thing had, rather surprisingly, found itself forgotten about. Perhaps it was something else, though. Alexander found himself wondering whether, in fact, he had detected a little reticence on his young friend's behalf, even before they left London, and he'd therefore just let the whole thing slip, deferred for the duration of the visit.

Alexander decided that there really was no need to make a decision about anything right now since, unless Ben cancelled, he was seeing him for dinner next week and all would be clear by then. Clear? What was he talking about? There hadn't been a falling out – what need was there for clarity? The boy probably hadn't any particular feelings about what had just happened anyway – he was just relieved that he'd managed to say what he wanted and didn't want and must be given his due for having the courage, because he was basically a shy young man who was clearly not at all fond of any sort of confrontation outside of a passionate political debate. And why the hell would it not still work, his little plan? Alexander was quite sure that Ben would be more than scrupulous about his duties, and his damned eyes meant that whoever it might be, he genuinely did need someone around now to help him out.

It suddenly struck him that there was another advantage to what Ben was insisting upon – without the hanky-panky, he'd eventually feel much freer to consider introducing him to Bridget because there was nothing now that needed to be hidden from her and nothing for her to suspect, of course. She was a shrewd old girl though, quite adept at working things out, and Alexander was sure that she'd had her suspicions in the past about various things – it was likely that she'd wonder where a nice-looking young man had sprung from without any warning. He might leave the introductions for a while, therefore, until all was in working order and a routine had been settled into. She would take to him, he was absolutely sure – he was presentable and clever and well-spoken. What was there not to like about him?

Best write the lad a note, he thought. *Immediately. Have it in the post before lunch. Yes, that's what to do.* Nip any unpleasantness in the bud with not a mention of the conversation they'd had – or indeed not had – as he was leaving. Pretend that nothing had happened.

Greatly looking forward to seeing you next Wednesday for dinner as usual, when we will firm up our arrangement. Just felt compelled to say once again what an absolute joy it was to be able to introduce Paris to you, dear Ben, etc, etc…

It was a shame, though, he had to admit. Alexander didn't quite understand – cash was cash after all, but the lad had made up his mind. But then the cash was to continue, of course, even though it might be for a different service. He had to come to terms with new facts, that was all. It happens. Enzo, without ever putting his foot down or even beginning to talk about it, had obviously begun to grow uncomfortable with an arrangement that had suited them both for a number of years. Well – a wife and baby recently added to the picture did change things rather. The initial contact with him had come about in quite a different way, too – no phone call to a discreet, well set up massage agency like the one that Alan ran. They'd made eye contact outside that dubious club in the Rue Sainte-Anne, a place notorious for a certain type of pick-up – not really that much different to approaching someone leaning against the railings under the arches at Piccadilly Circus. It now seems like a long time ago – indeed it is. It had been a rather careless act for someone in his position, even though he was misbehaving in Paris rather than London – what on earth was he thinking of, taking such a risk? Very lucky it all worked out.

Enzo was a young Sicilian with little education and no dosh at all, trying to make his way in a foreign city. It could have been a recipe for disaster, but that's not how it had turned out – he'd seen his chance and taken it, changing his life forever while at the same time never letting go of some innate sense of Sicilian honour. They were both quite comfortably aware of the basis of what their relationship was about, though Enzo had been able to put on a more than competent show in the bedroom for an awfully long time. He hadn't been completely averse to the goings-on, Alexander was quite sure. Keener than Ben who quite obviously wasn't much taken with all of that.

However, the arrangement had recently seemed to have run its course and looking back over the years, it can hardly be denied that Enzo had profited mightily – which is what Alexander intended. And the lovely thing about it is that the relationship was now changing into something else. Alexander had grown mightily fond of

Henriette after an initially shaky start and had gladly accepted an offer to be young Vittorio's godfather. Enzo was certainly extremely grateful for the financial help he'd had in setting up Il Delfino, heaping praise on his benefactor at every opportunity to anyone who'd listen.

Now, Enzo found himself in the enviable position of being the patron of a nice little restaurant in the centre of Paris, and he was probably well aware that his old friend would continue to indulge him in the way he always had in the past. Alexander knew he was sure to find himself inventing a good reason, in a year or two, for waiving the quarterly repayments they'd agreed on without causing embarrassment with his generosity – though frankly Enzo is not the type to bother with too much embarrassment. But anyway, it would be nice if the visits to the bank would no longer be necessary. Why not spread a little joy in this funny old life? And all this because of a naughty exchange of glances more than ten years ago!

Sex was such a damned good introduction because, having put it to one side, however reluctantly, one's left with all that warmth and affection that would never have come about had they just been introduced in the normal way. Well, that couldn't ever have happened with Enzo; the English milord and the mechanic's son from Messina –their paths would never have crossed anywhere but in the Rue Sainte-Anne. What a loss it would have been never to have known him! And now there was another young man who was well worth the investment. Just for the fun of it, the sweetness of the friendship, and all the stimulating conversation that would keep him on his toes. Bloody good thing – so he really could shut up about the sex business slipping away. Other fish in the sea, many more pebbles on the beach, etc.

And while his relationship with his dear friend continued to change and evolve, he was not altogether miffed to have sensed, during the course of dinner at Il Delfino last night, that there might have been just the slightest hint of jealousy apparent in Enzo's dealings with Ben. Very satisfactory. A slight clawing back of a little portion of the pride that had gone missing this morning, Alexander was pleased to observe.

∼

He didn't know it, of course, but later that morning, Alexander found himself sitting in almost exactly the same spot that Ben had occupied the day before in the glorious Jardin du Luxembourg. However, the fountain splashing busily away in the middle of the pond was not soothing him in its usual way. There'd been a change in the weather overnight, too; it was brisker, with more than a hint of autumn in the air, and Alexander was glad of his last-minute decision to loop a large red scarf around his neck as he'd left the apartment.

'I'll skip dinner at Enzo's tonight and go to Madame Claude's. Cheer myself up with one of those shapely, bright girls.' He was talking to himself. It was a habit that he'd recently adopted, as though the words, once spoken, automatically became an affirmation, a promise to himself that wouldn't be broken. He may have eventually managed to conjure up a laugh after his young guest had left this morning, but he had to admit to himself that as the days progressed, he was still a little out of sorts.

'Bloody postbox!' Out loud again, to confirm his annoyance. He'd written his note to Ben on one of the postcards from his carefully chosen stack bought from the artist's shop downstairs – the eyeglass had helped him pick a Modigliani figure of a woman in a dark hat with a red brim, and he'd found what he hoped was the correct stamp in the left-hand drawer of his desk. Ten minutes later, the card was deposited with a satisfied flourish into the postbox set into the wall at the corner opposite the entrance to the Jardin. But after he'd let it slip from his fingers into the yellow box, he'd realised that he had very probably dropped it into the slot on the left-hand side, reserved for local post, '*Paris – Banlieue*', rather than the right, '*Autres départements. Étranger.*'

'What does it matter – it'll get there eventually, for *fuck's* sake!' he'd shouted. An old french trout sat close by, wearing a thick dark coat that gave off a slight whiff of mothballs after having been retrieved from a summer spent in a wardrobe. She had glared at him before raising an index finger to her lips. 'Pardon, Madame', he'd boomed. 'And mind your own business,' he'd said (this time silently).

He wouldn't actually be going to Madame Claude's, of course, because the grand old house just off the Avenue de la Grande Armée in the 16th arrondissement that she used to operate from is now a hotel as discreet in its own way as the business she oversaw until the authorities finally caught up with her a few years ago (tax evasion rather than immoral earnings). The old girl had done a runner to America and a comfortable existence in Los Angeles, but she was still much missed in the upper echelons of international society. Tonight, though, he'd be visiting a nearly comparable establishment situated close to the old one, run by Huguette, one of Madame Claude's ex-girls who'd learned well from her old mentor and ran just as tight a ship but also paid her taxes.

It was not quite the same, of course; nothing could match the glamour and the hint of intrigue of the old place – Alexander recalled an evening when a handsome type in dark glasses with a walkie-talkie pushed against his ear had forcefully but politely put a hand out and stopped him halfway up the grand staircase to allow someone who looked uncannily like the Shah of Iran to go past. The young man had sported an air of something between a valet and a hitman. 'Merci de votre compréhension, monsieur,' he'd said after his boss had reached the bottom of the stairs. The names in Madame Claude's book of contacts were legendary. Valéry Giscard d'Estaing was said to be a client, even while he was president de la République, though it was quite likely that the girls would have visited the Élysée rather than him coming to the house; a persistent rumour always had it that JFK had photos delivered to the Oval Office direct from the Embassy in Paris and would pick one or two girls who would be flown over for an assignation in some townhouse in Georgetown. The girls themselves were wonderful – highly educated, often aristocratic, and no doubt short of cash because of living a little beyond their means while studying at the École polytechnique or the Sorbonne.

Those were the days. Marvellous atmosphere. Wasn't free, of course, by any means. Extraordinary that there really was nothing that compared to it back home. 'The French are so much more relaxed than we are about anything to do with sex,' Alexander liked to say to friends, taking a vicarious pleasure in his adventures over a drink or two in the Three Crowns after work. 'A president without a mistress is thought of as rather peculiar. Sex is nobody else's business to the French, a quite private affair that no one has the right to get in the way of.' He'd often relate a favourite story that Enzo had told him, insisting that it was true, concerning a young gentleman being berated by a policeman after having been apprehended for pissing against a tree in this very garden. 'Urinating in the Jardin du Luxembourg is an arrestable offence!' 'Officer, I'm not urinating – I'm masturbating!' 'Oh, I *do* beg your pardon, monsieur!'

～

Alexander, deflated, seated himself at what was becoming his usual table on the pavement outside Il Delfino.

'Good God! I've had enough of this, I really have. I can see practically nothing at all, and now I'm going round maiming people. What is it all coming to – really?'

Twenty minutes before, standing outside the gates of the Jardin du Luxembourg on the corner of the rue de Médicis and the Boulevard Saint-Michel, he'd decided that the effort of trying to identify the yellow light on top of a taxi and then flagging it down was going to be too much for him and that he would walk to Il Delfino instead. He was doing quite well, clearing a path before him with his stick, affecting what he hoped looked like a confident swagger. But halfway down the Boulevard Saint-Michel, while mounting the pavement from the road, he'd stumbled and thrust the stick out to his left to save himself, only to find he had stabbed it hard against the ankle of a young woman as she was browsing her way through the books set up on the tables on the pavement outside one of the many bookshops serving the student fraternity of the Sorbonne. She'd let out an anguished yell of pain and a heated altercation with her male companion, growing steadily in outrage and volume over the course of two or three minutes had followed, even after Alexander had profusely apologised. Unfortunately, his misplaced pride had found him quite unable to reveal the reason for the mishap, which, of course, was his atrocious eyesight. Eventually, having apologised yet again, he'd managed to break away from the young couple and had set off with gusto once more, only to find himself almost immediately marooned in the very middle of the Boulevard Saint-Germain, in mortal danger from the heavy traffic bullying him on both sides.

'Monsieur,' said a voice in heavily accented English as his elbow was cupped into the palm of a hand, 'will you allow me to help you? I'm so sorry – I understand now that it is difficult for you to see.' The young man who had been shouting at him just a minute before was now weaving him in and out of the traffic, guiding him towards the far pavement.

'Thank you so much, that really is most decent of you, and let me say again how very sorry I am for–'

'Monsieur, this is my fault. I had not noticed the trouble of your eyes. Have a nice day, and goodbye,' the young man had said with a courteous little bow of the head as they reached the safety of the pavement.

～

The incident had not helped his mood at all. His pride had been snatched away once more, and he'd turned up at the restaurant wanting the company of his old companion more than he cared to admit. But he'd quite forgotten that Enzo had told him last night that he'd be missing the lunch shift today in order to take young Vittorio to the clinic for the first of his inoculations.

Alexander was being fussed over by Paolo, no doubt because the young probationary waiter was keen to make sure that the boss's friend would report back favourably on his efforts to look after him. He'd been encouraged to order the plat du jour, a carbonara, but feared that the cream-coloured dish would blend itself into the white plate, a camouflage his eyes might not be able to deal with. He was not in the mood to enter into a struggle with pasta sliding disobediently around his plate and then refusing to sit on his fork – and asking for the services of a spoon was out of the question. He settled on a Margherita – red pizza against a white background – as his mood darkened further into a sulk at the compromise he was having to make. His pride took another severe battering when the pizza arrived already cut into portions. Was this just for his benefit? Did these people think he was a bloody child, for God's sake? Or was this the Italian way? At least he could eat the bloody thing with his fingers. He loosened his tie and tucked the huge white napkin well into his neck. No one dared pick him up on *that*. When in Rome as they say…

Having consumed a demi-carafe of the house white with his pizza, he took refuge in a further two glasses with a lemon sorbet – a strange but somehow comforting mismatch of tastes – followed by an expresso accompanied by a glass of port from the bottle that Enzo kept especially for him in the cupboard underneath the till at the service station. He stared into the river below. *At least I can see something of* that, he thought as the water dazzled in the late autumn sunshine. Sat at his table, nearly alone now that his fellow diners were beginning to leave, he allowed himself to descend into a thoroughly indulgent period of maudlin reflection.

'Can't be that long now, I suppose, before I pop my clogs,' he declared to the river. The water took no notice and indeed, in his heart of hearts, he knew that his pronouncement was probably untrue, since apart from the eyes, he was as fit as a fiddle. He was able to take the stairs up to his flat at least two at a time without becoming even slightly breathless, but he was putting that inconvenient fact to one side for the moment.

'Everybody's jumping ship. Only me and Bridget left, for God's sake. Monty Bernstein died two days after our anniversary jollies, the very same day that Philip Long had his stroke. Must have been the champagne we served. I suppose it can't be long now until we have to put ourselves away in some horribly expensive bin with dreadful food and no means of escape.' He shook his head in acknowledgement of the awfulness of what he'd decided must lie ahead. 'No car, practically no son, quite soon probably no London house, and no horse, damn it – no bloody horse! Flight's dead. Dead as a dodo!' he said, shaking his head in disbelief, as though he'd only just heard the news. He recalled the Saturday afternoon, barely a month ago, when Natasha Curtis-Nichols had phoned as he and Bridget were having their afternoon cup of tea, to tell him that his beloved horse was terribly ill. Bridget had driven him uncharacteristically fast up to the stables beyond Woodnesborough, where he'd been confronted with Flight kicking the wooden partition of his stall, biting his flank with flared nostrils, his eyes wide with terror and pain. By the time the vet had arrived, the animal was on his back, rolling from side to side, kicking out uncontrollably.

'There's not much we can do, I'm afraid,' said the vet as he, Alexander and Natasha stepped out of the stall. 'He has a badly twisted gut,' he confided in a low voice, as though not wanting Flight to overhear the news, 'and he's not a young horse. We can't put him through surgery.' The young man had rubbed his face hard with his hands, unwilling to break the news. 'We'll have to put him down, Your Lordship. I'm so sorry.' He was eventually able to administer enough of a tranquilliser to calm the horse down sufficiently so that Natasha and he were able to get him up and coax him into the paddock. Bridget and Alexander had stood at the entrance to the stables with their hands thrust deep into their pockets, saying nothing. Natasha had disappeared into the farmhouse to summon her husband who had quickly gone off to fetch his shotgun – a little too readily, as though he was enjoying the drama, Alexander thought later, perhaps unfairly. The old couple had turned their back on the scene before the shot echoed like an outraged accusation against the large barn to the side of the paddock; Bridget had gasped and Alexander had put his fists to his ears and then marched back towards the car with a face like thunder, an easier expression to adopt than the one that expressed his total devastation.

Later, Bridget had poured them an over-generous, much needed pre-dinner drink, taken aback by her husband's grief and not quite knowing how best to deal with it. 'We can find another, Alecky, I'm quite sure. Natasha's an expert and has all the contacts–'

'No, darl. No more horses. No more horses,' he'd said, struggling now to keep the tears from filling his failing eyes.

∼

There was a gentle hand placed on Alexander's shoulder followed by the tiniest of squeezes to bring him back to consciousness. He was immediately awake.

The waiters had busied themselves around him during the course of their lunch shift as the customers had thinned out and noon had progressed into mid-afternoon. Eventually, only Alexander remained, slumped back in his seat with his eyes closed and his mouth open. Came the time for the staff to close the premises for a two-hour break before the evening shift started, but no one wanted to disturb the old man's reverie. So it was Paolo, the new arrival, who had been deputised to give up his break in order to keep an eye on the patron's patron.

'Cappuccino, signore?'

'Oh – oh yes, thank you, Pietro, that would be lovely.'

'Damn – wrong name, but never mind,' Alexander muttered as the lad disappeared back into the restaurant. 'Paolo. Paolo. I'll say it once or twice rather loudly when he comes back. That should put it right.' Wrong name notwithstanding, Alexander was relieved that the young waiter had not had to shake him back to life, so he was able to pretend that he'd just popped his eyes closed for a fleeting moment or two, but was absolutely, fully with it now and raring to go. His pride would, in fact, have taken yet another turn for the worse had he known that

Paolo had spent his entire break, not with his new girlfriend as he'd promised, but sitting on a strategically placed chair just inside the open door of the restaurant, leaning forward, arms practically outstretched towards the old man, ready at any minute to rush out to prevent him from rolling clean off his seat onto the pavement and perhaps then onwards towards the gutter.

∼

By the time Enzo appeared for the evening shift, Alexander was a new man, sat upright at his table. He'd felt his way down the stairs to the gents with his walking stick once Paolo had supplied him with a surprisingly strong cappuccino. Then he'd rinsed his face in cold water and departed for a walk around Île de la Cité.

'Tell Enzo I'll be back for a little early supper, Paolo,' he'd announced to the young man holding the door open for him, who was relieved that he might now be able to stretch a leg after an afternoon of old-man-watching, certainly more challenging than the one he'd spent babysitting his little niece the week before.

The fresh air had enabled Alexander to solidify a decision. He'd decided that he would do all that he could to make Ben come on board. 'Sex – an extraordinarily efficient short cut to friendship, so let's move on. I'm going to give this a go, and never mind if eventually it doesn't work out. I'll have tried, dammit!'

What a day of ups and downs he'd had, but now, while waiting for his evening meal, a feeling of relief and then contentment washed over him. He was happy to see Enzo's smiling face and he was still glowing from the pleasure of Ben's visit now that he'd put the lad's unsettling departure behind him. And perhaps at last, with this decision taken about his young friend, he could finally begin to put the ghastly saga of his son, Owen, behind him.

～

'I'll raise it to two hundred pounds a week on condition he sticks to the agreement we made ten years ago and never contacts us again. That's the deal, Yarnton,' he'd said to his stockbroker two days after Flight's demise. Yarnton, still harbouring a misplaced affection for his friend's son, had offered to be an intermediary once Alexander had declared he was quite unwilling to talk to Owen face to face.

The two men were sat at the table in the dining room at Eaton Square; they'd finished their monthly catch-up about interest rates, government bonds and the rise and fall of the stock market, all the while knowing that their usual dealings were to be followed by one of the most difficult conversations that the two old friends had ever had. Papers were collected slowly and methodically enough to help waste a little time before being filed away. That task completed, a silence had descended before it was broken by Alexander noisily pushing back his chair to go to the kitchen. He reappeared carrying their usual lunch in a carrier bag – two bottles of beer, and ham-and-pickle sandwiches purchased first thing by Alexander from the Italian deli round the corner in Lower Belgrave Street.

The ensuing conversation had, in fact, taken no time at all since Alexander knew what he wanted to say. As Yarnton released the sandwiches from their cellophane wrappings and arranged them on two plates, Alexander laid both hands, palms down, on the table. A pause then, before the words that were to bring the tortured subject of his son to an end for what he prayed would be forever.

'Not a word about him, ever again. Bridget and I had enough of it years ago. The boy's dead to us.'

CHAPTER 11

'Bloody hell, Benjamin! How many sloppy old blow jobs were needed to secure this little number?' Aurelio, hands on hips and mouth falling open, was taking in his surroundings.

'Lelo – that's horribly crude and you know that's not what goes on...'

'I know, I know, I know. Sorry. My unfunny little joke. But, come on – just at the moment it's a little hard to believe. Wow!' There was a slow shaking of the head as he looked around the unfurnished flat where the noise of drilling and hammering was forcing us to raise our voices enough to muddle me into thinking we might be heading for a row. 'The boy's landed on his feet, I'd say – fancy being given a flat for a birthday present. Even when it isn't your birthday!'

A chill spring breeze was harassing the plastic sheeting stretched across the spaces that were awaiting the imminent arrival of new sash windows in the sitting room. I was standing in the middle of a spacious, empty flat with my old friend, who was in full architect mode, having arrived equipped with a measuring tape, notepad and a pencil which was lodged above his ear. There was nothing for him to do, since the builders had been at it since early January and were nearing the end of the renovation, but Aurelio was wanting to check things out, to make sure that all was well and that no one was being taken for a ride. He was surveying all before him, squinting his eyes to better see what might be a crack in the ceiling, banging his heels against floorboards, drumming his fingers on the new radiators and stopping abruptly now and again to poke and tap at the walls to check for loose plaster; he was noisily flicking light switches on and off even though a brand-new meter, installed this morning, meant the electricity supply wasn't being connected until the morning.

'I have *not* been given a flat, Lelo. It's just that things have been arranged a bit to my advantage, that's all.'

'Fuck me, you can say that again.'

∼

It was a proper financial arrangement I'd made with Alexander about the renovation of the property. We were strict about such things so there could never be misunderstandings – and indeed there never once had been in the four or five years I'd been around; he firmly believed that the better you know someone, the tighter the agreement must be to avoid even the slightest misunderstanding. Quite a lot of paperwork, therefore – no *'sealing of a deal with the merest nod of a head across a crowded auction room'* nonsense. I'd been more than happy to visit Alexander's old family solicitors in Fleet Street, all wood-panelled walls, fountain pens and bow ties, to sign various bits of paper that I didn't completely understand.

I found the three flats, all behind one front door and

in a frightful condition, just south of the Oval. The property was owned by an old Greek couple who had lived in the ground-floor flat and rented out the two above. They were retiring back to Cyprus after years of living in London where they'd raised their two kids – one now the owner of a large plumbing business, the other a successful wedding planner, though they didn't particularly seem to have helped out with keeping their parents' property in very good condition. It had taken a lot of haggling to get an agreement on the right price, the negotiations mostly conducted by Mrs Steffanides, trying to convince me that the incredibly tatty old furniture and fittings that she was willing to throw into the deal was a reason for adding another £5,000 to the price.

'Curtains and blinds is in the price, everything included with sofas and beds and mattresses. Is all for you and even the kitchen stuff with washing machine and fridges quite new. Very good for students, innit,' she insisted with an accent so heavy she might have arrived in London yesterday. I politely declined her offer, helped by an image of four or five nastily-stained mattresses having to be thrown onto a skip as soon as we took possession. She chain-smoked throughout our meetings while supplying me with endless cups of rather bitter coffee, puffing away while pursing her lips and screwing up her eyes every time she took a drag, as though she'd only just taken up a rather perilous habit and hadn't quite got the hang of it yet.

Alexander bought the property for £45,000; I'd found a competent builder with Aurelio's help through the architect's practice he worked for, and another £40,000 had been spent making the flats fit for purpose – new roof, plumbing, wiring, and plastering throughout. The top one was to be mine. Certainly not a gift, though – our agreement stated that I was to arrange the sale of the ground- and first-floor flats and then take out a mortgage on mine so that Alexander, who'd put up all the money, would get back his outlay of £85,000 and would be able to rejoice in the fact that he'd been able to provide me with a property I could never have afforded by myself, while the whole enterprise would have cost him not much more than a few months of no interest. Well, not quite – there was going to be a *bit* of a gap in his finances, but I might have just remained quiet and supremely grateful about that. I was overwhelmed by the prospect of being able to buy a place for nearly half the price it would have cost me on the open market, and Alexander was quietly pleased with his little scheme. 'Well, why not make the pennies work to our advantage, eh? Damned good idea of mine, don't you think, old boy?'

'Damned good, Alexander, damned good.'

He came for a second visit to the property last week after our return from Morocco, tapping his way round with his stick, trying to give the impression to the builders that he was testing the plaster and floorboards rather than feeling his way about. There was lots of talking to the three lads who were working here at the time, with Alexander displaying a degree of knowledge that for some reason I'd not quite expected, though after years administering various property companies it would be surprising if he didn't know a thing or two, even if he had been mostly confined to a boardroom. Bridget had wanted to come too, for her first visit, but I'd persuaded her to delay, with a promise that she would be my very first luncheon guest once I'd moved in and got things settled enough to entertain a lady from the right side of the river. 'Well, I'll be most offended if I ever find out I'm not the first to view the final result, dear boy.'

'I suppose I'm a bit jealous, Ben,' said Aurelio, lifting a mug of tea to his lips in the greasy spoon round the corner from the flat now he'd poked around for long enough to convince himself it was all sound. We were not having to shout any longer, and therefore the feeling we were heading for some sort of confrontation had dissipated. 'Funny, isn't it, what I was warning you against three or four years ago.'

'What do you mean?'

'You know – the whole rent boy thing. I was wrong, wasn't I?'

'Yup.'

'Well – good on you. It's fantastic – really, I mean it.' There was a pause as he put his mug down. 'Now – tell me about your holiday in Marrakesh.'

⌒

I was used to going away with Alexander now. Rome, Amsterdam, Morocco just last month and I'd lost count of how many times we'd been to Paris together – at least eight times in the past year for what was usually a long weekend – and nowadays, he was happier if we travelled together, rather than me joining him there. It became a set routine, with me taking the train to Dover and meeting him in the departure lounge of the hoverport, and I was very glad to be able to report that I seemed to be getting better at packing a little case these days.

Before I was introduced to Bridget, I'd make sure I was there early enough to make my way up onto the balcony beyond passport control where I'd watch the old couple, arm in arm, join the check-in queue below. Bridget – tall, wafer thin, her white hair enveloped in an Hermès scarf, and wearing her ubiquitous navy-blue Barbour jacket – would deliver a goodbye kiss to Alexander's cheek as he stepped forward with his ticket and passport, and I'd run down the stairs to greet him as he came through.

It was as if he were departing one life and entering another and that was a fair description of how things were for me when I was with him in Paris. I lived two lives there – one frankly rather debauched, if I'm being honest, which I'll momentarily come back to – and the other spent with my old friend, a half-speed existence of feeling our way around in his increasing darkness, his elbow firmly gripped as we stepped off pavements, the top of his head protected by my hands as he lowered himself into taxis, the telephone handed back to him once I'd dialled a number and checked that it was ringing. I'd learned to lower my voice to just the right level as I read out a menu, to search for the eyeglass after it had gone missing because it had slipped from his hands during his afternoon nap and ended up between the cushions of the sofa, and I'd become adept at tantalising descriptions of various pretty lads who might pass by on one of our walks. 'What sort of colouring has he?' Alexander would whisper excitedly.

'Well, that depends – what sort of colouring do you fancy today, Alexander? Do you want him dark or blond? Up to you.'

'Oh, you are such a damn tease, making fun of a blind old man…'

The Telegraph, bought by me from the paper booth on the Boulevard Raspail just before my visit to the boulangerie for two warm croissants, was read to him every morning, usually followed by a spirited discussion of the day's politics. 'I think we'll agree to disagree, Ben.' That little sentence used to be a necessary break to prevent things getting too heated. Now, it was no more than a mantra to get me to close the subject under discussion and move on to the next. No offence was taken by either party beyond the occasional adversarial bit of banter. 'Yes – and what exactly would you say to that, eh?' he would often enquire as he won a point in an argument.

'I'd say go fuck yourself.' A riposte that was guaranteed to make him shake with laughter.

We left the rue de la Grande-Chaumière at about noon, ambling arm in arm across the Jardin du Luxembourg for lunch at either The Rostand on the Rue de Médicis or at the Delfino with Enzo before returning to the flat where Alexander took a siesta – quite a short one when we first started coming here together, but much longer these days, now that he was a bit older and also knew he was not in charge of keeping me entertained.

With Alexander dozing on the sofa for part of the afternoon, I was off on my own, making the most of a fabulous city that could never be explored fully enough. I had a season ticket that got me into most of the Paris museums, which meant I was a great deal more knowledgeable today about French history and art than I was about that of my own country. Paris felt like my second home now, and by the time we returned to London, my head was pounding from a surfeit of beauty and my feet were often in need of serious attention after all the walking.

Every evening, at 7pm on the dot, I punched in the code to the side of the green door in the rue de la Grande-Chaumière, having had a quick nap and a shower in my room at one of the two hotels where my visits had become such a matter of routine that Hameed, the Tunisian receptionist at Le Raspail, long ago began to greet me as 'Monsieur Benjamin'. As the door opened, Madame Forestier glowered sullenly at me, even though I tried to be as friendly as possible. 'Bonjour, madame! Comment ça va?' I called out with the broadest grin pasted onto my face, but there was to be no winning her over. She glared at me from her plastic-flowered eyrie, her round, bulbous eyes set in a large, neckless head that floated above a great grey mohair jumper that put me in mind of ruffled feathers. *'The Barn Owl'*, I've taken to calling her. Seemed as though all those clichéd stories about fat old Paris concierges being unfriendly pieces of work were true.

It was after dinner that my second life began, though, once I'd seen Alexander safely home and practically tucked him up. I was free then, my legs allowed to operate at a normal, young man's speed after the slow, deliberate steps that Alexander's eyes demanded of us both. I became a creature of the night. I'm afraid I have to admit that I now knew my way around all the corridors of the Opera Euro sauna, together with the dimly lit paths that followed the Seine under the bridges of the city, various shaded (and shady) parts of the Tuileries Garden and a notorious nightclub called Le Trap in the rue Jacob, not much more than a short walk from the apartment. It was introduced to me by a friend who I just happened to bump into in a bar one afternoon in the Marais, a stage manager I'd worked with during a panto season in Leatherhead. Very old school, is Howard. Eton and the Brigade of Guards before a slip down the social ladder to what he really wanted to do, which was to play at theatres, though I believe that a trust fund made any profession not entirely necessary. 'What goes on there, Howard, at Le Trap?'

'Major willy-bashing, old man,' he'd said, leaning against the bar and pushing a fringe of the blondest hair from his eyes. 'Drinks downstairs with a pretence of deportment and decency, and all hell breaking loose in the darkness once you climb the stairs. Terrific fun. Nothing to compare in London, absolutely nothing. You'll have a spiffing time. But I say – don't go tonight. I'm planning a visit and we don't really want to catch ourselves interfering with each other in the dark, do we?'

Is it rather dishonest that I didn't divulge all of what went on to my old friend? Because I didn't. Of course, he knew quite a bit of what I got up to, but I didn't go into detail and certainly would rather have kept the extent of the debauchery and the hours I devoted to it from him. He might have been shocked to know that often I didn't get back to the hotel till the early hours, if at all – there had been the discovery of certain *arrondissements* outside the most central parts of the city, the occasional waking up in an unfamiliar bed, followed by the panic of trying to work out how long I was going to be on the metro before letting myself into the apartment with warm croissants and the paper under my arm. So, a bit of a white lie as I yawned over the coffee was not that unusual.

'Don't know why I'm so sleepy, Alexander. The Paris air, I think. It always happens when I'm here. A little too invigorating, perhaps – it's a funny thing because I slept quite well once I got to bed last night…'

The putting of my foot down with Alexander about the sex thing was never mentioned once we got back to London after that first visit. That was going so far back it seems like history now. I was prepared for some sort of embarrassing tussle where I might have to restate my case before perhaps leaving Eaton Square forever, but it never materialised, and it was not alluded to again. I loved him for it – for the knowledge that I was important enough to him to put the subject to one side even though I suspect his feelings for me were quite strong. He did his own thing, then, and had become not very shy about telling me about his various adventures. Now and again, he might cancel one of our Wednesday dinners. 'It's not convenient to meet up this evening' he'd say as I was packing up at the desk in the study. When it first happened, even though I had my suspicions about what was going on, I said nothing. Nowadays, I'd raise my eyebrows rather pointedly while he suppressed a grin. Indeed, more recently, there'd been the odd time when I'd helped out in the search for a little adventure – not always that successfully.

One evening in Paris – just before our trip to Morocco – after dinner at the Taverne Basque and our customary two bottles of Tavel, we both got rather carried away with the idea that we might find somebody to provide Alexander with a little nocturnal entertainment. This rather dubious enterprise saw us taking a taxi to a night-club that he knew from the early days of his friendship with Enzo. Le Sept is a near Parisian copy of the Embassy Club – now of blessed memory. It was taken over by someone who hadn't a clue how to run a club; it crashed and burned two or three years ago. All in the past now, apart from an enduring friendship with Nadia.

It was an important part of my life, and I'll always remember my time there with great affection. The Parisian club is a little smaller, and certainly a great deal older, but with the same mixture of high society ('bon chic, bon genre', I heard Enzo say about the clientele – the French equivalent of 'Sloane Ranger' I later found out), people from the arts and music scene, shady drug dealers and city-boy types overlaid with a heavy gay subculture swiftly making its way into the mainstream, just like its London equivalent. It was also well known as a joint where gentlemen with the right sort of money might be able to find a little company of an evening. I don't remember much of our disastrous visit, since we must have been there less than twenty minutes, but I do recall Alexander losing his temper very badly with a young waiter who he felt had been a little slow in taking our order as we stood overlooking the dance floor. It wasn't the case; the real reason for his frustration was his inability to see anything at all through the smoke and low lighting. I suspect he was comparing things to his last visit a few years before and was unsettled by the realisation of the extreme change in his vision. We walked around for a while, trying to keep our drinks in our glasses as we struggled with invisible steps, bumped into dark leather chairs, and were jostled by people careering on and off the dance floor.

Eventually, there was an unfortunate altercation with

a floor-length white tablecloth while we passed through the restaurant (we were lost). It got caught up in Alexander's foot and nearly saw him pitched to the ground, at which point we admitted defeat and managed to find two seats. We stared out at the dance floor for a while, an old blind man and a younger one also blinded by the strobe lighting and who was disappointed to find he was succumbing to a feeling of being very foreign. There was no chance of arranging anything for Alexander in such an atmosphere and I soon found myself desperately trying to judge at what point it would be politic to suggest cutting our drunken experiment short and exiting the hellhole of a building. The whole thing was rather sad – a bit of a defeat after the childlike excitement of the discussion at the Taverne Basque less than an hour before.

'How about we make our way out, Alexander?' I shouted through my cupped palms into his ear after about five minutes. No persuasion needed – he was on his feet immediately, heading with real determination, and no help, towards a door that he correctly sensed was somewhere behind us and which he quickly opened and entered. It turned out to be a broom cupboard from which I had to extract him, before we made what I hoped looked like a more or less dignified exit, with me checking the faces around us to see if we were being laughed at; nobody, of course, was even vaguely interested. The very cold air outside – Paris in February – quickly returned us to our senses, and I was busy trying to flag down a taxi when I noticed a comely youth probably in his early twenties sitting on a doorstep smoking a cigarette. He was wearing a tee-shirt but no jacket against the cold and had light-blond curls catching the streetlight, green eyes, sinewy smooth arms, and a knowing smile that revealed a becoming gap between his front teeth. A wink in my direction was enough to inform me that I might be able to enter into a little business proposition for the benefit of my old friend.

'Do you know, Alexander, I think all is not lost – you still up for a little adventure?'

'By Jove, yes. I certainly am.'

A minute or two later, we were in a warm taxi, rattling across the cobblestones down the rue de Rennes without a word being exchanged, the windows misting up with excitement, the boy's smile unchanging on his face now a financial transaction had been agreed, and me basking in the sense of no longer being at all foreign, having achieved something clever and risky in a dangerously cosmopolitan atmosphere – now not just overseeing my old friend's paperwork, guiding him around and arranging holidays, but also setting up illicit liaisons in foreign capitals. Some little dope deal next, no doubt, if we ever decided we wanted it. I was surely a man of the world.

Fucking disaster. The boy's smile faded at the front door to the apartment as I was saying my goodbyes and he realised that I wasn't included in the deal, but I didn't feel unduly worried. I left them alone having checked that there was the agreed number of notes held together by a clip-pin in the inside pocket of Alexander's jacket and went over to the hotel for a relatively early night, peeping up from behind the curtains in my room to see whether the lights were still burning above me in the apartment on the other side of the road.

'Darned boy ran orff,' said the voice from the

kitchenette the next morning as I closed the front door of the apartment behind me. 'Took the money from my jacket and skedaddled. Surprised he didn't run past you on the stairs on your way out...'

∼

Marrakesh, March 1984

'What did the old girl mean, Alexander? Rather an extraordinary thing to say, don't you think?'

We'd just sat down to dinner at our usual table in the dining room of the Es Saadi Hotel. I was leaning sideways towards Alexander, who'd made sure to be seated to my left during mealtimes for the last few days, a gallon of water from the pool having settled into his left ear. We'd summoned a doctor with a syringe for the morning. 'Blind and now fucking deaf as well,' he'd said in a matter-of-fact sort of tone as we stood at reception a little earlier to make the appointment.

'What?' he shouted, flicking his napkin and settling it round his knees in his customary manner. 'What did you say?' Perhaps the water had succeeded in flooding his right ear too.

'Lady Fountain,' I shouted a little too loudly. 'She just said, "I like your boyfriend". What's she up to?'

'Oh heavens. Just an expression, I think. She means she likes my friend who's a boy.'

'Yes, well I hope Bridget didn't catch it. Nosey old boot if you ask me. Fishing around for information.'

Bridget, whose hearing was definitely not what it was, had obviously missed the comment and was taken up with looking around to see who exactly was entering the room before reporting the comings and goings back to me, nearly as interested as she was. The gossip that would follow ('Wasn't she wearing the same frock last night?' 'Not talking to each other at all now – there's quite obviously been a falling out!' 'I say, isn't that Ludovic Kennedy and Moira Shearer?') was fast becoming one of our favourite holiday pastimes.

We'd been in the short queue at the entrance to the dining room, waiting to be seated, when Lady Fountain approached us, flustered about having to wait her turn.

'Oh, not again,' she sighed, 'you'd think they'd check the damn guest list to see what's what, who's who, wouldn't you? We had the very same thing last night, you know. In the end I had to tell them who I was–'

'And who were you?' said Alexander without a pause. She'd mellowed once she'd caught the eye of the maître d' who assured her that the table reserved for her and her travelling companion (a Miss Sprite, a tiny wordless thing in a beige cardigan with very straight white hair, clutching a tissue and dabbing at an angry red nose) was very nearly ready. She was certainly being flirtatious when she made the comment about me to Alexander, loud enough for me to hear while looking me up and down with her head to one side and a little sideways smile that put me in mind of a stroke victim. When they were fetched to their table, she'd veered a little off course as she entered the dining room in a cloud of chiffon, running her fingers along the side of the piano to the alarm of the resident pianist who braced himself as though preparing to have her land up in his lap.

'Who is she, anyway, Alexander?'

'Oh, sort of parvenue type. Widow of Michael Fountain who was chairman of Eagle World Insurance. Left her an absolute fortune. She was his secretary, then mistress. Rather a big scandal at the time. He was married to a sweet girl, too, awfully pretty – Lord Tyron's daughter, who I had a go with once, I think. Went orff with *her*, though, in the end,' he said, nodding vaguely towards the far end of the dining room where Lady Fountain was fondling the arm of the waiter who was taking her order.

'I think she's been over-refreshing herself at the bar,' I said.

'Maybe. But don't bother taking offence; she's not a bad old girl really.'

∼

It's a question in people's minds. Of course it is. How could it not be? Everybody must have been wondering who, but who, is this young man that the Bellaghys have taken up with. Amanuensis? Lover? Catamite? Alexander had told me that there was even talk of my being a long-lost and now rediscovered illegitimate son, and that it was being said that my presence had become acceptable to Bridget because of the bitter disappointment of her only child.

'Where are you hearing all this from, Alexander?' I'd said to him as we settled a last bit of business in the study at Eaton Square the morning before our departure.

'Oh, you know – from round about…'

'Round about where?'

'Well, let me think. White's, the clubhouse at St James's, various bars in the Palace of Westminster–'

'Bollocks! You're teasing me.'

'Well, yes, a bit, but I imagine that they might be saying that sort of thing. They must be intrigued. I know it from the fact that I'm *not* being asked any questions!'

'Not quite the same thing.'

'Perhaps not, but there's something about the general feeling of mystery that I'm rather enjoying,' said Alexander smiling while slipping further down into his chair now that the morning's work was over. 'Teddy Jessop is the only one of my friends who's actually asked any questions. Dying to find out, of course. I teased him by pretending not to get the point and then changed the subject, which, knowing Teddy, means it's certainly now being discussed in every corner of the Garrick. You ever been there, Ben?'

'Er – no, Alexander, not the sort of place I would have found myself frequenting in the past.'

'What? Good Lord! Marvellous collection of portraits. I'll take you to dinner there – think you'd rather enjoy it...'

I'm sure I would. I've often walked up Garrick Street and stared up through the windows at the huge, beautifully lit canvases lining the walls. I think I'd enjoy it nearly as much as the tittle-tattle that is turning me into a bit of an enigma.

⁓

We left Marrakesh – on what I can only describe as a road trip – the next day. Bridget was intending to drive us all the way to Tangier where we would be staying for the last week of our holiday, a journey just a little short of six hundred miles. We departed first thing in the morning, and we stayed overnight in Rabat. A packed lunch was prepared by the hotel kitchen, and we stopped on the way to eat it. It promised to be a social week; the Bellaghys went nearly every year and knew lots of expats in the city.

A few days ago, there was some dangerous talk of me helping out with the driving, but I was hoping that my face crashing to the ground when it was mentioned by the pool had put paid to any suggestion of that. I'd only been driving since January and really didn't fancy putting everyone's life at risk on those treacherous roads. I'd seen how some of the locals drove and I was not at all keen. Besides, how the fuck did they expect me to manoeuvre myself about on the wrong side of the road? I prayed the subject did not raise its ugly head again. Please. There was a little bit of dread that wouldn't be dispelled around the subject, but I thought I was probably safe. Fingers crossed and all that.

I'd loved the experience of Marrakesh – the lying beside the pool until way after lunch, and then wandering up in the cooling afternoon to the Jemaa el-Fnaa, the ancient market in the medina, where the stall-holders relentlessly vied for your attention. 'For the eyes alone, the eyes alone,' they'd say as they rolled open a dazzlingly coloured carpet or insisted on lining up a collection of brightly painted bowls and vases on the counter once they'd ushered you in to their premises. I'd learned not to catch anyone's eye – whether it be a merchant in the souk or some pretty boy. They were on to you in a flash, and it was difficult to get away. We'd made the most of our time here – I'd seen palaces and gardens, travelled up the Ourika Valley to eat lunch at a little hotel that my holiday companions discovered years ago, and taken a horse-drawn carriage with Bridget to wander round the Menara Gardens.

Yesterday, Bridget and I took tea on the terrace at La Mamounia, where we sat cross-legged on huge cushions under a vast fan of peacock feathers. I found myself fantasising about what it would have been like to stay at this extraordinary place rather than the more conventional Es Saadi.

'We stayed here once or twice many moons ago, before Morocco was so popular,' Bridget told me, 'but the place has gone frightfully upmarket now. Hardly recognisable from the days when Winston and Clemmie used to come after the war. He was very fond of the place – used to sit in the shade painting all those awful pictures. But now! All these silk hangings and stuff and the staff in ridiculous costumes, like something out of *Lawrence of Arabia*.' Bridget was casting her eye round disapprovingly. 'Far too opulent, don't you think? All a bit over the top,' she said, screwing up her eyes to study the latticework in the ceiling above us but resolutely failing to be won over. 'They say it's owned by the King, and if he turns up with his entourage, one's likely to find oneself turfed out with nowhere to stay, apparently.' My companion was on the point of admitting defeat in her struggle to get comfortable. The constant battle to maintain a straight-backed dignity on her cushion had soured her mood; she'd very nearly rolled off it earlier while concentrating on raising a cup to her lips. 'I think I probably prefer sitting in a chair for my afternoon tea.'

As we were about to leave, a woman of a certain age who should have known better tottered past us in the highest of heels. She was sporting a pair of vast sunglasses atop a blood-red turban matching her lipstick and nail varnish and wearing the skimpiest of yellow bikinis. Hanging from her bejewelled, liver-spotted hands were a bottle of Dom Pérignon and two glasses. 'Most unedifying,' said Bridget as the trembling cellulite on the back of the woman's thighs receded into the distance. A pause for reflection. 'I find the Es Saadi more restrained, more measured in its ways, don't you agree, Ben?'

'Yes – yes, I suppose I do really,' I replied, looking longingly across the lawn to the pool. On the far side, an attendant in a purple djellaba was delivering a jug of something ice cold and delicious to a table within reach of the languorous hand of someone swinging in a hammock between two palm trees.

∼

I'd spent a lot of time alone with Bridget during the past few days, and it changed things. Quite often, we'd left Alexander dozing by the side of the pool or in his room and struck out together. A little guilty pleasure, we admitted to each other, not having to compromise, to lower our speed to that of the slowest ship in the convoy. He was fine though. When we returned from the Menara Gardens the day before yesterday, we found him sitting in the foyer, his stick between his legs, and a victorious smile on his face. He was full of a story about being whisked through the Jemaa el-Fnaa on the scooter of the friendliest of the waiters we'd met at dinner, who'd obviously taken pity on him sitting alone by the side of the pool and insisted on inviting him home to tea to meet his wife and two small children. Alexander had been delighted at his little adventure, speeding through the market on a scooter with both legs splayed out, one hand clutching his stick and the other alternating between holding his hat to his head and encircling his host's waist to stop himself slipping off his seat. 'I've had my tea – fresh peppermint – with my new friends. I've gone much more native than either of you two,' he said proudly, turning his nose up at the pot that had been summoned for me and Bridget.

But he was going to be happy about the fact that Bridget and I seemed to have hit it off – I'd spent enough time with her now to allow me to think that, in her eyes, I was no longer just the chap who spent time downstairs at Eaton Square helping out her husband with his paperwork and who had appeared once or twice, needing to be entertained, for a weekend in Sandwich.

It had been much more than a year since Alexander had interrupted our work in the study at Eaton Square and ushered me upstairs into her presence for the first time. All very polite and straightforward, though I was ridiculously nervous about making a good impression, and afterwards, it occurred to me that Bridget may have been as aware as I was of the importance of the event. She'd quite obviously been preparing herself for the encounter and had delayed her departure for Sandwich. When Alexander ushered me into the sitting room, she was standing in the middle of the room awaiting my arrival, as though I might be a member of the diplomatic corps receiving my credentials from the sovereign before departing on a tour of duty.

'Hello there! Nice to meet you,' she said, breaking the Buckingham Palace code of behaviour by taking my outstretched hand in both of hers. 'I really have heard so much about you. Alexander rather relies on you these days, he tells me…'

By the end of that first meeting, I'd been invited to Sandwich for the following weekend, and found myself packing a little overnight bag on the Friday evening with the same sort of jitters that used to accompany my early trips to Paris. I wanted to get it right, knowing that Bridget would be making an effort to entertain me, and that there was the rather daunting prospect of a small dinner party being planned in my honour for the Sunday evening.

Alexander purposely took a back seat to Bridget after the short walk back from the station where he was waiting for me, proud to show off the fact that he knew this patch of ground so well that he got about without bumping into anything more than the odd parked car. As soon as she had greeted me, Bridget immediately adopted full hostess mode, insisting on showing me all the local sights. She was quite clearly making an effort – the two of us took a walk down to Sandwich Bay on Saturday morning; later, there was a drive to visit the Roman fort at Richborough followed by an inspection of Walmer Castle and Gertrude Jekyll's pretty garden that surrounds it. Before the dinner guests arrived on Sunday, Alexander and I walked along the Butts and the Ramparts – the old town walls – and giggled about how solicitous and welcoming his wife had been to me.

'You made the impression that I knew you would, dear boy. Plain sailing from now on!'

The dinner party was my first introduction to the sort of Sandwich society that I was going to get so used to in the years to come. Three guests. A pot-bellied gentleman with a shiny bald pate called Murray Frayne, the owner of an old family business – a chain of laundrettes – which was never to be mentioned on account of Murray's insistence on being a *bona fide* gent; a wonderfully rotund, gossipy and forthright life peeress called Lady Fulbourn, just widowed, and very merry. She'd been a Tory whip in the House of Lords and brooked no nonsense there, and later a baroness-in-waiting to the Queen, full of stories of having to greet ghastly foreign potentates at Heathrow on Her Majesty's behalf. I immediately took to her, but we wouldn't be talking politics.

'Now who the devil are *you*, young man, and what are you doing with my old friend Alexander? Spill the beans!' Plain curious and not ashamed of it – my type of gal. I walked arm in arm with her the few yards back to her house at the end of the evening and told her the acceptable version of the meeting with Alexander in Paris, which had doused her curiosity for the moment.

The last guest was a Diana Shalcroft, as sweet-natured as she was ancient, a delicate lady smelling of lavender and wearing evening gloves. Her eyes were bright in a palely powdered face, the remnants of a great beauty shining through. As she was shown into the sitting room by Mrs Smith, the housekeeper, I jumped up to relieve her of her fox-fur stole which I deposited in the cloakroom. The creature's eyes looked back at me as I draped him over the hat-stand; he wore a disconsolate expression on his flattened face, as though he was just coming round to the realisation that he'd been wrapped round an old lady's shoulders for much longer than he'd ever been a fox.

I more than survived the weekend, quite sure that I had made a good start with my relationship with the 'Baroness' as I took to referring to Bridget. I was genuinely pleased to find that I had been able to hold my own in the rarefied, genteel atmosphere. A little like play-acting, I thought to myself on the train journey home. One of my stock characters had been called upon, and it came easy to me. I thought I might have to be careful to avoid being typecast.

∼

We were in the hire car that was delivered to the hotel that morning, slowly making our way through chaotic traffic on the outskirts of Marrakesh. Alexander was in the back, sat dead in the centre like a maharaja awaiting a twenty-one-gun salute, and I was in the front next to Bridget, who was quite obviously ill at ease, snatching at the unfamiliar gear stick while all around there was a cacophony of car horns, only partly directed at her, but which she was taking personally.

'Oh, for heaven's sake, this is quite bloody impossible! The manners of these people!' She looked distressed, her hands rigidly gripping the steering wheel, shoulders hunched forward as though she was waiting to receive a blow. 'How do you feel about driving, Ben? Just part of the way, to help me out – once we're clear of Marrakesh?' A pause. 'Just as far as Rabat.'

Rabat? Bloody Rabat! That was three-hundred-odd miles – half the journey! Just the very thing I'd been dreading, of course. 'Um. Yes. Yes, perhaps once we're well clear of the city and properly on our way? Once I get a feel for the car and–'

'Get the feel of it? That's certainly not going to happen if you're just sat beside me looking out of the window!' A little sharp, the comment – not the first I'd been subjected to, but I was getting used to Bridget's plain-speaking ways and I was already unlikely to take offence.

Please let this not be happening, I prayed. A change of subject was desperately needed, or should I have tried plain flattery? A minute or two of silence, apart from a few words of encouragement from the back ('Well done, darl, that's the spirit! Ignore the fuckers!') and it seemed that things had calmed down a little. 'Golly, Bridget,' I said, 'you seem so used to all this! Did you actually tell me the other day that you once drove from Tehran to Isfahan? Extraordinary, but you're such a competent driver, of course…'

Last year, Alexander had insisted that I learn to drive, even when I declared I could not see the point. He'd paid for a course of lessons and to everyone's immense surprise, just after Christmas, I passed the test first time. 'That's the most unlikely thing I ever heard,' said Aurelio, rather unkindly. My success might seem to have implied that somehow driving came easy to me, but it didn't. I was a nervous, very new driver. The garage in Sandwich was instructed to provide me with a car as soon as possible, and a beat-up old Austin was quickly found, Alexander confidently declaring that if I had the odd scrape, it would be of no importance. 'All part of the learning curve.' Not sure if anyone in an 'odd scrape' with me would feel the same, however.

But I'd quickly got used to driving and had quite taken to it, with only a few mishaps – the most serious being my first drive down to Sandwich. Plucking up courage on an empty stretch of the M2 close to Canterbury, I found myself doing an exhilarating eighty-five miles an hour for the first time, at which speed the car suddenly began to vibrate quite violently before the bonnet unlocked itself, caught the slipstream and swung up towards the windscreen, totally blocking my view. I managed to stop and, promising myself that I was going to join the AA at the first possible opportunity, got out and secured the bonnet with a length of ribbon that I found in the glove compartment. I was still suffering badly from 'new driver syndrome' so I was constantly waiting for things to go wrong – the rumbly-bumping of a flat tyre rolling along the tarmac, a red light on the dashboard that meant there was going to be a fire, the petrol gauge stuck at three-quarters full when, silly bugger, the tank was actually empty. I'd quickly developed a healthy respect and a certain amount of fearfulness around cars, which, in my opinion, had a mind of their own, especially when they were elderly, like my old girl. I never got into a car without expecting the worst.

We were free of Marrakesh and picking up speed; Bridget had found her mojo; her hands had slipped lower on the steering wheel and her shoulders had come down a little. We were beetling along towards Rabat and I was beginning to relax. Then, without any warning, there was the tick-tock-tick of the indicator as Bridget pulled over and stopped abruptly in a cloud of dust at the side of the road. She noisily cranked up the handbrake and turned off the engine. 'Thank you so much, dear boy, for offering,' she said, adjusting her scarf in the mirror. She collected her handbag wedged beside the gear stick, opened the door, and stepped out into the middle of nowhere, heading round to the passenger seat.

There was an enormous storm brewing as I tentatively moved the car back onto the road. I was taking big breaths and wondering how on earth to deal with driving from what surely must be the passenger seat and with everything in quite the wrong place. Within a few minutes, the heavens opened, turning the rusty-pink landscape around us to an iridescent red. I soldiered on, hardly able to see a thing until it began to occur to me that this situation might just be survivable after all. I was showing a bit of gumption, pressing on through adversity. 'Well done, old chap, you're doing marvellously,' encouraged Alexander from the back as Bridget clapped her hands at the same time as there was a roll of thunder. 'You're a natural, an absolute natural!' she declared, patting my thigh.

I was pleased with myself. The storm abated as quickly as it arrived, and the sun came out.

'Extraordinary how this wet clay smells of burning rubber, don't you think?' I said, coming over rather chatty and carefree now that I was so obviously winning the day. I was picking up speed, too. A minute or two later, the smell was getting more powerful. I glanced down; I'd left the handbrake on.

∼

In the end, I drove the whole bloody way to the Hotel El Minzah in Tangier, would you believe! I was riding a bit of a wave after the success of my first foreign drive, even though we had to have a car change in Rabat – something wrong with the handbrake; I pretended to know nothing about it. Bridget was thrilled when I offered to complete our journey; the idea of getting us all the way to Tangier, she told me later, was spoiling her holiday and I have to say, from the experience of the first four or five miles out of Marrakesh, I was not sure that the three of us would have survived the journey. Guess it was fine for her on the familiar roads to and from Eaton Square and pottering around Sandwich and its environs, but she had a right to be losing her nerve on a foreign road at the age of 75. Tehran to Isfahan was, after all, twenty-five years ago! There was an element of forgetfulness around Bridget; I hadn't really noticed it before the holiday. It was especially apparent when she was stressed. There was a lot of faffing around in the car at the Es Saadi before we left – a studying of the pedals with a look of uncertainty, and even, just for a moment, a question about what the 'lever' on her right was for. Turned out to be the gear stick, so I did know that we were in for a little bit of bother.

I don't remember much of our overnight stay in Rabat, apart from a short pre-dinner walk from the Hilton towards the King's palace, where jittery guards blew whistles and gesticulated madly in my direction to warn me not to approach any closer to the green-tiled building with a monumental gate, the Royal Standard fluttering above it. Two nearly successful coup attempts just a few years back meant that Hassan II couldn't take things for granted. But my recollections of Rabat are hazy apart from (and perhaps because of) the fact that I was woken very early in my room the next morning before our departure for Tangier by Alexander, who, apparently third time lucky, had found the right door to knock on.

A shaken voice penetrated the closed door. 'Emergency, Ben! Bridget is stuck fast in her bath and I can't get her out!' I leapt from my bed and sprinted down the corridor. 'No time for modesty, young man. Avert your eyes and haul me out, please,' she declared as I hovered by the door to her bathroom in my underpants. 'Much easier than alarming the staff, don't you think?' For the sake of propriety, there was a flurry of bathroom towels which were thrown over Bridget as though she was a chip-pan fire on a kitchen stove, followed by a lot of yanking of wrists and elbows while Alexander offered encouragement from behind me by repeatedly shouting 'One-two-three – LIFT!' at the wrong time. After only a moment, the Baroness was freed from her slippery prison, and helped to her feet by the side of the tub, a ghost-like figure covered from head to toe by a huge bath towel. I was immediately a hero, lauded for my strength and no-nonsense approach. A triumphant breakfast for three was ordered from room service and taken with a fair amount of relieved giggling about what had just happened. From that moment, the importance of my role in both, rather than just one, of their lives became an accepted fact.

～

The day after the bath rescue and the completion of the long drive from one end of Morocco to the other, Bridget presented me with the prettiest little snakeskin wallet. A thank-you for services rendered having reached Tangier. The Order of the Bath and Road, you might say. There was a different quality to our relationship already; I noticed that now, as we stepped out of the hotel, her hand was likely to find its way round my upper arm and to stay there. I liked it; it felt like a sign of dependence and affection. 'We must introduce Ben to all the locals, Alecky – they'll be so taken with him, and I'm looking forward to months of post-mortemimg together when we get back home, too,' she'd said over tea after our arrival. 'I want to know exactly what they think of him and, more to the point, what he thinks of them…'

On our first evening, we were joined for dinner by a House of Lords acquaintance of Alexander's who was also staying at the El Minzah. Lord Sawyer, Bridget informed me on the way down to the dining room, owned vast acres of Yorkshire moors and, she said rather pointedly, 'has never married.' A pause then, and a significant look with raised eyebrows. 'I think he probably felt he'd prefer to shoot things rather than manufacture children.' He was with a very much younger companion called Toby, with whom he was sharing a room, the grandson of one of those Second World War commanders who ended up with the names of Asian countries or North African towns and deserts in their titles.

Sawyer was a bore, stout with a gammy leg and a nose that had been subjected to too much port; he talked incessantly about slaughtering pheasants and ducks, chasing foxes and about an ongoing row with his tailor in Savile Row. But Toby lit a bit of a fire in me. He was my age, studied law at Oxford and wanted to be a human rights lawyer. He had joined Sawyer, an old family friend, for a few days' break from an unpaid job with a children's charity in Meknes – but I'd no idea what their relationship was about as they seemed entirely unsuited. Toby swapped seats to be beside me at Bridget's insistence when dessert was served, and we found ourselves setting the world to rights together. Bright as a button and cute as hell. After the Bellaghys and Sawyer retired for the night, we went to the bar together and drank enough for him to become a little maudlin. At one point during the long evening, I was just sober enough to stop myself moving a lock of hair away from his blue eyes after they filled with tears when he told me how much he was missing his girlfriend. Later, I think I may have slipped up by putting my arms around him as we said goodnight.

It had been a social whirl, our visit. The Bellaghys had not been back here for a while, and I got the impression that the novelty of seeing old friends had been a welcome distraction for a diminishing, ageing population. Our first port of call was to the Villa de France, the hotel where Alexander and Bridget had stayed every visit but this one. The El Minzah, a name that conjured up comparisons with Raffles, Reid's, or indeed, La Mamounia, may have been chosen for this trip as a special treat for me, since whenever the Bellaghys mentioned their old hotel, they grew quite wistful. The staff at the Villa de France went wild with joy at the reunion, with cooks, chambermaids, waiters and even an ancient gardener holding on tight to a pot of geraniums collecting in the lobby to greet their former guests with hugs and a touching of hands to hearts. I stood there smiling sweetly, basking in the sunshine of their popularity while being taken for their son by several members of the staff who stroked my face as though I might be a seven-year-old.

Two days after our arrival and on the spur of the moment, I decided to abandon Alexander and Bridget and set off alone on the ferry from Tangier to Gibraltar. I stood at the bow where a spring shower, sea spray and dolphins accompanied me on the thirty-mile journey from

Africa to Europe across a surging sea. I hailed a taxi and embarked on the quickest of tours of the vast rock slicing into the clouds above. Quite by chance, outside a pub on Main Street that looked as though it might have been transplanted from a London suburb, I bumped into Aurelio's brother Albert, taking a short stroll between lessons at the primary school where he taught and where he insisted on taking me back to be introduced to his class of seven-year-olds. 'Hello Mr Teasdale, hello to you, hello Mr Teasdale, hello to you' they were encouraged to say in unison as I stood in front of the blackboard trying not to glance at my watch – I had all the time in the world but was beginning to fret about the time of my ferry's departure back to Tangier. It was my first day away from the Bellaghys in nearly three weeks – a strange feeling of heady freedom and slightly threatening rootlessness.

Lunch the next day found us at the home of the Hon. David Hervey-Smythson, the doyen of Tangier society, and an old friend of Bridget's from her coming out season in 1922. Doyen is the polite way to describe him, but Bridget was more forthright in telling me that he was generally known as the Queen of Tangier. 'David's also the most terrific snob,' Bridget told me in the taxi on the way, 'but he takes no offence whatsoever at either description.' He'd lived in Tangier since he was in his mid-twenties, after being ordered to leave England by his father after some scandal or other.

'Oh, do tell me what happened,' I said to Alexander who was sat in the front next to the driver. 'It's so much more interesting to know everything before meeting someone for the first time. Important to get things in context, don't you think?'

'Nosey bugger! Ask him yourself when we get there–'
'Oh, come on!'

'Well, the whole thing was hushed up, of course, but it was the usual sort of thing that queers get mixed up with, you know – a black frock, the rose garden at Hyde Park Corner in the early hours, and a trooper from the Brigade of Guards, that sort of carry on.'

'Oh golly!'

~

David lived just a mile or two from the centre of town on the Mountain, the district where most of the grand foreign residents of Tangier had their homes. It was a beautiful, tumble-down house filled with antique furniture from the family estate in Wiltshire. 'Oh, just tat, really – all pinched from the attic at Lullingworth,' he said when I complimented him on it, which was a bit of a faux pas according to Bridget. 'Best not to talk about people's furniture,' she said to me in the taxi home, looking out of the window. It must have been one hell of an attic. The three of us were greeted in the French style with numerous kisses to each cheek at the front door by our host – a thin strip of a man wearing crumpled linen and a Panama hat that didn't come off for the duration of our stay. I suspected that David was not well – some illness was eating at him; I could feel a desperately bony shoulder through his jacket when it came to saying goodbye and he had a long-toothed grin in a grey, cadaverous face; I tried to envisage it atop a black frock in the rose garden in Hyde Park, but I couldn't quite get there.

Aperitifs were served on the terrace where three large

arches set into salmon-pink walls were framed by a vibrant bougainvillea. There were olive-green shutters at the windows, palms and ferns in terracotta pots and wide stairs leading down to the exotically overgrown garden. We were attended to by two loose-hipped young Moroccans wearing crimson waistcoats and tight white trousers.

Suddenly, I was feeling uncomfortable and had to leave my chair. 'I must have a look at this glorious garden before lunch!' I said, heading down the steps from the terrace while wiping my damp forehead with a hanky and hoping that no one had noticed. I needed to be alone for a while. I took refuge by a marble bust of a Roman emperor in the shade at the far end of a shingle path; I scratched and loosened some lichen at its base as though it was important remedial work I was undertaking, while snatching cool breaths and telling myself that all was fine.

A little after my return to the terrace, we were ushered into a dining room where an eclectic mix of pictures hung on rusty-red walls. The table was groaning with silver, flowers from the garden and brightly coloured local plates charmingly clashing with each other. But my hand was still shaking as I picked up a glass of water, and I was wondering whether I might have to leave the table and take refuge in the garden again. An arm settled lightly along the top of mine.

'Isn't this exquisite, Ben?' Bridget, without saying a word, had ignored David's seating plan and made sure to sit beside me. The wine arrived and I took a gulp; it immediately revived and calmed me; I was able to take note of my lunch companions for the first time. David, supported by brilliant blue cushions, was enthroned at the head of the table on a gold-leafed armchair. Next to him was an elegant gentleman in green corduroy called Paul, entirely distracted and dragging hard on a cigarette in a holder between each of the several courses as if his life depended on it. He was morosely silent throughout the meal apart from a comment about his recently deceased wife. 'She was a wonderful hostess and quite a girl in the bedroom, but unfortunately not always just in the one that we shared...' he'd said wistfully, just loud enough for me to catch it when Alexander offered his condolences. 'Very famous,' Bridget informed me during the lengthy post-mortem on the journey back to the hotel, 'the most wonderful writer, and a damned good painter – though too, too sad after his wife's death.'

'Don't know quite why he made that comment about Jane as though he was some sort of aggrieved party,' said Alexander. 'It was the most open marriage you could possibly imagine. Open to all and sundry, regardless of age, sex, colour...'

Seated next to Paul was a very grand dame who was the guest of honour, a cousin of the King, and a former Moroccan ambassador to the United Nations. She talked in exquisite French only to the people to either side of her and never exchanged a word with me. She was next to a wrinkled old trout sat quite comically low in her chair (much more in need of the cushions than David), who was apparently an exiled Polish princess, brought up on a vast estate near Kraków, and now reduced to living above the stables owned by the Americans living next door to her host. She spoke with a heavy Polish accent, said 'cunt' three or four times during the course of the meal and was as far removed as possible from what might be a little girl's idea of a princess, but told a wonderfully exciting story of her escape from Warsaw in the mid-sixties. After the nationalisation of her father's estates by the communists, she'd worked in a menial capacity in the offices of the state airline but had managed to escape to the West in the boot of a French diplomat's car.

Opposite me was a loud, friendly couple, she an artist called Deborah with a Southern drawl and an extraordinarily loud laugh, who, as the afternoon wore on and the wine continued flowing, plonked her elbows on the table and let her very large breasts take up residence on the tablemat along with the coloured beads of her long necklace. Her husband, a professor of Byzantine studies at some German university, gave the table the most wonderful lecture on iconoclasm which quite banished the last of my panic attack.

Lord Sawyer and Toby were the last to arrive, just as we were sitting down to eat. I was thrilled to see Toby, who I wasn't expecting; later on, Bridget repeated her little trick of moving chairs.

'Good for me to circulate a little, Ben. And nice for you to have a young companion – you must be getting a bit tired of us old fuddy-duddies.' There was a squeeze to my hand as she got up. 'Are you all right now?'

'Oh perfectly! I was just a little hot for a moment, that's all...' Bridget didn't miss a trick and had more understanding than many would've given her credit for.

Toby and I made for the bar again once we returned to the hotel. We talked into the early hours with me daring to think that maybe something was up between us. A young man, a little lovesick, stuck in the middle of Morocco for months on end, unexpectedly finding a companion and perhaps loosening his constraints a little? Eventually, we said our goodnights, and I made sure to keep my arms by my side. A little after I turned my bedside light off, there was a tentative knock on my door. A pause, followed by another knock, even less sure of itself.

I let it be, though. I don't know why. Sometimes I can be such a curious fellow.

CHAPTER 12

A Thursday evening, January 1992

This afternoon, the wait for Ben's arrival in Sandwich had been testing Alexander's reserves of patience even more than usual. Ben was going to be reporting back to him on the disposal of the contents of Eaton Square and he was dreading it – he didn't want to have to face any of the facts around the packing up of his London home, but no doubt, Ben would have handled it with his usual tact, knowing how ghastly it was for him.

A good hour and a half ago, Alexander, who'd been sitting in his chair in the drawing room since Theresa, their housekeeper, left for her weekly break, had busied himself trying to locate the little talking clock that Ben had bought for him in Tottenham Court Road last year. In the process, he'd swept his teacup off the side table with his hand; it had bounced and then rolled about on the very stained carpet at his feet – certainly not the first time this had happened. While trying to prevent the cup from falling, he'd also knocked the column lamp; it had swayed like a drunk for a moment or two before settling with the lampshade at an angle.

'Oh, do be careful, Alecky!' Bridget had looked up from the *Daily Telegraph* crossword puzzle before leaving her seat and coming over to sort things out. After the lamp had been adjusted and the cup retrieved from the carpet, she'd judged that it was necessary for her to fiddle about behind Alexander's chair; the outside edge of the curtain had to be turned in on itself. Then she'd made her way over to one of the family portraits to cover it with a small blanket she kept for the purpose by reaching up and tucking it behind the top of the frame.

'Darl, what on earth are you doing?' There was a kerfuffle as the blanket refused to stay in place.

'Oh dear! That damned low sunlight. Time of the year.' She threw the blanket at the canvas, and it managed to lodge itself on the picture light above. 'Ruinously bad for everything – it's eating up the curtains and taking all the colour out of the paintings.'

'Oh, do let it be, darl. The sun's gone hours ago – and what does it matter anyway? We'll both be dead soon, thank the Lord,' he said as she made her way back to the sofa.

Much more carefully, Alexander embarked on another quest to locate the clock. He found it, right at the far edge of the side table and pressed the wide switch on top. '*The time is sixteen twenty-five*,' announced the lady with a Japanese accent.

'Jesus Christ. A whole hour and three quarters before he gets here!'

'What, Alecky? What did you say?' Bridget was fiddling around with her hearing aid, pressing it further into her ear; it was whining in complaint at its rough handling.

'Nothing, darl, nothing.'

'I thought you said something.'

'Talking to myself, really. I was just thinking,' he said, raising his voice to a level he knew she could hear, 'that Ben's not due for another hour and three quarters.'

'Oh dear. He is coming, though, isn't he? I do hope so. We've nothing in, you know – nothing at all.'

'Don't worry – Theresa will have done the shopping. It's just got to go in the oven, I expect. Ben will sort it out.'

'Yes, but we've nothing in. Do you really think he's coming? I haven't done any shopping.'

'Darl – it's done, and Ben will do his usual trip to Deal tomorrow morning.'

'That's if he comes, Alecky.'

'Oh Jesus,' Alexander muttered under his breath.

The dreaded Thursday afternoon wait for Ben. These days, even teatime was a cause for concern. Bridget was increasingly frail but didn't realise or couldn't admit it, and he could see the time approaching when the preparation of their afternoon tea might be beyond her. He'd recently become aware that she had to stop halfway along the hall to rest the tray on the round table outside the library before continuing her journey from the kitchen. Just a few months ago, they were both still taking a modicum of pleasure in the gap between Theresa's lunchtime departure and Ben's arrival – the last vestiges of a truly independent life. Now the wait was insufferable to him – their afternoon was taken up with endless panicky comments from Bridget about food not being 'got in' and her not being able to manage in the kitchen any longer as 'it's just too, too much for me!' although it was many years since she'd had to do anything domestic. It was Mrs Smith's retirement six months ago that seemed to particularly unnerve her, and even Ben's appointment of a live-in housekeeper had not put her at ease. She still couldn't quite get used to a new person in the annex, especially since spying Theresa's boyfriend, visiting for the weekend, strolling across the lawn one morning last November. 'We're quite obviously running a brothel here!' she'd said in despair as Jerry had disappeared through the garden door at the far end of the lawn. 'Anything goes these days, anything – that's all I can say about the matter.' But, as always, Ben's arrival this evening was bound to have the usual effect. There would be peace, and no more fretting about the lack of vegetables in the pantry. Thank God for the boy.

∼

'Here he is!' Alexander called out as he caught the sound he'd been waiting for since just after lunch – the lock turning in the front door.

'Hooray!' Bridget shouted almost at the same time. He knew that her relief was enormous; she'd no longer be alone with her unhappy husband. It was only Ben, in those days, who could lighten the mood in the house. Nobody else.

The routine had been the same for some time now. 'Hi there!' would come from Ben in response to the greeting that bounced along the hallway from the sitting room. He collected the garage keys from the bowl on the oak chest in the hall and called out 'See you in a min!'

before leaving the house again to struggle with the stiff doors of the garage round the corner in Church Street. A minute or two later there was the sound of the keys being thrown back into the bowl from a few feet away as he returned. It was a noise that used to alarm Bridget in the days when she thought she could hear it ('Careful not to chip that bowl, Ben! It's Qing dynasty, you know!') Now it seemed she couldn't care less. Ben was here, and all would be well.

There'd been the usual whirlwind of activity since his arrival dead on 6.15. He'd parked the car, darted along the hall into the drawing room to deliver a hurried but affectionate kiss to both of their cheeks. Then he'd disappeared into the kitchen to read the dinner instructions that Theresa always left for him before he'd laid the table in the dining room. A quick catch-up with Alexander and Bridget from his perch on the arm of the sofa had followed before his announcement that he'd be pouring drinks at seven with dinner at eight, as per usual. With the food in the oven, they'd gone their separate ways, for baths and to dress for dinner, the sound of clunking pipes and flushing loos heralding the turn in the mood that would accompany their return to the drawing room and the first glorious application of the anaesthesia of alcohol – a mightily generous whisky for Alexander, a large gin and tonic for Ben, and a more temperate vodka served with a saucer of water biscuits for Bridget.

∼

Ben had cleared the dining room, washed the dishes and made sure that Bridget had safely climbed the stairs on her way to bed. The nagging pain in her hip was not improving and these days, after wishing her goodnight, he liked to stand surreptitiously on the bottom step in the hall with his ear cocked, listening out for her safe arrival on the landing above – just a sensible precaution after the pre-dinner vodka and a glass and a half of wine. Now, sat on the sofa by the fire that Bridget had vacated, Ben was rustling some paperwork in his hands. He'd taken off the jacket of the suit that Alexander had made for him in Savile Row five years ago, throwing it over the back of the sofa before rolling up his sleeves and pouring them their first glass of port. He obviously meant to complete a little bit of business before anything was read from *The Telegraph* this evening.

'Christie's collected this morning, and I've already got from them the reserve figures that they are suggesting for the first sale. Just need you to okay them with me in the morning before I phone them back–'

'Whatever you say, Ben,' Alexander cut in. 'I'm sure you've got it all in hand. Might be a little bit of a tussle with the carriage clock from the sitting room, though. I know it's a good one, made in Edinburgh in the 1790s, and I won't be told otherwise. But you sort everything else, dear boy–'

'It's all going to plan, Alexander.'

'Oh, you are a wonder, Ben. What in hell's name would we be doing without you? But I say, old chap – let's not talk about Eaton Square till the morning. Do you mind awfully?' Alexander was looking towards Ben as though he could see him. 'Actually, you know what? I think I'll have an early night.'

He could sense that Ben was a little taken aback. Their time alone after Bridget had gone to bed was acknowledged by all to be Alexander's favourite part of the day. 'What, no *Telegraph* tonight – I was going to read you an extraordinary article about the war in Yugoslavia.' Ben waited for a reply from the big chair in the corner that didn't come. 'I guess it can wait till tomorrow, then.' There was a much longer pause. 'Sorry, Alexander. This is all very difficult for you, I do know.'

'You can bloody well say that again! Monstrous, just monstrous, really. The dismantling of a life,' he said, shaking his head to hide the break in his voice that he couldn't quite suppress.

'It's so tough, I know. But we have to press on with it, that's all. It must be done properly,' Ben said, slightly more firmly than he intended.

'I know, I know. And you're doing your absolute best to make it as painless as possible.' Alexander leaned forward in his chair and rested his chin on the handle of the stick that was placed firmly on the ground between his feet; he screwed up his eyes. 'Mind seeing me safely up the apples and pears? Sorry, Ben. Just not up to it tonight. I'll be in better shape to discuss it all before lunch tomorrow.'

Alexander climbed the stairs, feeling the way ahead with his stick. Ben was two steps below him, a flat palm resting encouragingly at the top of his old friend's back. When they reached the dressing room next to the bedroom, they started on the slow ceremony of undressing. The jacket of the suit was hung on the back of a chair and the trousers were folded and placed on the seat, ready to be easily rediscovered in the morning together with the fresh socks and pants that Ben would take from the chest of drawers. Alexander placed a hand on Ben's shoulder for support as first one leg and then the other was guided into pyjama bottoms. Ben rubbed Alexander's upper arm affectionately as they crossed the room for the ritual of the brushing of teeth followed by the pee into the sink. 'What a luxury, Ben! You really don't have to do this, you know. I'm quite capable–'

'I know, I know, but why not, since I'm here!'

'I'm being spoilt – don't have this level of service usually. Wonder what Bridget and Theresa would say about me peeing in the sink?'

'Well, let's keep that from the powers that be, shall we?' said Ben, running the tap and directing a quick squirt of bleach into the plughole. 'No need for the ladies ever to know,' he added while acknowledging to himself that he was, in fact, the only power around here these days. 'For heaven's sake,' he said, 'if a man can't piddle into the sink in the dressing room of his own house…'

As Alexander waited at the end of the bed, curtains were drawn, pillows plumped and arranged, and a glass of water was poured from the bottle left by Theresa and placed on the bedside table next to a second talking clock. On the other side of the bed, Ben checked the box of tissues and the radio, which was within arm's reach; he turned it on and adjusted the volume down so that it was only just audible.

'Now you go back downstairs and enjoy another glass of port without having to worry about the gerontocracy,' Alexander said.

'Goodnight, Alexander. Sleep tight. See you in the morning when I get back from Deal.' Ben turned out the light.

'God bless, dear boy.'

∼

The blackness into which Alexander was now plunged momentarily soothed him; it was preferable to the all-pervasive bleeding-flesh colour that his vision presented him with during his daylight hours. Sometimes, if he'd had enough whisky, the dark allowed him to tell himself that his loss of sight was just a temporary aberration and that the sun would be greeting him in the morning.

But it was going to be a tough night. He was too wound up for sleep, and there'd be little or no solace in the familiar voices on Radio 4 – the accompaniment to lonely, sleepless old people with its snippets of favourite items from the past week, world correspondents' reports, the shipping forecast, farming, and business; it would pass him by. His old home in London was going to be haunting him tonight.

Of course, he insisted to himself, it was quite impossible, a waste of money, to carry on with it, especially since the damned flood in mid-October. Heaven knows, he hadn't been up to town for nearly three months before the incident, and Bridget for much longer, which was why the whole thing went unnoticed for so long – a radiator had burst, and the communal heating system had pumped boiling water into the building for nearly four days without anyone knowing. It was done now. Ben had just signed the papers on his behalf that relinquished his tenancy with Grosvenor Estates and the place was empty but for a few boxes, thanks to his hard work. The damage by water and steam had been extensive. Perhaps it was a blessing in disguise, a fait accompli from which there was no way back and although he still wasn't up for a detailed discussion about it, there'd never been much doubt in his mind that it was the end of the road.

Everything of value had been removed, most of it to Christie's. The eight-foot-tall canvas by John Craxton would be finding its way into the Modern British Art sale in late March while the French Empire desk, the eighteenth-century bust that Ben loved and the Louis XVI commode with ormulu mounts would come up in the late eighteenth and early nineteenth-century French furniture sale a little later. The English sale was some time after that, but the items – the sideboard and dumb waiter, the grandfather clock, the table and Hepplewhite chairs from the dining room were to be stored in Christie's warehouse in New Covent Garden until then. Lots of other stuff would end up in Freddie Rothbury's shop at the top of Sydney Street where Ben could keep an eye on the progress of the sales, though Freddie was a great friend and absolutely above board, of course, and the ten per cent commission would be a great encouragement for him to do his best. Bastard thing, though, the whole bloody business.

At least his wonderful mezzotints would find a home with Ben. All forty-odd of them. They'd look quite magnificent ranged along every wall of his flat at the Oval. They were all to be heavily restored after a mighty insurance claim that Ben had to handle after the flood. He'd reported at the time that the whole collection looked as though they had been dunked in a hot bath, but now they were being professionally washed and restored, laid on acid-proof paper, remounted and returned to their Hogarth frames. Ben visited the restorers last week and was convinced that the whole collection was going to come out looking better than ever. So that was something.

Now, in these sleepless hours, he was casting his mind

back to the day that they'd first arrived at Eaton Square. He and Bridget had stood on the porch with Podge, their poodle, yapping round the ankles of the removal men who were carrying in their possessions that had just arrived from the cottage in Shere. It was during that extraordinary week of mourning for the King. February 1951. Or was it 1952? Alexander thought he remembered the all-pervasive smog outside while the furniture was being stacked up in the hall – or was it in fact just the times they were living through that made everything seem so gloomy? The poverty and indebtedness of the country, the never-ending years of rationing, the barbed wire round the acres of bomb-sites, the lonely surviving steeples adjoining roofless churches all over the City – and that poor girl having to take over from her dead father, swearing to do her duty by the nation. He'd never forgotten the sight of her as a tiny baby, just a few months old, when he'd visited the Yorks for a shoot at Glamis and peered into the pram in the rose garden. He'd have taken a longer look had he known what she was destined for.

That was the beginning of the trouble with Owen. The very same week that they moved into Eaton Square. Never-ending strife until fifteen years later, when they'd finally had enough.

It started with a phone call from Robert Birley, the headmaster of Eton no less, asking if he might take the train down as soon as possible, to discuss 'what is, I'm afraid, a rather serious matter concerning Owen.' The boy had been stealing – and not just the odd apple pocketed while passing the local greengrocers in town, or the careless long-term borrowing of a schoolmate's scarf, but a much more methodical lifting of goods from other boys' lockers and rooms. A camera had been discovered amongst his things, along with a purse of money and more besides – a pair of leather gloves, two fountain pens, a Swiss watch, a chess set with ivory pieces belonging to the head of house's fag, for God's sake – a much loved present from a doting grandfather, apparently. The meeting with Birley was not really to discuss anything at all, it was to give notice that Owen had to be removed from the school as soon as possible. Expulsion. Alexander was surprised that Birley hadn't said it over the phone to save him the journey to Windsor. On the way back home, he tried to formulate a plan of putting it about that the boy had been expelled for '*the usual thing*', but he quickly dismissed it, knowing that it wouldn't wash. A little bit of buggery would indeed have been more acceptable than stealing, but the word was out by the time Owen found himself on a train not that long after the one that his father took back to town.

Millfield School was next, but that went wrong very quickly when the boy was found in the bed of one of the under-matrons. A preferable crime to that of theft, but a bloody nuisance all the same, given how much covering up and lying had gone into securing him a place there. Sent home again, before the end of term. A little later, having languished in a bank in the city for a year while alienating a close friend of his father who had been prepared to 'give the lad a chance', strings were pulled in various places to get him a commission in the Irish Guards – hell of a palaver that was too, trying to get the powers that be to ignore the boy's asthma. Chucked out for pouring ink over the regimental sergeant major's head within a month. You couldn't make it up, could you?

After that, Alexander had been approached by a persuasive friend who Owen had worked with in the bank; he'd convinced him that a business supplying smoked salmon to high-end restaurants would be just the thing to give the boy a sense of purpose. Alexander came up with the money to start them off, but the business went under very quickly when the two young men and their friends ate all the smoked salmon. After that, he was in and out of their lives, living with various friends in Chelsea before disappearing to Cornwall for a year or two, but inevitably fetching up from time to time asking to be bailed out of some sort of trouble. There were drink-driving bans way before anyone regarded such a thing as much of a crime, a nasty fight in a nightclub, six months unpaid rent owed to an irate landlady who ended up banging on the door at Eaton Square, a Harley Street abortion for a pregnant girlfriend, a policeman knocked unconscious after an altercation in Sloane Square. He was forever running up a multitude of debts at tailors, gunsmiths, turf accountants and wine merchants, all of which had to be settled before the police could become involved. Why the hell the management at Annabel's allowed someone so obviously untrustworthy to run up a tab of hundreds of pounds was quite beyond Alexander; there was the most fearful row with the owner, whom he accused of being a crook; he'd taken a taxi to the club in Berkeley Square and pounded his fist on the desk in Robin Birley's office while threatening legal action. Bloody Birleys. No connection, as far as he knew, between the headmaster of Eton and this chap, but boy did he curse the damn name – the fearsome temper had surfaced that afternoon, that was for sure, but it didn't stop the bill from eventually having to be paid.

The boy was the black sheep of the family, except there wasn't anybody else in the family to be any other damn colour, of course. Just Owen going about his ruinous business. On top of all that, he became quite skilled at getting perfectly acceptable young women to fall in love with him. He married, quite against his father's wishes, who considered that he and his bride were far too young, but the couple could not be persuaded to wait. Alexander was at least a little bit hopeful for the first few months after the wedding that the marriage might temper his son's behaviour. It didn't work, of course. Having fathered two daughters as quickly as was biologically possible, Owen abandoned his wife. Another daughter was born of an even shorter second marriage before he moved on again. Yarnton had informed him recently that Owen apparently was now on his third marriage – to a former nurse who seemed to be more of a carer than a wife. Incredible what women will put up with. They lived in straitened circumstances somewhere in Norfolk apparently, where Owen seemed fairly determined to drink himself to an early death. His choice. They didn't see their granddaughters; the girls may have been perfectly sweet, but Alexander and Bridget were too old, too exhausted by their son's shenanigans to be able, at their time of life, to take an interest in three girls who could never be anything more to them than a reminder of the most chaotic of times.

The last straw was New York, sometime after the collapse of the brief second marriage. Dear friends of theirs, sympathetic to Owen because of his relentlessly winning ways – oh yes, he was quite capable of being mightily charming – invited him to stay at their brownstone in Brooklyn. They may well have been oil millionaires, and quite able to afford anything they wanted, but Owen's sale of articles of furniture from their house to fund certain nocturnal amusements while they were in the Hamptons for the weekend finally opened their eyes to his true character.

'Heir to title arrested in possession of drugs at Heathrow,' said *The Telegraph* a few weeks later when Owen was stopped at Heathrow on his way back into the country. He was found to be carrying two kilos of cocaine in his suitcase – wrapped in silver foil as though they were a workman's sandwiches – and was jailed for eighteen months, a light sentence given the quantity he was caught with. By the time the case reached the courts, Alexander and Bridget had decided to make a binding financial arrangement with Owen and then cut all contact.

～

Alexander turned over in bed, one hand stretching out to feel for the talking clock while the index finger of the other was poised to press the button on top. '*The time is 3.07,*' the curt voice informed him. 'God almighty,' he said, 'I've been lying here for half my life!' He wondered if his young companion in the room at the end of the corridor might just possibly still be awake. Unlikely, he thought, but decided to clear his throat loudly to bring attention to the fact that he himself was still very much awake. He coughed, trying to make it sound like a biological necessity, as matter of fact as possible – but as loud as permissible without turning it into a summons. He cocked his ear and listened in hope. A relentless silence. He sighed heavily and now reached for the radio; it needed to be turned up to drown out the noises in his head. What the hell was it that was so exercising him? Giving up the house? Ghastly, of course, but why was his son also on his mind after years of freedom from worry? There was a running commentary going through his head tonight – some sort of obituary, a macabre review of his life, and he was not coming out of it at all sympathetically. Too late to change anything now, of course, especially since we were on the home straight. Jesus – was he going to make it till morning? Perhaps he'd attempt another clearing of the throat. The boy was a bloody deep sleeper, quite obviously.

Was it all their fault? Might it have been different if he'd been stricter with Owen – or less strict? Was it his terrible temper that had an effect? Suppose Bridget had been a bit more maternal, perhaps? Or was it something in his own past that made him unsuitable father material? Perhaps the boy was just born that way; now, they might call him autistic – a word much bandied about these days, but God knows what it means. It was probably just another fancy word to help one pass the buck. But surely, they couldn't have got it all so terribly wrong, even if they weren't the most ideal of parents? And who the hell does it all right, for God's sake?

It had not exactly been a love match, the marriage to Bridget. His father had been pleased, of course, because her people were proper aristos, not yeoman farmers from Northern Ireland like his; she was the descendant of nabobs who'd made their fortune in cotton and silk with the East India Company, been granted a baronetcy and had returned home at the beginning of the nineteenth century to buy a large country estate; Bridget's father had married someone who could claim three dukes among her four great-grandfathers, a mightily pleasing thing to Sir William Lowther MP, in his upward trajectory through society.

Alexander, at the age of twenty-six, had little idea what it felt like to be in love, having never come close to experiencing it, and was therefore quite capable of convincing himself that this was what he felt for his handsome young bride. It was probably the same for her, too. He certainly wasn't marrying into money, old or new – the Indian rupees had long since been spent, so it probably had a bit more to do with social caché than he was prepared to admit to himself at the time. Sir Arthur, Bridget's father, had been struggling throughout the twenties and thirties to keep the vast old Palladian mansion near Cirencester from going under, and, indeed, the whole estate had to go as soon as he died some little while after the war. The new baronet, Bridget's brother, who wasn't the sort to relish much of a struggle anyhow, found he was quite unable to keep the show on the road. Talk about a trajectory in the opposite direction to Sir William's – to be fair, he was landed with huge death duties, but then quickly gambled away whatever was left after the sale and was now the doddery old concierge of a block of flats off the Bayswater Road where none of the residents knew that the impoverished old man who sorted the post and organised the window cleaner was a baronet; Alexander sent him a monthly bottle of a good whisky to keep his spirits up. Swanley Court was now an old people's home, the once elegant stucco exterior painted an unforgiving gloss white while the grand entrance hall was graced with swirly-patterned carpets, a stairlift, several arrangements of plastic flowers and an overfamiliar receptionist. They visited a few years back and quickly retraced their steps down the long drive in horror. Some nice porcelain pieces, including the Qing bowl in the entrance hall here in Sandwich, together with a few portraits and pieces of furniture were the only reminders of the draughty old place, all bought at auction by Bridget during the sale of the contents held in a marquee on the west lawn in the mid-fifties.

∼

It was a quite conscious decision not to have a child for a while after they married. They were young and carefree, and having far too social a time to burden themselves with parenthood. Alexander was ambitious too, doing well at the bank and convinced in those early days, after ditching the law, that his career in finance was important to him; he'd been delighted to receive a telegram from his boss during the honeymoon in Venice offering him a short-term, in-house contract in New York, which he readily accepted. Bridget, however, was not interested in relocating – she made it quite clear that she didn't want to be uprooted for seven or eight months right at the start of her married life and put her foot down.

'I want to get the cottage together – there's just so much to be done. Leave me be and the whole thing will be simply spiffing by the time you get back. Clarence Wendover is marrying Bobby Hornby in May, too, and I absolutely promised I'd be there. How about if I come over for September, instead, on the *Aquitania* or something? Such fun – we'll stay at the Algonquin!' There was money to spare at the time since Alexander's maternal grandmother had just left him a very tidy fortune, which meant that Bridget's new independence could be well funded by her generous husband – who'd also quite quickly come round to the idea of being in New York by himself.

So off he went, and it wasn't long before he found himself indulging in the sort of infidelities that he just couldn't consider to be very important. He'd recognised practically on their wedding night that Bridget was never going to be that much of a star in the bedroom department; on their honeymoon there had certainly not been any hurrying back to bed after a bit of sight-seeing on the Grand Canal, and by the third or fourth night, it had become apparent to him that during their 'lovemaking', his new wife's gaze was not directed into his own eyes but straight past them and into those of the cheeky-looking putti painted on the ceiling of the bedroom in the palazzo in which they were staying. Easily distracted. Not very interested in *'having a go'*. But always good fun in her own way, right from the beginning.

However, Alexander had not long settled into a shared apartment overlooking Central Park when the financial markets started to rumble and then ended up in the full-blown catastrophe of the Great Crash. He was hit hard by it; the Chase National Bank had long made it clear to their employees that they should show faith in their employer by heavily investing in their stock. For most, that meant borrowing a large sum of money, usually from the bank itself. When the crash came, Alexander was in the relatively fortunate position of having sunk a good part of his inheritance from his grandmother into the bank rather than sliding into debt to raise the funds, so he wasn't one of those chaps who took to flinging themselves off skyscrapers like ticker tape during that extraordinary autumn. Both Bridget's passage on the *Aquitania* and the stay at the Algonquin had been paid for months before, so when she swanned down the gangplank from the boat, waving at him and wearing a new fur coat in the eighty degrees of an unexpected autumn heatwave, it was obvious that she had no idea about the new state of impoverishment that awaited them. But the facts were so dire that Alexander decided to ignore reality and carry on partying with his young wife as though there was nothing amiss, rather like drinking champagne in the first-class bar on the top deck of the *Titanic* while paying no heed to the rapidly increasing slant of the floor beneath their feet.

He'd underestimated her, though. The truth was out within a day or two and the no-nonsense side of his wife that he'd not particularly been aware of before quickly came to the fore. 'We'll stay here till the end of the week and then move to something much cheaper. This hotel's eating dollars and there's no point to it,' she declared when appraised of the true situation. He'd forgotten that she was quite used to poverty, however genteel; she'd lived in a house that had cost a fortune to heat during winter and where the family, before dinner, would collect in the drawing room and practically climb over each other to catch just a little of the meagre warmth of the only fire in the place, in the hope of staving off the inevitable chilblains. Later, she'd lived in London with her Guinness cousins and knew from that experience just what it must have been like for Cinderella and her wait for a glass slipper. Poverty for her would be reverting to the norm.

Alexander had never been much of a gambler, so he still had no idea what possessed him, just before leaving London, into thinking it was a good idea to invest a fair portion of his grandmother's inheritance in the most unlikely proposition you could possibly imagine. A goldmine in Venezuela. *Well, why not?* he'd told himself. *Three quarters of what I have is in the Chase National Bank – safe as houses – and a ludicrous flutter on something unlikely can't do much harm. Just for fun, just for once in my life.*

On the last day of their stay at the Algonquin Hotel, they decided to eat dinner in the restaurant downstairs. It turned out to be a bleak affair; for some reason the room was half empty, as though weeks after the financial crisis had broken, the resolutely bohemian clientele who usually frequented the place and gave it such an exciting air, had only just caught up with the news and stayed away. They ate in silence, the oysters chased down by nothing more than soda water. It was the first time since his arrival in the city that he'd found himself resenting prohibition; he was suddenly seriously missing a drink to soothe his growing anxieties, and as they returned to their room, he decided that the gnawing feeling in his stomach was due to alcoholic deprivation. But by the early hours, he was in terrible trouble – so much so that a doctor had to be called. It felt like the end of the world; quite apart from the hideousness of his physical condition, he was at a loss as to what to do about the medical fees that would be chasing them forever if he were to find himself in hospital. He was just a little better in the morning, however, so that after half a cup of weak tea, he felt strong enough to glance at *The New York Times* that had been picked up outside the door to their room by Bridget, on her way out to the pharmacists. He'd hurried into the bathroom with it for what was his umpteenth visit within a few hours. '*LOS CRISTIANOS MINE IN VENEZUELA STRIKES GOLD*,' he read, gripping the paper while enduring something like a labour contraction.

Alexander couldn't recall the rest of the course of his illness. He did remember, however, that a cursory working out of figures on the back of the newspaper while he sat on the lavatory showed that his lost fortune was much more than restored, that he never fetched up in hospital and that later, after telling her the extraordinary news, he noticed that his wife had returned to their room no longer wearing the fur coat in which she had left.

'My sweet darl,' he said, close to tears, 'you shouldn't have done that. I shall be getting you another, anyway – and it'll be even more splendid than the one you've just sold.'

'I don't think so, Alecky. It was just for show. Not really my sort of goings-on, you know, a fur coat.'

～

No more banking. Alexander gave in his notice, wrapped up his commitments in New York and then climbed aboard the very same ship in which Bridget had sailed back to Europe in a month before, partly chosen with the knowledge that there was none of that prohibition nonsense aboard, the ship being British. The experience of the last six months had helped him come to the conclusion that the financial sector really was not 'as safe as houses', as he'd taken to saying before the crash, and that perhaps it was indeed houses, or more strictly property, that was. It didn't bother him that, within a few weeks of his return home, strings were being pulled for him around his father's contacts; he had enough self-regard to know that he was quite worthy of a helping hand up, being willing to work hard and aware that his diligence would eventually be appreciated. Not as exciting a project as the bank, for sure, but steady, safe and well paid.

He found a broker (the very same one who years later was still trying to give him advice about Owen) who invested his capital in a varied portfolio with only a minimal sum risked in the sort of ventures that had restored his fortune; they were a good combination of talents – Yarnton was a plodder who also knew when not to restrain the more playful side of his client's impulses, with the result that by the time that Owen was born in 1936, the Lowthers were more than comfortable and settled into a bland domesticity (save for the odd inconsequential infidelity on Alexander's behalf) that neither had any reason to doubt would continue for a lifetime.

∼

Reminiscing, reminiscing, reminiscing, and each memory rendering him more awake. Another few coughs were thrown into the void beyond his room in the forlorn hope of raising his young friend from the dead.

CHAPTER 13

One loud cough had woken me, a second had alarmed me, and the third, quite a while later, saw me throwing back the duvet, quickly pulling on my dressing gown and feeling my way along the corridor in the dark. '*3.40*' shone luminously from my watch. I didn't want to turn the light on and disturb an eternally vigilant Bridget, who had recently taken to sleeping with her door open in preparation for catastrophe – these days, she devoted her life to worrying about her husband, about who was going to be doing the food shopping and then cooking it once it reached the kitchen. That was me or Theresa, of course, but Bridget descended into some sort of purgatory of her own making if there was the slightest doubt about anything. The open door to her room was a declaration of uncertainty. That might have been a tiny bit unfair since perhaps I was also fine-tuning myself at least for mishaps, if not catastrophe.

I'd tentatively entered Alexander's bedroom and turned on the light, my heart thumping in my chest while I prayed hard that we were not facing some sort of ghastly medical emergency. I found him propped up in bed, looking composed, with the usual three pillows behind him, the radio dutifully humming to itself in the background.

'Alexander? Are you okay?'

'What? Oh, hello there, Ben! What on earth are you doing up at this time in the morning? Must be close to half past three!'

'Is everything all right? Anything I can get you? Glass of water?'

'Good Lord, no. I'm just whiling the night away, as per usual. You having trouble sleeping?'

'No – not at all. It's just that I heard you coughing fit to burst!'

'Oh really? No, no – everything's fine. Just waiting patiently to shuffle off this mortal coil, you know. Can't be long now. Sit down and have a chat, though, if you can't sleep...'

∽

Well, the chat in the early hours that morning turned into a marathon, and then I was really late for my shop in Deal – and speeding when there was no real need. Bridget's anxieties were infectious; there was absolutely plenty of time to do everything – shop for the weekend, get back to Sandwich and make a little lunch, a stint at the desk to write cheques out for Theresa's wages and the gas and telephone bills, a walk with Alexander along Sandwich Bay if he was in a bright enough mood after our late night, then a sorting out of supper things in late afternoon before my own shorter walk along the Butts.

I was still dead to the world at 10 that morning when Bridget roused me with a polite but urgent knocking on my bedroom door – she was accustomed to a chat over coffee and digestives in the sitting room with me before I went off to do the shopping, so was quite put out when I was 'absolutely nowhere to be seen.'

'I've not done any shopping you know, Ben. I thought I could leave it to you.'

'Don't you worry about that – I'll be off as soon as we've had our coffee and a chat,' I reassured her as I put the tray on the coffee table in front of the sofa and sat down beside her. Her anxiety, however, turned to delight when I told her that I had overslept because I'd been keeping Alexander company through the early hours.

'But is he all right? He sleeps so little these days–'

'Oh, we had a great chat, everything's fine!' I was making light of it, knowing that my old friend was not happy at the moment, but pleased that by the time I left his room that morning he was both sleepy and comforted.

'Oh, dear boy, thank God for that! You've no idea what it's like when you're not here, you know, watching him from the sofa with his chin on his stick for hour after hour, just staring at the nothingness in front of himself. Awful. Makes me feel so bad for him. Quite unnerving, you know, because what can I do? I can't pull him out of the slough of despondency anymore. Just can't. But absolutely everything changes as soon as you get here. I hate it when you're away...' Bridget had stretched forward then, fiddling with the tray, edging it back and forward by an inch or two as she carefully chose her next words.

'I think it's the worry about him that affects my memory, you know, Ben. I know there's a problem there, and it's getting worse.' Typical of Bridget not to be dodging the issue.

'Just a little, perhaps, but not enough to get in a state

about,' I said, not altogether sure that what I was saying was true but taking her hand on the cushion beside me and giving it a squeeze. 'Don't you think perhaps one of the reasons I'm here is to remember for you?'

She'd returned the squeeze and taken a breath before resolutely announcing, 'I've decided I'm going to join an organisation for people with impaired memories. It's called CRAFT.'

'CRAFT?'

'Can't Remember A Fucking Thing,' she said with the straightest of faces. Dear Bridget – still mostly with us.

~

Well, I was on my way back from Deal, but there'd been an interruption to my progress, and now I really was in a hurry. I was lugging the shopping through Sainsbury's car park when I heard that urgent, high-pitched whiney sound that a vehicle in reverse gear makes. I looked up just in time to see a car hurtling towards me and knew immediately what was going to happen – no chance of escape. A newly vacated parking space, a woman spotting it, reverse gear selected with said woman looking over her shoulder aiming to reach the gap before anyone else and completely failing to see me. Next second, I was looking down at the boot of her car with various bits of my shopping as high up in the air as I was. There was a thump as I returned to earth, followed by a close-up look at the gravel before someone was turning me over and apologising for the damage she'd caused. Then I was being helped to my unsteady feet and sat on a chair in the entrance to the supermarket to be fussed over by a lady with a bosom like a fortress wall and a tall, skinny youth with acne, both in St John Ambulance uniforms. A bit of prodding, poking and twisting quickly revealed the frankly extraordinary discovery that I'd sustained no broken bones. After I'd managed to dismiss the little crowd of helpers and rubberneckers ('I'm fine, I'm fine – no harm done!') who had collected around the spectacle of a gentleman amid his ruined shopping, I found a phone box and, without giving any alarming details, let Alexander know I was delayed while I did a re-shop for the flattened Marks and Spencer's chicken Kiev that was going to be our evening meal. I was accompanied along the aisles by the guilty woman who'd run me down; she was holding my shopping, periodically rubbing my arm and making too bright conversation in the hope (successful, given the wimp that I am) that I was going to put the incident right behind me. Jesus, she must have been as relieved as buggery that I didn't seem to be the suing kind. Stupid not-looking-out-properly old bag – I wanted to tell her to fuck off, but there was a people-pleasing little smile painted onto my face that just refused to be budged. What the hell was that about?

It all came out, of course, because I was out of sorts in the kitchen when I got back to Sandwich and Bridget was not so scatty that she didn't notice a limp and a rubbing of a buttock that wasn't there over coffee this morning. There was a further delay to lunch when both Alexander and Bridget insisted that I go and get checked out at the surgery which involved an interruption to Dr Melchett's lunch and a quick lowering of my pants; there was already a large bruise on my bottom and a lot of wobbly skin with blood underneath it, but no open wounds. 'A massive, rather nasty oedema developing,' Dr

Melchett said, with what sounded like relish. Later, I managed to put lunch on the table which was accompanied by lashings of sympathy from my old friends followed by a bit of a telling off that I'd come back without the phone number of my nemesis. I was instructed to leave the washing up (still to be done later, of course) and take to my bed for the afternoon which was where I realised that I was feeling slightly tearful and sorry for myself.

~

I was lying on top of the continental quilt in my room, feeling not only physically sore but also discomforted in some other way. Something about my little accident that morning had unnerved me more than it should have.

I have two old friends in Sandwich who are totally reliant on me, so I can't come to your hospital with you, I'm afraid. I was imagining a conversation in the ambulance that would have been summoned had I not put my foot down. Time for reflection, I suppose, about what happened and how stuck the three of us would have been if I'd been really hurt.

The Bellaghys were now utterly dependent on me. That was a fact that had been stated by them more times than I could count, and to whoever may have been listening. They said it with pride and affection – usually within earshot of me – as if they were expecting to be congratulated on working things out so well. I liked it too, of course, this feeling of being so revered. Those last few years had given me a delicious feeling of worthiness, a pride in the fact that Alexander and I had worked things out so practically, and that my old friends completely trusted me to handle everything about their lives. Two or three years ago, Alexander and I sat down to make his will together. No embarrassment, no evasion of the fact that I was to be the major beneficiary. 'Well,' Alexander had said just before signing the document in Geoffrey Barnes's office in the high street, 'you've been scratching my back, and I'm scratching yours, Ben. You're going to be in your forties before too long, and I'm determined that you'll have the means to be free of worry about work when we've gone. Who the bloody hell else am I going to leave my money to anyway?'

But something about what happened in Deal that morning, together with the long chat with Alexander during the night, had shifted my perceptions. It felt as though I was succumbing to some sort of grief at what would soon be left behind. Alexander was eighty-nine and in good health but that was a fair age. Bridget, at eighty-six, was less sprightly than she was even a few months ago, and her mental faculties were worryingly compromised; we could have carried on, of course, and there was quite enough money in the kitty to pay for all the help that I may have needed to look after them both. No problems there. But this life – our lives together – could not be forever, and that fact began to wrap itself around me like a shroud. I guess a large part of me didn't want anything to change.

'No London house, no car, no son,' was Alexander's opening gambit last night as I took up his offer of a chat and sat myself down on the chair by his bedside. 'Can't be long now. Just a few more months.' I was used to rolling my eyes whenever he repeated those words – I'd heard them for thirteen years – but that night, I remained silent. It had been the strangest feeling to find myself having to pick out what to tell and what not to tell him about the process of closing down the house in London. I was having to take so many decisions without referring things back to him; it was not fair to burden him with something he was finding so difficult, and besides, there just wasn't the time – there was just too much to be done. I'd made mistakes of course – there was a break-in the week before last, and a beautiful grandfather clock and two eighteenth-century side tables from Bridget's bedroom had disappeared. The caretaker from next door hadn't interrupted the two men in white coats and highly polished black shoes he saw loading the things into a smart van; they looked far too professional to be up to anything untoward and had even greeted him with a cheery 'Good morning!' as they went about their business of robbery. I blamed myself for having the things waiting in the hall by the front door for a Christie's collection that I'd arranged for that morning. Not my fault really, but the lapse in the contents insurance policy certainly was. Alexander somehow seemed to take it on the chin; there was not a long discussion about it. A little bit of an avoidance of the awfulness of it, I think.

Then there were the books I amassed on the floor of the drawing room, ready for the appropriate person to offer to take them off my hands. I thought I'd been meticulous about what was to be transported down to Sandwich, sold or just thrown out but just after shaking hands on a deal with someone who described himself as a 'house clearance specialist', I realised he was packing away five or six books the sight of which jolted some memory that forced me into picking one of them up. There was nothing to distinguish this particular volume from any of the others, and he'd not had time to take proper stock, so my vaguely underhand removal of Winston Churchill's volumes on the Second World War – one of Sir William's most prized possessions, signed by the author himself – from the pile of books at the front door passed by unnoticed. 'Holy fuck and shit and bollocks, thank you, thank you, God, for stopping that one!' I whispered to myself as I transferred the dusty books into a box marked '*Sandwich*'. God knows how many things must have slipped the net.

They had been lonely days in those emptying rooms. I'd been haunted by now distant memories of happy Wednesday evenings with Maria serving us dinner, of my feet curled up on the sofa opposite Alexander as we talked late into the night, glass in hand and of all the laughter and chats downstairs in the study – discussions and arguments about stocks and shares, Thatcherism, Lloyd's names, the right to anonymous funerals and everything else.

I hadn't revelled in the task of dismantling the house; I thought I might – imagining myself dealing in an authoritative voice with the people from Christie's and Sotheby's and sitting cross-legged on the floor in the drawing room going through the books, the crockery and silver, deciding what was to stay and what was to go. That's exactly how it was, but there was no enjoyment in it, that's all. Everything was left up to me. Bridget lost interest in the place so long ago that over the last few years she'd been stealthily stripping her bedroom of the things she valued and driving them down to Sandwich. The wall above her dressing table in Sandwich has become a veritable kaleidoscope of pretty little watercolours that used to hang in her old room in London – their disappearance the first indication to me, way back, of changing times. I'd asked her some time ago if there was anything she wanted me to keep and send down to Sandwich.

'Nothing. Absolutely nothing. I can't think of a single thing that I want and haven't taken already. Everything's here in Sandwich, now.' Not quite true. There had been the odd phone call to Eaton Square – the ring now a startling echo in the emptying drawing room – that was interrupting my afternoons of sorting.

'I say, Ben – I thought my first edition of the Beatrix Potter books was in the attic here in Sandwich, but I can't lay my hands on them. Would you be a dear and have a thorough check?' They were rediscovered on my next visit to Sandwich in the downstairs cloakroom where they had been living quietly for very many years. The previous Monday, there was a much more panicked call about a bracelet, an heirloom inherited from her grandmother.

'I know it's there somewhere, Ben. I can just picture it on the side table – the one on the left. I left it out, you know! So silly of me! Oh dear, what a worry! You simply must find it!' I'd never seen it, but later remembered talk of a bracelet being deposited in a safe; a quick phone call the next day confirmed that the item slept peacefully in the dark in a strongbox in the NatWest in Sandwich.

Now and again, with a slight feeling of dread, I'd had no choice but to consult a reluctant Alexander from the house, inserting my finger into the dial of the ancient Bakelite phone while trying to lengthen the cord which now knotted itself into such a state I couldn't raise it to my ear without a struggle.

'What about your suits, Alexander? I'm counting twenty-one of them. Are they all coming down to Sandwich?'

'What are they? London suits?'

'What's that?'

'London suits, Ben! What material are they? What colour?'

'Well, you know... wool, I suppose. And grey, lots of grey–'

'Yes, but what material?'

'Erm–'

'Oh, for heaven's sake, Ben, hasn't your tailor explained these things to you?'

'No, Alexander, my tailor has not explained these things to me...'

～

It was finished now; the previous morning, before leaving for Sandwich I signed the papers with the representatives of the Grosvenor Estates ending the Bellaghys' connection with the place that went back forty years. Another visit next week and I would be done. The Grosvenor Estate must have been overjoyed; they were losing a tenant who had been paying the same rent for decades – £5,000 a year and the most frightful row whenever an increase was suggested.

In the desolate house, there were great, melancholy smudges on the walls where the mezzotints used to hang; I'll never forget the panic on the day after the flood, after I'd contacted Emma Talling – a childhood friend who's now an expert in conservation – with a plea for help to save the prints. She'd appeared within an hour or two; we'd manhandled the collection off the walls and thrown them into the back of her small van. 'Time is of the essence,' she'd said as she jumped into the front seat and dramatically revved the engine. She took off like an ambulance driver with forty patients on life support aboard, accompanied by the sound of the haphazardly stacked frames noisily shedding their glass and squeaking and buckling in complaint at their treatment. Their shadows will haunt the walls until the house is turned upside down by the renovations that must be just round the corner. The builders will come in and pull the place apart on behalf of new occupants who will be inviting interior designers in to reassemble the place in a new guise – en-suite bathrooms, a bigger kitchen, underfloor heating, fitted bookshelves and Farrow and Ball finishes.

∼

After dinner, with my bruising settling in, it was me who was thinking of an early night. I'd cocked my ear at the bottom of the stairs to make sure that Bridget had reached her room, I'd done the washing-up, poured Alexander and myself a large glass of port and gingerly lowered my less bruised buttock onto the sofa.

'Why don't we stay up and continue our conversation of last night, Ben? Just occurs to me how many things I've not told you. Nothing to do with secrets – just a bloody long life with things going on that you don't know about, that's all…'

'Oh, golly – I was rather thinking of two or three paracetamol and an early night, actually, and I doubt very much there's anything I don't know about your past after all this time anyway…' There was a crestfallen look on the face with the closed eyes on the other side of the room.

'That bloody boy,' he said, his chin settling onto its usual position on the stick anchored between his knees. 'For some reason I just can't stop thinking about him...'

'What boy, Alexander?'

'Owen. My son, Owen.' Three deep breaths then, and a slow shaking of the head. 'How could it possibly have gone so wrong? Was it my fault, do you think, Ben? Be honest. Perhaps something to do with my wayward behaviours?'

'Good Lord – what on earth are you talking about? I don't believe that for a minute. Not a minute. He was bonkers, Alexander, a lost cause. Very, very sad, but I'm quite sure I'm right.' I eased myself up from the sofa, walked across to where he was sitting and placed my hand gently on his shoulder. 'Tell you what, though – how about a change of plan?' I wasn't really up for it, but needs must. 'If you're in the mood to entertain me with some salacious stories from your past, why don't I see you safely up the stairs and then come back down to fetch two glasses and the bottle of port?' Joy breaks out on the face in front of me.

'Absolutely excellent idea!'

CHAPTER 14

September 1940

'Lowther, isn't it – Sir William's son?'
'Yes indeed, it is, Mr Churchill. I'm most flattered that you should remember me, sir. How are you?'

Alexander had spotted the prime minister about to cross the road between St James's Park and Clive Steps. He couldn't have missed him since he looked like a parody of himself – he was wearing a pinstripe siren suit, a spotted bow-tie and a homburg hat, and his hands were clasped behind his back, the ubiquitous cigar clenched between his teeth. Alexander had politely averted his eyes, having noted that Churchill was in deep conversation with four or five colleagues, amongst whom he recognised Mr Atlee and Lord Halifax. But Churchill had stopped and called out, waving the cigar in a circular motion. He was taken aback to be recognised since they'd only briefly been introduced by his father while they were lunching together at the House of Commons the previous April, the day before Alexander, now in the Irish Guards, was to rejoin his regiment in Belgium. Mr

Churchill had approached Sir William's table to thank him for his support for the tough line he had taken against Sir Oswald Mosley and his wife, and his vociferous contributions in the house against the attacks he was having to endure from the left of the Labour Party. It was a relationship that went back quite a few years; Sir William was a staunch believer, like Churchill, in non-appeasement, and had therefore been overjoyed when his colleague was called to the palace by the King to be offered the premiership. Alexander, in uniform, had risen from the table to shake the prime minister's hand. The briefest of introductions.

This second meeting, conducted as Churchill made his way with his colleagues towards the entrance to the Cabinet War Rooms, was not much longer than the first. There was an exchange of pleasantries ('Remember me to your mother,' Churchill had said, forgetting perhaps, the famously unpleasant divorce of his parents) and a lifting of hats in farewell before Alexander resumed his journey across the park to his club in St James's Street. To his astonishment, within twenty-four hours, a message was passed to him by his father, with whom he was staying in Ladbroke Square Garden, asking him to contact the prime minister's private secretary. Two days later, he had been seconded from the Irish Guards and was an assistant secretary in the War Cabinet.

He was glad of it, since he'd been twiddling his fingers, bored rigid by duties in the army that, just for the moment at least, seemed pretty pointless. Thoroughcoat Property Investments had let him go temporarily when he joined the Irish Guards and now, after the debacle on the continent, he really did seem to be at a loose end. So much had changed in such a short space of time. It seems an extraordinary decision now, but Bridget and he had decided during the winter of that first year of the war, that while escape was still possible, she and Owen would sail for Canada. It had all happened so quickly – their decision, the very last-minute booking of a berth on the *President Roosevelt*, the haphazard flinging of belongings into three suitcases and a frenzied drive down to Southampton docks – in what seemed at the time to be a hopeless race against the clock to board the ship before its departure.

Less than an hour after their arrival in Southampton, he was shading his eyes against the sun with his hand, waving goodbye to Bridget and Owen standing high above on the deck of a vast ocean liner. The little boy with a mop of red curly hair and bewildered eyes set in a face of freckles had waved back vigorously, following instructions from his mother who was doing the same. To either side of them, Alexander took note of the alarmed-looking children, some even smaller than Owen and accompanied by brothers and sisters not much older, shouting down to weeping parents now preparing to endure a second separation which they had hoped to avoid when they had fled their old lives in Europe.

∼

It was the strangest of times; there was nothing that Alexander could compare it to either before or since. Having waved goodbye to his wife and child, he'd returned alone to the cottage in Shere. However, within a week, he was handing the keys over into the safekeeping of Mrs Byers, their cook. He'd volunteered, endured a medical and immediately been accepted into the Irish Guards before going into the office at Thoroughcoat Property Investments to clear his desk; he had then reported to Hounslow Barracks for basic training.

Almost immediately after his arrival in France, he was plunged into the horrors of the evacuation of Dunkirk. During the chaotic retreat from Belgium, he'd found himself holed up in a barn some miles inland, separated from his platoon after a frenzied firefight. It was a hellish introduction to real warfare after the make-believe games of training; he was utterly shocked to find himself the only officer amongst a small group of men – or boys, rather, since at least three of the seven didn't look old enough to be out at night. He was well aware that after only a few weeks of rudimentary instruction he was the least likely person to be able to get them out of the mess they were in and felt right out of his depth.

Just before nightfall on the first day of their scramble towards the coast, two of the men had rushed back to the barn after an interrupted recce to tell them that the Germans were approaching; clutching their rifles with white knuckles, they had all just managed to hide themselves amongst bales of straw on the other side of a flimsy barn door when a tank entered the farmyard outside. It filled their hiding place with the terrifyingly loud noise of the tracks rattling over splitting cobblestones before coming to a halt within a few feet of the barn door. They'd all pressed their hands to their mouths as they listened to staccato German voices yelling commands to subordinates. There was a lot of running around, chickens squawking uproariously, empty drums been kicked, a door being destroyed by rifle butts, and a woman screaming in anger and fear. A few long minutes later, the tank roared back into life and left the farmyard in a great cloud of black smoke that entered through the gaps in the barn door and threatened to choke them. Alexander had never been a praying man, but that's what he found himself doing until the sound of the huge machine faded into the distance and silence returned. How it was that they were not discovered he would never know. Much later, they'd set off again in the pitch black, heading towards what they hoped would turn out to be the coast, with Alexander issuing stern orders in a rasping whisper in the hope that he might be able to convey to the men that he really was in charge.

'You done us proud, sir, getting us out of that. You done us proud,' a baby-faced trooper from Northern Ireland with cheeks wet with gratitude and relief had shouted to him when they caught sight of the sea in the early morning. Alexander wasn't to know it until later, but they had arrived well ahead of many of the stranded troops and were spared the ordeal of being trapped on the beaches while Stukas dived out of the clear blue skies.

As they queued to climb aboard some old rust-bucket in the harbour, they'd watched Viscount Gort – the leader of the British Expeditionary Force – being piped aboard, followed by his horse, a magnificent black charger which was unceremoniously hoisted into the air; he'd been left stranded for a while far above the deck, motionless, his tail limp and doleful eyes sad with the acceptance of the indignity to which he (and everybody else) was being subjected.

∼

'I live round the corner. In Glebe Place.' The young man had broken the silence.

'Alone?'

'Yes. Of course!' he said, a broad smile spreading across his face, revealing his youth as his nerves melted away with the contact. 'Would you like to come back for a little while?'

Until this moment, there'd been a lot of walking very slowly with hands thrust deep into pockets; there was overtaking and falling back, stopping for brief moments, sideways glances. It couldn't go on like this for very long; it was freezing and there was a drizzle being driven by a cutting wind. Now, at last, after a journey that had started on the far side of Victoria Station, they were side by side, so close their shoulders were touching. They had finally come to a stop, staring into a tobacconist's on the King's Road, both pretending to take an interest in an uninteresting row of pipes in the window. Happy Thoughts, Alexander noticed the shop was called when he passed by early the next morning on his way to Godfrey Street for a shave and a hurried change of shirts before work.

What on earth had possessed him to accept the offer to go back to the young man's house? He'd not set out with any intent to have an adventure, after all – he was on his way back to his rooms in Chelsea in the late evening, a half hour's walk he'd done nearly every day for the three or four months since he'd started work in the Cabinet War Rooms below Whitehall. An opportunity had presented itself to him – and he'd gone along with it. At first, he was truly shocked that he had done such a thing and yet very quickly he was aware that he had thoroughly enjoyed everything that had happened – the delicious danger of the chase, followed by the outrageous sexual abandon, the easy affection, the laughter. But before leaving the following morning he'd made it quite clear to Nicholas that they would not be meeting again, and indeed, the young man had looked nonplussed at his comment, as though it had never occurred to him that there would be a repeat.

'Married man, eh?' Nicholas said after a moment of reflection. He was lying on the bed under a pile of blankets to ward off the cold in the frozen house. He laced his hands behind his head as he smiled up at Alexander who was adjusting his tie in front of a small mirror.

'That's right…'

They'd spent the night in Nicholas's childhood bedroom at the top of his absent parents' house in a room filled with the detritus of boyhood – a signed cricket bat attached to the wall, a shelf of tarnished cups celebrating different athletic achievements, a battered cello case taking up space in a corner, a single bed with a tartan rug saved from prep-school days. It occurred to Alexander that this was a room not vacated quite long enough ago for his parents to have bothered to reclaim it, perhaps a needed reminder in wartime of the boy their son used to be. There was a small, open suitcase on an armchair with pyjamas, shirts and pants spilling out; it was to be repacked as soon as Alexander took his leave so that Nicholas could return to his air squadron in Lympne. This was a kid playing a death-defying game in a toy that was a killing machine. He'd survived the Battle of Britain, Alexander told himself, but would have lost so many of his companions; talk about living life on the edge. Anything goes when you know that any day might be your last.

Any day might be your last. Perhaps it was the same for Alexander, too. Perhaps his adventure was just as much down to a devil-may-care attitude as Nicholas's. Less than a week before his meeting with the prime minister in St James's Park, the Blitz had begun in earnest. Thunderous warplanes crossed over from the continent to let loose their cargoes of bombs as they ranged up and down the Thames almost unopposed, setting the city on fire night after night. He was glad to be underground in Whitehall, taking shelter in the nerve centre of the war effort. During those two months of relentless bombing, there was a feeling of unshakeable, stoic calm underground that Alexander submerged himself in like a warm bath, but that would drain away into uncertainty once he returned to the surface, to the dark and cold air of a winter's evening.

At the beginning of December, he'd moved to Chelsea; he'd not been able to stay in the old family home in Notting Hill, finding his father quite impossible to deal with – a hangover from the feelings he'd had to endure while witnessing his mother's pain at the divorce she'd insisted on after years of his father's open philandering. Constance, his father's mistress and now wife, fussed around him, trying to get him to approve of her which only exacerbated his resentment and the feeling that somehow, his presence in the old family home was a betrayal of his mother. There were tiresome dinner parties two or three times a week that he felt compelled to attend – old fuddy-duddy House of Commons colleagues of his father's trying to get him to talk about the goings-on in the War Cabinet while being served dreadful food in the semi-dark imposed by the blackout. The two basement rooms in Godfrey Street rented from a colleague's parents ('I need to be closer to work, Pa – I'm there at all hours, you know...') were a godsend, though once he'd moved and spent much more time alone, he realised, somewhat to his surprise, just how much he was missing Bridget and Owen.

Not long after his adventure with Nicholas, however, his wife and son were on their way home from Canada. Bridget had written to Alexander explaining that she felt as though she'd done a runner, and wanted to be of more use, which was quite impossible trapped on a cherry farm in Ontario where she was sure she was about to succumb to terminal boredom and where Owen seemed quite unable to settle into his new school – a harbinger of things to come, perhaps. She'd insisted on returning and seemed quite willing to risk the idea of the odd U-boat on the way home – *Heavens, I'm sure our ships can outpace those damned Huns sneaking about under the water*, she wrote when he'd pointed out the danger. She wouldn't have said that a few months later, but at the time, it seemed like a reasonable comment.

Alexander was pleased. They'd open up the house in Shere again. *What might be best*, he wrote once it had all been decided, *is if I were to carry on with the rooms in Godfrey Street for the time being. It means that if I'm kept at work, as seems inevitable, I have somewhere to lay my head rather than struggling to get down to the cottage. Such jolly japes at the weekend, though, when I'll come down to join you both.* Just a little bit of independence, he thought. Damned good idea.

∽

À la Recherche du Temps Perdu. The title of a book Alexander had never got round to reading, but a perfect description of how he felt about the memories that were stirred up after his night with young Nicholas. *Young* Nicholas. Jesus – the boy was not more than one or two years older than he and his Oxford contemporaries had been during his university days, but he quickly decided to stop berating himself about taking advantage of someone so much younger than himself – it had been Nicholas who had made all the running, so there was no point in getting into a load of self-recrimination about what had happened; he was the one who had been seduced, he decided.

It wasn't the first time he'd felt like an ingénue – he'd gone up to Oxford knowing very little about the world in general, and even less about sex. Desire, however, never much present during his schooldays at Winchester, had hit him like a freight train in those first few weeks of liberation from his old life. He was a late developer who had catching up to do.

'Didn't you get up to any mischief at school?' he was asked by Bertie Thornton as they settled into a sofa in the Hypocrites' Club to reacquaint themselves. Bertie was an old schoolmate from Winchester now in the year above him at Oxford who was a rare example of someone who professed to be an aesthete and was also a sportsman – an Oxford rowing Blue, along with sundry other things, was firmly in his sights. 'God, I was an absolute tart at school – I was had by practically everybody. Lovely time.'

'What on earth are you talking about? I never saw anything like that going on.'

'Really, Lowther? How could you have missed it all

– were you going round with your eyes closed? What an innocent you are – it was everywhere!'

'Oh, Good Lord. Trust me to miss out!'

It was Bertie who had invited him to join the Hypocrites – a recently established student's dining club that met in two down-at-heel rooms with a kitchen attached, above a cycle shop in St Aldate's. The members liked to see themselves as aesthetes – some of them were, but they were mainly a dissolute, bohemian crowd who were chasing sexual adventure and a great deal of drink (and a few drugs) as much as they were discussing philosophy, which was the high-minded purpose they'd espoused at the beginning. 'They call themselves an artists' club, but all they draw are corks,' Alexander once heard one of the serving ladies saying to the cook. 'The Bright Young Things.' That's what the press had started to call them after commenting on their fancy-dress parties, treasure hunts through London and the clubs they formed. It was a world that Alexander felt he never quite belonged to, though he formed relationships with many of his contemporaries that were to last a lifetime. His ambitions were a little too prosaic for him to be totally identified with the set – admittance to the Inner Temple to practise as a barrister before making some money in banking wasn't quite the right mix for him to have been included amongst the poets, artists, novelists, photographers and professional dandies who made up this stellar crowd.

There was a hefty joining fee for the Hypocrites that he was made to cough up beforehand, but on this, his first visit, he was pleased to see that the wine was flowing freely and there was the smell of good food being prepared on the premises. As Bertie was informing him of all the fun he'd missed out on at school, Alexander was transfixed by the scene on the leather sofa opposite him. Two boys were necking furiously, rubbing each other's crotches while writhing about on the squeaking leather. They were quite obviously putting on a bit of a show to make an impression on their fellow members, most of whom seemed to be pretending not to notice, as though it might be par for the course. However, the whole thing worked a treat on Alexander who quickly, to his immense surprise, decided that he would very much like to try the same thing.

And he did. The opportunities were endless, too. To be sure, there were quite a few chaps in the Hypocrites and other similar clubs who were not available for that sort of carry-on – the hard-drinking fraternity who were in it for the hell-raising – but a large minority were up for anything, especially after a lot of good Burgundy. Perhaps the same sort of abandon that Nicholas was to show years later had infected them – might it be something to do with wartime? How many of those boys, his companions at Oxford, had lost older brothers in the ghastliness of the trenches? Were they living just for the moment, convinced that propriety was pointless, best put to one side?

He spent a little more of the allowance that his father gave him and also joined the Railway Club – just as much fun, with the same sort of crowd. Black-tie dinners on the Penzance to Aberdeen Express. They'd catch the train as it passed through Oxford and make their way to the pre-booked dining car where they'd have the first of their three courses. There was a little bit of rowdy behaviour – the odd bread roll being thrown about and some drinking straight from the bottle, but there was also a lot of good conversation, reading of extracts from books, and the would-be poets among them declaiming to an appreciative audience as they went on their way to Leicester; there, they'd leave the dining car, cross the platform and resume their dinner on the train back to Oxford. Rather silly way to carry on, but great fun at the time.

His discovery of the joys of sex didn't take up all his waking hours. He was ambitious after all, attending lectures and tutorials and determined to work towards a good law degree. But when the opportunity presented itself, he was up for it.

First, there was Charlie Falkirk, who he'd met at a supper given by a don who'd plied them both with a great deal of whisky and saucy conversation about the sexual habits of the ancient Greeks, perhaps in the hope that one of them, or indeed both, might not bother to go home at the end of the evening. The don's readings from Xenophon and Herodotus did indeed have the desired effect, but not until the young men had left him to clear up and had reached Charlie's room at Balliol. It wasn't a grand passion or any sort of commitment they'd agreed upon, just something they easily fell into when the opportunity presented itself. That had carried on for a few months until Charlie developed a grand passion for a rather horsey-looking bluestocking from Lady Margaret's.

He then, rather surprisingly, took up with Bertie Thornton for a while. It was rather an unlikely alliance – the desperately sporty Bertie, up at first light for training on the river whatever the weather, and Alexander, who's idea of sporting activity at the time wouldn't have stretched much beyond the odd bit of seasonal shooting at a friend's estate in the country followed by a very good dinner. They'd stumbled back to Alexander's room at Magdalen in torrential rain after a late evening at the Hypocrites' Club. Freezing and wet through, they'd stripped off all their clothes, tried to dry each other with the only available towel and one joyous thing had led to another. But that too ended when Bertie took up with a very pretty but rather ordinary girl, an assistant in a hat shop near the Covered Market.

Then there was Miles Eversley, who he'd taken a great shine to the moment he saw him cavorting on the sofa on that first visit to the Hypocrites' Club, but the fresh-faced young man was having none of it since he was carrying on with a beautiful youth from Brasenose who'd spotted him in the Bodleian and had sent him a naked photo of himself – *Come and drink with me somewhere*, he'd written on the back.

If Alexander had dared to be really truthful to himself, he would have had to admit that he was wounded by the rejection in a way that he hadn't experienced before – lovesick enough so that just for a little while he had to avoid Miles, even skipping the Hypocrites for two weeks running while he sulked, hoping that he might be missed and that Miles, who was quite obviously fond of him, might come knocking on his door to check whether there was anything that he could do for him. It didn't happen; his friend never noticed his absence.

Alexander had no choice but to move on from the rejection; the two eventually became friends instead and so he was able to observe Miles as his cherubic features quickly faded as a result of his generally debauched lifestyle. After Oxford, Miles taught for a year or two before finding extraordinary success as a writer, becoming a brilliant and witty chronicler of the upper-middle-class life and mores he observed at Oxford and beyond. Alexander rushed out to buy every new book of his on the day it was published and could never decide whether he was relieved or disappointed when he was unable to recognise himself among the many familiar characters that inhabited the pages.

Over the years, Miles grew progressively more melancholy, selfish and brittle. Success failed to mellow him, either in public life or at home. Alexander remembered visiting his old friend in mid-winter not long after the war and observing him as he warmed his backside by the fire while his children (from a second tempestuous marriage) looked on longingly as he ate, with ostentatious relish, a banana – something not widely available in those days of rationing. It reminded him of the young Miles on the sofa in the Hypocrites, showing off his disregard for propriety all those years before. Later he converted to Roman Catholicism; absolution's handy if you need a device to excuse yourself of bad behaviour without ever having to apologise to anybody but God. But he was always the most delightful, acerbic and cynical companion – he was long dead now and still missed. He hadn't stayed around long enough to be invited to the jubilee at Eaton Square.

∼

Alexander never thought of himself, or indeed most of his friends, as pansies. Indeed, they weren't. There were a few obvious ones, of course, swanning around Oxford with silver canes, floppy hair and affected accents, people like Harold Acton, Brian Howard and their set within a set – 'The Homosexualists', Mark Patten liked to call them, over-enunciating the vowels with a disdainful expression. Alexander was doing 'homosexual' things now and again, and greatly enjoying it all, but without even bothering to think of it as a phase, he knew he'd be moving on, like practically everyone else. There would be women. It was as simple as that. The fooling around was fun while it lasted and then, somewhere towards the end of his second year, it was no longer happening, as though they'd all grown up rather late and found themselves moving on from boyish pursuits. There was much less staying up until the early hours, drunken throwing up on pristine quadrangle lawns, losing keys and climbing up drainpipes – and much less fiddling around with other fellows. No decision was made to stop. It was just time to move on.

However, for a novice like Alexander, there was much to be learned when it came to the wooing of women; it was a great deal more complicated than what had preceded it. Unlike the casual falling into bed (or thereabouts) with chaps not long out of school, a measure of pre-planning was deemed necessary when it came to the fairer sex, and even that didn't mean that his endeavours were to be blessed with success. Far from it – it was all quite hit and miss, and it soon seemed apparent to Alexander that a lot of young women were not that bothered about sex in the way that a lot of young men were. The whole courting thing seemed to have to involve a great deal of conversation before moving on to candlelit dinners, the presentation of flowers, endless walks on the water meadow and then, if success were achieved, the bribing of the odd janitor to help with the turning of a blind eye to late night (and early morning) comings and goings on the staircase – no more climbing into various rooms through windows.

Alexander couldn't now recall exactly who was the first of a series of girls that saw him through the rest of his Oxford days, but perhaps the fact that his memory didn't conjure up that many names and faces was an indication that none of those dalliances were of much importance. There was Judith Vane-Templeton somewhere along the way, whom he did manage to seduce during what was meant to be an introductory walk on Port Meadow before dinner for two. By the time she was pulling her stockings back up after the event, Judith had decided she was appalled that he'd encouraged her into such brazen behaviour (Alexander had been delighted by her dragging him to the ground as soon as he'd given her what was intended to be a chaste kiss) and the walk back into town was accompanied by silence apart from the odd muffled sob, a whiff of horse manure from the back of his linen jacket and then a slap to the face as they parted. Dinner was cancelled.

Before or after Judith was Charlotte Semprey, blonde, full-bosomed and red-lipped with a demeanour that convinced Alexander that she was up for anything. It didn't go his way, though, and weeks were wasted in sexual fantasy before he realised that nothing was going to happen; she had an extraordinary ability to string things out conversationally until there was no time for anything but sleep. One morning, after an evening in which Alexander had sneaked her into his room and plied her with champagne, he woke to find himself stretched out, fully clothed on the floor, having fallen asleep during a long, one-sided discourse on scientism and reductionism, which was her thing, apparently, but which made no sense to him at all. He'd struggled very hard that last night to stay awake in the hope that things might take a turn for the better, but it wasn't to be. Charlotte had stepped over him and taken to his bed once he'd succumbed to sleep, snoring blissfully until he made her a pot of tea in the morning. Perhaps she was waiting for a proposal of marriage before the first kiss.

And then there was Hermione de Sainte-Claire, a friend of Judith's at Somerville, with whom he imagined himself quite taken. Judith's slap had been forgotten and she had recast herself as friend and matchmaker to Alexander – possibly so that he would never try anything on with her again. Hermione was introduced to him at a little Sunday tea party in Judith's room and they had quickly embarked on a relationship that was to see them nearly to the end of their student days.

She was ravishing – a tall, willowy girl straight out of a Pre-Raphaelite painting, her auburn locks framing her delicate features as they tumbled about her shoulders. The caché that came his way with this beautiful creature on his arm was immensely pleasing to him, but in fact the victory was not quite what it seemed. Hermione may have had a French name, but she was in fact as English as a rose and without any of the Gallic passion that her name hinted at. Certainly, the most exciting part of any of the nights they spent together was the subterfuge required to smuggle her into his room. Once there, and before bed (always the bed – there were to be no sofas, blankets spread out on riverbanks, back seats of cars, and certainly no fumbling or tumbling around on the floor), she'd attend to her nightly toilette of face-washing, cream-applying and brushing of her lustrous hair before asking him to turn away while she undressed, neatly folding her clothes before putting on the nightdress which had found a permanent home in the bottom drawer of his chest of drawers; the bedside light would be turned off when she joined him in bed and there might be a conversation about the day's events. Eventually a bit of rather rudimentary sex would take place; her eyes would be closed for the duration and her hands, prettily placed next to her ears on the pillow, never dared to lower themselves under the blankets to explore what might be going on below.

The relationship ended when she ran off, immediately after her finals, with an Italian who had been reading History of Art at New College. It was the most horrific surprise to Alexander who had not seen it coming at all, though perhaps he should have. Her weekly visit to his room had slipped into becoming a fortnightly event a while before she abandoned him, and even that had recently been shifted to a rather safe hour in the middle of a weekend afternoon, with the nightdress resolutely staying in its place in the drawer. When they'd been gone a few weeks and the hurt had started healthily morphing into resentment, he wondered how the fiery young Italian with the V-shaped torso and solid thighs (Alexander may have moved on, but he wasn't averse to the odd bit of ogling) was going to come to terms with Hermione's somewhat lackadaisical approach to the arts of love.

Many years later, just before the war, he was to bump

into the couple during a fraught, unexpected meeting during a soirée at the Italian Embassy in Grosvenor Square where it turned out that Lodovico was the cultural attaché. They both looked as beguiling as the day that they'd fled Oxford – he'd maintained his physique and looked no different at all except for a dash of white hair at his temples, and she was even more alluring than he remembered, her hair swept up above her head revealing her milky white shoulders and a long neck graced by a brilliant diamond choker. He'd smiled gracefully as he introduced her to Bridget at his side, but was taken aback to feel, just for a fleeting second, the return of a hot resentment filling a space in his diaphragm. There had been an exchange of pleasantries during which Alexander learned that the Count and Countess De Piscopo had become the parents of six children within fifteen years, which is an awful lot of missionary position if that's all they ever got around to.

Some time after Hermione left and Alexander felt up to a post-mortem, he started to ask himself if perhaps the failing was a little more to do with him than he'd been willing to admit – perhaps he was the one who was a bit of a letdown. Was he lacking in passion, or skill? He came to acknowledge that, quite apart from the obvious mechanical differences, sleeping with women really was not the same as sleeping with men. Strange, when he thought about it, that before getting down to the business of sex, there was always so much talk with his girlfriends, followed by a usually rather silent, straightforward act, never that memorable. It was the exact opposite with what used to happen with his male partners. During the course of an evening together, there might be some tacit acknowledgement of what might be going to happen later, as though it was important that actual plans weren't seen to be being made. Later, sheets would be thrown back impatiently, lights turned full on, acknowledgements made about what was working well, breathless instructions to do this and now that, and what might be nice to try next. Alexander remembered the seduction of a young Frenchman from Balliol; he'd taken him out on a punt on the Cherwell and had tied it up in the shade of a willow tree. In his unabashed excitement Christophe had never shut up for a minute, and then, at the critical moment, had threatened to reveal their hiding place by shouting out at the top of his voice, 'I am arriving. I am arriving!'

CHAPTER 15

Late April 1992

Alexander needs my company most of the time now, especially since Bridget's accident. She comes home today after nearly three months away, but Theresa, Alexander and I really don't know how that's going to turn out. We're nervous, but we've done our best to prepare for her return. There's a starkly bright pine handrail twisting its way up the stairs now like a fresh scar on an old body after an operation; it clashes with the seasoned dark brown of the wood panelling it's been attached to. In the bathroom, a low plastic stool sits in the middle of the bath and large chrome handles have been installed on the tiles above the tub; a faux-rosewood commode is taking up a snug space in the corner of Bridget's bedroom next to the sink and the long runner outside the drawing room together with the Persian rug in the hall have been rolled up and taken to the attic – best to be overcautious with things that might create a hazard until we know better. We've been assured that, at least for the moment, she can get up the stairs with help, and knowing the old girl as I do, she'll be quite determined to stay put in her beloved bedroom, so we're not doing what seemed to be the most practical thing – moving her into the small room next to the utility room downstairs – and stairlifts, etc are postponed to a future date. Last week I sat at the desk with Theresa, and we worked out a rota of staff from the nursing agency recommended by Dr Melchett; an armchair, a little desk and a portable TV have been placed in the corridor outside her room so there doesn't have to be a moment when Bridget need be alone. If there's any of her old self left, she'll take umbrage, of course. She can't bear strangers in the house, but we'll just have to deal with her discomfort.

Since her accident and prolonged absence in the nursing home, I'm here for much more of the week than I used to be, especially now that Mrs Smith – our old housekeeper – has moved to her daughter's. Her old cottage, just a little down the street from the big house, was made over to me last year so that I have a little bit of an independent life when I'm here; Alexander sorely needs my company, and I'm not sure if I would be able to manage if I didn't have the little place to escape to at the end of a long evening. It's my refuge – a two-up, two-down cottage that I've painted white, carpeted green and hung modern prints in. I sleep in a narrow bed in the narrow room that looks down onto the strip of garden at the back that I'm enjoying nursing back to life; I'm living in a doll's house, and I cherish it. Theresa and I do a half-week each now – I come down on a Wednesday evening and leave when she gets back from her break after lunch on Saturday. Last week, without calling to let me know, she didn't turn up until Sunday afternoon, by which time I was feeling more trapped than I can ever remember. A dereliction of her duties, to be sure, and the first time I've found myself having to be quite clear with her about how pissed off I was, and that it can never happen again. It's hard though, on both of us, watching someone we're very fond of slowly slipping beyond us; this is a less happy place to be these days.

Alexander and I have made a habit of our 'port nights'. There are times when I put my foot down, and I try to limit it to once a week, whereas he would be up for it every night. They are such a comfort to him that I'm loath to turn him down when he suggests it, knowing how much he dreads the small, sleepless hours these days. If that entails drinking port for a large portion of the night, so be it. I've been uneasy about leaving the house for my cottage at the end of every evening while Bridget's been away; it feels as though I'm neglecting my duties, so often I've climbed into my old bed along the corridor from Alexander's room. But from now on, there will be a carer here every night so a little independence and relief from worry at the end of each evening will be returned to me. Ostensibly, the lady will be here to look after Bridget, but I have an agreement with the agency that a bit of an eye is to be kept on Alexander, though I'm not, of course, mentioning that to him.

I'm still rewarded with a glimpse of the old Alexander, though every week that passes I'm more aware of his growing physical frailty – the lingering to catch a breath halfway up the stairs, the hand that's gripping his stick or holding a glass shaking ever so slightly, the slight confusion over dates, people, places, the descent into sleep in the drawing room after supper in the middle of an article I'm reading from the *Daily Telegraph*.

'Have I been asleep?' he'll say, coming to abruptly and looking perplexed.

'I don't think so, Alexander...'

～

Our 'port nights' have mostly been about reminiscence, but sometimes I think he's testing the ground, trying to find out whether I'm going to be shocked about something he's done in the past. I never am, of course – I've heard most of the stories before, I'm not very shockable, and besides, I'm far from convinced he's done anything particularly shaming. Now and again, he'll repeat a tale that I've undoubtedly heard before, and as he finishes, there will be a tiny displacement of his head to one side, as though he's waiting for me to voice my disapproval. It's new, this; it seems that some devil in his head is trying to persuade him that he's cheated Bridget and Owen of security and happiness and needs me to confirm it.

'Have I ever told you about my criminal stupidity in Ireland after the Washington Conference in 1943?' he said during a particularly late session last week.

'Yes, Alexander, but it's one of my favourite stories of all time, so tell me again...'

～

'The most perfectly stupid thing I've ever done,' Alexander had said to me the first time I heard the story.

It was May 1943 – the height of the war, but with things perhaps just on the turn after the Soviet victory at Stalingrad. All the British and American bigwigs – headed by Churchill and Roosevelt – had met up in Washington for top-secret talks concerning plans for the invasion of Sicily and D-Day – the fight-back against the Nazis in Western Europe. The politicians gathered at the White House, while the military, headed by Eisenhower and Lord Louis Mountbatten, met close by in the Federal Reserve Building in Constitution Avenue. Boy, how the Americans had taken to the glamorous team headed by Lord Louis, all swishing around in dashing white naval uniforms with acres of gold braid and caps set at jaunty angles – panache was all the British had at that point in the war; there had lately been important victories in North Africa, but there was still an awfully long road ahead. Alexander had flown across the Atlantic with Lord Louis, his job to be part of the team that was to liaise between the Cabinet and the military planners.

Perhaps it was his recent adventure with the young airman in London that had begun to wake him up to new sexual possibilities, and during the two weeks he was away, he found himself struck by the aura of indefinable sexual ambiguity that hung around the dazzlingly handsome Lord Louis and the younger members of his staff. It was almost as though they'd set out to seduce the Americans by stealth, with their hosts eventually succumbing to something they weren't even conscious of, like sixth-formers at public school developing an entirely innocent crush on the fresh-faced new intake in the third form.

∼

He had caught Alexander's eye at Gander Airport while the aircraft that was to take them back across the Atlantic following the end of the conference was being refuelled. Alexander had first noticed him as they waited to climb down the ladder from the plane; the young man had run a hand through a shock of unruly blond hair that had taken flight in the sudden gust of wind as the door was opened; he'd then tamed it with the firm application of a hat before his descent to the tarmac – an incongruous figure in a dark brown double-breasted suit, quite out of place among the surrounding military uniforms. He might well have been a civil servant, finding himself mixed up with the service personnel for the flight home. Or a foreigner? He had the slightly mysterious air of someone not quite British – Northern European, perhaps, a delegate from King Haakon of Norway's government-in-exile? In the vast hangar where they'd been offered refreshments before continuing their journey, Alexander had watched as the much younger man had helped himself to a mug of coffee from the large steaming urn at the top of the queue, smoked a cigarette and then, after their eyes had met for a second or two longer than mere curiosity might permit, had followed him out into the fresh air.

Alexander had trailed him at a distance, for the length of the runway and beyond, to the edge of a grey lake where busy little waves, whipped up by a keen wind, were slapping against the shoreline. They stood many yards apart, both looking out over the water with hands deep into pockets while Alexander half kidded himself that he was doing nothing more than stretching his legs and enjoying the brisk cool air of a late Newfoundland afternoon after the escape from a relentless Washington heatwave. The walk was doing him good, he told himself, as he readied himself again for the noise and discomfort of the journey and the long haul back across the Atlantic to Ireland; the five Avro Lancasters in the convoy had been converted to hold people rather than bombs, but it was an almost impossible task to rest while being subjected to the bone-rattling roar of the engines; there was very little comfort to be found in the single line of rattan chairs that had been secured into place in the windowless space above what was usually the bomb-hold.

There was no contact between them during the walk, though the young man surely must have been well aware that he was being followed; no acknowledgement was granted to Alexander, who kept enough of a distance to make sure there could be no accusations of any sort. A walk was being taken, that was all. But he'd forgotten himself and an hour had easily slipped by – the sudden onset of dusk and a glance at his watch told Alexander that take-off time was fast approaching. In the distance, the Lancasters, readied for departure, were turning from grey to a flaming red in a late spring sunset and both men, still keeping up the pretence of not noticing each other, had had to break into a run. Alexander, returning swiftly to reality, was suddenly very conscious of what was securely tucked into his armpit. Within the slim leather folder that had been entrusted to him by Churchill himself in Washington was a copy of the top-secret papers that were a result of the conference – the outlines for the invasion of Sicily, and the beginning of the plans for the Normandy landings.

As he reached the top of the ladder into the Lancaster, he turned round to offer his hand to the figure just behind him; a firm grip was returned, though their eyes had not met. But as Alexander passed him while he was settling into his seat, the grey eyes above the scarf wrapped round the young man's face had finally met his again for another fleeting moment of acknowledgement.

∽

'Might I leave a message for Lord Liscasey?' Alexander was on the phone, making his excuses to His Lordship's butler from the reception desk at the inn where he'd just booked a room. The crew and passengers were spending the night in Shannon before continuing their journey back to London, and he had been invited to stay with his old friends nearby, along with the more senior members of the party.

'Will you tell him that I've booked into the Joymount Arms in the village for the evening? Really don't want to bother him when he's got a houseful of people and might be needing more space. I'm thinking that he might be quite grateful for the cancellation!'

'Not at all, sir; we've plenty of space and–'

'I insist. I'm booked in here now and quite happy to stay.'

'Very well, sir. Might I ask who's calling?'

'Alexander Lowther.'

'Ah yes, indeed, Mr Lowther. How nice to hear your voice again. But you'll still be joining us for dinner I hope?'

'I most certainly will. Looking forward to it.'

Lord and Lady Liscasey were not only old friends of his father's, but actually distant cousins of Bridget's, and he'd been a frequent visitor to Cloncolman House since before his marriage. Teddy, the Liscaseys' son and heir, had been a friend at Oxford who had been tragically killed in a car crash in the South of France in the summer of their first year. Alexander had often been included in shooting parties at the house both before and since Teddy's death and had always been treated with the greatest affection by the now elderly couple and their younger son Freddie. His change of plan would be a disappointment to them, but he was on a mission now, and had made his mind up. He'd promise to catch up with them during a proper, longer visit another time. Soon.

On arrival at Shannon Airport, they'd been hurried towards a fleet of waiting cars. 'Vehicles to the right for Cloncolman House, vehicles to the left for the Joymount Arms,' bellowed a very young woman in uniform, looking pleased to be important enough to be directing the traffic. The airport personnel were no doubt eager to have them packed away as quickly as possible – the Irish Free State being neutral in the war, the staff were perhaps being cautious about being seen to be associating with personnel from one of the belligerents. As Alexander was dipping his head into the back seat of the car that was to take him to Cloncolman House, he caught sight of the figure in the brown suit walking towards one of the cars that was going to the inn.

'I'm in the wrong party! I'm staying at the Joymount Arms,' he shouted as he'd jumped out of the car and retrieved his suitcase from the still-open boot.

～

'The fucking brazen stupidity of it.' Alexander took a breath while reacting to his recounting of the incident as though it had happened yesterday, fiddling awkwardly with the pillow behind his back as though he were hoping its new position might just lessen the impact of the memory.

'I was so enamoured at the thought of some sexual adventure that I quite forgot myself. Lost in the whole bloody thing, I was. Right through dinner, until the chap sitting next to me brought me round during the dessert. Rhubarb with meringue we were having. Imprinted on my memory.'

∼

'Be careful.' Alexander's portly neighbour had finished his pudding earlier than anyone else, placing his spoon and fork together on the plate before relaxing back into his seat and fiddling with the top button of his trousers as if he were tempted to undo it. It had been a fine dinner, unencumbered by any rubbish about rationing that was an all-pervasive fact of life at home.

'I'm sorry?'

'O'Donoghue. Proprietor of the Joymount Arms – you're staying there, you said? Loathes the British with a passion – Liscasey's fairly certain he was one of the crew that came up to the house to try and set it on fire during the Troubles, though they've put it behind them now. Easier for everyone to pretend there's nothing to it. But I reckon he's a wrong 'un, that man. Rumoured to be spying for the Germans...'

Alexander heard himself making implausible excuses to his hostess as he pushed his chair back and got to his feet, his napkin held in a tight ball in his fist.

'Do excuse me, Lady Liscasey, but I have to leave this

instant! So stupid of me but I've just remembered I absolutely promised to speak to Bridget about Owen. He's been frightfully ill with measles and–'

'But my dear Alexander – use the phone in the library! You'll be completely alone in there.' His hostess was looking bemused.

'No, no, I'm so sorry – I have to dash. I'll pop back in the morning before we depart for London, I promise.' It was a lie – the Lancasters would be taking off for London before daybreak; the passengers were to be present at a late morning meeting of the War Cabinet.

'Are you not feeling well, old boy?' Lord Liscasey looked as concerned as his wife. 'This is most unfortunate. Are you sure we can't make–'

'No, no. I must go this instant…'

His hands were shaking and sweating as he paced up and down the cavernous entrance hall where long-dead Liscaseys looked down on him from the walls; he was now horribly conscious of the gap under his arm where he wished the leather folder might still be. Hat and coat snatched from a tiny maid who had been summoned from the kitchen in the middle of dinner to retrieve them for him, he flung himself down the stairs beneath the grand portico of Cloncolman House and raced down the drive, aware of nothing but his pounding heart and the sound of his feet on the gravel. He ran past the two soldiers posted at the gatehouse, one of whom looked askance, hands deep in his pockets, at the fleeing figure, while the other belatedly snapped his feet together and raised his hand to his temple in a crisp salute.

Earlier, knotting his tie as he'd dressed for dinner, he'd

looked down from the window of his room just in time to see the back of the tall figure from the plane striding out purposefully along the small country lane in the direction of Cloncolman House. Alexander had pulled on his dinner jacket and coat, seized his hat and hurried out of the inn in an attempt to catch up. He was determined to make contact, carefully preparing breezy words of introduction that might make a midnight drink after their return from dinner a possibility. But he had disappeared; there was no sign of him during pre-dinner drinks at the house and looking up and down the long table as they sat down to dinner, Alexander realised with great disappointment that he was not there.

∼

'That run back to the inn, Ben, was undoubtedly the ghastliest few minutes of my life. When I reached my room, I can remember trying to get the key into the lock with my hand shaking, followed by the horrific shock as the door swung open and I could see that the folder was not on the bed where I was quite sure I'd left it. But then, in the rising panic, I'd caught sight of my open suitcase on the armchair under the window, and there the folder was, partly hidden by my pyjamas. Just before I saw the young man from my window, I'd placed it there with my little silver hip flask on top of it. Jesus, the relief of finding it. But then the agony, once the doubts started crowding in – had someone come in and read the bloody thing, taken it away for photographing before putting it back in the exact position that they'd found it? And *was* that the exact position? Was the hip flask on top of it? Hadn't I hidden it completely under the pyjamas? I can still remember the return of the feelings from relief to awful, gnawing doubt again. It ploughed me up inside for months. Right up to D-Day over a year later, in fact, until I heard the news that the Germans had been taken completely by surprise in Normandy.' There was an outbreath, a reliving of the relief.

'I should have been shot for such stupidity. Really, I should have. You're the only person I've ever dared to tell this to, you know.'

'Oh well. It all seems to have worked out in the end. We won the war, I believe.'

'Yes, yes indeed we did. But it wasn't the last of my stupidity.'

And then Alexander told me of the affair that he'd started just before the end of the war. He'd fallen deeply in love with the young widow of a colleague in the Irish Guards who'd been killed at Anzio. Her dead husband was yet another relation of Bridget's – the very rich banking side rather than the very rich brewing side of the family, and so the bereft young lady was close enough to be invited down with her two little boys to the cottage at Shere. They'd thought that the children would be cheered up by the slightly older Owen, and that the Surrey Hills would be a distraction from the vast house in Suffolk that Anthony's parents had handed over to the young couple just before the war, all but a wing of which had been requisitioned for war-wounded. Bridget had persuaded Alexander that Esmée might need a break from the constant reminders of her dead husband that were provided by the mangled survivors she could see every time she looked out of a window. But within a week of her visit, they had arranged to meet up in Hyde

Park while assuring themselves they were just seeking out old familiar company. Soon after that they were enjoying passionate trysts at his rooms in Godfrey Street and Esmée's London home in Grosvenor Place.

'Eventually, she gave me an ultimatum. Leave Bridget and Owen and be with me. Well – she was alone with two small boys and needed a husband.' Another weary sigh. 'What a bastard I was, really, stringing everyone along–'

'So, Bridget knew?'

'No, thank God, I really don't think she did. Oh, I suspect she knew of most of my other flings, but they were never serious, of course, and I don't think she gave a damn about them. But for some reason, the thing with Esmée turned into something else. I was terribly smitten. I remember, after her ultimatum, walking from Godfrey Street to the East End and back again in the middle of the night, trying to work out what to do about the whole damn thing. Anyway, by the time I climbed into bed back in Chelsea as the sun came up, I'd decided to put an end to it. Ultimately, I just couldn't bear the idea of abandoning my wife and child. So that was that.'

'So, you did the right thing, then, didn't you? I think you should be proud of yourself. Why the recriminations now, after all this time? And hardly as serious an issue as the Normandy plans going astray, surely? I don't think you've anything to tell yourself off about, I really don't. I very much doubt that's the reason that Owen is such a tosser – if you'll pardon the expression.' Alexander didn't look convinced and took refuge in another large mouthful of port.

'Do you think that Bridget ever strayed, Alexander?'

I said, wondering whether I might dig up a little something that would help assuage the guilt.

'Well yes, I rather think she may have done. Someone we met during a holiday in Cannes in the early fifties – a black painter from Harlem, much younger than both of us, who we kept coming across at a series of cocktail parties. Something was up there, I think.'

'Golly. Did you mind much?'

'Well to be quite honest, no. In fact, in some extraordinary way, I was rather taken with the idea. Found myself walking around in a semi-tumescent state whenever I thought about it – very nicely put together young man, he was...'

CHAPTER 16

Three months earlier, mid-January

'Just wondering if it's a terribly good idea, Alexander?'
'What?'
'Bridget's afternoon cigarette. Seems to have an extraordinary effect on her – has it always done that?'
It was just the quickest of conversations with Bridget out of the room, but, God, how I wish I'd taken it up more seriously. I'd never known anyone who smoked in the way those two did. Two cigarettes each a day. That was all. One each, sometime after lunch, and another with their afternoon tea, though I was never witness to it since I was always out for my daily walk in the break between clearing up after lunch and coming back to prepare dinner. But this one afternoon, having detected a rather nasty smell in the cloakroom, I had to cut short my walk to let in the plumber I'd summoned, and while he put things to rights in no time at all, I found myself being included in the four o'clock tea ceremony. I was already a little perturbed by the sight of Bridget struggling along the corridor, bang on the hour, with the tray

in her hands at a perilous angle and the crockery clinking noisily together as it slipped towards the edge. I'd offered to carry it but was firmly rebuffed; it was one of her little tasks that demonstrated a continuing independent existence. Straight after tea, having meticulously extinguished her cigarette, Bridget got to her feet and made her way over for the afternoon fiddle with the curtains. On her way back towards the sofa, I noticed her swaying to and fro as though she was on a channel ferry in a storm, arms reaching out to either side to steady herself.

'Are you all right, Bridget?' I said, alarmed.

'What do you mean?'

'Are you dizzy? You seem a little unsteady–'

'What on earth are you talking about? I'm perfectly fine!'

∼

A few days later, our lives changed forever. Just after six o'clock, coming back into the house to start dinner after my walk, I was presented with a chaotic scene in the hall. Bridget was splayed out on the floor at the bottom of the stairs and Alexander, stick in one hand, was leaning over his wife, trying to pull her to her feet with the other. She was grimacing with pain, her back against the bottom step, legs stretched out in front of her. There was smashed crockery all around her and the tea-tray had rolled away and taken up a position leaning against the skirting board by the kitchen door.

'Jesus – what's happened? How long have you been there, Bridget? Alexander, leave her be! Don't pull her hand, just let her be. Bridget, don't move, be absolutely still. I'm phoning the doctor,' I shouted.

'Can't you just pull me up, Ben? I'm fine,' she said, the look of anguish distorting her face telling me otherwise. 'I just lost my balance, that's all.'

'I don't think there's anything much wrong, Ben,' Alexander said, trying for a reassuring tone, 'but you're probably right – might be an idea to have her checked out by Dr Melchett.'

It occurred to me later that evening that perhaps they had descended into a state of denial after she'd fallen, as though they knew that their lives were never going to be the same again, and so they were both making light of what had just happened in an attempt to keep the inevitable at bay. Alexander, in my absence, had pottered back and forth from the drawing room collecting, one at a time, an assortment of cushions that were scattered around the victim and serving no purpose at all. He'd managed to locate a glass in the kitchen, somehow filled it with water from the tap, and placed it on the step beside Bridget; it was now on its side with the contents adding to Bridget's misery by being soaked up by her blouse. 'Oh – do get up, darl, I'm quite sure there's nothing wrong, you know,' he said in an exasperated tone as I glanced over at the scene, phone in hand, waiting for the surgery to answer.

Dr Melchett, accompanied by the district nurse, had arrived promptly after my call and the three of us had managed to get Bridget up the stairs in a fireman's lift, into her nightie, and settled in an upright position with the aid of a mass of pillows. General relief all round.

'As I was saying, my feeling is she's just rather badly bruised,' Dr Melchett said as I opened the door to let him and the nurse out. 'A few doses of paracetamol and a rest will put her to rights, I'm sure. I'll pop back tomorrow morning to see how she is.'

～

'This is quite ridiculous! I'm perfectly fine – and what about dinner?' Bridget said to me as she pushed back the bedclothes a little later. 'Why can't I come down?'

'Just this once, Bridget. Dinner in bed. And you'll be fine in the morning, trust me.'

'Don't keep saying "trust me" – you've no idea how annoying it is!'

She seemed to settle then, trying to look a little vexed and not really succeeding when I brought up a tray with her supper. I thought a little bit of her was relishing the attention after nearly two hours on the floor in the hall, but there was no way she was letting on.

By Alexander's bedtime, I'd managed to calm him – and myself – down; as I folded back the bedclothes in his room, I told him I was abandoning the cottage for the night and moving back into my old bedroom down the corridor.

'Better safe than sorry,' I said, pouring him a glass of water.

'Don't be ridiculous, Ben, nothing's going to happen,' he said, twiddling with the knobs on the radio and losing Radio 4 in the process. It was the only station that he listened to and the messing around was enough of a display of his unease to convince me I was doing the right thing.

'She's had a bump, nothing more. Just went over at the bottom of the stairs. I think you thought she'd fallen all the way down, but she hadn't. It was just a sort of controlled descent to the floor, a buckling of knees, that's all. Back to normal in the morning, I'm sure. You go off for the evening, now.'

'I'm staying the night. Made up my mind.'

'Good God – talk about Grand Guignol. We're just a bloody nuisance, aren't we?' he said, failing to hide the relief at my insistence.

∼

'Coo-ee!'

I was awake immediately.

'Coo-ee!' again. I propped myself up in bed and glanced at my watch. It was just before half past three in the morning. I'd left four doors wide open, which meant I was able to see straight out of my room, along the corridor, through Alexander's dressing room, across the landing and into Bridget's bedroom where there was a light on. But there was something odd about it. I sat straight up then and tried to focus on what might be happening. To my horror, I realised that the lamp on the bedside table was no longer where it should be; it was on the floor, throwing ghostly, elongated shadows.

'Bridget?'

'Coo-ee!' I couldn't make her out amongst the tumble of blankets and pillows on the bed, but then I saw an arm slowly being raised from the floor at the end of the bed – like a wave to attract attention from someone in a lifeboat after a sinking. Just for a tiny second, I turned over and buried my face in the pillow, not just to prepare myself, but also in the forlorn hope that when I looked again, just a few seconds later, I would have got it all wrong and nothing would be amiss – the lamp would be off and the dark, far-off shape of a contented, sleeping Bridget would fill the bed.

∼

It was the longest night of my life. And the loneliest. I tried to make her as comfortable as I could, not knowing whether to move her or not, before deciding to keep her in the awkward position I'd found her in on the floor – her left leg at the strangest angle, turned in as though it might be that of a little girl's broken doll – and deciding on a covering of blankets with a single pillow that I carefully manoeuvred into position under her head. She'd wet herself and was shivering both from cold and shock; it wasn't long before she descended into a delusional state, imploring me to tell her why Napoleon's army were camping on the lawn, and insisting that I get in contact with the Emperor himself to ask him to move on.

I fucked up, unforgivably. I knew not to wake Alexander – what would be the point of adding his fear and frustration to the scene? But perhaps my decision-making would have been better if I'd not been alone for those hours. I decided immediately that, since the Bellaghys had medical insurance, I would be phoning for a private ambulance. It would be fantastically efficient, no doubt; pick her up within half an hour, and transfer her to the private ward of the Kent and Canterbury Hospital. The biggest mistake of that awful night, and nobody at the end of the line willing or able to put me on the right path. Two hours and numerous panicky phone calls later, I was still waiting for the ambulance to arrive, and then, deciding that Bridget was either falling asleep or losing consciousness as I sat on the floor stroking her head and telling her that help was 'just round the corner', I did what I should have done at the beginning of the ordeal and phoned the NHS emergency services who took another thirty-five minutes to reach us.

The two burly, wonderfully attentive men had trouble getting Bridget, moaning softly on the stretcher, down the narrow stairs; I followed behind, hoping they would take notice of my finger against my lips as I whispered, 'As quietly as possible, chaps, if you can. The lady's husband is in his room, and I'd rather he not be disturbed...' I could just hear Alexander's radio talking to the night. Whether he was asleep or awake, the sound was just enough to muffle the drama in the hall.

I went into the kitchen after they'd gone, thinking that waves of relief would break over me now that poor Bridget had been delivered out of my hopeless care into capable hands. But it didn't happen. Instead, as I sat at the kitchen table clutching a mug of tea waiting for dawn to break and quite unexpectedly trying to keep tears at bay, I was enveloped by the crushing sadness of what might now be lost forever; a little later, anger began to bubble up about having had to wait with a very sick old lady for three hours, and at Dr Melchett's mistake in leaving me in charge of someone who, as the X-rays were to prove within an hour or two, had badly broken her hip and was unlikely ever to walk again.

∼

Napoleon's visit to the garden that night was only the beginning of the real downward spiral of Bridget's mental faculties, so that the forgetfulness that had frustrated us before the accident began to pale into insignificance.

Three weeks after her fall, I had her moved from the private wing of the Kent and Canterbury Hospital to a nursing home closer to us. I visited every day, having to accept, at the same time, that Alexander was now quite incapable of making the journey with me. Bridget retained enough of her faculties to know that the getting in and out of a car and having to be helped along corridors bumping into things was not an option for him; Alexander, however, was less sanguine about it and was, at least for a time, consumed by guilt at not being able to visit.

⁓

'Thank God you're here, Ben – what on earth is going on? Where have you been all this time? Why am I in this place?' These same imploring questions, before a slide into indignant anger, would quickly follow the look of utter relief that would come across her face once I'd entered her room and planted a kiss on her cheek.

'Because you've broken your leg, and it needs to be in traction so that it heals properly.'

'Oh – I – see!' she'd say with a *'dawning of realisation'* look on her face, 'I had no idea!' She would ask the same questions and respond to my explanation in the same way every day, but worse was to follow once she started to regain a little of her strength. The steely part of Bridget would battle to the fore so that sometime during the night, the no-nonsense part of her character would compel her to somehow unhook herself free of the traction, slip gently, head-first, from the bed onto the floor and power herself on her elbows towards the door of her room, dragging her legs behind her. Two or three times she was discovered in the corridor outside, relentlessly making her way to the place where she believed there would be a car waiting to take her home.

'Bridget, it's of the utmost importance that you stay in bed. All night long,' I'd say in a hopeless quest to get through to her.

'But what is this thing on the end of my leg, Ben?' she'd say, pointing to the cable attached to her ankle, with a look of utter bewilderment.

'It's something that's pulling your leg to help it get better, so it heals in exactly the right position and–'

'But what on earth went wrong with it in the first place?'

'You broke it where it meets the pelvis.'

'Oh – I – see...'

A little later, the doubts were to set in about what I was reporting. 'Are you sure about that, Ben? Broken?'

'That's it, Bridget. Broken leg,' I'd say, with the idea that I might show her the X-rays coming into my mind and being discarded immediately as beyond pointless – it would be an explanation that would be taken on board for only as long as my visit.

'If it's such a nuisance, can't we just cut the damn leg *orff* and go home?'

～

She was a tough old bird, and the assessment made soon after the accident that she would never walk again, proved to be quite wrong. On the day she came home, Theresa and I helped her out of the ambulance I'd hired and up the two front steps into the hallway; she took in her surroundings, steadied herself for a moment within her walking frame, and then struck out with gusto down the hall, past the site of her accident, towards the drawing room. 'Alecky, I'm home! Coo-ee! Here I am!' she called out as she made her way towards the reunion with her husband who was standing waiting to greet her by his chair in the drawing room. They'd been apart for nearly three months; I watched, close to tears as Bridget dared to let go of her frame for a moment and put her arms around her husband.

In a matter of days, she'd not only conquered the stairs (one walking frame left at the bottom, another awaiting her arrival on the landing), but was spending time in her garden, though she showed a keen frustration when being reminded that she was not able to pick up and move her pots of geraniums. I always made sure that there was a carer hovering close by in case a wobble threatened to turn into something more dramatic. She'd often get overconfident and dispense with the walking frame. 'Bloody thing!' she'd say, pushing it away so that it clattered onto the York paving stones.

'Bridget! Please, please, no walking – no standing, even – without the walking frame!' I said to her one day at the end of May as I saw her weaving unsteadily across the lawn to inspect some begonias that Midge had just planted. 'Always Bridget with frame, Bridget with frame!'

'Why?'

'Because you might fall without it!' She looked quite perplexed and, five minutes later, she was crossing the lawn again, the walking frame held high above her head. Bridget with her frame as commanded, but not quite in the way I wanted it.

We were living in different times, and it wasn't long before Bridget's troubles became an endurance test for all of us, especially Alexander. Theresa and I handled it better – but we'd not been married to her for over sixty years.

The days of the joyous greeting wafting down the hall when I threw the keys into the bowl were over. Now, Bridget would be waiting for me, standing within her frame, so close to the front door that I would have to be careful not to knock her over as I opened it on my arrival. Somehow, she'd never fail to remember that I was coming, but then, having waited in the hall for hours, she'd quite forget that I was going to prepare dinner.

'Oh, thank God you're here, Ben! We've a real emergency – we've nothing in! I don't know what we're going to do. No one's done any shopping!' I was used to that, of course, but there was panic in her voice now, rather than anger and frustration. 'It's all right, Bridget – Theresa's left me stuff in the fridge for this evening and I'm going to Deal in the morning to stock up. Everything's all right, I promise you. Go back to the drawing room and just relax – I'm getting on with dinner now, and there's nothing for you to do or worry about. How about a nice glass of vodka a little earlier than usual?'

'Shopping's done? Thank God! And *you're* doing dinner, Ben? Oh, you are a dear...' I'd steer her back to the drawing room, greet Alexander, who'd be looking harassed, and pour them both a drink – still a lifesaver for Alexander but perhaps less so for Bridget these days, now that she was permanently adrift in her own version of purgatory. Drinks at 7 were brought well forward in an attempt (mostly successful) to calm fraught nerves, meaning that an enormous gin and tonic was now accompanying me back to the kitchen a good half hour before the old, appointed time. Needs must. But Bridget's relief would only last a few minutes before the panic would return, and, from the kitchen, I would hear the thump-shuffle-thump-shuffle-thump of the walking frame making contact with the floorboards in the hall as she was compelled to return to the kitchen. 'Coo-ee! Who's there? Is someone making dinner? I can't do it all by myself, I just can't...'

~

Before very long, we were settling into a sad routine that was never really to change. Bridget had physically rallied, but spent all her days in a trance of anxiety about food, shopping and bankruptcy, about 'that strange gypsy' (Theresa's boyfriend, Jerry) she'd see crossing the lawn every now and again, about where I was when I wasn't in Sandwich, and about the state of the roof – which was retiled absurdly slowly over the summer by a two-man outfit that had grossly underestimated the time it would take to complete the work on a listed building. They'd first arrived soon after Bridget's return, and were still there at the end of September, two not very young men growing more and more sullen as they endlessly lugged terracotta tiles onto the roof with bangings and hammerings going on from early morning till sunset and having to endure a ghastly row with an exasperated Alexander at least every third day. 'When the bloody hell are you going to be finished?' was a constant refrain delivered to the skies through the open French doors. Whenever one of the men came down the ladder from the roof into the garden, there would be a shocked outburst from Bridget that meant there would have to be an explanation – swiftly forgotten – about who these strange men were, what they were doing and why.

'But no one's told me about it!'

'Lord give me strength,' Alexander would mutter under his breath, especially when Bridget's confusion went a little further and led to the resurfacing of worries about Napoleon having set up camp in the garden with his spies on the roof, etc.

At the same time, she developed some rather ghastly little habits that even I found hard to endure. Settling ourselves at the table for dinner, she took to clearing her throat and then spitting into her soup before patting the corners of her mouth, ever so daintily, with her napkin. No words from me or Alexander seemed to make any difference and after some time I gave up serving soup for something more solid. It seemed to do the trick – quails' eggs were never spat upon, but Bridget's growing confusion about almost everything to do with dinner made the evening meal a mighty test of endurance.

'What are these great big things under the table?'

'Oh Jesus, here we go,' Alexander would say with a sigh.

'They're Alexander's shoes, sweetheart,' I'd say.

'But what on earth are they doing here?' she'd reply, prodding hard at the offending items with her husband's stick.

'Well, just at the moment, Alexander's feet are in them…'

∼

I'd been advised that a strictly adhered-to timetable might help Bridget ground herself a little, and I did my best to comply. There was coffee and chats at 11 in the drawing room, like the old days, which Bridget would somehow never forget to attend, however confused she was about everything else. She'd wait for my arrival and after we'd finished, a game of patience would be set out on the tray once I'd removed the cups and sugar bowl; lunch was served dead on 1 after a glass of sherry and a few choice articles had been read from the paper to Alexander, with Bridget glad of my voice whether she understood or not. More patience before teatime at 4, now always prepared and overseen by me after a shortened walk, and then the never-changing routine of the *Daily Telegraph* crossword, which had given both my old friends the greatest joy ever since I first met them. Now, though, Alexander would be slumped forward in his chair, his forehead resting on his stick as he half-heartedly took part, with Bridget repeating the same clue time and time again. 'They've obviously got a new man,' she'd say, when the answers eluded her, which, as time went on, was more and more often. I'd go back to the cottage then; a little time to myself before dinner for which we invariably still dressed – it was noted if ever I let standards slip.

'Not dressing for dinner, tonight, Ben?' said Bridget to me as I summoned them into the dining room on a night when I'd been rushed off my feet and had inadvertently left my jacket hanging over a chair in the kitchen.

'Well – since Alexander is wearing his suit jacket with his pyjama bottoms, and you are wearing your frock both inside out and back to front, I thought perhaps an element of informality was being permitted this evening…'

'Grand Guignol, Grand Guignol,' Alexander said, laughing aloud for the first time in a long while.

But soon after that, at the end of the summer, he'd had enough and started to spend an increasing amount of time in his room, not only weary of the repeated conversations that we were all subjected to, but also, I believe, guilty at his impatience and reactions to a situation that he found too difficult to deal with. Theresa informed me that when I was not there, he would sometimes only bother to dress and come down once it was time for the pre-lunch glass of sherry.

∽

I had a permanent headache that summer. Port is a notorious creator of hangovers, and I'd made up my mind to keep Alexander company and as happy as I could, which meant that our standing order for wine and port from Averys of Bristol had to be revised upwards. It was worth it, to witness him rally a little after Bridget was escorted off to bed every night, though it sometimes meant that I would spend the morning in a haze while having to deal with pressing concerns, especially having to endure the incessant noise from the roof while I dealt with the paperwork around the Lloyd's names debacle that we had so mercifully just managed to avoid.

'Holy shit, Alexander,' I remember saying to him in the study downstairs at Eaton Square years before, 'why are all you nobs taking the risk of losing your shirts for the sake of a tax wheeze? Unlimited liability? Totally mad, in this litigious age. It's only going to get worse, you know. Bad, bad idea!'

'We all do it. I've made tens of thousands...'

'But you and your mates stand to lose *hundreds* of thousands, perhaps millions. "A sound, almost blue-chip investment", this thing says. I don't think so. Bonkers idea,' I said, making my point by waving a glossy brochure that had just arrived in front of his face, creating a waft of air that made him blink.

'You know nothing about it, Ben. It's been going on for hundreds of years. Since the time of the South Sea Bubble.'

'Fuck me – not a good example if I might remind you of how all that ended up!'

Incredible that he was to take my advice, since he was quite right about me knowing so little about it, but very soon after our conversation, I was sending out handwritten letters to the syndicates he'd belonged to for years, informing them that he wished to withdraw as soon as possible.

One of the best bits of service I'd ever done for my old friends, even though I had little idea at the time of just how immense it was. By the time I was packing up the house in Eaton Square, the 'insurance' train was hitting the buffers hard. First, there were the plethora of asbestosis and environmental claims, followed by the Exxon Valdez oil spill, Hurricane Hugo, Bhopal and everything else. The world had changed, and Alexander got out of the one or two worst affected syndicates just in time, though we had to keep our nerve when the letters from the panicking administrators started to arrive, disputing the dates of his withdrawals. Yarnton, Alexander's old stockbroker, was one of his friends who, by 1990, was heading for ruin. He'd phoned me while Bridget was still away, remembering that I'd talked to him about an acquaintance whose girlfriend was the editor of a knitting magazine.

'Look, old chap, I'm just wondering whether your friend the publisher might like an article I've written about fly fishing in Scotland. I'm turning my hand to a bit of writing now.' Desperate times, poor soul. Quite recently, I had delivered a bottle of whisky from Alexander to his flat in Chelsea where I was confronted by a broken-down old man who I hardly recognised in a sitting room stripped of anything of value. Windows crying out for a clean, damask curtains shredded by sunlight from top to bottom, walls denuded of his much-prized collection of Munnings sketches and an ancient fitted carpet, very faded but for large patches of its original colour now seeing the light of day after the removal of some fine old rugs.

'It doesn't have to be fly fishing, you know. I can write about a lot of things if you think you can point my jottings in the right direction. I know an awful lot about the raising of Merino sheep...' He wasn't the only one we knew who was in trouble. I went to visit Bridget's old friend Mrs Martin, the widow of a Tory MP and golfing friend of Alexander's who'd once had a home in The High Street. Her son had been a member of one of the worst affected syndicates and had had to sell practically everything he owned; he'd been forced to relocate his mother from a wonderfully comfortable room in Sandwich Bay with a view of the sea, to a much more affordable 'bin' in Canterbury. I went to visit her quite soon after her move; she was very muddled, not quite sure of who either of us was, but unlike Bridget, mercifully appeared not to be at all unhappy; we sat talking nonsense over a very milky cup of tea and a ginger biscuit, and I was grateful that she didn't seem to mind, or even know about her change of circumstances – her small, overheated room overlooked a car park, beyond which was a stream with an upturned child's buggy in it, its wheels poking up above the surface of the water.

∼

'I'm ready for you!' Some time at the end of November, a little while after the cacophony from the roof had ended, I'd triumphantly summoned Alexander, who'd been waiting in the sitting room for me. A final victory over Lloyd's, the end of a nightmare! It hadn't come at all naturally to me, the two-fingered tapping on the electric typewriter borrowed from the solicitor's office, but now I'd completed the last two letters to the syndicates; I'd abandoned my handwritten letters and filled up waste-paper basket after waste-paper basket in a quest for typed perfection and had finally got there. Two handsome pages of A4, both awaiting a signature. Alexander tapped his way with his stick along the hall from the drawing room and I gently manoeuvred him into the chair in front of the desk, placing the pen in his hand and lowering it towards the paper. 'So finally, Alexander, two letters – one to Gooda Walker, concerning 298, and the other relating to RJ Bromley 475. It's the end of the matter, that's for sure. We've done everything to the letter of the law – Goodrights are confirming both syndicates don't have a leg to stand on and will insist that they'll have to pay any costs. They have absolutely no claim on any of our money. This is just a formality – something with your signature that basically says, "Fuck off and we're out of here!"'

'You are a marvel, Ben. We'd very possibly be out on

the street if I'd ignored your advice all those years ago, you know...'

An oversized signature was delivered to my first letter, starting off horizontal before dipping perilously towards the bottom of the page. Blotting paper then, and the same slanted signature was applied to the second. I felt like an enormously proud ADC, standing respectfully behind a victorious field marshal and his defeated enemy before collecting up the all-important signed documents of surrender. When he'd finished, Alexander slowly and deliberately screwed back the top of the pen and placed it to the side of the blotter, but it rolled towards the edge and fell onto the Persian carpet.

'By the way,' he said as I bent to pick up the pen, 'Owen's dead.'

'Owen who?'

'My son. Owen, my son.' The pen dropped out of my hand, this time hitting the floorboards before noisily skittling away under the desk as though it was taking refuge from what had just been said.

'Good God, Alexander! I'm so, so sorry. What on earth happened? When did you hear?'

'This morning. Yarnton called. I don't want to talk about it.' A pause. 'What's for lunch?'

'Erm... cottage pie. Is Bridget in the drawing room? I must go to her...'

~

I sat in the armchair outside the drawing room for a little while, taking deep breaths and wondering what on earth I was going to say to a mother who had just heard she'd lost her son. Eventually, I went in and sat down beside her on the sofa while she continued with her game of patience, for a while not seeming to be conscious of my presence. 'Are you all right, Bridget?' I said, clumsily taking her hand and squeezing it in mine.

'What?'

'Alexander has just told me the news. About Owen.'

'Oh yes, he's dead now, isn't he?' she said, returning the card that I'd inadvertently crushed in her hand to the others on the tray in front of her. She looked out across the lawn.

'He lived here once, I think, didn't he?'

~

Months went by; I don't remember them well because nothing very dramatic happened for quite a while, though there was a steady but slow decline in both the 'patients' (as Theresa and I found ourselves calling them) rather than a graph tumbling earthwards at an alarming rate. If I'd ever talked it through with Theresa, we might have referred to that time as a holding operation, though, of course, we knew where it was all inevitably heading. There was the odd event that shook us up, that we thought might be heralding the end – soon after Owen's death, Bridget had to have a tooth removed because of an abscess that sent her so doolally I thought she wouldn't get over it; having endured an agonising night that saw me back in the bed at the end of the hall, she had the culprit molar removed and then returned for three nights to the same nursing clinic that she'd tried to escape from after her fall. Whilst there, she shouted to the staff in schoolgirl French, was bothered by Napoleon again, insisting that a cavalry regiment was galloping back and forth across the wall opposite her bed, and demanded a bedpan because she was quite sure that the white thing below the lavatory seat in her en suite was a huge mouth that was going to take a bite out of her.

She rallied, though – as did Alexander who fell while getting out of bed one winter night, cracking his head badly on the bedside table. Yvonne, the carer for the night, knocked at my cottage door in the early hours wrapped in a cloak with a hood against a howling gale – looking like a figure from a Brontë novel – to tell me that 'His Lordship has fallen over, and I can't raise him from the ground.' A very black eye was to follow the next day, but a few paracetamol soon had him sat up in bed, twitching the radio dials and telling us to 'stop all this fussing, for God's sake!' It's part of my nature, I suppose, that following Yvonne back to the house with my heart in my shoes, I was already preparing a funeral before feeling silly about it the next day.

Bridget took to falling now and again, but mercifully, we always got away with it. 'Yer boss is rollin' aroon' on the green,' Jerry, Theresa's Scottish boyfriend announced to us one morning in the kitchen. Interrupting her game of patience, she had managed to open the French doors in the sitting room while Alexander dozed in his chair, wandered out without her frame and had keeled over on the lawn. The garden was a constant temptation to her; sometime later, I was sitting at the desk in the hall with my paperwork before lunch when I heard a gentle – but rather insistent – tapping coming from the door into the garden. Nothing seemed amiss at first, but on looking through the glass panel at ground level I saw Bridget hard up against the door like a draught excluder. 'All I had to do was roll and roll and roll across the lawn and here I am. Get me up, dear boy, will you...' Again, no damage done, and quite a good strategy for getting about if one's walking frame was out of reach.

The gnawing anxiety was forever taking its toll on her, though, however brave a face she tried to present. I could see the total bewilderment at what was happening to her that accompanied the panic that had set in to ruin her last few years.

'Really, Ben – what *is* the point of it all?' she said to me one afternoon as Alexander eased himself up from his chair and shuffled out into the hall without words, driven out once again by the endless repeating of crossword clues.

'What do you mean, Bridget?'

'This life. This awful ending to a life – it's quite intolerable. Only a sadist would inflict this on someone.'

'Oh, come on, sweetheart. You still love your games of patience and your coffee, and a lovely glass of vod in the evening, don't you?'

'No, Ben, it's not enough. And *I've* had enough, I really have...'

I wondered how long I'd have kept her going without the stay in the nursing home in the bay. I'm not blaming Alexander and Theresa for being tempted to move her for that long weekend while I was away. Perhaps I would have agreed to it too, had I been in Sandwich and at the end of several combining tethers.

～

In the cottage that morning, I'd given up on sleep in the early hours, disturbed all night by the unhappy vision of the previous day – Bridget tossing and turning in the overheated, airless room at the nursing home in the bay. I dressed, deciding on a quick cup of coffee in Clarence House before driving down to the bay to sit with her, hoping my presence would calm her more than it had the day before. As I sat alone in the kitchen, I heard the soft timbre of Theresa's voice coming from Alexander's bedroom. She was sitting on the side of the bed, holding his hand in both hers, which was not something I'd ever witnessed before.

'Good heavens – you're an early bird this morning, Theresa!' I said as breezily as I could, while trying to ignore a feeling of rising panic. I took a breath then, collecting myself for startling news.

'Tell him, Theresa,' Alexander said, without a pause.

'Ben, I have bad news. Her Ladyship passed during the night. The matron just phoned a few minutes ago…'

'Oh my God, Alexander, I'm so sorry. Oh God. I wanted to be with her…'

∽

I think I arranged her send-off pretty well, seeing that I'd never done anything like it before. Only a little band of relatives and my helpers from the house were there, since everyone that Bridget knew was now dead or too old and frail to make the journey through the fog to the middle of Kent. The service was held in a soulless, red-bricked crematorium, with its sparse arrangements of dried flowers inside and frosty, dormant roses bordering the car park outside. We laboured our way through a hymn, a prayer was intoned by a smiley clergyman with a shiny bald pate who referred to someone called 'Briony' rather than Bridget for the duration of the service; I did a little reading ('I have only slipped away into the next room. Nothing has happened...') that I'd tried to choose carefully but would have meant very little to my sweet friend in her coffin waiting patiently to be on her way. The old Bridget would have said it was all quite ridiculous but she might just have been pleased with the spread of sandwiches, cake and tea that I'd arranged in the pub across the road after the service.

Twelve of us, I think, including a middle-aged niece – daughter of the broken-down old baronet who was Bridget's brother – with a quarrelsome reputation, accompanied by her daughter who was interrupting her studies at Edinburgh University to attend. Her memories of her great aunt meant her face was mostly obscured during the ceremony by a large hanky. I loved her for her tears – I felt the same way but was too preoccupied to be able to join her. I wanted to get it right, this day; I'd already said my goodbyes, though. I'd left the house the day before and gone to sit beside the coffin in the undertakers in the high street where I'd assured Bridget that in her absence I would look after Alexander as well as I possibly could. An hour passed with me resting my hand on the coffin while talking to a dead person without once feeling silly; the pre-dementia Bridget would definitely have thought I was giving in to nonsense.

I never mentioned it to Alexander, who might well have been furious, but through Yarnton, I contacted Ella, Owen's eldest daughter, and let her know that as far as I was concerned, she was more than welcome to attend her grandmother's funeral. She arrived in Sandwich the evening before the service, and we arranged to meet in the bar of the local hotel. I was nervous of meeting her, slightly unsure of my decision to go behind Alexander's back, but was immediately put at ease by the tall, very beautiful young woman. She greeted me with a kiss to both cheeks before thanking me effusively for arranging for her to stay with an old friend of the Bellaghys who felt I was doing the right thing by inviting her and wanted to support my decision. It turned out to be one of the best decisions I've ever made. Our deep friendship, born of my secret invitation, endures to this day and was one of the greatest gifts that Alexander unwittingly bestowed upon me.

Perhaps my efforts made up just a little for the fact I wasn't with Bridget when she died. I have to work on forgiving myself for that; it felt like some sort of dereliction of duty, though no one blamed me for my absence, just me.

I don't quite know how it was that I was able to persuade Alexander not to attend the funeral; I'd imagined that I had no chance of dissuading him, but in the end, I think he realised that it would be an almost impossible task for him, unsteady on his feet and bumping into people he couldn't see who he'd have to be reminded of, including the niece that he couldn't abide. A tentative suggestion of a wheelchair was met by a stony silence, as though the idea was so preposterous that it didn't merit an answer. I mentioned it once and knew not to do so again. 'I'm going to be there for both of us, Alecky,' I said later, for the one and only time using Bridget's pet name for him, 'because I just don't believe you have to put yourself through this ordeal. It's too much for you to deal with,' I added, observing an old man definitely rather grateful that I was making my point so firmly.

Theresa and I had left Alexander alone in his chair in the drawing room to go to the funeral together. I'd felt a keen panic as we drove back to Sandwich through the darkening Kent countryside, suddenly aware of my old friend waiting for us to return from his wife's funeral. Yvonne had suddenly been struck down by a migraine; it was too late for us to find a replacement carer, which meant leaving him utterly alone at the last minute. 'I'll be fine. I'll be fine. Off you go!' he'd insisted, perhaps glad to be left with his own thoughts for a while. At first, the blackness and silence we encountered on our return made me panic that he wasn't there, but as I entered the drawing room and turned on the light, I found him sitting bolt upright in his chair, his stick in its usual place between his knees and his unseeing eyes wide open. I sat cross-legged on the carpet at his feet then, neither of us saying anything at all until Theresa came in with a cup of tea for us.

'Tell me what happened, Ben. Tell me all about it,' he said eventually. I recounted every detail to him – apart from the presence of his granddaughter – even making him laugh a little about the niece berating me for arranging the funeral for a time that meant that tea rather than lunch had been served. 'Typical Claudette – typical!'

A little later, when I heard Theresa laying the table in the dining room, I'd reached up from my position at his feet to take his hand.

'The last year or so was ghastly for her, Alexander, you know that – and very hard for all of us; for you, of course, but also for Theresa and our little band of helpers who were all quite devoted to her. But it was hardest of all on her, you know. She'd had enough, she really had.'

Alexander nodded slowly, allowing himself to agree with my words. 'She would be thrilled to be out of it, I promise you. And do you know what I'm going to do now? I'm going to go down to the cellar to get a bottle of Moët which I'll put in the freezer, and while it's cooling, I'm going to have a bath. When Theresa calls us into dinner, I'm going to open the bottle, pour three glasses, and then you, Theresa and I will make a toast to sweet Bridget and wish her God speed…'

∽

They were desperate, unhappy times, those ten months after Bridget's death. Christmas was upon us almost as soon as we'd recovered from the funeral, and I took the decision to stay with Alexander alone while Theresa spent the holiday with her family in Glasgow. I thought it wouldn't be a great sacrifice for me – I'd be avoiding the usual thing of turning up at the very last minute to Pa's underheated house in Woking on Christmas Eve where we'd watch repeats of *Morecambe and Wise* with me laughing a little too loudly in order to hide the fact that there was nothing in particular that either of us had to say to each other. I'd be silently counting down the minutes to departure once the 'cold collation' had been consumed on Boxing Day. God – those two evenings of looking at my empty glass and wondering how long I might leave it before asking whether there 'might be a chance of a refill.' 'Help yourself, boy. Don't bother asking,' Pa would say without averting his eyes from the telly. But difficult to ask, for some reason. Family history, perhaps. No such pretence in Sandwich, of course, where I was master of the cellar.

But it was awful, that last Christmas in Sandwich, truly awful. I'd arrived the day before Christmas Eve in time to see Theresa on her way, a turkey crown and all the trimmings in the boot of my car, having shopped in Marks and Spencer's a day or two before. I ate alone though, late on Christmas afternoon after Alexander had refused to come down from his room. I sat in the dining room, a napkin over my lap with an unpulled cracker above my plate while I served myself a lonely Christmas dinner with the sound of his radio wheezing its way down to me from his room. Early in the evening, I managed to persuade him to try a small portion of turkey together with a glass of champagne, taken up on a tray. I'd decorated it with a little sprig of holly that he quite rightly complained about when it drew a pinprick of blood from his thumb as he grabbed it thinking it was a spoon.

'I want to listen to the radio,' he said rather crossly as I applied a Kleenex to the wound. 'Alone!'

'It's Christmas Day and you're allowed to do whatever you want, so I'll leave you to it and bring you another glass later,' I said, relieved to be returning to the company of the television downstairs.

I spent the rest of the long, miserable evening quite alone, not having to bother laughing at the same sort of telly that I would have been watching with Pa, while telling myself off for wishing so hard to be tucked up in the cosy little cottage across the street that I'd abandoned for the duration of the festivities.

∽

'Piping hot coffee, Alexander,' I announced as I opened the door to his room the next morning.

'Who the devil are *you*?'

I thought at first that he'd come round, that this was a little joke to cover up the awfulness of the day before – but the surprise and outrage on his face persisted, reminding me of the ghastliness of Bridget's last few months. I did what I usually do in times like these – I stepped out of the room, closed the door, screwed up my eyes and prayed this was not happening. Then I took a breath and went back in to confront a new situation. It wasn't actually the first time that he'd been a bit confused, but this was on another level, and I was freaked by it; we were alone in the house together, he was angry and confused – and I immediately had to deal with the situation while feeling as bereft, scared and lonely as I had been the night of Bridget's fall.

'Whoever you are – I want you to phone my mother and tell her to send the car over to fetch me. I've had enough of all this!' Round and round in circles the conversation went as I tried to persuade him that he was in bed in his own house and that I was his best friend.

'I want my mother to send her car round NOW!'

'Alexander,' I said finally, 'how old are you?'

'I'm ninety. *You* know that perfectly well!'

'Ah! So you do know who I am!'

'Of course I do – I'm not demented!'

'And so, if you're ninety, how old do you think your mother might be now?' A long silence and a grudging return to sanity. An apology followed later, and an admission by lunchtime that he was 'really rather muddled this morning.'

'Hope I'm not going the way of Bridget…'

But I'm not sure I ever really got him back after that; something had gone forever after that Boxing Day morning. It wasn't that the dementia was an issue – it certainly never reoccurred in quite as dramatic a way, though I know from that moment that I was never free of the dread of having to deal with it again. Perhaps things had changed before that, and it was this occurrence that brought it home to me. I'd always prided myself, in those last few years, with being able to change his mood whatever the circumstances, as though I was a skilled fisherman reeling in a struggling catch from some toxic lake before transferring it to sweeter waters. But there was precious little I could do in those last months to make it all right for him, and I was keenly aware of that. The only job left for me to do was, with Theresa's help, to look after his physical needs.

After Christmas, there was only the most infrequent of forays from his room to join me downstairs – no more arm-in-arm walks, no more laughter or readings from the *Daily Telegraph*, no suggestions of the opening of another bottle because there was still too much to talk about. Just a silent, unhappy old man, confusing night and day in his darkness, propped up in bed half listening to his radio, with his broad hands stretched over the quilt in front of him as the sadness and loneliness flowed out of the room and made its way down the stairs to fill every corner of the house.

EPILOGUE

I rush down to Sandwich, full of the most overwhelming feelings of guilt. When I open the front door, I'm poised to throw the car keys into the Chinese bowl, but it's no longer there. I look around and gasp with shock when I see that the house has been stripped of all its contents – it's been transformed into a desolate, dark place reeking of betrayal and disappointment; there are threateningly low beams that I don't remember, strategically placed to knock me out, and the staircase twists and turns on its way upwards; it narrows into a hardened artery, constricting me from both sides. With a pounding chest, I reach the landing outside Alexander's room. Then I hear a familiar sound.

'Coo-ee!' Bridget, in her nightie, is standing in the corridor just outside the door to her bedroom, white-knuckled hands grasping her walking frame. A full moon, shining through the window behind her, silhouettes her.

'We're both still here, and we're so pleased to see you, dear Ben. Where have you been? We've been waiting for months on end for you. Why haven't you been to see us? We've missed you so much. We've nothing in for supper, though, so I don't know what we'll do...'

I walk up to her and kiss her cheek. Over her shoulder, through the half-open door, I catch sight of Alexander inside her bedroom. He's wearing a filthy grey suit and is lying on a bare, stained mattress, the only thing in the room apart from a white stick that lies beside it on the floorboards. He's kicking his legs about in a vain effort to sit up.

'Good Lord, Alexander – what's happened? Why's the house empty? Where on earth is all the furniture?'

'You've got it, Ben. You packed it up and took it all away, don't you remember? But it doesn't matter; we're just so pleased to see you – so pleased and relieved.'

I had that recurring nightmare two or three times a week for a year after Alexander died. It had a quality of such intense reality that I would wake up sweating, struggling to return to myself and to identify the room I'd woken up in. It eased over the months, of course, but took its time; I was settling into my new house and still a little bit of a stranger in it – sitting on the edge of my crisply new sofa not yet feeling that I quite belonged in a brand new and rather opulent setting. Early on, the dream forced me to leave my bed in the middle of the night so I could fully wake up before starting the process of wondering why I was being haunted by my old friends. They were both dead, and I was still dreaming of them alive – alone, abandoned, frightened. I spent months asking myself whether I was guilty of something truly shocking; was the dream accusing me of something? Was I the conniving perpetrator of some plan of deception?

It wasn't that, though, I know it now. It was much simpler – my subconscious was accusing me of not really caring, hinting that I'd forgotten about them, that's all;

I'd shunted them to one side in order get on with my new life – and so every now and again I was being tapped on the shoulder and reminded of how much the three of us had meant to each other.

Sitting on the side of my bed having woken from the dream, I'd endlessly tell myself I had nothing to be ashamed of – even though I'd prospered mightily. It's what Alexander had always intended, after all. Everything about my future (and theirs) had been properly arranged after extensive, open discussions. The whole thing couldn't have been tidier.

The dream became less intrusive over time. After a while, I was able to dismiss it by a move from one side of the bed to the other, rather than having to take a calming flannel to my face in the bathroom. Weeks could go by without it, but then there would be a spate of visitations, though there would be a subtle variation as it tried to catch me unawares by using a change of location. I'd find myself summoned to a lonely old mansion in a wooded valley that leads down to the sea – shades of Manderley crossed with Wuthering Heights. A gale would torture the trees that surround the house into grotesque shapes and whip the sea below into mountainous waves; I'd have to bend my shoulder to the door to force it open, battling wind and unyielding wood. When I felt my way with outstretched arms through the pitch black, I'd come across a staircase and climb it; a ghostly Bridget would then reveal herself, waiting for me on some unfamiliar landing by a door into a room that would then turn out to be the same as the one in Sandwich. And there Alexander would be, illuminated by moonlight in the empty room, lying helpless on the mattress.

Now and again, the dream would summon me to the apartment in Paris where I'd sneak past the disapproving Madame Forestier, run up the five flights with great trepidation, realising, as I unlocked the door, what I was going to be presented with. I'd walk into Alexander's bedroom, but it had once again been transformed from Paris to Bridget's room in Sandwich, empty but for Bridget in her nightdress, the white stick on the floorboards and my old friend in his grey suit stretched out on the mattress.

For a whole year after they'd gone, somewhere in my head I carried on accusing myself of neglecting them. No lying or cheating, theft or fraud – I'd just put my dead friends to one side and moved on to embrace a new life free of the responsibility of looking after them. I don't know why, but even now, after all these years, perhaps I still feel a little that way. The dream still visits me every so often, though the intensity has faded, like a painting from the drawing room in Sandwich that Bridget had failed to protect from the sun.

∽

Sandwich, January 1996

Jesus. Three months since Alexander died. There wouldn't be time for grief even if I was feeling it, which I'm not. I'm just not. Is that peculiar? I'm lost in it still, telling myself off and lying about it because it seems so heartless not to be feeling bereft. How the fuck did I turn into this person? But I'm being hard on myself, I know that. I am beginning to see that it is impossible not to find relief in the fact that Alexander's death finally allows three old friends to escape from a very difficult situation.

I've returned to my cottage; Clarence House was just too big and empty and cold without Alexander and Bridget, and since Theresa and her boyfriend packed up and left on New Year's Eve, this little place has become my haven once again, just as it was before I moved back into the big house last Easter to be close to Alexander. So much to be done, but I knew I could deal with what was facing me only if I could spend my nights here – though that's not going to be for very much longer, either. I put this little place on the market the day Theresa left, and I've already accepted an offer. Clarence House will be next, too. It's not under offer yet, but it will go in the next few weeks. *'A beautiful, early Georgian house with six bedrooms. Ideally located in the old town of Sandwich, conveniently near to the famous Royal St George's golf course, this property of a noble gentleman with a stunning garden is in need of just a little attention to bring it up to standard,'* the estate agent's blurb says. All sorts of nobs – banking types, retiring brigadiers and QCs, all mad on golf – are being shown around, so it won't be long.

I shall be gone soon, too. I didn't have to think very long about staying in Sandwich – I'm quite sure I'll never be interested in golf and the sort of old people who are. 'Not my goings-on,' as Bridget would have said. Nothing but memories to keep me here, which isn't a recipe for a future. So – how's this for pressing down full on the accelerator? I've already made an offer on a house in

Clapham! I couldn't resist it, having seen it and fallen on the place with a notebook and measuring tape to check if all the bits and pieces I wanted to keep from Sandwich could be accommodated in the gaps either side of fireplaces and windows, etc, and to make sure there was acres of free wall space for prints and paintings. It has fabulous high ceilings and cornices and mouldings to die for. But why the hell am I in such a fucking hurry? I'm behaving like a spoilt child who wants his ice lolly right now – and I'm not sure if I'm much taken with that person.

Okay, there's a little bit of justification for my haste. A few days before Alexander's funeral, Theresa was woken during the night by what sounded like clunky footsteps on the roof. She'd opened a creaky door at the top of the staircase into the attic, shone a torch onto a window and sworn to me that she'd seen two legs in shadow outside being hauled upwards and out of sight; there were three or four smashed tiles outside the garden door the next morning. Obvious, isn't it? Big house, newly dead owner, full of lovely things, sometimes uninhabited with ex-staff coming and going. A sitting duck.

So, I've had to get a move on, and now, already, the house is empty but for a few odds and ends that I'll get a local clearance company to deal with in the next day or two. Everything has been packed up after being valued by Christie's and finally taken away today by a removals firm made up of rather jolly, well-formed young Australian backpackers on their gap year. There have been agonising decisions about what I'm putting into storage to reach my new house later, and what will go to auction, though I've already taken some of the stuff back to the flat in

London after surreptitiously filling the car in the garage and leaving after nightfall. I've felt like a pirate, slipping out of harbour in the dead of night with a treasure chest full of goodies. Paintings and prints, candelabras, porcelain, a Georgian mirror, column lamps, carriage clocks, Persian rugs, books, snuff boxes and busts. At times, I've hardly been able to close the car windows, let alone the boot – if the police stop me, I'm likely to be hauled off to the local station for questioning and no doubt will find myself stuttering incomprehensively because I'm sure I'm guilty of something, though I'm not quite sure what it is.

My flat must look extraordinary, as though it belongs to an old Prussian aristocrat – forget the pirate – who's escaped from the advancing Red Army, having loaded up his carts with as many heirlooms as he could before striking west from the ancestral estate; he's squeezed his treasured possessions into a space not nearly big enough or grand enough to accommodate them all. I've cleared it with Barnes, of course. The estate is under probate – which might well be another word for limbo. He told me very early on that all Alexander's goods and chattels belong to me but that has yet to be 'proved' – I can move around the assets, etc, as long as there's a comprehensive list and it's quite clear where everything is. Only another week or two before it's all settled; Barnes says we've done well, and probate will be one of the shortest he can remember. That side of things has been as straightforward as Alexander intended.

Three months on and perhaps bits of the old friend that I remember from before those last wretched eighteen months begin to return to me. When I think of Alexander, a hint of a smile is now and again superimposed on the lifeless features I last saw on his pillow; I've found myself beginning to laugh at old anecdotes that have come back to me as I've picked my way through the house wearing gloves and with a knotted scarf round my neck – the heating's off and so it's freezing in there. Now and again, I've come close to tears as I've gone about my work, but it's the sadness of the emptying house that catches me in the throat, not the memory of my old friend. Perhaps it's enough, for the moment, that I'm amused when I remember him regaling me with stories.

I came across his old golf clubs in the attic last week. I haven't been sure what to do with them and they belong to a time in Alexander's life when I didn't know him – his glaucoma had already put paid to his game before I came along. I'm going to take them to the clubhouse tomorrow. Yes, of course I could sell them, but perhaps they might make a nice present to some promising young chap down there who'll really appreciate the gift? Something for the secretary to decide upon. They have an old-fashioned air, even to me who knows nothing of golf, but I'm doing the right thing.

The sight of them had me sitting down on the dusty old abandoned armchair on which I'd found them while I recalled the story Alexander told me about accompanying the Duke of Windsor down to the clubhouse in the early fifties soon after the Queen had succeeded to the throne – they'd met up after some ceremonial involving Sir Winston at Walmer Castle during one of the duke's rare visits to the country after he and the duchess had settled in Paris, and thought they might fit in a game. As Alexander and the duke entered the dining room at

Royal St George's for lunch, all the old colonels had got up from their seats and made for the door in disgust. 'Bloody quitter!' one enraged old soul with a face red with anger had spluttered as he passed his former monarch. They'd been friends ever since their prep-school days, though Alexander was adamant that a bullet had been dodged with the abdication; the duke was not up to being king, he told me – 'All those cabinet papers returning to No. 10 from the palace in their red boxes, stained with rings of whisky where the King had put down his glass during a party. You really couldn't take him seriously.' During one of our port evenings, he told me that a little while after the clubhouse incident he'd met up with the duke again at the British Embassy in Rome – for a commemoration of the Irish Guards at Anzio – and had later somehow found himself accompanying him to the crypt of St Peter's Basilica to visit the grave of the Old Pretender and his two sons. Alexander and the ex-crowned head of the usurping Hanoverian dynasty had stood together, heads bowed, at the tomb of the last Stuarts. 'A little brush with history,' the duke had said to him.

I spent the rest of the afternoon up there, going through old photograph albums that I'd never seen before, full of unfamiliar faces, but with the names written below in Bridget's hand, jogging memories of people and places that Alexander had told me about over the years; hunting weekends in Ireland, tall-masted yachts in Greek island harbours and croquet players on the lawn in Shere; there were pictures of Owen, with nannies, with cousins, on his first day at school, Owen in a large toy tin racing car wearing goggles, pictures of a bright-eyed boy with curly red hair and freckles, wearing a bow-tie – '*HIS NIBS'S SEVENTH BIRTHDAY PARTY!!*' was printed in capitals below. What to do with records of a family that mean nothing to anyone apart from the person who had so diligently worked on putting them together? I've decided to take them with me, to keep them together with the ashes I collected from the undertakers a few days after the funeral. Last spring, a few months after her death, I scattered Bridget's in the garden she loved so much, but for the time being, Alexander's are going to stay with me.

As the attic room grew dark, I threw the bag of golf clubs back onto the armchair; an already compromised leg collapsed under the weight and the chair tipped backwards, crashing into something propped against the wall behind. They were five large mezzotints covered with a blanket, leaning up against the very damp wall beneath the window. There's a crack in the glass of one of them after the little accident, but apart from that, they're in really good condition, considering that they've been left standing under a leaky window for as long as I've been coming down to Sandwich. How on earth was it that Alexander had never mentioned them to me when he was so proud of his collection? He was usually so diligent about cataloguing them all. I laid them out carefully on the dusty wooden floorboards for an inspection – more horses, more generals and sons of George III – and I was as thrilled as a small child to find them, because I've inherited the bug from their owner. 'I'm so glad you get the point of them, Ben,' he used to say to me. The sight took me away from the attic in Sandwich back to the hallway at Eaton Square on the very first night I met Alexander; he's leaning up against the wall opposite a row of his fabulous mezzotints, arms folded. A comprehensive lecture about printmaking in the late eighteenth century is being delivered to an entirely receptive audience of one, and as I remember his enthusiasm to educate his young visitor, I'm smiling again, perhaps for the first time since he died.

∼

'I think, you know, that this might be it,' the agency night nurse had said to me and Anne when we entered the bedroom at the end of her shift. It was very early morning; I'd sat at the end of his bed with a bottle of port through the night, listening as Alexander's pattern of breathing had changed. Now, his heels had turned a dark crimson and there was the strangest aroma filling the room, of damp autumn leaves, tobacco and cleaning fluid – a hodge-podge of smells masking something else, sinister and sweet. A bit of me didn't believe what was obviously going to happen in the next few hours; I could hear Alexander's voice from as far back as I can remember, saying 'Can't be more than a few months now, just a few months.' Why would this day be any different? Might it just be that Alexander was immortal, and we'd carry on with our way of life forever? Except that our old way of life was already over, of course.

Whether I believed it or not, I was outside the solicitor's office at nine that Friday morning, doing my best to ignore the port-induced hangover that was gnawing at my brain as I waited to inform Mr Barnes, who had drawn up the will, that Alexander was dying. We sprang into action, visiting the bank and using our power of attorney (Barnes and I were joint executors) to transfer all Alexander's funds to his current account. I can't remember exactly why, all this time later, but it was something to do with making sure that since our power of attorney enabled us to write cheques, a large sum would be available to us during probate, so that any death duties could be paid immediately to avoid interest on what the estate owed.

'Gosh, seems a little bit calculating,' I said to Barnes as we left the bank manager's office having achieved what we'd set out to do.

'Not at all. We're His Lordship's executors and we're efficiently fulfilling our duties as he would have expected, that's all.' But even before my dear old friend was dead, I was taking action to safeguard something that was to benefit me. Busy, busy me.

∼

Alexander had died as I stepped into his room sometime around midday, having been summoned by some unknown force from the garden. I was transfixed for a minute, conscious of the sound of my own breath and the silent stillness of the body of my old friend in front of me. I stood at the end of the bed for a short while then took his warm hand, and kissed his forehead; a few minutes later, Anne, the carer who'd been helping me during Theresa's absence, placed her hands on my shoulders and guided me, as I'd guided Alexander for these last years, downstairs into the sitting room where, having sat me down, she poured me a large whisky.

'I think you're entitled to a drink, too, Anne,' I said, suddenly aware that my hand was shaking so badly I was in danger of spilling the contents of the glass.

'I'll have one later, thank you, Ben. First things first – we need you to phone the doctor; he'll come and issue the death certificate, and when we've got that, we can phone the undertakers in the high street. Are you all right with that? The same ones who did for Her Ladyship last year?'

'Yes, that's fine, Anne. Thank God you're here. I wouldn't have any idea how to go about this...'

∼

'Ah, we've lost His Lordship, have we? I'm so sorry, Mr Teasdale. Are you all managing there?' The receptionist's voice at the other end of the line in the surgery was almost a whisper – out of respect for the newly departed, but also perhaps to keep the news of a death from cocked ears in a busy waiting room.

'Yes, yes. All fine here, I think. It wasn't entirely unexpected, of course...'

'No, indeed. Dr Turnbull is on his rounds at the moment,' she said, the voice abruptly returning to its usual slightly abrasive tone, 'but I'm sure he'll be with you as soon as possible.'

I left it to Anne to answer the doctor's knock at the front door while I hid alone in the drawing room clutching the medicinally large dose of whisky and feeling uncomfortable that I was pretending to be too distressed to greet him. But in fact, looking back on that day that so utterly changed my life, I think I was probably in shock, not knowing how I felt and how I was meant to behave – what is the face to be adopted when someone dies, and you're taken aback to be experiencing a range of emotions including relief, even some sort of perverse excitement, rather than the expected overwhelming grief?

Dr Turnbull's arrival was followed by such a silence that after a short while I felt compelled to leave my chair and creep along the hall to try and find out what was happening. The calm that had settled upon me straight after Alexander's death immediately crashed and was overtaken by a feeling of intense anxiety. Did the ghostly silence mean that Anne and the doctor had abandoned me, gone to seek some further help – and if they had, what might that mean? I tiptoed along the hall to the bottom of the stairs to discover that I was not alone in the house after all – there was a muffled conversation going on behind the closed door of Alexander's room upstairs, and almost immediately the sound of floorboards creaking, the door into the dressing room opening and then water tinkling into the sink and through the pipes as the doctor washed his hands.

I scurried back to my chair then, for some reason not wanting to be discovered waiting in the hall as Anne and the doctor came down the stairs. Once there, I adopted the face of someone in grief, lost in the deepest contemplation. Jesus. I felt like a fraud, guilty at what I was feeling and not feeling. Eventually, Dr Turnbull came into the drawing room; a puzzled look took over his face as he quite obviously had no idea where I fitted into the picture.

'Ben Teasdale,' I said, rising to my feet and shaking his hand without saying anything more, which still left him clueless as to who I might be. I guess I gave him no choice but to address me in the same matter-of-fact way in which he was talking to Anne – perhaps he thought of me as just another carer, someone who'd witnessed death many times and would now be moving on to new employment. It certainly was not his fault if he assessed the situation wrongly, and I didn't take offence – he wasn't being unsympathetic; he'd recently taken over from Dr Melchett and he must have been uncertain about our history in the house. How could he know what the old man was or was not to me?

'Now here's the death certificate that the undertakers will need to have a look at, and once you've instructed them, I expect they'll be round very fast,' he said, waving the piece of paper between my hand and Anne's before, with a hesitation, placing it in mine because it was the closer of the two. 'Well, there we are – another of our old residents gone,' he said, as I stared at the piece of paper burning into my fingers. 'When was it that Lady Bellaghy died?'

'Ten months ago, now. Last November,' I said, respectfully placing the certificate on the little table in front of the sofa where I used to put the tray of coffee I made for Bridget and myself every morning.

'Extraordinary, extraordinary,' he said, sounding as though it wasn't in the least. 'Oh well, I'll leave you both to get on.' He was already making his way out of the drawing room, the leather briefcase in his extended hand seeming to take charge of him, guiding him towards the front door and his next patient.

'Thank you for coming so promptly, Dr Turnbull. Anne – you'll see the doctor out? I think I ought to get on with some phone calls–'

He stopped at the door then, quite abruptly, and turned back to me.

'I'm so sorry – I'm not quite sure who you are. You're a relative of Lord Bellaghy's?' Just curiosity, I'm sure, but for a moment I felt threatened, as if an incorrect answer might see me ejected from the house after some sort of hurried assessment at the police station.

'No, no – I'm not. I'm – I *was*, er, his secretary. Companion, really,' I said clumsily before finding my voice again. 'Actually, I was his friend. I was his great friend.' A reminder to myself as much as to anyone else. I wanted the doctor gone then so I might be left alone with another glass of whisky in this room that I knew so well but that had suddenly become so different.

'Ah, yes, I see. Sorry for your loss. Sorry for your loss,' he said, as he continued on his way.

∽

I didn't go up to the room with the undertakers when they came to take Alexander away from his home. 'It's a job for the refuse disposal people,' I could hear him saying in my head as they went up to fetch him. 'Put me in a black bag and leave me outside the back door. No fuss and no bloody nonsense...'

I held the front door open for the two reverentially polite young men in dark suits while they were leaving. Anne's comforting hand rested on my shoulder as they stepped out into the late-afternoon sunshine with the zip-up bag carried on a stretcher between them. It seemed to me to be almost weightless, as though it was a less than half-full bag of dry autumn leaves that had been swept up from the patio beyond the garden door.

∽

Barnes, Theresa and me. Just the three of us, that's all. I could have whipped up a few people, but absolutely knew that it was not what Alexander would have wanted. 'Please try to understand that the funeral is very strictly private,' I said to the few who felt they had to insist on being present. I got my way. We returned to the same place that had received Bridget nearly eleven months before, but this time it was on a glorious, blustery day in early October with the windswept roses around the crematorium way past their best, but still putting on a little bit of a show. I'd asked the undertakers not to close the doors after the coffin was brought in, and a bracing breeze swept through the building and ruffled the petals of the dark roses on the small wreath I'd had placed on his coffin – my only concession to any type of funereal decorum. My wishes had been made quite clear to both the undertakers and the staff at the crematorium; they were, above all, Alexander's wishes, and I was determined to do right by him.

'As the coffin is brought in, I wish there to be absolute silence. There are going to be no priests in robes or any sort of ceremony – just the quickest of goodbyes, so not a word will be said. We are going to sit still, just for a little while, and then, when I decide the time is right, I will raise my hand, and that will be the sign for the coffin to disappear. We'll be done and dusted in less than five minutes.'

And that's how it was. The three of us returned to the house, and we had lunch using the best dinner service, all laid out in the dining room for the very last time. I had bought armfuls of flowers, retrieved the lawn-mower from its hibernation to give the grass its last cut of the year and had my band of helpers dust the place from top to bottom; I wanted the house to look as beautiful as it had been when I visited it for the first time all those years before. Later, Theresa and I saw a slightly tiddly Barnes on his way back to his office for what must have been a rather unproductive end to his afternoon before we cleared the dining room and prepared a goodbye tea party for our departing helpers. The very next day, I started dismantling the house.

∼

As the sun came out after a late spring shower on a May morning in 1996, I left Sandwich. The car was loaded up once again, this time with some of the contents of my little house; a hired van was to follow, bringing some larger bits of furniture to the new house in Clapham, which I'd just taken possession of. Having dusted and vacuumed the cottage ready for its new owners, I'd locked the door and had started walking towards the car; then I'd hesitated and returned to kiss the oversized brass knocker goodbye, looking to either side to make sure I wasn't being watched. 'Thank you for looking after me,' I'd whispered. As I passed Clarence House in the car just a few yards further on, I gave a crisp, theatrical salute to the front door, above which a sign declared 'Sold'.

I have been back to Sandwich once or twice since, as a visitor – and also, some years after his death, to scatter Alexander's ashes which I kept in a cupboard at home for far too long. One day, remembering Alexander's total lack of sentimentality about such things, I came to the conclusion that he'd think it quite ridiculous that I'd not got rid of them, so I booked myself into the Bell Inn on the quay, drove down and got drunk during the evening alone in the local Indian restaurant – three or four years on from my departure, I was growing terribly fond of a drink or two, partly the result of keeping up with my old mate's consumption – and early the next morning drove down to the bay to scatter along the beach the light-grey powder that had once been Alexander. 'Good God – what on earth are you up to?' That's what the dear sweet man would have said about that, I'm quite sure.

It was a long time after. Perhaps it needed to be. I'll make a guess now, given the benefit of hindsight, that I was worn down at the end, not just by the whole thing of looking after two old people, but also by death. Three deaths. Owen, whose death hung over his parents' house like a silent curse, was never talked of again after the day Alexander announced the news to me; a tacit understanding forbade his mention. Then Bridget's. And Alexander's lastly, releasing us all. There were two or three others too, in those last months – ancient friends of the Bellaghys whose funerals I'd attend, sometimes with Theresa, to make sure Alexander and his dead wife were represented.

Four deaths in the end, though, not three. The day in April, five months after Bridget died, that I moved back into Clarence House from the cottage to be nearer to Alexander, I'd had a phone call from Jonny Falcone, Aurelio's oldest friend who he'd grown up with in Gibraltar.

'He's got pneumonia, Ben, but it's not AIDS, so he doesn't want you to worry. He's going to be fine in a couple of weeks.' When the call came, I was sitting downstairs in the drawing room with Alexander, a rare occurrence by that time.

'I'm going for the shortest of walks, Alexander, just to clear my head a little,' I said, in a hurry to be alone. I didn't tell him, though he knew Aurelio and was very fond of him. Enough of bad news.

Men in their early forties don't usually get pneumonia, and though I pretended to be reassured by Jonny's words, I immediately knew that my dearest friend was desperately ill. We'd seen very little of each other for the previous few years – he'd embarked on a tortuous relationship with a much younger guy in the East End who was so consumed by jealousy that it became almost impossible for Aurelio to see anybody at all, let alone old male friends with whom he might have shared a 'past'. Terry was not at all well, found life quite impossible to bear and eventually took his own life; a grief-stricken Aurelio had reappeared in our lives, wanting connection and comfort, just before the time that he became ill. Once I'd heard the news, in between my stints in Sandwich, I'd take the Tube out to East Ham to visit him every week while he made meticulous plans for an uncertain future, cashing in an insurance policy which would enable a very early retirement for what would probably be a long, slow illness with good days and bad, cushioned by the support of loving, newly rediscovered friends.

But it was not to be. Just a few weeks before Alexander died came a late-night phone call from Aurelio's father and mother, who had come over from Gibraltar to look after him, telling me that one of the opportunistic viruses, almost unheard of before the epidemic, but now commonly seen in AIDS patients, was galloping up his body towards his brain and that he would be dead within the week.

I was holding his hand when he woke in the hospital bed soon after my arrival from Kent the next morning. He smiled at me, and we sat in silence for a long, long time, not feeling the need for words.

'Are you frightened, Lelo?' I eventually said.

'Not in the slightest.'

They were amongst his last words; by the next day the virus had robbed him of speech. His lack of fear somehow freed me to be able to be with him at the end, and, on his insistence, but against the advice of the doctors, we moved him back to his home for his last few days. We made his bedroom as comfortable as we could, took the television he couldn't watch upstairs from the sitting room, placed a bowl of fruit he couldn't eat on the bedside table, and sat around trying to be light-hearted, to amuse him with jolly banter that he might have heard but couldn't respond to. Five endless days stripped of hope, waiting for the inevitable.

~

A funeral with a crowd of inconsolable friends. A cloudless day as hot as the Sahara with white lilies, piled high on the coffin, trembling at the movement of the horse-drawn hearse on the cobbles. It makes its way through the cemetery to the chapel where Jonny plays perfect Bach on the piano, his face set in grim determination to complete this last favour to our friend; a mother, until this point unable to cry, throwing herself onto the coffin of her son just before it is lowered into the ground; a mound of fresh clay next to a gaping hole and me, blinded by tears and losing my footing as I drop a handful of earth onto the coffin, saved by my friend Richard whose hand encircles my waist to stop me from falling into the grave.

∼

It's over twenty-five years now since I left Sandwich.

There's the smoothest two-mile stretch after you leave the town, a shiny black racing track of road begging to be taken at speed. I remember that last journey – another shower followed close on the one that had witnessed my goodbye to the cottage; a few minutes later, it tumbled out of the sky to lash the windscreen, the tyres on the wet tarmac singing as I swept myself away from my past at close to a hundred miles an hour before slowing for the abrupt corner that takes you into Wingham. The car slowed because I applied the brakes, but I had the feeling that something else was impeding me; it was as though there was a mighty elastic band attached to the rear of the car, and the further I went, the more it tensed, waiting for the maximum moment of stretch before it would catapult me back to Sandwich where I still belonged. But I didn't stop, of course; I picked up pace again through the village until I had to tell myself to slow down to avoid a possible confrontation with the police car that was often waiting in a little layby on the far side of the village.

I wasn't just running towards a new life, a new home. I was fleeing my old life and some sense of disapproval of myself that I couldn't shake off. I was confused about my lack of grief for my old friend, but there was something else too. In those upside-down months – my description now, though I wasn't aware of it at the time – I treated someone badly and it's preyed on me ever since.

It must have been an inbuilt fault in the dining-room chairs, but that last dry, hot summer of Alexander's life saw them all beginning to give up the ghost. He had sketched out a design for the chairs himself after a visit to Harewood House and a Mr Prickett in Ramsgate had made them for him very soon after his arrival in Sandwich. Now, forty years on, they had decided, en masse, that they'd had enough and needed attention. Over the course of a couple of months, they were becoming unstable, cracking – all in the exact same place – where the support bars crossed beneath the seat. One could be ignored, but after four had succumbed in the space of a month, I decided to do something about it. It became a quest to distract me during that lonely summer just before Alexander and Aurelio's deaths, and so I set out to find someone who could repair them.

I found him in King Street in a busy workshop that I'd never noticed before. He shared it with an upholsterer who had owned the premises for years but now was semi-retired and hardly ever present. Joel was in his mid-twenties, had a mass of floppy blond hair on his head with a sharp tan line where his tee-shirt met his neck, and a constant smile that showed off the dimples in his cheeks; he was wearing baggy, faded dungarees with jangling tools poking out of every pocket – a bit of rough with a ready smile. The cutest guy I'd ever seen in Sandwich, with all my senses screaming *'not available'* – no gay vibes and anyway probably too young to be interested in someone approaching forty – and that meant

I was free to let my imagination run riot without ever having to do anything about it, which perhaps had become a bit of a pattern with me in those times. 'For the eyes alone', as a Moroccan shopkeeper in Marrakesh had said to me.

'Yep – easily sorted, I reckon; I'll put a small steel cross underneath, where you can't see it, which will hold the structure together. They'll be right as rain for another forty years!' I wasn't listening very hard; I was glad of a solution and very pleased to have such a pretty man in the dining room explaining it all to me.

First appearances were deceptive, since he wasn't 'a bit of rough' at all. He had a Masters in English Literature from Cambridge but had given up the promise of a career in academia to work with his hands and had left the family home in Nottingham – Dad a lecturer at the university, and Mum a GP – under a bit of a cloud, to become an artisan.

The day after his visit to the house, I'd gone back to the shop and had sat on a stool that Joel cleared a space for in front of a desk with tottering columns of papers and books. He sat close beside me, jotting down figures while pausing now and again to suck the end of his pen while he got together an estimate of the work that I was giving the go-ahead for. The place was full to bursting; tea caddies without lids; a copper bowl holding an enormous selection of ancient keys; a grandfather clock case without a clock; a chest missing any sign of its drawers; stripped, warped panels from the hall of a local Elizabethan sea captain's house; a bank of tools ranged along the far wall in case there weren't quite enough hanging from Joel's clothes; a multitude of frames of chairs, stacked high, stripped of varnish; a low chaise-longue piled high with papers (*The Economist*, *The Guardian*, *Private Eye*) with horsehair sprouting from great rips in the leather. Above the chimney piece hung a large, dark wooden crucifix with an emaciated Christ in agony staring down towards Joel's desk, as though deeply pained by something he'd just discovered about the young man below. The place smelt of flowers (rosewood, Joel explained later), Danish oil, varnish, beeswax, and fresh ground coffee.

All these years later, the room is still imprinted on my brain, as is the memory of his knee pushing hard against my thigh as I peered down at the completed estimate, my heart beating in a way that I had quite forgotten was possible. I may have been a little out of practice and fearful of how to take things forward, but it was only a few minutes later that he was leading me to a room at the back of the shop not much bigger than a cupboard, where I was reintroduced to pleasures that I had begun relegating to the past.

It became a bit of a thing, for a while – a mid-afternoon visit while Alexander napped, with me leaving him with his carer drinking tea in the kitchen. There'd be the turning of the key in the door after my arrival, with the *'back in ten minutes'* sign swung round to face the street, followed by a hurried retreat to the room at the back where I'd slip the denim straps of his dungarees off his shoulders; heavy with his tools, they'd fall to the ground leaving him naked but for his boxer shorts, the sparse golden hairs on his chest catching the light of the single bulb above us. It was wonderful – naughty standing-up sex with grunts and groans, with me convinced that this was what it was like to be truly alive again after what felt like years of abstinence (not quite true, but there'd certainly been nothing as good as *this* for several years). Afterwards, there would be the disapproving tinkle of the little bell attached to the door as I left with a saucy, self-satisfied grin on my face.

~

A month or two into our back-room assignations, I could feel things were changing a little. One Saturday afternoon I was hurrying away to say goodbye to Alexander before leaving for London and my weekly visit to Aurelio. Joel had used his thumbs to haul the straps of his dungarees back onto his shoulders after a particularly steamy session (it was a very hot summer) and had then hugged me tight and put his head on my shoulder.

'Stay the night with me, Ben. I'll make us supper. It would be cool, don't you think?'

'I can't, Joel – I've got to get back to town and anyway, I'm not really much of a one for suppers,' I said, mumbling into his hair that smelt of sawdust and shampoo.

'Come on – take a risk. I'll make us something nice. Perhaps next week, when you're back?' As I reached the door, I was aware of a wistful little smile that I'd not seen before.

We did have supper, as early as the following week; I returned to Sandwich a day early, without telling anyone at Clarence house, and spent the night with him in the single bed pushed under the eaves in a room as tidy as his workshop below was not. There were large Miró and Kandinsky posters Blu-Tacked to the walls above shelves of orderly paperbacks; I put my head to one side to glimpse them as he cooked a vegetarian risotto for us on a gas hob in the far corner of the room, trying to work out who this boy was, working with his hands during the day and reading his way through Trollope, Hardy, George Eliot and Edith Wharton at night.

I remember his grey eyes in the early morning light as he stroked my cheek; I remember being struck by the fact that there had been as much affection as lust during that first full night together; I remember him tentatively telling me that he 'might be in a bit of trouble' if I didn't care for him the way he cared for me.

I don't know why, what happened to me, at that time when there was enough sweetness and warmth within Joel's soul to melt the most calloused of hearts. But not, just at that moment, mine. I wanted the single light bulb, the exploring hands, the hurry, the naughtiness that made me think of two small boys doing something they shouldn't, and afterwards the squeaking of the opening shop door and the finality of the tinkling bell telling me I'm gone, I'm alone, I'm free.

I wasn't being intentionally cruel. We spent lots of time together – the night of Alexander's funeral I stayed with him, glad of his company and chat after the farewells to the carers. Our trysts saw me through the winter, the emptying of the house and the settling of the estate with Barnes; in the months before I left, he always made sure to find a gap in his heavy work schedule so he could be with me on my walks along the bay, past Royal St George's towards Ramsgate in the distance and then back to the waiting car as night descended.

'We're fuck buddies!' I said on one of those four-hour walks. No idea what prompted me to say it, but it escaped my lips, feeling immediately like a falsehood that correcting would make into too much of a thing. He made sure his pace didn't alter, but I saw his face redden with disappointment and pain as he looked towards the ground.

'I'll phone in a couple of weeks. When I've settled a little,' I told him the morning I left. He gave me a wry smile and a tender hug. He was hurting, his soft eyes filling with tears, knowing he'd never see me again.

⁓

Now, I ache to be able to say sorry, to tell him that just at that time it wasn't possible for me. After I'd scattered Alexander's ashes along the shore where both Alexander and Joel had both walked with me, I drove back into Sandwich and parked the car outside Clarence House, now under new ownership. I hadn't really figured out that I was going to go back to the workshop in King Street, but that's what I did. *Just to have a look at the place before driving away. He won't be there of course, not four years on...*

There was a sign hanging listlessly above the door, belonging to the same agents that had dealt with the sale of Clarence House and my cottage. '*Under Offer*,' it proclaimed hopefully, looking as though it had been announcing the news for many months. I pressed my nose up against the glass in the door, trying to look beyond the long horizontal rip in the old pulled-down blind. The place was empty, surprisingly large now it was stripped of the chaos of busyness, with the door at the back hanging open and receding into the darkness of the room beyond. It was just curiosity, I'd told myself as I walked over – *I'm taking in the changes to Sandwich since I was last here.* Halbert's the butchers is now a craft shop, with wicker baskets hanging at jaunty angles above a collection of greetings cards, a pyramid of small jars of local honey, glove puppets and tulips about to bloom in prettily painted pots; the hardware store – '*Sedgwick's, Established 1924*' – has housed a pizza restaurant that has opened and closed in the time since I was last there; there are chairs stacked on tables, rows of dusty wine glasses on shelves, a mound of post on the mat and a repossession notice stuck to the inside of the door; the fisherman's tackle shop is now a scrubbed up architect's office – the old shopfront has been removed, there's a plate glass window and inside, a sweep of monochrome-grey broken by two large weeping fig trees in terracotta pots between desks with large screens on them.

I couldn't let it be, in the end, and found myself in the estate agent's office asking questions.

'Yes – it's under offer yet again now, but it's been empty for ages. Some dispute with the land registry about the backyard not being included with the premises,' said the same over-chatty soul with a hint of a moustache, wearing a tartan skirt. She had dealt with my sales four years before but didn't seem to remember who I was. I couldn't be bothered to remind her. 'Fingers crossed it all goes through this time, though. Third time lucky.'

'Any idea what happened to Joel?' I said nonchalantly, pretending to concentrate on a photo in the window of a newbuild in the bay.

'Who?'

'Joel. Think he was apprenticed to old Mr James–'

'Oh, God yes – he's been gone ages. I think he went off to Spain,' she said, having theatrically screwed up her face to help her recall the young man. 'Went into business with another young chap, I think. Thought they'd try their luck in Bilbao – Bilbao? Somewhere in the north anyway. That's right, yes – that was well before Mr James died, too. Nice young chap.'

'Yes. Yes indeed.'

∼

A day or two after I'd moved from the big house into my little cottage in Sandwich, I bought some simple click-on frames and a collection of small prints by Modigliani, Schiller, Van Gogh and Picasso from Habitat in Canterbury – a pretty assortment, chosen quickly, to dress the wall behind the sofa. I remember an evening of getting it all together, clicking the prints into their frames, wobbling around on a chair trying to maintain my balance with tacks in my mouth, a tape measure in one hand and a hammer in the other after marking the wall with faint pencil lines. After I finished, late at night, I stood at the far side of the room, hands on hips, to look at my handiwork. I was confronted by a cacophony of clashing images making no sense at all. It was an angry and disappointing muddle that saw me throwing down the hammer, turning off the light and thundering up the stairs in a sulk. 'Fucking waste of time and money!'

But when I came down in the morning, expecting the same rush of disappointment that had driven me to bed, all was calm. It was as though I'd left it to the room – sofa and rugs, mirror and prints – to make peace with each other, to compromise and find common ground. And truly, that is what had happened. Order, harmonious colours and symmetry – all agreed on while I slept.

And so it was with the new house. A longer process, of course, but over two or three months, I had to insist on remembering the experience with the cottage, while all the bits and pieces from Clarence House declared war on each other and everything else, before finally making peace with walls and floors and higher ceilings, newly bought rugs, wallpaper and curtain treatments. It took up every moment of my time. But what took even longer was settling into the place, waiting for the day it would feel like home. It happened slowly over the summer – the shift from something bizarrely new, a house full of things that I remembered from a past existence, to a place where the objects eventually came to an agreement with others around them and then allowed themselves to feel they were now owned by me and occupying their rightful place. Eventually, the evening arrived when I was able to settle back deep into the sofa with an outbreath, a dinner tray on my lap and a growing realisation that all the things that had been gifted to me by Alexander were now becoming mine.

But still, any feeling of grief about my old friend continued to sidestep me. Perhaps it really is just not possible to grieve for old people in the same way. It must be that a life coming full circle is so much easier to mourn than a life ending prematurely?

~

'Do you remember the day you showed me around your house?' Angie had popped her head round the door of the sitting room, taken a breath once she'd seen that I was alone, and then come over to sit beside me, easing herself down to my level on a sofa so low it was practically on the floor – so far down, in fact, that once she reached me, there was a sudden impression of forced intimacy, as though we'd climbed into bed together without knowing each other very well. We were at a party next door – three or four months after moving in, I was slowly getting acquainted with my neighbours.

'I do, Angie – the day I gave you the key, you mean?'

'Yes – yes, that's it.'

There was a happy hubbub from outside in the garden. Our hosts had set the bar up on a trestle table beneath twinkling fairy lights with two large speakers positioned to either side which were regaling us with a bizarre mixture of heavy metal and Dolly Parton. I'd taken refuge from the noise and evening chill for a while, with a large glass of Pinot Grigio – sneakily poured from the very same bottle I'd arrived with. I'd been alone on the sofa only a moment or two and was more than a little tipsy, so it was probably beginning to occur to me that I might leave and continue the party by myself, accompanied by nothing more than the second of the two bottles of Pinot Grigio I'd bought earlier. I'd had a nice time though, flirting with a primary school teacher who was making eyes at me, which I was rather pleased about. Not really my type – *'three-gin-and-tonics'* attractive, so best to go home before a mistake was made, since I'd had a great deal more alcohol than that. At home, I'd be able to indulge alone in a jolly post-mortem that I was going to come out of rather well. '*In his late twenties. Made a beeline for me. Obviously still got it, etc, etc.*' The really good thing about the evening was that I'd met a few more neighbours that I'd probably been avoiding a little since I moved in. Nice folks. Don't need to be around them too much, but great to be able to bellow a 'Hello' in future to the other side of the road or up into a porch now and again.

'Did you think there was anything odd about my behaviour that afternoon?' Angie said slowly and deliberately, not looking directly at me while kneading a bare foot curled up beneath her on the sofa.

'You mean when I was showing you round?'

'Yes.'

'Not at all...' Not the truth. Halfway through the tour of the house four months before, Angie had practically done a runner, my front-door key clutched in her hand. She'd told me she was sorry, but she had to leave immediately, suddenly concerned about a pan she was certain she'd left on the hob. Definitely an excuse, because she didn't come back. She was up the stairs from the basement and standing by the front door in an instant, fiddling desperately with the lock in an effort to get out as soon as she could.

'Horrible to be woken by an alarm in the middle of the night and have no way of turning it off if I'm away,' I said, glad of the opportunity to banish the awkwardness that had hung around ever since – in fact, we'd not spoken since, and I had been wondering about asking her for my key back before learning she'd been away, looking after a terminally ill parent for most of the summer. 'But listen – I more than understand that you might not want the responsibility – rather imagined afterwards that I'd bulldozed you into it.'

'Ah – so you did think it odd–'

'Well, perhaps a little bit.' Of course I'd thought it odd and couldn't decide what had happened. A little jealous, perhaps? Something she'd realised about her new neighbour she didn't like? Overtaken by the need for a pee and too shy to ask a virtual stranger where the loo might be?

'I have to tell you what really happened.' She was looking straight at me now. 'I think I told you about myself when we first met – in Debbie's garden, the day after you moved in last July.'

~

I remembered it. It was meant to be an introductory Saturday mid-afternoon gathering at Debbie's – my nearest neighbour who I had decided after a quick chat over the garden fence was to be my primary keyholder. 'Come over tomorrow afternoon before you show me the alarm system,' she'd said, 'nice excuse for a bit of Victoria sponge with us.' Debbie, taking a break from her art studio in the attic, her husband, daughter, with boyfriend – and Angie. The lesson about the alarm keypad had to wait for a day or two; once the Victoria sponge had been eaten with a mug of tea, there was a suggestion of something stronger and the evening had fast degenerated into a rather drunken event involving numerous bottles of cava with an interruption around dusk for an emergency resupply from the off-licence. Angie, slightly slurring her words and using a confidential tone, had trapped me on a small bench in the garden while the others were in the kitchen indulging in the spliffs being rolled by the monosyllabic boyfriend with soulful eyes. Out of the blue, she had announced to me that she had a special gift – she saw and felt things that others didn't.

'I'm a medium,' she'd declared, *sotto voce*.

'A medium what?' I replied, knowing exactly what she meant but not being able to stop my hackles rising. I can't really be doing with that sort of nonsense. Drunk talk, I decided, and boring – not Angie herself since leading up to that we'd had a good old gossipy chat about the part-time help in the corner shop – an elderly lady the size of a mountain, covering a deep Cockney accent with something she thought posher who always wore more make-up than a pantomime dame, and, it was rumoured, had once been a 'woman of the night'. It was also rumoured that she just *might* have had a sex change many years ago in Morocco when such a thing was still rather experimental. All that was well worth a giggle on the bench, but then, unfortunately we were obviously getting to that part of the evening when a fun companion was going to let herself down and disappoint with a ridiculous fairy tale about herself and the occult. It coloured my view of my new acquaintance, though not enough to exclude her from being the second candidate who might have the honour of being a keyholder for me. A medium. Silly, but reliable, perhaps; I left it a few days before knocking on her door and asking her – she accepted the key duty immediately, and we'd made a date for a quick tour of the house.

∼

'We weren't alone.' Angie loosens the linen scarf at her neck with fidgety hands and looks away from me again as a gentleman with a bushy beard enters and quickly excuses himself from the room with an apology. He's thinking he's interrupting something intensely private and retreats back to the party in the garden.

'What do you mean?'

'In the house that afternoon. We weren't alone.'

'Are you sure? Oh! I suppose my cleaner might have been around, but not sure if she had started working for me when you–'

'No, there was someone with you. I mean beside you. The whole time.'

∼

She'd looked put out even as I opened the door, I remember now, looking over my shoulder along the hallway at the newly hung pictures as though one of them was skew-whiff on the wall.

'I don't know why I felt awkward about it, Ben. I see things all the time, so it's not as though I was frightened or anything like that. I just wasn't expecting it and I didn't know quite what to do. Caught me off guard – and I suspect you're highly sceptical about that sort of thing. I remember you looking down your nose at me at Debbie's when I told you about myself. So when I saw him I was sort of embarrassed and flustered, I think.'

He'd followed us around apparently, sometimes a pace or two behind, sometimes just a bit in front while I babbled on about this and that, proudly showing off, all three of us stopping now and again to admire the things I'd so carefully placed around the house; through the sitting room, back into the hall and up the stairs we went, his hand apparently now and again reaching out and just stopping short of caressing a treasured remembered object. A tall man, Angie said, with a kindly face and whitish curly hair, holding a walking stick and wearing a grey suit.

'Have you any idea who this person might have been?' Angie's relaxing now that she's aware that my nose is not rising into the air.

'Yes. I used to know someone who had about fifty grey suits. London suits he called them.'

'London suits?'

'Yes, but don't ask,' I say, beginning to smile. The longest of pauses, then, that didn't need breaking.

'He was a dear friend of mine,' I said eventually, 'and rather extraordinarily, it's the first anniversary of his death today.' Another very long silence. 'Angie, this old chap you saw – did he look bewildered, unhappy?'

'Good God, no. Exactly the opposite. Smiling all the time. Particularly after we went back into the hall to look at those lovely old prints and you started to give me a wonderful lesson about them. I wasn't paying attention, I'm afraid. Too caught up in his presence. But *he* was listening, all right. Nodding his head and loving every single moment of it.'

∼

Fuck knows. Really. I can't tell you quite what I believe about all that, but that's the way it happened. Another run-in with folksy occult bollocks. You'll know full well after what I've told you about Alexander that he wouldn't have any patience with it, and yet here I am, telling you at the beginning of my story about rattling windows, banging shutters, children's feet on floorboards and a howling wind, about being summoned up creaking stairways to deathbeds and blardy blardy blah. Now I'm telling you a story about a medium and the same old gent wandering around a house in Clapham. God, I wanted to catch up with Angie afterwards to grill her about the whole thing, but I never did. Funny old thing she's become all these years later, with her shaved head, great spangly earrings and her insistence on feeding the foxes in the garden and declaring three days of mourning every time a goldfish in her pond dies. Now it's all antivax, 5G masts and suspicious vapour trails and me keeping well out of the way. She's lonely, I suppose, and settling into the bananadom of late middle age with no partner to anchor her to reality. But there was something about her reticence in telling me the story – perhaps her sensitivity to the fact that I might dismiss her as a charlatan dreamer – that touched me in some way, making it more difficult for me to put it to one side.

'Make of it what you will.' I'm repeating a little phrase from my first chapter here to assure you that I'm just relating the story that Angie told me, that's all. I'm not going in for a general conversion about the metaphysical.

I gave Angie a drunken kiss on the cheek after our conversation and left the party without saying goodbye to anyone. Nothing unusual about that – I'm used to slipping away (and then apologising for my bad manners later), but I think I was in an extra hurry to be gone and really not knowing what to make of what I'd just heard.

Alexander on his horse. It was the first picture I saw as I turned on the light in the hall on my way back into the house that evening. The painting seemed to be glowing, showing off, demanding my attention above all the others ranged along the wall; the jigsaw puzzle of frames (my relocated Habitat collection from the cottage) and watercolours, ancient maps and family photos, bits and pieces collected from art fairs, little shop windows in country villages and talented friends. It's a small painting – he's sitting comfortably on his beloved Flight, slightly turning towards the viewer with one hand holding the reins while the other rests on his thigh. I don't quite know how good it is, but I do know it's quintessentially Alexander, confident in his seat, seeing and not seeing all at the same time. And present, extraordinarily present. I unhooked it from the wall and looked at the back. '*Alexander, Lord Bellaghy on his horse, Flight. Timothy Whidborne, 1980.*' I remembered the talk of him sitting for it, the discussions about whether the look of him had been captured or missed, the decision to place a windmill in the distance, the sky being altered to look more like one you'd expect of a hazy summer's day above Sandwich Bay.

And that's when the tears started. The grief came down upon me like heavy rain, a startling but wholly welcome moment that I'd stopped ever expecting. Yes, of course I was drunk, and drunker still a little later when the second bottle of Pinot Grigio succumbed to the corkscrew. But it was there at last, a grief of the purest and sweetest kind, utterly uncomplicated and unthreatening, stripped of tragedy and regret.

God knows how long I cried for, walking round the house attaching memories to the things around me. I opened my wardrobe and took out the suit that Alexander had had made for me, kneading the cuff, remembering his fifty suits, and wondering when I might ever wear mine again; I went down to the kitchen, sat on the little sofa that had come from my cottage, with Bridget's old patience tray on my lap, remembering the intense concentration on her face when she was playing, and the sight of Alexander's death certificate lying on it as we waited for the undertaker; I found myself polishing the old wine cooler, now a bedside table, that Alexander had spilt so many glasses of port over in the drawing room; I picked up the Chinese bowl from the hall of Clarence House, looking closely for any sign that my car keys had damaged it as Bridget had insisted, and lastly, I took from the wall – hanging slightly further along from Alexander and Flight – a little drawing that the couple had sat for in Venice. It had been banished to the downstairs cloakroom in Clarence House, but I'd now promoted it to the hall after a reframing. A street artist, in pastels, had quite brilliantly captured a moment of the young couple's honeymoon; they're sitting in St Mark's Square with the Doge's Palace behind them. Alexander, leaning forward with arms folded and holding a cigarette, looks straight out at the viewer with a serious expression while Bridget, in profile, is seated beside him but turning away; she's pointing upwards with one hand while the other clutches a light scarf that catches a breeze.

∼

I woke up just as dawn was breaking the next morning, dazed and hungover. The picture of my old friends on honeymoon was on the pillow beside me; Alexander's Japanese companion in the clock I'd kept from Sandwich told me it was 5.30, but I left my bed and went down to make myself a cup of tea, rehanging the little picture on the way. Mug in hand, I unlocked the French doors and stepped into the cool garden in my bare feet; new trellising, York stone and shingle, luminous in the semi-dark, framed by flower beds empty but for a few struggling shrubs that would be brought back to life after a heavy pruning during a large planting a few weeks later. I sat down on the old Georgian garden bench I'd brought with me from Bridget's garden and stared at the brown earth and the weeds that had been making themselves at home during the summer while I mapped out my plans with Gilly, my gardener.

'I'm going to do a planting that will give you a choice,' she'd said over the noise of the tree surgeons' chainsaw a few days after I'd moved in as two lime trees at the end of the garden were reduced to let in more light. 'You'll either be interested in becoming a gardener or not. If not, I can come every now and again and keep things in order. But I'm going to make a guess, Ben, that you'll love it, and I won't be required that much. Bet you fly with it!'

I sat there drinking my tea and trying to envisage what this space might look like in the years to come. Would it bloom, make demands on me that I'd be ready to meet – or fade, not able to catch my imagination?

As the new day began to impose itself, I went back into the house, carefully locked the doors behind me and then pressed my forehead up against the cool glass, looking out at the blank canvas of my garden.

But just a minute later, I was unlocking the doors again, flinging them wide open to let the air in. Then I climbed the stairs to my bedroom, slipped back under the duvet and quickly fell into the deepest sleep.

ACKNOWLEDGEMENTS

My heartfelt thanks to all those who read my chapters and buoyed me up with suggestions and encouragement. My siblings – Bruce Parker, Viv Parker and Stella Parker-Bowden; Nicola Aplin, Matt Barry, Kathleen Costello, Neil Daglish, Nina Deerfield, Emma Davison, Glyn Dillon, Ruthie Henshall, Elizabeth Lewis, Ruth Milligan, Edie Reilly, Baillie Walsh, Susan Williamson. Lastly, I'd like to thank Angel Belsey at Deixis Press, who dared to see the possibilities in my manuscript and let it see the light of day.